The carriage made anothe[r]...
ing on this wave of exube...
kissed Alexandra on her p... ...
and she lifted her hand to cup his cheek. Her fingers slid to
the nape of his neck, curling into his hair, and he groaned.
God, she felt so good, tasted better. Desire coursed through
him, and he wrapped his arms around her body and crushed
her to him, deepening the kiss.

Alexandra's eyes flew open and she stared into his, wide-
eyed and still.

His lips curved into a smile against hers.

She pushed against his chest, straining away from him.
"Stop that," she cried. "You can't keep kissing me."

"But I like kissing you. And your response tells me you
liked it, too."

"I was half asleep!" she protested.

He lowered his voice and pulled her back against him,
liking the feel of her soft body against his. "Then imagine
how much better it will be when you're awake."

She averted her face. "Lord Kendall, I told you—"

"Garrett."

She looked at him, frowning in confusion.

"That's my name. You used it earlier today. And now
we've been intimate."

She gasped and shoved against his chest so hard that he
released her. "We most certainly have not! A few stolen
kisses do not constitute intimacy."

"Good, then let's do it again."

"Absolutely—"

Absolutely worked for him . . .

For the Love of a Soldier

VICTORIA MORGAN

BERKLEY SENSATION, NEW YORK

THE BERKLEY PUBLISHING GROUP
Published by the Penguin Group
Penguin Group (USA) Inc.
375 Hudson Street, New York, New York 10014, USA

USA / Canada / UK / Ireland / Australia / New Zealand / India / South Africa / China

Penguin Books Ltd., Registered Offices: 80 Strand, London WC2R 0RL, England
For more information about the Penguin Group visit penguin.com

FOR THE LOVE OF A SOLDIER

A Berkley Sensation Book / published by arrangement with the author.

Berkley Sensation Books are published by The Berkley Publishing Group.
BERKLEY SENSATION® is a registered trademark of Penguin Group (USA) Inc.
The "B" design is a trademark of Penguin Group (USA) Inc.

For information, address: The Berkley Publishing Group,
a division of Penguin Group (USA) Inc.,
375 Hudson Street, New York, New York 10014.

ISBN: 978-0-425-26423-2

PUBLISHING HISTORY
Berkley Sensation mass-market edition / March 2013

PRINTED IN THE UNITED STATES OF AMERICA

10 9 8 7 6 5 4 3 2 1

Cover art by Gregg Gulbronson.
Cover design by George Long.
Interior text design by Kristin del Rosario.

ALWAYS LEARNING   **PEARSON**

*To my mother and my sister,
my earliest and biggest cheerleaders.*

ACKNOWLEDGMENTS

I couldn't have completed this journey without my husband and children. Thank you for your incredible patience while I disappeared for days at a time. (Told you it wasn't all about martinis with my writers' group!) Special thanks to the New England Chapter of the Romance Writers of America and to my incredible critique partners, the Quirky Ladies—Kate, Nina, Tara, Michelle, and Liana! They kept telling me . . . *'This is the one, this is the one.'* I would also like to thank my fabulous agent, Laura Bradford (www.bradfordlit.com), and wonderful editor, Leis Pederson, at Berkley Publishing Group. They believed in this story and helped turn my manuscript into the best that it can be.

Chapter One

><

SOMETIMES a woman runs out of choices.

Alexandra Langdon glowered at the door, willing herself to turn its brass knob. She didn't belong inside the chamber. She risked discovery, expulsion, and scandal. Her stomach growled and reminded her why she was entering anyway. What did the pampered heirs inside their exclusive enclave know about hunger? The hollow, empty rumble of it. The slow, insidious gnaw of it. She had experienced it for so long, it was like a familiar adversary. One she vowed to conquer.

That is, if she could open the damn door and cross the forbidden threshold.

There was money to be had inside the gentleman's card room. The Duke of Hammond hosted the grandest balls of the season. The cream of society attended, and while wives and debutantes danced the night away, husbands and bachelors sought refuge behind these doors. Rich men with fortunes to win or lose at the turn of a card. Alex just needed to possess the winning hand—and she would.

Her father had given her a gift and she planned to use it. It was the only thing he had given her. For this, she loved and hated him.

She shook her head, wiped her clammy hands down her black dress trousers, resisted the urge to readjust her masculine wig, and once again, crossed into forbidden territory.

The familiar smells assaulted her first, a mixture of cigar smoke, whiskey, and men. The noise hit her next, the murmur of conversations, the rumbles of masculine laughter, and the crack of billiard balls striking together.

Burgundy carpet covered the floor, and dark wood-paneled walls were crowded with the familiar paintings of foxhunts. Red-coated riders leaned over straining horses, galloping after their prey. Alex's sympathies lay with the fox. She knew the desperation of seeking safety in hidden crevices, the terror of being hunted. Her lips pressed into a determined line. Like the fox, she needed to keep alert for fear of getting caught.

Alex stepped farther into the room, eyes locked on the card table in the far corner. A game had broken up and new players were claiming the vacated seats. One of those chairs was hers. If she reached it in time.

A group of men blocked her path. Her head barely topped their shoulders as she circled them, threads of their conversation drifting to her.

"Kendall is back."

The name echoed, ringing familiar to her. It had circulated throughout the house since her arrival downstairs, voiced in hushed tones that reverberated through the guests like a rippling tide.

"I thought he had returned last fall."

"Well, he's in town. And word's out that he's here tonight."

"Christ. Does Monroe know?"

"More important, does Monroe's *wife* know?" Laughter followed.

"*Only* Monroe's wife? What about all the other women?"

Alex had no interest in the antics of some Casanova. The room overflowed with them. Oiled hair neatly groomed, snow white cravats, and hands curled around crystal brandy glasses. It was no surprise that these men would be petticoat chasers. The sport didn't give blisters, mess their hair, or soil their jackets. Bitterness washed over Alex as she sought to bypass the group, but their next words brought her up short.

"Last time he sat at a table, he lifted a fortune off Lambert and Eldridge."

"Didn't Samson challenge him to a duel?"

"Rumors have circulated, but unlike you, Peters," a man drawled, "Kendall is mute on the gossip he generates, and Samson has disappeared."

"Remind me to avoid Kendall's table," someone muttered.

A gambler and a rake. Her dislike for the man grew.

Dismissing him, she continued forward, intent on her goal. Two seats on opposite sides of the circular card table remained vacant.

She set her sights on the closest empty chair. As she neared it, she studied the four men already seated. She recognized the two viscounts conversing with each other, Lords Linden and Chandler. Lord Richmond, an earl, had been introduced to her once before. Lord Filmore was a welcome sight. She had lifted fifty pounds from the rake in their last encounter.

But that was over six months ago, and the money hadn't gone far.

None of the gentlemen rose to greet her, nor did they draw back her chair. It always surprised her, but it shouldn't have. They nodded, murmuring her surname in that familiar greeting men exchanged, dropping titles and first names.

Before she breached society's rules and claimed her seat, she studied her surroundings. A mahogany bar lined the wall opposite her. Light from the chandelier danced off the crystal decanters and glasses littering the bar surface. A gilded frame mirror hung above the setup. Alex didn't immediately recognize the stranger staring back at her. When she realized it was her own image reflected in the glass, she drew in a sharp breath.

A young man with brown hair, startled blue eyes, and a crisp white cravat tied about his neck returned her stare. A red flush climbed her throat and stole over hollowed cheeks. She tore her eyes from the reminder of her gaunt appearance.

Her blue jacket had needed to be taken in further, only the padding filling her out now. It was little wonder she sweltered and yearned to yank off her cravat and draw a cooling breath.

The disguise was a necessary evil if she wanted to play for these stakes. Card rooms existed for women. She could try her hand at the genteel games of piquet or whist, but no fortunes would be laid on the tables, no hundred-pound bets. She needed to be here where serious money could be won.

She lifted her chin in determination and braced herself to wish the man in the mirror luck, but her view was blocked.

A new player had claimed the remaining chair opposite her.

Her eyes rose from his pristine black evening jacket, tailor-fitted over a tall, muscular frame to study his face. This time, she did retreat a step. Not because the man was handsome, though his classic aristocratic features were striking. He had chiseled cheekbones, sensual lips, and an enviable mane of thick, raven black hair. The room held a banquet of beautiful men, and while Alex was aware of them, her hunger was directed else-where. There was something more about this man, something beyond a handsome face and figure.

It was in his eyes. They were storm-cloud gray, cold as slate and hard as steel. Alex couldn't look away. They were hypnotic, riveting. He frowned, shattering the spell that had held her transfixed.

Weak-kneed, she circled her chair to drop into her seat. The hairs on the back of her neck prickled.

He knew.

It was the only possible reason for the black scowl directed at her, for she had never seen the man before in her life. Her eyes snapped back to his but he turned away, dismissing her. He collected a brandy from the tray of a passing waiter and folded his tall, lean body into his seat. He set the glass on the table but did not drink from it, instead shoving it out of reach and turning to respond to a comment from Richmond.

This man had no interest in her. Her tension eased and she exhaled. She needed to remain focused. *Focused players win.* She eyed his untouched glass of brandy. *Sober players win.* Her father's words echoed. Drawing a steady breath, she started to remove her gloves, but paused. Her hands would give her away but it couldn't be helped. The risk had to be taken. She slipped the pair off and lowered her hands to her sides.

Richmond addressed the group. "Kendall, you know every-one?"

Her eyes shot up.

Kendall.

The womanizer and gambler. But of course. It was inevitable that fate would seat this man at her table. Of late, fate had been less than kind to her.

"Actually, I don't." Those compelling eyes leveled on Alex.

"Right. Alex Daniels is new to you," Richmond said by way of introduction. "Daniels returned from abroad last year, grand tour and all." He addressed Filmore, a slow smile curving his lips. "Filmore, you remember Daniels, don't you?"

Daniels. She had chosen the name from a stallion who had triumphed at Ascot despite one-hundred-to-one odds against him. She hoped for similar luck.

Filmore grinned. "I do. You left with my money the last time we shared a table. You've been scarce these last few months. Good of you to make an appearance. I like to be given the chance to recoup my losses."

She opened her mouth to respond but noticed Kendall frowning at her again. She didn't like it, or the effect it had on her pulse. If she'd had a fan, she would have snapped it open and given him the cut direct. Without her fan, she turned away from him to respond to Filmore, lowering her voice to do so. "My apologies, Lord Filmore. I so enjoyed spending your money that I've returned for more." She couldn't bring herself to drop his title, cross over into the intimate address of men.

Chandler grinned. "The gauntlet has been tossed. Let's hope you brought your purse, Filmore." He lifted his glass in a mocking salute.

Filmore settled back in his chair and eyed his friend. "Did you bring yours, Chandler, or are you wagering another one of your father's prized stallions?"

Chandler laughed, unperturbed. "The earl managed to reclaim him. Admittedly, not at the bargain price at which he'd originally purchased him." His grin was unrepentant.

"He must not have been too upset over your bartering his prime bloodstock. After all, you still live," Linden commented dryly.

Chandler shifted in his seat. "There was a bit of a row, but there are benefits to being the earl's only heir—no spare."

The men laughed, with the exception of Kendall. Alex didn't

know where Kendall had left his sense of humor, but she abhorred these fops' cavalier attitude to betting their estates, their father's stables, or treasured family heirlooms. If they didn't need their pampered luxuries, there were those less fortunate who did.

"Shall we deal the cards, gentlemen?" Richmond asked, lifting the deck and waiting for Filmore to cut before he dealt the first card to Kendall. "Opening bid is twenty-five pounds."

Beneath the table, Alex's hands clenched her thighs, her fingers digging deep. She had pawned her last piece of jewelry to enter this game, hoping to double its value. Glittering baubles were of little use, for there would be no more Seasons for her.

The round circled and returned to Kendall, who drew two cards and addressed the group. "Gentlemen, I'll raise you fifty."

"Aren't you missed in the ballroom?" Linden muttered as he tossed in his note, flicking off a piece of lint from his bright blue jacket. "Not by the men, but by the ladies?"

Kendall merely raised a brow, refraining from comment.

Alex ignored the banter. Good Lord, seventy-five pounds. Her necklace had garnered a mere hundred. She studied her cards. It was a good hand. *Langdon luck*. Her father's voice bolstered her flagging courage, and she added her note to the growing pile, stamping down her nerves.

"Recently returned to town, Kendall? I haven't seen you at White's or the last few balls," Linden said.

"Unlike you, Linden, I'm selective in the invitations I accept," Kendall returned, his eyes on Chandler, who scowled at his hand.

Filmore suppressed a laugh, but kept his attention focused on his cards.

"You have something in common with Daniels here." Richmond nodded to her.

"He's been scarce as well."

"Yes. Well, I've had other priorities." She waved a hand. Her eyes met Kendall's, and his narrowed as if he heard the lie in her words. She cursed him for appearing to read her so well, for looking so damn arrogant and handsome.

He was a distraction she didn't need.

"You both missed quite a spread at Warden's." Chandler

added his note to the pile. "This season's debutantes are prime stock. I fully intend to sample a few of the fillies."

"Bloody hell, Robbie, haven't you had enough problems with horses?" Filmore snorted. "Gentlemen, shall we raise the bet another twenty-five?"

The cards circled to Linden and he folded his hand. "I'm out."

Alex did the math, calculating that after the round she would be left with . . . with nothing. Nothing didn't go very far. Past experience had taught her that stark, bitter lesson. But she only needed one more card. *Just one more.* She wondered where her heady rush of Langdon luck was and feared it sat at another table.

She gnawed on her lower lip, then froze—no tells. She surveyed the table, but they appeared unaware of her frayed nerves.

The room was stifling. Why did men wear cravats? Like a noose around one's neck, they choked. She glanced up and noted Kendall appeared to have once again read her mind, for he removed his black evening jacket.

The man proceeded to brazenly roll up his sleeves and bare his forearms. She was riveted to every movement of his crisp white dress shirt sliding back to reveal his muscular, bronzed arms. She swallowed. Good Lord. It was indecent. He cocked a brow at her, and she stiffened. It was her move and all eyes rested on her.

She was suddenly grateful for the hateful cravat, as it hid the burning flush stealing up her neck. She met the bet and turned to await Richmond's play, avoiding Kendall. Why did his return to town have to coincide with hers? Like an ominous shadow, he darkened her mood and her hopes.

"Have you received news from the front?" Richmond addressed Kendall.

Alex turned, surprised by the question but glad for the sobering distraction. News of the Crimea should help her regain her focus, cool her burning cheeks.

Kendall's hand paused in placing his bet, but then he shrugged. "Nothing the papers haven't covered."

Linden leaned forward, his expression thunderous. "That bloody Russell should be fired for his libelous dribble. He's—"

"Accurate," Kendall cut the viscount off, his eyes hard. "Pity Lord Raglan's command wasn't as competent as Russell's pen. It might have saved a lot of bloodshed."

A taut silence stretched over the table.

Alex was stunned. Kendall hadn't served up the usual loyal drivel glorifying hard-fought campaigns or extolling a long life for the empire. Kendall voiced the dark and bitter truth.

She had heard murmurs of William Russell's reports in the *Times* publicizing the troops' suffering from shortages of food, clothing, and medicines, but she didn't need to read his accounts. She had heard from the soldiers themselves, and her heart had bled for them, for the carnage the Light Brigade had left after its disastrous charge at Balaclava last October.

She swallowed and glanced up to see Kendall's enigmatic eyes resting on her. She dropped her gaze and blinked furiously, cursing her momentary lapse and his words for touching her. But they had. Contrary to the opinions of some, she was not made of stone.

"Yes, well, to those who fought with courage." Richmond broke the silence, raising his glass in a toast, the others following suit. "Their glory will not fade." He echoed the poignant line of Lord Tennyson's tribute to the fallen men.

Kendall's hand tightened on his glass before he lifted it in response, but he set it down without drinking and turned to Chandler. "I believe it's your bet."

Frowning at Kendall's untouched brandy glass, Alex's head shot up. For a span of time, she had forgotten the game. That had never happened to her before. *A bad omen.*

She shook off the thought. She had a good hand, a solid hand. Her last card had completed her full house. The Langdon luck had come through.

Chandler sighed and tossed his cards onto the table. "My glory has faded. I fold."

"No more prized bloodstock to throw into the pot?" Filmore quipped.

"Not tonight. This evening my sights are set on the fillies downstairs, but I won't be riding them if I waste my time and money here with you gentlemen."

Inwardly, she cringed at the vulgarity.

"I'm out as well." Richmond folded his hand and leaned back in his chair. He withdrew a cigar from his jacket and waved a passing servant over for a light.

"Gentlemen, shall we call this hand?" Kendall asked.

Alex edged forward in her seat, heart pumping. She would win.

Fillmore tossed down his cards. "Pair of kings." At Linden's snort of laughter, he shrugged. "Worth a bluff. But I believe I'll join Chandler downstairs."

"Gentlemen, let's hope you have more luck with the ladies than at cards," Kendall said, spreading his hand on the table. A straight flush.

Linden whistled, shaking his head. "Christ, Kendall, tell me you're joining the others downstairs. Leave a man something to hope for in the next round."

"There's still hope. Daniels hasn't laid down his hand," Richmond said. "Alex, any chance you have a royal flush?"

Alex jumped as all eyes locked on her. She concentrated on drawing a steady breath as the room spiraled around her, a whirlpool sucking her down.

She had lost. *Lost everything.*

One hundred pounds; her meager fortune gone. She couldn't move. Couldn't think. She blinked at the cards. Heat flooded her body, and the smell from Richmond's cigar gagged her. In a flash, she knew what ran through the condemned's head before the noose tightened and their feet flailed beneath them in those final seconds of life. Nothing. Absolutely nothing.

It took all her strength to spread her cards over the table rather than grip the edge of it and hold on for dear life as the room spun. After she ceded victory to Kendall, Filmore slapped him on the back, but their words and laughter barely penetrated her dazed fog. She had never seen a straight flush. Hoped to never see another.

Chandler and Filmore shoved their seats back and rose.

It took her a moment to realize Filmore had addressed her. He had to repeat her name and his invitation to join him and Chandler downstairs.

She moistened her lips, not trusting herself to speak. Willing her legs to support her, she slid back her chair and stood.

Yes. Escape. Flee the scene of her ruin. Find a private place to think or curl into a ball and will the world away.

She cleared her throat and managed to voice an appropriate

parting to the table. Her feet followed Chandler and Filmore while she marveled at her body's ability to function when her mind could no longer.

Voices and masculine laughter floated through the room, a river of life flowing by without her. She jumped at the explosive clatter of billiard balls, the noise shattering her daze. In a flash of clarity, she sent her companions ahead under the auspices of getting a stiff drink to drown out the bitter taste of her loss.

She had faced ruin before. It had not beaten her, and it would not beat her now. *The Langdon well of luck might be bone-dry, but the Langdon spirit will revive.* She heard her father's words and closed her eyes.

She wished he would shut the hell up.

He had gotten her into this mess in the first place. She slid a finger underneath her cravat and tugged at the tie.

A waiter carrying a tray of drinks passed. Alex summoned him over when suddenly a steel grip curled around her upper arm and she was dragged to the side of the room. Speechless at the audacity, she stumbled, gasping when the hold tightened to steady her. Before she could recover, her captor reached across her and shoved open the adjacent window. A blast of cool air whipped in, fanning her flushed cheeks and shattering her shocked immobility.

"Still going to pass out?"

Her head jerked back at the words. Enraged, she yanked her arm free and whirled around to confront her assailant. Her words died in her throat and she staggered back a step. Steel gray eyes bored into hers.

Kendall.

Why had he followed her? What more did he want?

His eyes narrowed on her. "When's the last time you ate?"

"I beg your pardon?" Indignant, she met his gaze before her eyes strayed to the pulsing beat in the column of his throat, mesmerized by the strip of golden skin. He had discarded his cravat and opened the top buttons of his shirt. It was scandalous. She smelled Richmond's cigar on him. His linen shirt stretched over broad shoulders and clung to a rock-solid body standing intimately, dangerously close. Too close.

Towering over her, he was formidable. She stepped away until the wall braced her back and cut off further retreat.

"Christ." Kendall spun her around again to face the window, prodding her toward it. "Breathe."

She cursed the man but sucked in deep, calming breaths of the cool air. She damned him for being right and herself for being a fool. She couldn't afford to pass out or lose her wits. Thanks to him, she had lost enough this evening.

The urge to faint passed along with the fleeting hope that Kendall would disappear. Collecting the shattered remnants of her dignity, she planted a hand on the windowsill and braced herself to face the man, ignoring the staccato rhythm of her heart.

His brow furrowed, the now-familiar frown curving his lips. Minus the scowl, the man was striking. She noticed he was thin, not gaunt, but pure sinew, hard angles and whipcord strength held in tight rein.

Confused at her train of thought, she pressed her hand to her temple. Suddenly aware the gesture made her appear as if she still planned to faint, she jerked it down.

She drew in a steadying breath before meeting those eyes. "Thank you." The words nearly choked her, but years of ingrained etiquette forced them out.

"Christ. You fools get younger every year. How old *are* you?"

She stiffened and thrust her chin up. "Old enough."

His lips pressed into a firm line, but he did not question her further. After an interminable silence, he spoke. "I've ruined enough men's lives, but I draw the line at boys. Here."

She stared at him blankly until she realized he was shoving something at her. She nearly gasped at what he held. Her notes. Blood rushed to her face. He was returning his winnings to her.

"Take it," Kendall demanded.

Her hand lifted, then snapped back to her side where she curled it into a fist. No, she couldn't. If she accepted it, she could never show her face in a card room again. She bit her lip. She felt like the fox fleeing those hunters, wondering if the escape route before her led to safety or another trap.

She needed to think, but he never gave her the chance.

Swearing, he caught her hand and dumped the notes into it, curling her fingers around them. He wore no gloves, and she shuddered at the touch of his bare skin against hers. His hand was hard, his fingers calloused.

"Next time, don't bet what you can't afford to lose." He turned away.

"I'll pay you back." Finding her voice, her words bounced off his broad back.

"Don't bother." He didn't break stride as he answered. "I don't want it." He was clearly done with the matter. Done with her.

Stricken by his response, she stared at his retreating figure in silence. His gracious gesture burned to ash under his scorching dismissal. The transaction meant nothing to the man. To her it meant everything.

Everything.

To Kendall she was simply a prick at his conscience, a blister he felt compelled to lance. While surprised he possessed a conscience, she hated him for it. She recalled his comment about the men he had ruined. His words disturbed her, but envisioning his cold, slate gray gaze, she believed them. After all, he had nearly ruined her.

Realizing she stood blankly staring at Kendall's back, she searched her surroundings. She feared facing censure for not honoring her bet. But no one glanced her way. Only Kendall was privy to her loss of face.

All the more reason to detest the man.

She blinked away the moisture blurring her vision as she shoved her notes into her trouser pocket, hiding the incriminating evidence. She withdrew her gloves and shoved her hands into them. Damn him. He wouldn't make her cry. She never cried.

She needed to get out of here.

Ducking her head, she fled the room, suppressing the urge to run. Why bother? There was no escaping the man. Storm gray eyes were branded in her memory. No matter how fast she fled, they would follow.

Chapter Two

~≈≼~

LIGHT from the sconces flickered over the hallway outside the gaming room. Alex's stomach churned and she feared losing its meager contents. She needed to find a ladies' parlor room and recompose herself. Stopping short, she nearly caused the gentleman behind her to collide with her. She murmured an apology, her cheeks burning under the man's curious regard as he passed.

For goodness sake, she couldn't enter a ladies' room. Rattled, she pressed a hand to her stomach. She needed to get out of here, preferably without encountering anyone with whom she'd be forced to converse with a modicum of intelligence, for she had left hers in the card room.

Changing plans, she whirled to retrace her steps. She had visited the Duke of Hammond's estate before, thus was familiar with its layout. Once upon a time, she had been a guest of the duke's daughter, Lady Olivia, and she recalled a side patio along the back entrance to the estate. There she should find little traffic to hinder her flight.

With renewed purpose, her steps quickened. The duke

housed many guests during the ball and some throughout the Season, so the servants paid her little heed.

She traversed the portrait gallery. The click of her boots on the hardwood floors reverberated throughout the empty chamber while the eyes in the portraits appeared to follow her flight with disapproval. She opened a hidden door to descend a dimly lit back stairway. Her tension didn't ease until she crossed the parlor and flung open the French doors leading to the deserted patio.

Alex closed her eyes and drew in a deep breath. A towering oak abutted the patio and blocked the moon, veiling the area in ink black darkness. The back of the estate opened to an award-winning garden lined with sculptured topiaries, mazes, and a rainbow of flowers. It was an oasis in the midst of London's fog-blanketed environs. A cool breeze ruffled the hairs of Alex's wig and brushed free the heavy yoke that had settled over her shoulders.

The ballroom was on the opposite side of the house. Laughter and voices from guests strolling into the garden and its maze mingled with the distant sounds of the orchestra. Alex listened to the soothing melody of a waltz. She would be all right. She had not won her fortune, but neither had she lost one thanks to Kendall. More important, she had escaped her uncle's sordid plans for her. She had eluded his greedy grasp, and she vowed to continue to do so no matter the cost. Her stomach growled, reminding her that sometimes the price was dear indeed.

She strolled toward the massive oak tree and removed her gloves to slide her fingers over the immense trunk. The gnarled bark was a solid comfort beneath her touch. In another lifetime, her brazen behavior would be considered scandalous. She stood under a cloak of darkness where dangers to an innocent, unchaperoned young woman could lurk in hidden corners, like wolves ready to pounce.

Predatory gray eyes invaded her thoughts and Alex grinned ruefully. She had met the beast and survived the encounter, bruised and battered, but still alive. As for social etiquette, she had breached those boundaries years ago.

With a sigh, she leaned against the trunk and struggled to collect her thoughts. As she contemplated her present plight, the French doors swung open. Instinctually, she ducked behind the oak, out of sight from the intruders. While cursing the interruption of her solitude, she peered around the oak.

Two men stormed outside, the taller of the pair groomed in uncompromising black. He blended into the night with only his pale features, snow white cravat, and silk gloves outlined in the darkness. He turned to pace the patio, anger etched into his impatient strides.

The second man, a footman, was shorter and wore the maroon-and-gold jacket of Hammond's livery. His lighter jacket and the white stockings beneath his formal knee breeches carved his stout silhouette into the dark backdrop.

"What the hell are you doing here? How did you get in? It's invitation only, and I know damn well you don't work here." The tall man broke stride, his voice, low and nasal, hissed with barely restrained fury. "Need I remind you that we shouldn't be seen together? I'm not paying for idiocy. I'm—"

"I know wot yer be payin' me for," interrupted the shorter man, unruffled. "A few quid greasin' the right 'ands opens most doors." He glanced around. "Least those downstairs." His coarse speech was of the East End or Seven Dials. "An' thot's why I'm 'ere," he added.

The tall man went deathly still. After a prolonged silence he sputtered, "What? Why?"

"I've reconsidered me fee." The would-be footman thrust his hands in his trouser pockets and rocked back on his heels.

"What?" his companion breathed. Alex could almost hear the man swallow before continuing, his next sentence forced out between clenched teeth. "Christ. What the hell are you talking about? I've paid you. My terms are nonnegotiable."

The shorter man grunted. "Murder's always negotiable. 'Less yer be takin' me ter the magistrate o'er the terms of our agreement."

Silence met the brazen words.

Alex dared not breathe. Her fingers dug into the bark.

"Not likely, eh? Magistrate's not partial to gents 'irin' killers, particularly when their target's a wounded war 'ero, survivor of Balaclava and all." His words became more heated. "Yer ferget to mention thot, guv'nor? Didn't yer be thinkin' it might increase 'is value? After all, ain't no ordinary bloke we be dealin' with."

Pinned to the tree, Alex's eyes widened, her heart thundering. They discussed murder. Murdering a soldier. A Crimean War hero! She bit back the protest that sprang to her lips.

Another lengthy silence ensued. Only the distant sounds of the music dared interrupt it. A light nocturne drifted to them until the taller man sliced into it with his curt response. "Forget it. There's no more money."

The stout man stormed over to his companion, crowding him. "Then get yer bleedin' wounded war 'ero to sell 'is commission. There's money to be 'ad there, and the poor sod won't be needin' it no more. My price went up 'nother five 'undred quid. Find it. Thot's if yer wantin' the bloody job completed." The man spun away.

A wounded soldier. Alex's heart squeezed. To survive the carnage in the Crimea only to be killed through this sordid arrangement. She closed her eyes. Faces of the men for whom she had cared loomed before her.

This man, this nameless man they planned to kill, was one of them. A survivor when but a third of the soldiers had walked away from the suicidal charge that marked that tragic battle at Balaclava.

Her throat constricted. She couldn't let it happen. She wouldn't.

But who? Whom did they wish dead?

The maroon-coated footman had reached the French doors when the taller man's words halted him. "Wait." He fumbled with something. A flash of gold streaked across the black night before the footman's hand snatched it from the air. "Once pawned, that should cover the fee."

The footman examined the item, flicking something open and closed.

A snuffbox? Watch? Card case? Alex squinted into the darkness, struggling to identify the object before the man's jacket pocket swallowed it.

"Good 'nough."

"What about the job?"

The footman gave a curt nod. "Kendall be taken—"

"Christ, keep your mouth shut!" the gentleman swore, his head pivoting, scanning the area.

A short, guttural laugh escaped his adversary. "Right touchy, guv'nor."

"Do we have a deal?" he hissed.

"We do."

There was a grunt of acceptance from the taller man. "Good. Now, get the hell out of here before you're spotted. We should both leave. Better if I had never come," he muttered the last.

"Good 'nough." The French doors opened and closed, and the short man disappeared, leaving his companion alone with his thoughts—and Alex.

Kendall.

She closed her eyes. It had to be *him*. *Again*. But of course. Fate had delivered him like a plague to ruin her night, and the night was far from over.

Alex's eyes flew open and her head jerked around at a movement from the patio. She leaned against the tree as if seeking to merge into it. Sweat pooled between her shoulder blades, dotted her forehead. A branch snapped in the distance, and she bit her lip to swallow back her scream.

The man whipped around.

Alex froze, holding her sharp intake of breath. Stark white shards of fear pierced her.

"Christ, bloody cat!" her adversary spat.

Cleo! Olivia's wretched black cat. Alex sagged against the tree, weak-kneed.

The man withdrew his handkerchief and flicked it at the cat. Cleo lifted her paw to bat at it, hissing her feline disdain before she scampered away.

Alex eyed the cat's escape with jealousy. Time moved at a tortoise-crawl until the man emitted a vicious curse and stormed inside.

She waited a beat before she followed. She needed to see him. To identify this man who wanted Kendall dead.

She eased open the doors in time to glimpse him striding down the corridor. She lengthened her steps, hurrying to pursue her prey. When he turned right, candlelight from a corner wall sconce lit his greased dark hair.

She followed him to the balcony overlooking the ballroom.

Should he descend the grand staircase, he would be swallowed up in the sea of black evening jackets crowding the floor.

Heart thundering, she rushed to the railing. She could not catch up with him, but when he fled down the stairs, she might see his profile. She held her breath.

His strides were quick and purposeful.

She gripped the railing, her eyes locked on the man's black evening jacket and she willed him to look up.

As if hearing her plea, the man turned. His eyes swept the upper balcony, briefly lighting on Alex before sliding past. Whirling around, he hastened down the last steps. In minutes, his head and shoulders were engulfed in the waves of guests blocking the edge of the dance floor. He was gone.

Alex expelled her breath. She did not recognize him.

His long, lean features were hawkish with an aquiline nose and thin, bloodless lips. His brows were thick and arched. He was but another mirror image of all the other distinguished gentlemen who composed the ton. She would have had to have gotten closer to get a better look at him; she doubted she could identify him again.

She sagged against the railing. What had she expected? A brand to enable her to recognize him again? A jagged scar lining his cheek? She snorted. Her Langdon luck had run dry, and she had best remember it.

Straightening, she pondered what to do next. Murder conspiracies were out of her realm. Poverty, hunger, and near ruin, well, she had some experience with those. This was different. Lives were in jeopardy, or rather, the life of one man. One despicable man.

Kendall.

She fisted her hands. She couldn't sit by and let the man be murdered. Pity there. He was a war hero. Who would have thought? She recalled his lean body and now realized his determined strides resembled a military gait. And his whipcord-thin frame. The man had been wounded and might still be regaining his strength. For what? To have it snuffed out by the hand of that treacherous little man? She shuddered.

She would go to the authorities. Let the magistrate deal with the sordid matter. There was no time to waste, for she did not know how long she had, or rather how long Kendall had. The murderous trap could be set for him this very night. The way her evening was going, that would be the case.

Intent on her plan, she started forward only to stop short. She could not speak to a magistrate. He would never listen to her because she was nobody. Lady Alexandra Langdon had never attended the Duke of Hammond's ball, Alex Daniels had. She cringed at the thought of donning her disguise in the light of day before the authorities of the law, no less. No, absolutely not. She drew the line at how far she was willing to go. Deceiving the ton to relieve them of surplus funds was one matter; lying to an official of the law another matter altogether. One was a case of survival, the other suicidal.

Blast it. She should just let Kendall be killed.

She spun and paced the long corridor. No, she couldn't. She owed him. Now she could repay him. Her debt would be wiped clean. Her life in exchange for his seemed a fair exchange. She would warn Kendall about this murderous plot, but she could give him no more, unable to accurately identify either man if ever located. A warning was all she had to offer.

She started forward but again paused. Like the magistrate, Kendall would never listen to her. He hadn't earlier when she offered to repay her debt.

He wanted nothing from her.

Typical arrogant male. She pursed her lips and reconsidered the matter. Well then, she wouldn't tell him to his face. She would write him a note, sign it anonymously, and have a butler deliver it to him in the card room. She ventured forward once more. It was a plan . . . of sorts. The best she could muster under the circumstances.

The man had survived the Charge of the Light Brigade. He had ridden through the valley of death, the mouth of hell, cannons storming him with shot and shell. He must have a talent for facing life-threatening situations and surviving against all odds.

Chapter Three

≈≥

GARRETT Sinclair, the Earl of Kendall, scowled at the man sitting opposite him. What was his name? Viscount Currans? His cologne seeped across the card table. The fop must have bathed in the scent. And what in God's name was he wearing? Since when had peacock-colored cravats come into style? Though, it looked better than Morley's dazzling green jacket. Its glare blinded a man.

Garrett stiffened in his seat, appalled at his thoughts.

Bloody hell. He didn't give a good Goddamn what the dandies wore. His only concern lay in what lined the fops' pockets or, rather, filled their trust funds. And he was fast losing interest in that.

He never should have come. He'd known it the minute he had arrived and the Duke of Hammond's butler announced his name in that portentous, booming baritone. The shock of it had plunged like a boulder into still waters, creating a ripple effect that spread across the room. Silence had been followed with the slow rising crescendo of murmurs. He had forgotten how fast and furious tongues wagged at the slightest whiff of news.

And sadly, he was news.

Ever since he'd stepped out into society, he'd had the unfortunate penchant for greasing the gossip mill. Years later, he still paid the price for his younger days of carousing stupidity. One would think his two-year absence would have eradicated people's memories or supplant them with some other fool's exploits. Currans, for example. The ass bragged about the actress he had brazenly escorted to Lady Monroe's garden party. Shouldn't that trump his rumored duel with Samson?

Garrett couldn't even remember who the hell their duel was touted to have been about. Samson's wife or his mistress? He did recall that neither woman was worth it. Thankfully, Samson had agreed, and they had both gotten amicably drunk toasting their mutual opinion. Even if he lived down the story, there were others to top it and that explained why he had purchased his commission. Joining the lancers had also had the added benefit of thwarting his imperious, pompous ass of a stepfather.

But once again, Garrett had been the only one to pay the price for his stupidity. And he was still paying it. He would pay it until he was dead and buried with the hundreds of others who'd been lost on that blood-soaked battlefield.

Christ, the loss. The senseless slaughter. One drop of their blood was more valuable than the combined lot of that which flowed through the men at his table. Their gravest decision in life appeared to be which color cravat to wear and even in this they blundered. It was little wonder they wagered their fortunes on the turn of a card. All too often, these were stakes they couldn't afford to lose.

Stormy blue eyes interrupted his thoughts, and Garrett clenched his jaw.

What was his name? Alex Denny? Dannel? What haunted Garrett about the man?

Damned if he didn't evoke memories of the lost boys in his command. The false bravado. The youth and incredible innocence. The flash of undisguised panic before pride stamped it down.

Why the hell had he followed him from the table?

Because having seen countless death stares riddling the corpse-strewn battlefield, he had recognized the despair in Denny's eyes and he had refused to be responsible for another man's demise. Not over money he didn't want or need.

He didn't appreciate Denny affecting him like that, nor would he forget or forgive the man for it. Life hardened those strong enough to survive it. Similar to battle, the soft got trampled, literally mowed down by the wave of men behind them. He smelled something soft about Denny and he didn't like it.

Thankfully, the man wasn't his concern, nor his responsibility. But Christ, the bloke was young. Garrett had never been that young. At age six, he had been ancient.

He tossed down his cards and collected his winnings. Ignoring the complaints of his companions, he made his excuses and fled. He'd had enough.

He had returned to town to regain the rhythm of his life, but it wasn't here. Damned if he knew where it was, but the room and company stifled him, catering to too many fops like Currans or fools like Denny. He didn't belong there. Not anymore.

>==<

GARRETT STEPPED OUT of the front doors of Hammond's estate and savored the cool, evening breeze. His shoulders loosened, his body eased, and he breathed deeply. He eyed the line of coaches cluttering the drive, squinting into the blanket of fog that fell like a smoke-colored curtain over the city. Music drifted to him. The notes mixed with the night's murmurs, the occasional whinny of a horse, and the clatter of traffic rumbling through the streets.

Garrett directed one of Hammond's footmen to call for his carriage. While he waited, he noticed another footman conversing with a gentleman.

Something familiar about the man's slim build and royal blue jacket tugged at Garrett. Hammond's man nodded in his direction. The gentleman stiffened in reaction to the servant's response. Slowly, almost haltingly, the man turned to face Garrett and he straightened. Bloody hell.

It was him. Denny.

Hadn't the fool had enough? Garrett noticed the man clutched a folded sheaf of paper. A promissory note? He cursed under his breath. Damned if he'd take it.

Denny faced the servant and leaned forward, thrusting the paper at the man and speaking in low tones.

A clatter of hooves slapping the pavement drew Garrett's

attention as his coach rolled into sight. Both his coachman, Ned, and his man, Havers, sat on the box. The glow from the torchlight illuminated the Kendall coat of arms, the two crossed swords in the shield on the side of the gleaming burgundy carriage.

Garrett walked over to the vehicle. As he passed Denny, he didn't break stride. "I told you, I don't want your money." He waved Ned back into his seat, forgoing the assistance to make a faster exit. When he reached his coach, he turned back to rake his eyes over the young man. "Take my advice and go home. Then stay there until you are grown." He reached for the carriage door and tossed his parting words over his shoulder. "It might save you some money."

He heard the footsteps closing the distance between them. He had to give the man points for perseverance. Persistent as the vultures circling the dead and wounded.

"If you value your arrogant life, I suggest you read this. However, the choice is yours."

Garrett turned at the challenge, studying Denny's flushed features. Spots of pink dotted the man's smooth cheeks. Hell, had he even shaved yet? He studied Denny's slim build and short stature, his head barely meeting Garrett's shoulders. Christ, he doubted the boy had reached manhood yet. He nodded toward the note. "A few more shillings can't save me, but if you insist."

He cocked a brow when he accepted the folded sheet and Denny's gloved hand briefly tightened before he relinquished his grip. Garrett meant to shove the paper into his jacket pocket and be done with the matter, but seeing Denny edge away from him, his expression guarded, Garrett changed his mind. He flipped open the note and scanned the contents. *Christ Almighty.*

What game was this?

Burning rage filled him. His body vibrated from its heat, and he raised his eyes to blast Denny with it. The man staggered back and pivoted to flee, but not soon enough. War trained, Garrett had often had only seconds to react in battle.

His hand shot out and curled around the younger man's arm in an imprisoning grip. The same jolt bolted through him as it did when he accosted him earlier in the card room, and he instinctively loosened his hold. The man was reed thin, Garrett's hand almost able to encircle the width of his arm. With a twist of his grip, he could easily break bone. Damn, if he wasn't tempted to do so.

The conniving, murdering, bloody bastard.

"Why don't we step into my carriage where we can discuss this matter more privately?"

Fear flashed in Denny's eyes. "That's all I know. I don't know anything more." Denny tugged at his arm, struggling to free himself.

Garrett leaned down, watching Denny's eyes widen as he towered over him. "If you refuse to talk to me, you can explain this note to the magistrate. The choice is *yours*." He tossed Denny's words back at him. "Get in the carriage."

Denny stiffened, panic draining his face to sheet white. "With you?" He swallowed and moistened his lips. "Alone?" The word croaked out in horror.

Patience snapping, Garrett growled, "Move. Now."

He prodded Denny forward. When he made no attempt to climb the steps, Garrett gripped his jacket and practically swung him off his feet. He gave his rear end a shove as he flung him inside, ignoring the man's shriek of rage. Shriek? The boy definitely hadn't reached manhood yet. He squawked like a woman. It confirmed his earlier opinion. The man *was* soft.

Before he climbed in behind the boy, he called to Havers, who leaned over the box to peer down. The sight of his familiar craggy features, shock of dark hair, and steadfast brown eyes calmed Garrett. "Drive around. Don't head home immediately." He moved to enter the carriage but turned back again. "And Havers, keep a sharp look out. There might be trouble. Be ready for it."

Havers didn't blink, nor did his expression alter as he nodded. "Right, sir."

Loyal, obedient, and unquestioning. They didn't come better than Havers.

Garrett vaulted into the carriage as Denny's fear turned to anger.

"How dare you put your hands on me!" Denny cried, lunging for the door. "I won't go anywhere with you. You're mad."

Talked like a woman, too. Garrett grabbed him by the scruff of his jacket, yanked him back, and thrust him onto the cushioned seat across from him. He decided against retrieving the revolver out of the compartment under his cushion. He carried a good four stone over his adversary, so had little need for the extra threat.

"I'm mad? You're the one setting yourself up to swing by the neck outside Newgate." He watched in satisfaction as Denny's anger drained in the dim carriage light, and he retreated into the corner of the compartment as if seeking refuge there. "Who the hell do you work for?"

"What?" Denny breathed, his whole body going still, blue eyes wide.

"You heard me. I want names. And I want them now."

"What are you talking about? I don't know anything more than what I wrote. I overheard two men talking. I barely saw their faces and they neglected to give their names. Good Lord, they were discussing fees for a murder! Your murder! They weren't exactly exchanging calling cards." Denny's words finished in a choked cry, and his head turned to the window as he furiously blinked watery eyes.

Disgust filled Garrett over the man's pathetic reaction. "Listen carefully, Denny. You're not going anywhere until I get names." He reined in his own anger, but his words were implacable.

Denny whirled back to him, a spark of his earlier defiance lighting his eyes. "It's Daniels, not Denny. You might start with getting *my name* right."

"Why bother? After the magistrate finishes with you, your name's irrelevant. There's no need to address the dead."

Daniels gasped and made another lunge for the door.

Garrett's hand shot out again. Cupping his forehead, he shoved him back. "Stop that. You're not going anywhere. We can sit here all night—or until you remember what you've forgotten."

Daniels edged back on the seat, his eyes shifting over the carriage before turning a mutinous expression on Garrett, his gloved hands fisting. "You can't extract information from me that I don't have. If I was involved in this plot against you, why would I be here now? Jeopardizing my own life? Why in heaven's name would I warn you of something that implicates me? Do you take me for that big of a fool?"

Garrett scowled and made a threatening move toward Daniels. He backed off when the man flinched and pressed farther into the corner, holding up his hands. Bloody hell. He felt like he had attacked a wounded man. Daniels was either one hell of an actor, or he spoke the truth, damn him.

Sighing, Garrett leaned back in his seat and raked a hand through his hair. "Start at the beginning and tell me everything you know."

Daniels eyed him warily for a moment before, in a slow and steady tone, he recounted the conversation he had overheard on Hammond's back patio.

Garrett snorted. "A tall man wearing black formal attire, and a shorter man with coarse speech dressed as a footman? The tall man stated he knew the footman didn't work for Hammond?" At Daniels's nod, Garrett continued. "The man you followed had dark hair, an aquiline nose, and thin features?" Another nod from Daniels. "That could describe half the fops there tonight. That's it? The only information you have?" Christ. The man was a useless idiot. Intelligence won battles. It won wars.

How the hell was he to fight an unknown enemy without it?

Spots of pink flamed on Daniels's smooth cheeks. "It was pitch-black, and I stood some distance away. But with a guest list of over three hundred, it's little surprise I didn't know the man. You may be on a first-name basis with all the members of the ton, but I, thankfully, am not." He finished the last in a heated tone and looked away.

Garrett cocked a brow at the blatant insult to the exalted aristocracy. Perhaps the man was not a complete idiot after all. "Why didn't you speak to Hammond immediately? We could have caught them leaving. You should—"

"If I can't identify the man, whom are they to apprehend?" Daniels interrupted him. "As I've tried to explain, the only information I have to pass along is a warning for you."

"Why didn't you follow him onto the dance floor?"

Daniels recoiled. "Once on the floor, he blended in with all the other guests, and I lost track of him." He dropped his eyes. After a moment, he lifted them to meet Garrett's. "I am sorry."

"So am I," Garrett muttered before turning to brood. The clatter of the horses' hooves and the lumbering creak of the carriage as it rolled along the pavement filled the silence. The night watch bellowed out the time and the weather.

"You said the man tossed something for payment. You didn't catch what it might be?"

Daniels shook his head. "Only that it was gold."

"That narrows it down." Sarcasm riddled Garrett's response. "I'm sure if you were there, you would have asked for a closer inspection."

"If I were there, they'd be dead and we wouldn't be here."

Daniels's eyes shot to his. "Yes, well, not all of us are military heroes."

"You don't need to be a hero to show courage, man," he snapped.

After a moment, he heard Daniels shift in his seat and clear his throat. "Can you think of anyone who would want you harmed? A jilted husband? Someone with whom you've dueled? Won money from?"

Garrett's eyes narrowed on Daniels. "I see you've managed to catch up on the gossip since you've returned from abroad."

"I'm not deaf, sir. If I were, we wouldn't be here, would we?"

"Point taken. However, if we go by that, it circles back to you. I won money off you."

"But you gave it back." The words were barely audible.

Garrett cocked a brow. "So you won't kill me?"

"Again, if I wanted you dead, why would I be here? Warning you?" After a moment of silence, Daniels sighed. "Look, I'm trying to help you. You don't have to trust me, but it's important that you trust this warning. You need to heed it. That is, if you value your life."

"Now there's the question," Garrett murmured and watched Daniels's eyes widen at his cynicism. "But reminding me there is a queue of men who'd like to put me six feet underground is help I don't need."

"Don't forget women." Daniels lifted his chin. "I'm sure with your charm and grace, they must just swoon at your feet."

Surprised by the taunt, Garrett eyed Daniels, whose bravado faltered under his pointed stare. He shrank back in his seat and again averted his gaze. Garrett frowned, something nagging him about the man's reaction. He slung his arrows, but then braced himself as if unable to bear the brunt of a return salvo. Like a mouse swatting at a lion. The man would never survive a day in battle.

"They swoon all right, but it's not from charm. When you're older and more experienced, you'll understand." His eyes raked

Daniels with derision. "Or perhaps not. But by all means, add women to the list. Like Herodias's daughter, I'm sure one or two of them would love my severed head on a platter."

A wine red flush stained Daniels's cheeks as he stared out the carriage window.

Frowning, Garrett studied his profile. He was an odd bugger. There was something effeminate about him with those long-lashed eyes. The blue of them so bright and deep you could swim in them. His pink cheeks were almost gaunt, the man reed thin. His lips were the only thing full about him. They were too full, almost sensual, a luscious red and . . . He stiffened. Daniels was right. He was mad. Contemplating the man's lips, for God's sake. He didn't give a good Goddamn if the man was light on his feet.

What mattered was if he was a lying bastard.

Damned if he knew if Daniels spoke the truth. Before Garrett could question him further, there was an explosion outside.

The unmistakable sound of gunshots ripped into the silence of the night.

All thoughts of his passenger fled Garrett's mind. He fought to maintain his seat when the horses bolted into a breakneck pace, tossing them about like sacks of seed.

Shouts and curses rent the air.

Swearing, Garrett lunged for the door. The coach veered sharply around a corner and slammed him into the unforgiving barrier, his hand gripping the latch. The carriage tipped at a precarious angle. For one dangerous moment, it hovered suspended half upright. It tilted toward Garrett, before it flipped onto its side. Well sprung and luxurious, the vehicle was not constructed to take city turns at full speed.

Garrett's shoulders slammed into the doorjamb and his head snapped back. Before he could draw breath, Daniels's body catapulted onto his. The man's screams echoed through the cabin, then instantly died when his head smacked into the door-frame above Garrett's shoulder. His body slumped against Garrett's, still and silent.

Shouts drifted in from outside, men's voices yelling to one another.

He recognized Havers barking a response and trusted him to handle the clamor while Garrett eased Daniels's crumpled body off of him and scrambled to his feet. He knelt on the door now flush with the ground between the two carriage seats and leaned over Daniels's unconscious figure. His screams still echoed in Garrett's ears, rattling him.

His palm slid over the man's temple and shoved his hair back, feeling the beginning of an egg swelling. The skin was not broken, but as he studied Daniels's temple more closely, he discovered the thick brown hair was but a wig. Underneath, blond strands were drawn back from the man's head. Surprise filled Garrett. Other than bishops and barristers, wigs were long out of fashion.

The thump of noises against the side of the coach distracted him, and he looked up as the door above him swung open. His coachman Ned's anxious features peered down at him. "My lord? You all right?"

"Yes, fine. Havers?"

"He's following one of 'em two bastards who shot at us. Havers took one down."

"The horses?"

"Fine, sir. Skittish, but I settled 'em down."

"What happened? Where are we?"

"Few blocks from Mayfair, sir. Close to home."

"There were two men? Is the one Havers hit wounded or dead?"

"Dead, sir." Ned frowned, his blue eyes darkening. "A gent went to fetch the night watch. Said he'd take care of the body."

Before Garrett could reply, clattering noise buffeted the carriage side and Havers joined Ned, his cheeks flushed, his hair standing up in tufts. "I lost the other one, sir. One dead, one gone."

Garrett cursed. Any leads or information he could extract from the men were lost.

"Some blokes are here to assist with the carriage," Havers said. "Heard the crash. Shall we give you a hand out?"

Garrett frowned down at Daniels. "Not yet. Ned, you said we're close to home?"

"Yes, my lord."

"Good." He leaned over and lifted the cushion on the seat to reveal the compartment underneath. Extracting the revolver, he stood and handed it up to Ned, knowing Havers carried his own. *Armed* and *Ready* were Havers's middle names. Serving as Garrett's adjunct for two years in the Crimea, he'd lived up to them.

Used to taking command, Garrett quickly snapped off his orders. "Ned, take this and go home. Saddle up Champion and return with him. My companion has hit his head and is unconscious. No point in moving him until I have a ride. I don't trust any hired hackney. And Ned, watch your back. Havers, stand guard. Keep an eye out for the night watchman. I don't know if there are others, but plan for it. I don't want to be outflanked again. Inform any man who remains to help with righting the coach that he will be paid handsomely for his troubles. Those who can offer any information on the dead man will be paid double. And Havers, alert me to Ned's return."

"Right, sir," the men replied simultaneously.

He watched them disappear from above, the sound of their steps against the carriage reverberating through the coach.

Left alone, Garrett's attention returned to Daniels, and he knelt beside him. He slid his hand behind the young man's shoulders and gently propped him into a sitting position. At the close contact, something prickly climbed the back of Garrett's neck. It was similar to the feelings he had experienced before riding into battle, minutes before the hidden ambush mowed down half his men.

Daniels groaned and his eyes opened. Pools of watery blue blinked up at Garrett before fluttering closed.

The vulnerable look touched Garrett, tugging at something buried deep inside him. Compassion? Disconcerted, he sat back on his heels and rubbed his neck. And then he froze. His eyes shifted over the pale features inches before him, reassessing the cream-colored skin, the pink cheeks, and those full, sensual lips in a heart-shaped face.

He removed one of his gloves and leaned over to loosen Daniels's cravat, sliding the material free. He slipped his hand into the open collar of Daniels's white dress shirt, feeling for his pulse at his throat. Daniels's skin was warm and soft against his fingers, delicate and smooth as silk.

An ominous chill swept Garrett. Almost unconsciously his hand lowered until he encountered a swath of bandages encircling the man's chest. He paused, the chill deepening as he slipped his hand beneath the tight binding. When his fingers slid over the beginning mound of soft, round flesh, he jerked his hand free and dropped onto his heels. He spit out a string of expletives as he swiped his hands down his face. The answer to what disturbed him about Daniels plowed into him. Bloody hell.

Once again, he had been ambushed.

This explained why he was drawn to Daniels the minute their eyes locked across the card table. Why he had followed him across the room. Why Daniels didn't dare confront the men he had overheard on the patio. Gut instinct sharpened by years of battle had warned Garrett there was something different about Daniels. He had attributed it to his being so damn young, peach-faced soft, and fresh out of the schoolroom. Not once in his wildest imaginings did it occur to him that the man *was a woman*.

His mind rebelled against the revelation. It was as if the enemy before him had suddenly switched sides. Garrett clenched his jaw.

What the hell was she doing gallivanting around dressed like a man?

And more important, who the hell was she?

And why the hell did she have to crash into his life when it was already in pieces?

Chapter Four

≈

GARRETT had little time to contemplate this disturbing turn of events, for Havers bellowed his name and the carriage echoed with the clamor of someone again scaling the side of the cab. Moments later, Havers's face appeared framed in the open door.

"Ned's in sight. Shall we haul you up, sir?" Havers spoke with his usual blunt eloquence.

Garrett blew out a breath, struggling to collect his thoughts. The shock of his discovery still pulsed through him. "Yes, ah, we'll assist Daniels out first. I'll lift him up to you. Take care with his head. Take care with her," he muttered the last under his breath. He slid an arm beneath her knees and another around her back, carefully cradling his burden as he rose to his feet. Her body was warm, featherlight, and he curled his arms protectively around her.

It had been so long since he had held a woman, two years too long.

Gritting his teeth, Garrett yanked his attention back to the task at hand.

With Havers pulling from above and his assistance from below, Daniels slid free of the coach.

Havers returned to grasp Garrett's hand and drag him out. Built like an ox with arms the size of tree trunks, hauling over fourteen stone barely extracted a grunt from Havers.

Outside, Garrett leapt to the ground and circled to where Havers had propped Daniels against the coach's roof. A cool breeze brushed over Garrett, and he shrugged off his evening jacket and knelt down. Easing Daniels forward, Garrett wrapped his coat around her, the large garment engulfing her body. Frowning, he studied the pale, still features before him.

Damn, he should have seen it. *Why hadn't he seen it?*

Long lashes swept her cheeks and her lips were lightly parted. He recalled those deep pools of blue blinking up at him, and the jolt at the feel of a slim hand warm in his when he'd returned her wager.

A woman. A Goddamn woman.

Twice in one night she had caught him by surprise. Despite the gentle features before him, this young woman held some mettle. It took that and more to have done what she had this evening: infiltrating a gentlemen's card room, following a man plotting murder, and then confronting Garrett with the plans. All three scenarios had placed Daniels in danger, if that was indeed her name.

Garrett swore. He didn't like to be ambushed. He had never liked puzzles, and he sure as hell didn't like the idea of being some bloody bastard's prey.

Once again, he was at war. Different location, different players, but the goal remained the same—kill or be killed.

Garrett clenched his jaw and vowed that this time, he'd be damned if he'd make for easy prey. An image of his blue lancer uniform flashed before him. The sun had gleamed off it, lighting it like a bright beacon for the Russians to use as target practice. With it, came the inevitable onslaught of memories. Shot and shell rained, death screams deafened, and the rank smell of gunpowder and corpses suffocated him.

He bolted to his feet and staggered back, shaking his head to dislodge the images. Christ. He had burned what remained of his bloodied and battered uniform. Pity, he couldn't burn his memories with it.

He felt a touch on his arm and whirled to find Havers beside him. Calm brown eyes steadied him. Once again, Havers dragged him back to the present, regardless of whether or not he wished to return.

"My lord? All right, sir?"

He swiped an unsteady hand across his face. As right as he'd ever be. That was the way of it for those pitiful few who had survived the carnage of Balaclava.

He turned to face Daniels's slumped figure and nodded. Right. New war, new players. He needed to draw up a battle plan—one that included Daniels.

She possessed the only intelligence Garrett held, and Garrett refused to let her go. Not until he knew more about her.

He let his eyes roam over her slim figure in the masculine disguise. An image flashed before him of those luminous blue eyes spearing him with defiant scorn. For the first time since his return home, a woman had caught his attention. While he had no plans for a woman in his wreck of a life, she intrigued him, and he'd be damned if he'd let her go before he knew more about her. His mind was made up. He was keeping her.

He recalled their exchanges in the coach, the jabs, parries, and retreats. The arrangement might lead to a few skirmishes. Good thing Daniels had some mettle to her. She would need it for the upcoming battles.

Garrett left Daniels and joined Havers to assess the damage to his coach. There would be nicks and dents on the side flush with the street, but nothing permanent. His attention shifted to the horses. He ran his hand over the coat of one of the four hefty bays, assuring himself they had weathered the ordeal as well. As he did so, his eyes scanned his surroundings.

A group of men stood a few feet away, waiting as Havers had directed, to assist with the coach. Gas lamps lit the immediate vicinity but little breached the veil of fog coating the evening. A prostrate body sprawled on the cobblestones a few yards from the coach. Garrett left the horses to see to the man Havers had shot.

Sightless pools of black stared up at him from a pockmarked face. Garrett didn't recognize the man but had no expectation he would. He was a hired lackey, one of many patrolling London's seedier districts, ready to do any dirty job to earn a quid. Poor sod. The only information he could provide was corroboration for what Daniels had overheard. Someone wanted Garrett dead.

Ned drew up beside him, holding the reins to his stallion, Champion.

"My lord, is he all right?" Ned nodded to Daniels, his brow furrowed under his mop of black hair.

Garrett hesitated before replying, his eyes following Ned's. "Yes, he'll come round." Explanations would have to wait until he knew more. The more information he collected, the better to form a strategy.

He walked over and mounted Champion. "Havers, lift Daniels up to me. I'll take him home. When the watch comes, should he have any questions after speaking with you, direct him to my address. No, wait." After the recent ambush on his coach, plans needed to be changed. "Direct him to Warren's. I'll be staying there tonight."

Garrett recalled his brother-in-law, the Earl of Warren, was in town, having plans to meet up with him later in the week. His sister, Kit, remained in the country, awaiting the birth of their third child. His eyes strayed to Daniels, and he thought Kit's absence fortuitous. The last thing he needed was his half sister's inevitable barrage of questions, needling him for answers he didn't have—yet.

Havers bent and slung Daniels into his arms, turning to lift him up to Garrett with Ned stepping forward to assist. Between the two of them, they managed to drape Daniels's body across the saddle.

Garrett studiously averted his eyes from the round buttocks before him. Later, free from prying eyes, he would readjust her position, but the intimacy of cradling Daniels in his arms and between his legs would raise a brow as well as a few snickers. Garrett didn't need to draw any more attention to himself. What he was receiving thus far was already deadly. Disguised as a man, Daniels had to exit like one. There was no help for it.

"Sir, should I inform the watch about the trouble you warned me about?"

Havers was as shrewd as a hawk; nothing escaped the man. Garrett frowned. He'd be damned if he'd repeat Daniels's story to the city watchman. He preferred to arm himself with more information before loading others with the paltry bits of conversation Daniels had overheard. He tightened his hands on the reins. "No. For now, tell the watch the usual footpads overstepped their territory in search of easy prey."

Havers nodded and stepped back.

Garrett gave his overturned coach a last glance and then nudged Champion in the direction of his brother-in-law's residence. He rested his hand on Daniels's back as he walked Champion a few blocks to place some distance between them and the accident. Once free of witnesses, he slipped his hands beneath her body and with a grunt, lifted her up to settle her into the saddle before him. Her head lolled on his shoulder and he drew her closer. A slim thigh pressed flush against his, and the feel of her posterior cradled intimately against his loins awakened dormant areas from a deep sleep. Cursing, he shifted in the saddle and urged Champion into a gentle walk.

All the while, his mind scrambled for an answer.

Who the hell is she?

⤛⤜

GARRETT REINED IN before the Corinthian pillars framing the imposing entrance to Montclair, his brother-in-law's London residence. The hour neared one in the morning, but being early in the Season, the night was still young. He doubted Warren would be home, but the doors were always open to him.

Warren's marriage to Kit linked them as family, but their real bonds were forged during their early days at Eton. Garrett never understood what had possessed him to intervene for the skinny boy floundering in a fight with his spectacles knocked askew. At ten years, Garrett had been an angry loner. Toss a dark dose of mean into the mix, and he was left to himself and had preferred it that way.

He would have kept out of it when the fight was two to one. That fight was fair, considering the bullies pounding on Brandon wielded their verbal abuse better than their fists. Small, wiry, and with those ridiculous spectacles, Brandon Andrews wore a target symbol like a brand burned on his forehead.

The loss of Brandon's spectacles combined with a third boy jumping into the fray had forced Garrett to take exception to the odds. He had joined the battle to even things out. When the bullies had sulked off, Brandon clipped Garrett's cheek before he clarified friend from foe. And that was that. Like a tenacious dog, Brandon had trailed Garrett's footsteps until he had chiseled away at his solitary fortress and breached his defenses.

Brandon had gained in height and weight, took a slab of Garrett's mean for his own, and discarded the spectacles except for reading. Soon where one boy was found, the other followed, both leaving a trail of trouble in their wake.

Years later, after Cambridge, Brandon gained his earldom and married Garrett's sister, Kit. The couple had two boys, with another child soon due.

Once again, Garrett was alone.

He cursed his detour down memory lane. For God's sake, Kit hounded him often enough so he'd never be alone, even if he wanted to be. Needed to be. His hand tightened on Daniels's waist and he grunted. And he certainly wasn't alone now.

He shook his head and shifted Daniels to lay her gently over the front of Champion's saddle. Pressing a hand to the small of her back to hold her steady, he dismounted. He eased Daniels from the horse, sliding his arms beneath her legs and swinging her into his embrace. With quick strides, he ascended the steps to Brandon's front door and banged its brass knocker with a heavy hand. If Brandon was out, a servant should be up awaiting his arrival home, or so Garrett hoped.

When both his hopes and the door remained unanswered, he shifted Daniels in his arms to rap the knocker again.

An irritable-looking Poole, Brandon's butler, yanked opened the door. He jerked his burgundy robe closed with one hand while the other grasped a brass candleholder. The scowl creasing the older man's face changed to surprise upon recognizing Garrett.

"Sorry to drag you from your bed at this late hour, Poole," he said, "but due to an unusual turn of events, my guest and I are in need of temporary lodgings for the night."

"Of course, my lord," Poole recovered quickly. He retreated from the door to allow Garrett entrance into the marble-floored foyer. "Lady Kristen always has your room ready for you." He used Kit's proper name. "We can settle your guest in the blue room, next to yours. If you'll but follow me." Poole turned to lead Garrett across the foyer and up the sweeping staircase to the second floor.

Brandon's ancestors followed their passage from their seats in the portraits climbing the stairwell. They were an imposing, austere bunch of old codgers, quite like Poole.

"I'll need someone to see to Champion as well," Garrett said, repositioning Daniels as his body temperature rose with their combined heat. His boots echoed on the marble stairs, while Poole's light cast dancing shadows over the staircase.

"Certainly. Will the gentleman be requiring the services of a surgeon or strong coffee?"

Garrett's lips twitched at the veiled reference to his last visit when both were required. "Ah, no, neither will be necessary. We had a bit of an accident with the carriage, and my companion was tossed about. However, a maid would come in handy." He nearly collided with Poole when the butler stopped short, turned, and cocked an imperious brow to peer down at Garrett from his lofty perch a step above.

An available maid for a gentleman guest clearly was not a request the butler felt obliged to honor. No surprise there. Poole might be loyal to Brandon, but his service to Brandon's late father had been decades longer. Thus the elderly servant had no compunction in spearing Brandon or Garrett with a look that reminded both men that he'd known them since they were in short trousers and deep trouble. His expression also managed to wordlessly convey that for the late earl's sake, nothing illicit would transpire under his watch.

Garrett shifted his feet under the penetrating stare, bracing his weight against the mahogany banister behind him. "It's of a delicate nature. You see, *he* happens to be a *she*, and while that appears quite damning to me in this situation, for once I am innocent of any foul play. When Warren returns home, I will explain everything to him. But first the lady is in need of a bed and a maid to assist her if that can be accommodated."

Poole's rheumy blue eyes fell to Daniels and narrowed speculatively. After a moment, he gave a curt nod and turned to continue up the stairs. "The earl is home. He returned and retired early." He paused before a third door at the end of a long corridor and opened it, stepping back to allow Garrett to precede him inside.

"So Brandon's keeping country hours?" Garrett laid Daniels on the immense feather bed jutting into the middle of the room.

She barely made an indent on the plush comforter. He leaned over and slid his evening jacket from her still form and tossed it to the end of the bed. Her lack of response did not yet concern Garrett. Experience had taught him that a knock to the head could render a man unconscious for hours. Often longer for those who didn't wish to return to reality too soon, or so Garrett believed, well aware that oblivion was safe and pain free.

"No, my lord. He complained of a pounding headache brought on by bad drink and bad company." Poole lit the lamp beside the bed. "My apologies, my lord, but I had assumed he was with you."

Garrett met Poole's blank expression. It was a wretched state of affairs employing servants who couldn't be dismissed for brash impertinence. But there you have it. "Please. I only drink the best liquor."

"Again, my apologies. You are quite right. It was quantity, not quality, with which you had the problem. Permit me to say I'm glad to see that is not true tonight. Welcome back, my lord. You have been missed." Poole's blue eyes sparkled before he crossed to the door. He paused with his hand on the knob. "And I trust that you have not abandoned one vice only to return to another." His gaze pointedly landed on Daniels, then returned to Garrett. "I shall send Molly in to assist your friend. Shall I have Shelby wake Brandon?"

Garrett barely recovered from his surprise at Poole's dual compliment and condemnation, cursing the man and his memory. It was too damn long. "Yes. I'll wait for him in his study."

He was happy to let Brandon's valet have the honors of waking him. It might take the edge off some of his temper, though Garrett had no compunction over interrupting his friend's precious rest. The last time Garrett had a full night's sleep was over six months ago.

Before October 25, 1854.

Before hell had opened up and spilled all its horrors.

Garrett rubbed his neck and wondered if he had made a mistake in coming here, but it couldn't be helped. He needed reinforcements, and Brandon had always covered his back.

Stirring from the bed drew Garrett's attention. Daniels groaned and shifted restlessly, but did not wake. Garrett removed his gloves and pressed a hand to her forehead, sliding her hair back and fingering the lump on her temple. Her skin was soft and warm, the bump the size of half an egg, hard and mean. He frowned.

He ran his hand over her head to find the fastenings of her wig, which he unclipped and slid off. A linen cap covered her hair, and he removed this as well, releasing the pins holding her hair up. Long strands tumbled free over his fingers, an undulating wave of golden honey. He leaned over and held a curl to his nose, inhaling a light floral fragrance he didn't recognize. He closed his eyes.

Moments later, his eyes snapped open and, appalled by his actions, he jerked back from the bed. Spinning on his heel, he opened the door and nearly collided with the maid, Molly, who stood outside, her hand poised to knock.

When she recovered from her surprise, she bobbed a quick curtsy. "My lord, Poole told me ye be needing my assistance."

"Yes, ah, that's right." Garrett waved his hand toward the bed. He had to clear his throat before he could string together a coherent set of directions for the maid. Once delivered, he bolted from the room.

Storming down the hall, he tugged at the knot of his cravat and yanked it free. Christ. He'd be damned if a mere slip of a woman distracted him.

He flew downstairs to the wing housing Brandon's study.

It was time to get his reinforcements in line, for he was in more danger than he realized—and it wasn't from those trying to kill him.

Chapter Five

※⧓⧓⧓⧓⊱

"WHAT the hell is wrong with you? Can't you behave like a civilized person and wait to discuss things in the bloody morning? Your life better be at stake because anything else can wait." Brandon Andrews stormed into his study and slammed the door shut behind him. "And get out of my chair. If I can't have my bed, I want my chair."

Garrett wryly noted that Brandon hadn't shot off all his temper at his valet, for he appeared fully loaded. His green eyes blazed, his dark brown hair stood up in uncombed tufts, and a scowl contorted his usually amicable features. His white linen shirt was unbuttoned to the waist, his shirttails draped loose over buff-colored trousers.

"Stop whining. For God's sake, you sound like a country bumpkin. It *is* morning. Just early." As Brandon glowered at him, Garrett unfolded himself from Brandon's leather chair and circled his desk. He moved to the table dividing the bookshelves that towered from floor to ceiling and lifted the brandy decanter and the glass beside it. "You should be at your club drinking. Since you're not, you can catch up here." He thrust the glass at Brandon, who scowled at it before snatching it from Garrett.

"What the hell do you want?" Brandon grumbled, slumping in his seat and eyeing Garrett over the rim of his glass as he took a sip.

"It so happens that my life *is* in jeopardy, and you're going to help me save it."

Brandon lifted his hand and pressed it to his temple. "Not sure I heard correctly, but I'm listening and the pounding in my head can't get any worse."

"At Hammond's tonight, someone overheard a conversation between two men haggling over the fee to murder me. The killer thought the price too cheap for a wounded war hero."

Brandon paused in the act of lifting his glass to his lips. "Someone has been hired to kill you?"

"Yes, and they attempted it tonight. Two thugs ambushed my coach en route home." Garrett paced the width of the room as he recounted the accident, his discovery of Daniels's disguise, and his decision to come to Brandon's.

"What a strange turn of events," Brandon murmured.

Garrett stopped. "What do you mean?"

Brandon set his glass on his desk and leaned forward. "Considering you've been trying to kill yourself for the past six months, I'm surprised to hear you have issues with someone being paid to finish the job."

Garrett stiffened and opened his mouth to deliver a scathing setback, but under Brandon's piercing stare, he clamped it shut.

With Garrett's history of carousing, gambling, and philandering, it was little surprise that some people wanted him dead. Since his return from the Crimea, he might have included himself among this group. It wasn't that he wished to die during his period of self-imposed seclusion and inebriated exile, but rather that he hadn't cared if he lived. There was a fine line separating the two and he had been walking it.

He closed his eyes but opened them to meet Brandon's steady gaze. It was time to take a different path. He had survived while so many others hadn't. If it took a murderous plot and the courageous young woman lying unconscious upstairs to remind him of the value of his life, so be it.

He was alive; it was time he started living.

He cleared his throat to respond. "Well, I *do* take issue."

After a beat of silence, Brandon nodded. "Good, because I do, too." He raised his drink in a toast. "Welcome back," he said and downed the contents.

Brandon slammed his glass down, leaned forward, and grabbed a paper and quill from his desk drawer. He lifted a pair of silver-framed spectacles and slid them on. "Now then, let's go over the information we have and draft our plan of attack. A good defense is often dependent on a strong offense." At Garrett's silence, Brandon lifted his head and leveled his stare on him. "Don't just stand there. Let's get started."

Garrett studied his friend. When Brandon's eyes gleamed from behind his spectacles, Garrett frowned. It was little wonder the man had married his half sister, for the two of them had the uncanny ability to rip his feet out from under him. They would not have allowed him to walk his line of indecision for much longer. If he hadn't come around on his own, they would have hauled him back to the living, ready or not.

Good thing he was ready.

≫≪

ALEX FLOATED IN a hazy void as impenetrable as the thick fog layering the city. She fought to emerge from it. Disoriented, she blinked as her gaze drifted over her surroundings.

She lay in a spacious feather bed, the covers drawn up to her chin, a floral canopy above her. A dresser stood across the room, a comfortable easy chair beside it, and a wardrobe in the corner next to a commode. Dim light from the bedside lamp played over the bouquets of rose carnations climbing the wallpaper. The room was warm, welcoming, and totally unfamiliar.

Alex's heart thundered. She fought the choking fear that curled around her as she struggled to piece together the events of the evening. Like grasping at shadows that refused to slide into focus, the memories blurred and stumbled into each other.

She was in the card room at Hammond's. She had lost the hand against . . .

Kendall.

His name doused her with a chilling blast of awareness. She

sat up abruptly, her head pounding. Closing her eyes against the pain, the images flooded her. A murderous plot, the confrontation with Kendall, the carriage accident, and then merciful blackness.

Good Lord, had Kendall been killed after all?

"Shh, Miss. Ye be all right. Lay back and rest. Ye be safe now."

The words were soft and soothing with a lyrical country cadence. The hand pressing her shoulder was gentle but firm.

A wet cloth pressed against her forehead, the touch calming Alex. Her breathing leveled, the pain receded, and for the moment her fears were held at bay. When she opened her eyes, a maid leaned over her, her white cap perched on her head and her expression one of concern.

"My name's Molly, and I've seen to ye. 'Ave a nasty bump on ye 'ead, but 'twill mend. Could 'ave been worse. Whot a fright ye 'ad." The maid stepped away to dip the rag into the porcelain basin on the commode and wring it out. Short and plump, her pear-shaped figure swayed as she walked. She returned to the bed carrying a glass. "'Ere's a dollop of brandy. Can be the devil's drink, but the angels claim it as well ta ease aches and pains."

Gingerly, Alex sat up. If she kept her movements slow, her head remained on her shoulders and did not topple off as she half expected. She clutched the glass with both hands and braced herself to voice the question she couldn't avoid. "And Kendall? He also survived the . . . the accident?"

The maid waved her hand as if to brush her concerns aside. "No worries there. 'Twas Lord Kendall that sent me to ye. Would take more than a tipped carriage ta harm him. 'E's survived far worse." Her voice lowered and she spoke in hushed tones. "The 'orrors of the war and all."

Alex sagged back into the bed. The weight of her burdens might cause her to stagger, but shouldering the news of a man's murder would have dropped her to her knees.

She lifted the brandy to her lips and drank. Liquid fire burned a scorching path down her throat. Bolting up, she blinked furiously as her eyes watered, and a spasm of coughs erupted from her. She clutched her head. An ease for aches and pains indeed. One would forget their own mother if they imbibed enough of this potent brand.

Needing to keep her wits clear, she set the glass on the bed-side table and froze. Her lips parted at the sight of her bare arm.

Good Lord, was she naked?

She snatched her hand back to press it to her chest and exhaled at the feel of fabric against her breasts. She glanced down. She wore a deep royal blue satin nightgown, whisper thin and baby soft against her skin. Of the finest quality, it was rich, decadent, and designed to please a man. The round curves of her breasts peeked above the plunging neckline. Heat burned her cheeks, and she drew the covers up to her neck.

Kendall. Womanizer and rake.

How dare he! How dare he give her one of his mistress's castoffs as if she'd step into the role. Her memory was fast return-ing and with it, her relief at Kendall's survival faded. He may have discovered her to be a woman, but he had yet to discern what sort of woman she was. She was most certainly not *this* kind of woman, or rather *his* kind of woman.

Not now. Not ever.

"Miss? Miss, ye be all right? Ye be lookin' a mite flushed."

Alex started at the voice. "Ah, yes, it's the brandy."

"Ach, I shouldn't 'ave given it ta ye on an empty stomach. It's a mite early, but I'll do some foragin'. See if I can scrounge up a wee morsel. A bit of meat on ye is wot ye need. Ye be skin and bones. Lie back and rest for now." Molly fluffed the pillows behind Alex and tucked the covers securely about her before she left. Food in Molly's world was clearly medicinal, as her stout build attested.

Alex closed her eyes, cursing her stomach's betraying growl at the mention of food. Pity a person had to eat. Poverty would be so much easier if one could forgo that expense.

She shook her head, bemused. Clearly, the accident had addled her wits. She winced as her fingers probed the bump above her hairline. She ran her hands through the tangled strands of her hair, wondering what had happened to her wig and clothes, wondering what Kendall had thought when he discovered her to be a woman.

She hoped he'd choked. At the very least, he should suffer wrenching guilt over his callous treatment of her in the car-riage. She squirmed at the memory of his shoving her into the cab, his hand bold and intimate upon her buttocks. Her cheeks

burning, she curled her fingers around her upper arm where
Kendall had handled her. His grip had been punishing before
he eased it, as if he had sensed her frailty.

Just when Kendall appeared ready to wring her neck, those
gray eyes nearly flaying the skin from her with their razor-sharp
scrutiny, he had retreated. Of course, with her cowering before
him, Alex hadn't presented him with a fair fight. But still. The
man had been filled with a boiling cauldron of anger, yet it had
never overflowed onto her.

A seasoned soldier, Kendall might be cold, hard, and un-
sympathetic, but he possessed control. He would not hurt her.
He had proven that tonight.

The man baffled her. Regardless of his distrust of her, he
had kept her safe. And that was something she hadn't felt in a
long, long time. Not since leaving home over a year ago.

Her eyes drifted over the room and settled on a garment
draped over the end of the bed. Recognizing her evening jacket,
she leaned forward to draw it to her only to realize it was not
hers. A familiar masculine scent identified its owner. Kendall.
After a brief hesitation, she slid it on, drew it closed, and folded
back the long sleeves covering her hands. It felt as if she were
enfolded in the man's arms, held safe.

She froze, the intimacy blindsiding her. The doorknob
rattled and Molly returned. Alex silently thanked her interruption, not wishing to be alone with her betraying thoughts, for
they tread into forbidden ground.

The maid carried a tray and wore a broad smile. "Cook is
a cheap, untrusting old biddy and locks up most of the cabi-
nets." Molly snorted. "A body would starve on her rations."
She winked at Alex. "But I managed ta dig up some bread and
cheese and best of all, fresh custard. Now miss, that should
return the pounds ta ye."

The maid had heated up a cup of cocoa and Alex cradled
the steaming mug in her hands as she sipped, forcing herself
to wait until Molly departed to attack the food. It was a feast,
and her mouth watered just looking at it. She planned to regain
her strength, rein in her straying thoughts, and later deal with
Kendall. Much, much later she hoped, and not on an empty
stomach.

When the custard crossed her lips, she couldn't resist closing her eyes to savor it. She settled back into the plush pillows of the feather bed and for the first time that evening, a smile curved her lips.

"Molly must have told you I died."

Alex jumped, blinking at the sight of Kendall standing in the doorway. He leaned his tall figure against the doorframe, his arms crossed over his chest. The bedside lamp cast flickering shadows over his handsome features, but she didn't need much light to know those slate gray eyes were locked on her. She swallowed, returned her fork to her plate, and hastily wiped her mouth. "No, of course not."

Straightening, Kendall closed the door behind him and strolled to her bedside to inspect her platter of food. "Ah, custard. Molly jeopardized life and limb to venture into Cook's domain, but considering Molly believes food is the cure for all ailments, she'd risk it." He lifted his eyes to hers and his voice lowered. "She might be right, for here you are awake, not looking like death warmed over, and smiling, *Mr.* Daniels."

Alex's hand closed the collar of his jacket, feeling heat rise to her cheeks. Kendall's linen shirt clung to his broad shoulders. A stray lock of hair curled over his forehead and his lips pressed together as he studied her. In the dim light and towering over her, he looked even more formidable than he had in the carriage.

She shifted, feeling as if his perusal stripped her bare. Alex cursed him and his effect on her pulse rate. She no longer feared Kendall would physically harm her, but he was still too handsome, too familiar, and too close for her comfort.

"How is your head?"

His obvious concern for her welfare caught her off guard. "Fine, as long as I don't move."

"Then we'll have to make sure you don't." His eyes dropped to her hands clutching his jacket closed. "Nice robe."

She caught the gleam of amusement in his eyes and stiffened. "Thanks to you, I have no robe and no clothes." She lifted her chin. "I'd appreciate it if you returned them immediately, as I'd prefer to change out of your mistress's castoffs and be on my way."

She spoke quickly, fearing she'd lose courage if she hesitated. "Tonight's accident confirms I spoke the truth. We both could have been killed, so you can't suspect me of being part of the plot against you." She lowered her hands and sat up straighter, hoping she presented a braver front than she felt. Like a card game, no tells.

Kendall raised a brow. "Yes, you're definitely much better." He slid a chair from the corner of the room and drew it beside the bed. He spun it around, straddled it, and rested his arms along the back. "Are you quite sure you're wearing a castoff? Why don't you return my coat and let me be the judge of that?"

Her grip tightened on his jacket collar as she sank back into the pillows. There was something different about him, something she couldn't quite put her finger on. Of course, he was no longer furious with her. He appeared more relaxed, but there was something else. She realized she was staring at him, and when she saw his lips twitch, she flushed.

"No?" He raised a brow. "Fine, keep the coat; just don't wear it on your next visit to Hammond's card room."

He was baiting her. *That* was the difference. The other Kendall would never have teased her. He didn't possess a sense of humor. Her eyes widened, wary of this new tactic, this different Kendall. What was his game?

In a flash, he became serious. "While it appears you spoke the truth about what you overheard tonight, you still lied about so much more, *Miss* Daniels, if that is in fact your name?"

She bristled. "That wasn't a lie. It was but a simple deception to earn a few quid. No harm done, other than to the gents' deep pockets and perhaps their dignity, as no man likes to be bested by a woman. However, that would only be if I had won, but as you are well aware, I did not."

"Filmore's an ass and Chandler has no dignity. But what about you?" He nodded toward her. "Don't you have a care for your own reputation? You risk scandal should your deception be discovered. That damage is harmful and irreparable."

Once again, those gray eyes narrowed on her. She stifled her retort that she didn't give a scrap for society's judgment. Her gaze dropped to her platter of food, and she recalled the deep, gut-wrenching cravings during those times when she'd stretched out a single loaf of bread for days. She no longer lived in the society to which Kendall referred. In her world, a sterling reputation couldn't put food in one's belly, clothes on one's back, or a roof over one's head, so what good was it?

She clenched her jaw, unable to hide the bitterness coloring her words. "Some risks are worth taking."

This time when she met his eyes, she didn't look away. The silence stretched as he continued to study her in his infuriating manner, as if he could see through her bravado.

It was then she noticed his eyes weren't a solid slate gray, but ringed by a pale blue circle and unusually long lashes. His features were all sharp angles, his cheekbones chiseled into the hard contours of his striking face. Her eyes dropped to his mouth and she noticed his top lip was fuller than his bottom, softer, almost sensual. Suddenly those lips curved into a smile, a bright beaming flash.

She sucked in her breath at the impact of it. It softened the hard lines of his features and did disturbing things to her body. Her pulse rate spiked, heat suffused her cheeks and slid up her neck.

"Some risks are indeed worth taking, on that we are in agreement," Kendall said, his eyes warm.

Disconcerted, Alex shifted. There were risks she was willing to take, lines she was willing to cross, and there were those she was not. Kendall stood firmly on the other side of the line, deep in forbidden territory. He was a soldier wielding many weapons, all of them dangerous. She needed to get far away from him. But her traitorous body didn't move, couldn't move. Kendall held her captive without laying a finger on her.

Suddenly his smile vanished, his brows lowered, and suspicion clouded his eyes. "You're not dodging debt collectors or running from the magistrate or a vengeful husband, are you?"

Surprised by his sudden mood change, it took a moment before his words registered. "Certainly not," she protested. "And unlike yourself, no one wants *me* dead. I'm also not married, so that is one less vengeful husband for you to worry about."

He cocked a brow. "You're sounding more and more like yourself. Good. We'll get to your story later, or not, if you so choose. As long as you are not wanted by the law or involved in anything illegal, I won't force the issue—yet." Again he peered at her, letting his words hang in a question.

"I'm not."

"I'll have to trust you on that, for as you say, some risks are worth taking. Now if you're still willing to gamble on the odds, I'd like to raise the stakes."

She stilled. What was he talking about? She wasn't crossing *that* line. No words or devastating smiles could change her mind. She rubbed her temple, struggling to deduce his intent. "What are you talking about?"

"I want your help in apprehending the men planning my murder."

"What?" she breathed. "*Me?* But I've told you all I know. I don't—"

"You hold the only intelligence I have. I can't afford to lose that. Hence, I can't afford to lose you."

His words were like a strong wave, knocking her feet out from beneath her. In its wake, a cold, damp chill washed over her.

Kendall stood and began to pace the room. "You have something I want, and I have something *you* want."

"And what, besides my clothes, can that possibly be?" she said, her eyes narrowed.

He stopped and faced her, curling his hands around the footboard and leaning forward, his expression intense. "Money. You need it enough to risk scandal and expulsion from society. I have money, my own as well as the money I returned to you, which, if you recall, you did vow to repay."

She raised her chin. "You said you didn't want it."

"I don't *need* it." He corrected her. "You can keep those funds if you are willing to earn more by assisting me in this investigation. I will reimburse you for your time. Otherwise"—he shrugged—"I'm afraid I'll have to call in your debt as my bargaining chip."

She raked him with a contemptuous look. "Your word means nothing to you, so why should I trust you?"

"I'm trusting you," he pointed out. "I'm willing to forfeit your wager, but are you? Do you truly wish to be in my debt?" He straightened and peered down at her. "You don't strike me as someone who likes to be indebted to anyone. You chose to gamble for higher stakes and earn your own fortune, rather than have another bail you out. You didn't enter a profession suitable for a woman to earn an income, such as a governess or a paid companion. Well, if you want to play like a man, you have to pay like a man."

Anger suffused her. Damn him. He didn't know anything about her, her choices, or the risks she was willing to take.

She had spoken the truth when she had told him that neither the law nor a vengeful husband pursued her. She sought to escape her greedy, mercenary uncle, her late father's brother. He never would have allowed Alex to step into a respectable household as a paid companion or a governess. He had shut off those avenues when Alex had thwarted his plans for her and fled her home, barely managing to escape with the tattered remains of her hide. She wasn't willing to risk it again by entering into a murder investigation.

"If you assist me," he continued. "I will pay you for your time. You will be well compensated, or at least have enough monies to keep you out of gambling debt for the foreseeable future."

She ignored the unwelcome reminder of her recent card loss and struggled to digest his words. For someone starving, the offer of a steady income was like being delivered a full-course meal. She had to swallow before she could manage a response. "What? Why?"

"Consider it an exchange of sorts." He shrugged. "My life, for yours." He paused and his gaze leveled on hers, his gray eyes darkening. "And after last night, you as well as I are aware of the dangers inherent in assisting me. I will do all in my power to keep you safe, but someone is trying to kill me, and they don't give a damn if their murderous course sacrifices anyone else. You need to be aware of the risks you are facing in your choice to assist me. It's another reason why I'm willing to compensate you so generously."

She blinked, those horrible moments in the coach before her world went black flashing before her. She pressed her hand to her temple, her thoughts spiraling. Reviewing her ill-fated gambling foray and her own perilous situation, she wondered if she would be exchanging one form of danger for another? Some risks were worth taking, but at what price? Toss in Kendall's lethal smile and another danger assailed her. Her eyes snapped to his. "I can't be seduced. I won't be your mistress."

His lips parted. For the first time in all of their confrontations, she had caught him off guard. After an awkward silence, he collected himself. "I don't believe I asked for that, but fair enough." His eyes drifted over her, a teasing light in them. "Perhaps when we know each other better."

Heat suffused her. She drew the covers to her neck, again unsure of this Kendall. His relaxed features, soft and amused, stirring something beneath her breast.

His expression once again became serious. "So, Miss Daniels, if that is your name, do we have a deal or not?"

She struggled to keep up with his quicksilver mood changes, but she recognized the gleam of challenge in his eyes. He held the advantage now, but she might surprise him. It was past time for her to do just that.

She lifted her chin, straightened up, and met his damn dare. She had risked much this past year and survived with little money and no protection. Kendall offered her both. She liked those odds—and she wanted his money. She had plans for it. "Yes, I'll help you."

Kendall's smile returned, quick and sharp.

Alex caught her breath, cursing it and him as her words echoed back to her.

Some risks might be worth taking, but at what price?

Chapter Six

❧❧

GARRETT noted the slim thrust of his adversary's jaw and the determined glint in her eyes, and nearly shook his head. He hadn't played her wrong. She had mettle all right, sharp as steel and strong.

For now he'd settle for her willing participation in his plans, for they coincided with his. He vowed to eventually pry Miss Daniels's true identity from her. The enemy you know is better than the one you don't. Or was the expression, keep your friends close and your enemies closer? Either way, he was keeping her.

"For your assistance in this investigation, I will reimburse you for your time as well as any expenses you may incur. You have my word that you will not be hurt again and will be under my protection. I expect . . ." At her frown and furrowed brows, his words tapered off. "What is it?"

"I don't see how I can assist you further than I already have. I've told you everything I know."

"Right now, you are the only link to these men and their murderous plot against me. You heard their voices and got a look at one of them. You might remember something more about them, something distinctive about their voices, their walks, or an odd mannerism. The knock on your head also might have dislodged a detail you didn't recall earlier. After suffering a trauma in battle, some men speak of seeing things. Their lives flashing before their eyes, so to speak. Maybe something will return to you that will help you recognize one of them or assist us in finding them. So I need you. If not," he shrugged, "it's a gamble I'm willing to take. Unlike you, Miss Daniels, I don't wager what I can't afford to lose."

Her eyes narrowed at his reminder of her circumstance. "What about other risks?" she shot back. "What will your mistress have to say about this arrangement?"

The question both surprised and amused him. "You mean the mistress of this house? Whose castoff you protested wearing?"

She gave a curt nod.

He grinned at her mutinous expression. Too bad he had left his jacket on the bed. He would have liked to see the gown she wore. His sister had lovely clothes, and her nightgown would be no exception, something as sheer as silk. His eyes drifted over Daniels's features. Blue fabric would enhance the shimmering pools of her eyes, but a rich, deep red would provide a brilliant contrast against her fair skin.

He jerked back, stepping away from the bed. Christ. Hours ago, he had believed her to be a man. He now knew otherwise, but that was all he knew about her. He needed to retreat before she further lowered his defenses and he pictured her naked.

He returned his attention to Daniels's question. Kit, with her perverse sense of humor, would delight in being mistaken for a courtesan. "If you assist me in apprehending those wishing my neck in a noose, I'm certain you will win Kristen's full blessing and support." He crossed to the door, but paused and faced her, unable to resist a parting line. "After all, she loves me."

A flush climbed up the slim column of Daniels's neck and she dropped her eyes.

Discussing one's mistress in mixed company was bad form, but Kit wasn't his mistress and he'd spoken the truth. Besides, he had cradled Daniels in his arms, stood at her bedside, and his jacket cloaked her nearly nude body. They had long ago dispensed with formalities and proper etiquette. They would have to draw up new rules in which to navigate their strange alliance.

However, for some reason, he wanted Daniels to know that while he might not be worthy of it, there were those who loved him. Not everyone wanted him dead.

"Why don't you get some sleep? I need to tie up some business matters, and that will give you a day to rest and recover. I've arranged for a doctor to stop in to check on you, and Molly will see to any of your needs. We will depart tomorrow morning." He turned to the door.

"Depart?" She cried, sitting up in the bed. "Where? Why?"

He faced her as he responded. "I want to leave London. It's too dangerous here. I can't guarantee the places I frequent aren't being watched, as was my exit from Hammond's. I have a manor house in Kent only a select few know about. We need to go to someplace safe where we can strategize a plan, and then we will return to catch the bastards. If our flight surprises you, the same surprise might keep us one step ahead of our adversaries. Molly said your clothes are in the wardrobe, but we'll stop at your residence for you to collect more of your belongings."

"Kent? Just the two of us? Alone?" Her voice rose, her fingers twisting in her sheets.

He raised a brow. "It is perfectly acceptable for two gentlemen to be traveling together unchaperoned, *Mr.* Daniels. With your disguise, *Miss* Daniels's reputation is safeguarded. We'll take advantage of it for another day. Though it's a bit late to be worried about your reputation, considering you neglected to do so before you embarked on your charade."

"You *are* right," she retorted. "It was foolish and reckless of me to venture into the esteemed sanctuary of a gentlemen's card room to lift a few quid from a bunch of supercilious imbeciles. Never mind that if they didn't lose their money to me, they would have tossed it away on a fashionable cut of a new cravat, their current mistress, or a losing wager at Ascot. They do need deep pockets for such necessities."

Her eyes blazed. "Perhaps I should have starved and let you be murdered. Then we'd both be dead and I wouldn't have to worry about my reputation, which until you pay me, is now my only asset."

There was that mettle again, a sharp sliver of steel with

which she stabbed him. She had good aim. Damned if he didn't admire her for it.

He was unable to suppress the smile curving his lips. "My apologies, you are right. Far be it for you to starve. You should have robbed those fops blind. Had I known that was your plan, I would have assisted you." He grinned at her expression. "Perhaps another time."

She looked stunned by his capitulation. She didn't believe he'd retreat while she was in full battle mode. After Balaclava, he'd learned the life-or-death lesson of when to fall back and when to recklessly charge forward.

"Do you think you can manage a trip tomorrow morning?" he asked.

She stared at him blankly, looking like a soldier braced for battle only to be informed there wasn't one.

"Your head?" he clarified. "You did mention moving it was not an option. Do you think you could survive a coach ride after some rest?"

She recovered her voice. "Yes, I can manage."

"Good," he said. "Then I'll leave you to get some rest." He made a brief bow and opened the door. He turned to step into the corridor, when a thought struck him and he looked back. "Those supercilious imbeciles, the reference would include me?"

"Of course not." She gasped. "You're a soldier, you fought in the Crimea."

He paused, disconcerted. A soldier who fought in the Crimea? That was how she saw him? Hell, buying his commission was the biggest mistake of his life. One he would pay for forever. He pressed his lips together, swallowing the bitterness that rose like bile in his throat. With a curt nod, he departed, not trusting himself to speak.

≫≪

ALEX BLINKED AT the closed door, groaned, and collapsed in the bed. For goodness sake, she shouldn't provoke the man. It was unwise to bite the hand that feeds you.

Though she hadn't really bitten his hand, but rather swatted it down. She hadn't meant to, but when he taunted her about having no regard for her welfare, she had seen a wide and vivid streak of red. Good God, if she didn't have her welfare to consider, why bother risking all to save it?

She closed her eyes and pressed the heels of her hands into them. She needed this arrangement, and she had agreed to assist him. She couldn't go into it with fists raised and daggers drawn or else they'd kill each other before the day was out.

It was Kendall's fault. He had chastised her like she was an errant child who hadn't considered the repercussions of her actions. When she protested, he had agreed with her. Baffled, she lay down, exhaustion settling over her like a heavy blanket.

What was the man's game?

It didn't matter. This was a temporary business arrangement. She'd survive it and him. They had one thing in common; they both may have been wounded in battle, but they were survivors.

≫≪

LATER THAT AFTERNOON Garrett returned to Brandon's house, his mood foul, his temper black. Damn useless police. They couldn't extract information on a couple of murderous, thieving footpads unless the bastards stood right before them. Even then, Garrett doubted they'd be able to learn the culprits' names much less pry loose any information they might harbor in connection with the assault on Garrett's carriage.

With irritable jerks, he began to shrug off his jacket but paused as the absence of the ubiquitous Poole filled him with unease. The old goat guarded Warren's sanctuary like a tenacious bulldog, so the lapse was curious if not disquieting.

Slipping his coat back on, Garrett followed the sound of low voices to the back drawing room. He paused in the entranceway and observed Poole's stiff frame half blocking a man whose back was to Garrett and who appeared intent upon helping himself to a glass of brandy.

"Quite right, sir," Poole's voice carried to Garrett. "But I worry that Lord Warren might not be returning anytime soon. I understand your necessity in wanting to see him, but he is in the middle of resolving a rather delicate matter. It might be best if—"

Back still turned, the man lifted his hand to wave the butler's words away.

Garrett grinned at his audacity but lost his amusement when the man spoke.

"Yes, yes, but I'm sure he will make time to see me. I am his father-in-law. I should take precedence over any colleague of Warren's."

Garrett crossed his arms and leaned against the doorframe in a deceptively casual pose as he regarded his stepfather from across the room. "Still an imperious prig—and brazen, too, helping yourself to Brandon's best brandy."

His stepfather lost his grip on the decanter, and the sound of glass clattering onto mahogany answered Garrett.

Poole was quick to intercede, adeptly rescuing the crystal before its descent onto the Oriental rug. For an old coot, he was fast.

Arthur Brown whirled on Garrett, his face sheet white, his golden catlike eyes blazing. "You!" He gasped. "What are *you* doing here?"

"You mean, what am I doing in town? Or what am I doing sober?" His stepfather's silent glare met Garrett's query. "What? Isn't that what had you losing your grip on your drink?"

Arthur closed his eyes and took a deep breath, as if he could draw in the patience he lacked. "I did not say that, nor did I imply that with my question. But leave it to you to interpret the worst."

"On the contrary, interpreting the worst is your forte. Or is that just in regard to me?"

Arthur snatched the brandy decanter from Poole, turned his back on Garrett, and poured himself a generous glass.

Well versed on when his presence as mediator was effective versus futile, Poole made his departure but not before he arched a brow at Garrett. Bastard or not, Arthur was a guest under Warren's roof, and Poole expected him to be treated as such. Garrett would have to lay down his sword and do battle another day. Sighing, he envied Arthur's draining of his drink.

A spasm of loose coughs choked his stepfather, and he removed his handkerchief as he doubled over.

Garrett frowned at the congested cough, noting the grayish tinge to Arthur's skin and the nasal tone in his voice. There was a wild look in his eyes that Garrett had never noticed before. He frowned. The man was sick, should be in bed. Another man might mention it, but Arthur had long ago rejected personal overtures from Garrett, not that he could dredge any up. That reservoir was bone empty.

Recovering his composure, Arthur returned his glass to the sterling silver tray, sank into the armchair beside the table, and cleared his throat. "It was a civil question. You have avoided town. Made it clear it held no interest for you, nor has much else captured your interest since your return. It should be little surprise that seeing you here caught me off guard."

Garrett eyed his stepfather, wondering if he could evict him without Poole's awareness. Impossible. Pity that, as the man was sick. Garrett didn't want to catch what he had, let alone have any other exchange with the bastard.

He crossed to the hearth and draped his arm on the mantelpiece, too tense to sit in his stepfather's presence—or rather to lower himself to the man's level. "Meaning, I have been a drunken recluse for the past few months." He held up his hand to cut off Arthur's interjection. "However, I am sober now. I arrived last week, but you need not worry because I'm leaving today. You won't have to acknowledge me at any of your clubs or sit across me at a card table."

"I see. So Poole was being diplomatic in suggesting I not wait for Warren. I should have known he was trying to head off an altercation. Very civil of him."

"Poole doesn't like bloodshed."

"Well, perhaps for Poole's sake, we can avoid that."

"We can. Allow me to show you the door." Garrett strode to the exit, turned, and lifted his arm to gesture Arthur ahead of him. "After you."

"Still as impertinent as always. But I came here to see Warren to discuss a business matter that has come to my attention. However, considering it involves you, perhaps I should go right to the source."

Garrett dropped his arm and warily eyed his stepfather.

"Certain rumors have come to my attention."

"I see." Garrett nodded. "No, I didn't sleep with Lady Beaumont, ruin the virginal Miss Peoples, or proposition the Dunford twins, either separately or together. Yes, I relieved both

Lord Bradbury and Viscount Morrell of over a hundred pounds each, but I gave them fair warning that I held the better hand." He shrugged. "Of course, they were too drunk to listen to reason. Unfortunately for them, I was sober, which is the real news. Now, shall I show you out or give Poole the honor? I wouldn't—"

"The talk concerned a business venture," Arthur's voice rose. "Regarding your pursuit into the manufacturing of ale on one of your properties."

Garrett didn't respond.

"Well?" Arthur snapped. "Is it true?" He lifted his handkerchief and irritably swiped it across his sweat-drenched brow.

Garrett pursed his lips. The man should be bedridden, rather than delivering lectures that Garrett had long outgrown. He really was a brazen ass. Pity that he was his half sister's father. However, if arrogance killed the man, it would save Garrett the trouble—and Kit's anger. He shook his head. "No."

"No, you're not manufacturing ale, or no, you're not venturing into trade?"

"No and yes."

"For God's sake, man, give me a straight answer. You are a peer of the realm. You cannot venture into trade and be accepted at court. More important, you cannot tarnish the Kendall name and title with whatever sordid business machinations you are dredging up when deep in your cups."

Garrett clenched his teeth but bit off his rebuttal.

Arthur rose and began to pace the room, gesturing with his hand. "Kendall Ale," he sneered. "It's scandalous! Particularly as your presence here to discuss a 'delicate matter' with Warren, as Poole phrased it, tells me that you're dragging him down with you. Well, I won't have you bringing a stain to the whole family. Think of your nephews. You could lose everything. Think of Beau and Will."

"Maybe I am. Should I make a success of it, I'll give the profits to Will." He shrugged. "Seems only fair, as Beau inherits Warren's title, Will as the spare heir might need the income."

Arthur's eyes nearly bulged from his head, and his mouth opened and closed before he could put voice to his anger. "Stop being an ass and answer me straight, man!"

Garrett straightened to his full height and peered down at his stepfather, his words cold. "You forget yourself. I no longer answer to any man but myself."

"That's right, and how has that been going? Holing yourself up in one of your country estates, drinking yourself into a stupor, entertaining who knows how many lightskirts and doing God knows—"

"You go too far." Garrett's voice did not raise, but the arctic dip to it gave Arthur pause. "I suggest you stop, as Poole wouldn't like your blood soiling the Oriental."

Arthur clamped his mouth shut, his cheeks vibrating with the force of it. He studied Garrett and then sighed. "I waste my time speaking to you. I came to see Warren. You don't perchance know when he is due to return?"

Garrett crossed his arms over his chest and shook his head. "No."

Arthur nodded, and refolding his now balled-up handkerchief, he returned it to his jacket pocket and crossed to the door. "I will return another day."

"You do that. My current *lightskirt* and I will be gone, so you can harangue Warren in peace." He couldn't resist goading Arthur. It provided the only pleasure in his relationship with the man.

Arthur paused. After a beat, Garrett heard him mutter under his breath. "You'll never change. God help us."

Garrett had no doubt Arthur meant for him to hear the indictment, for his stepfather always liked to deliver the parting salvo. For once, Garrett agreed with him, sharing the opinion in regard to his stepfather. Once a bastard, always a bastard.

Garrett waited until the front door closed before leaving the drawing room. With his stepfather's departure, the tension coiling through him loosened, and he quickened his pace to escape up the back staircase before Poole could waylay him. He'd had enough lectures for the day.

He dismissed Arthur as he had learned to do throughout the years. He had also spoken the truth about his imminent departure, or rather the partial truth. He didn't have a mistress waiting, but he and Miss Daniels were leaving.

Garrett's lips curved as he pictured her reaction to his

calling her his current lightskirt. *I won't be your mistress.* She'd probably take up the sword Arthur had just laid down and skewer Garrett through. He didn't understand why the thought improved his mood, lightened his steps, and made him smile, but it did.

All the more reason to keep her near.

Chapter Seven

A FTER a full day and night of rest, Alex awoke clearheaded and free of pain as long as she didn't move too quickly. The doctor whom Kendall had sent to visit her had assured her she would be fine. When she sat up and stretched, she believed it.

True to Kendall's word, Molly had checked on her throughout the day and she had never arrived empty-handed. She had brought a book of poems, tea laced with her medicinal brandy, but most important, large, plentiful, and mouthwatering meals.

Alex had perused the poems, avoided the tea, and eaten with a gusto that had delighted Molly. Despite the feasts before her, Alex hadn't been able to resist slipping a few rolls under her blanket. The memory of not knowing when her next meal would arrive was raw, and it had dug a hole in her stomach she felt she could never fill.

She had inquired about Kendall only to be informed he had left the house and had yet to return. Molly didn't know his whereabouts, and Alex did not probe. She thought he would have stopped in at least once to inquire about her welfare, but when he never appeared, she decided she didn't care.

It was of no interest, nor any concern of hers how Kendall

spent his time or where he went. However, it was a relief to wake up the next morning and be informed that Kendall expected her to meet him in the drawing room at nine o'clock sharp.

Despite it sounding like a military directive, as if she were one of his soldiers to command, Alex was prepared to face him—until she opened the wardrobe and faced her gentlemen's attire. Oh, dear. It would be slow going to deal with the pads to thicken her waist and bind her chest. And without Gus to assist with her cravat . . . she froze. *Gus.*

Sad, sweet, useless Gus.

She sank back onto the bed. Kendall had said he would escort her home to collect her things and there would be . . . Gus.

More important, how would Gus be? Sober? She doubted it. Not since Meg's death. She closed her eyes against the wave of grief at the memory of her cherished nanny, who had all but raised her. Dearest Meg, whom her aunt had callously dismissed after her uncle had inherited her parents' estate. It was to Meg that Alex had escaped when her uncle had closed all other doors to her.

Months had passed since Meg had died of the influenza. While Alex's grief remained raw, the damage to Meg's husband, Gus, had been irrevocable. A war veteran, Gus had taken the loss of his leg and the sale of her father's stables with stoic fortitude. But Meg's death had broken him, taking the reliable, hardworking Gus with her. The Gus left behind periodically roused himself for the odd job, but more often than not, the most he managed was a trip to the local tavern.

At least drowned in a bottle, Gus wouldn't worry over Alex's disappearance. He could also be sleeping off his drink at a friend's, one of the other veterans who haunted the same tavern as Gus.

Ignoring the stab of guilt at the traitorous thought, Alex stood. It was time to get dressed. Time to leave and move forward.

Her future lay ahead with this enigmatic man and their odd alliance. With a fortune hers to gain, her future looked brighter. That is, if she reined in her temper as her father had so often advised her to do. She frowned, for she had never been good at heeding her father's advice. Then again, her father's advice had never been good to her, either.

She needed to play her cards right, and perhaps, just perhaps, she could change her fortunes and salvage her future.

≫⋖

With Molly's assistance, Alex was once more dressed in her masculine disguise, minus her cravat. The complicated necktie eluded both Alex and Molly's attempts to form it into any semblance of a fashionable knot. In the end, Alex draped the material around her neck, squared her shoulders, and followed Molly from the room. She'd deal with it later.

As she traversed the long corridor, her eyes drank in her surroundings. A home reflected its owner, and she looked for signs of Kendall and keys to unlocking the man.

Light stole through the window at the end of the hall and cast a soft glow over the Oriental carpet. A statue of a toga-draped beauty lounged in a sinuous pose on a hallway table, while the marble staircase wound its way to the front foyer. The house exuded wealth, but not an ostentatious display. It was elegant and understated, lovely.

Alex paused, unable to resist glancing behind her. When her eyes fastened on the painting gracing the back wall, like Lot's wife, she regretted her action. She didn't need to see this portrait. To see this woman whom she instantly identified.

Kristen. Kendall's mistress. Whom else could she be? It was brazen to so prominently display it, but that was Kendall.

She was beautiful. Thick auburn hair tumbled over her bare shoulders, and her golden eyes were warm and bright. A Madonna smile curved her lips, teasing Alex, taunting her. Her skin looked as porcelain smooth as the alabaster Greek statue Alex had passed. Her gown was a deep emerald green and pearls draped her neck.

Alex noted her beauty, but it was Kendall's words that resonated with her. *She loves me.* Something lurched in Alex's chest and she spun away from the woman's laughing, knowing gaze. She hastened her steps to catch up with Molly. In the back recesses of her mind, she wondered if Kendall returned the sentiment. She squelched the thought. It really was of no import to her.

Before she reached the first floor, she glanced up in time to see Kendall emerge from a room to the right of the landing.

He was impeccably dressed in black-and-gray-striped trousers and a pristine black jacket that hugged his broad shoulders. He leaned against the doorframe, flipped open a gold pocket watch, and scowled down at it. "You are twenty minutes late and"—his eyes lifted and dipped to her loose necktie—"not finished dressing." He snapped the watch cover closed and straightened, watching her expectantly.

Alex stopped a few steps above the landing, her hand resting on the mahogany banister, and peered down at him, appreciating her superior position. "My apologies. Had I known I was being timed, I would have sent Molly ahead to inform you that I needed more of it."

Kendall arched an imperious brow, while returning his watch to his trousers pocket. "Come here." When she made no move to obey, he crossed to her.

Before she realized his intent, he had caught both ends of her cravat and tugged her before him. "What are you doing?" She gasped. Her hands clutched his wrists as she staggered down two steps until she stood on the bottom stair. She regarded him balefully.

"Getting you dressed." Without another word, he proceeded to flip the ends of the linen cloth together.

She turned her head to hide her mortification. His fingers were warm against the bare skin of her neck, branding where they touched. His movements were quick and dexterous, dispensing with a neat four-in-hand knot. She could smell his masculine scent mixed with his cologne. Heat suffused her cheeks and her breathing became shallow. Once again, the man was too damn close for her comfort.

Undoubtedly, Kendall, being a rake, didn't give the intimacy of their situation undue thought. No matter, Alex gave it enough for both of them. With the exception of dancing, standing this close to a gentleman was scandalous, and she didn't dare contemplate what etiquette lines his touching, let alone dressing, her crossed.

As soon as he moved away from her, she would speak to Kendall about his familiarity. It had to stop. While she had agreed to their arrangement, she had not agreed to anything else. She thought she had made this point clear when she told him she would not be his mistress. His memory must be short, or he was too accustomed to women tripping over their feet to be near him.

There was no denying his magnetism. He was undeniably handsome. His thick black hair mere inches from her looked soft as silk and . . . she blinked. She had lost her train of thought. Something about mistresses?

She couldn't think when he stood so close. His finger tipped her chin up, her perch on the bottom step placing her almost at eye level with him. Her breath caught as she stared into those compelling eyes, storm-cloud gray and locked on hers.

"I don't like to be kept waiting. Remember that next time."

Just who did he think he was? She removed his hand from her chin. "Next time ask me, rather than order me. You forget, you are no longer in the military, and I am not one of your men to submissively obey your directives." Heat burned her cheeks, but she did not back down, even when his eyes narrowed and his lips thinned.

He studied her like some curious specimen in a laboratory or one of those newfangled machines on display at the Great Exhibition. After a drawn-out moment, he stepped away. "You're right again. You are certainly not submissive. Pity." His eyes roamed over her, lingered on her trousers. When they lifted to hers, a slow and devastating smile curved his lips. "But I can teach you."

She sucked in a sharp breath.

"Again, perhaps when we know each other better." He grinned and turned to the door. "We should go. We are late."

She glared at his broad back, adding arrogance to his annoying qualities. They were adding up, and it did not bode well for a smooth working relationship.

He glanced back. "You coming? Oh, my apologies, was that an order? Please, *will* you join me?" He bowed, but not before she caught the twitch to his lips and the gleam in his eyes. He swept his arm out for her to precede him.

She lifted her chin and strode ahead of him. There were advantages to being dressed as a man. She need not wait for the door to be opened for her. She unlocked it, swung it open, and let herself out. With great delight, she slammed it shut behind her.

On the front stoop, she withdrew her gloves from her jacket

pocket and jerked them on. Arrogant, insolent, and impossible. She didn't know which would top Kendall's list of character flaws, but its growing length worried her.

≫≺

GARRETT BLINKED AT the closed door. By God, they could have used her at Balaclava. When Cardigan had commanded the Light Brigade's charge through the valley of death, Miss Daniels would have flatly refused the suicidal directive and told the Ignorant Ass to go to hell. Think of the lives she would have saved.

Over six hundred seventy men had ridden into the valley of death. After the battle, only one hundred ninety-five remained fit for duty. The latter hadn't included him. He rubbed his side, the jagged scar from his near-fatal wound a stark reminder.

He shook his head, admiring her courage. Admiring her.
Who the hell was she?

He wanted to know more, needed to. He frowned, recalling her earlier reference to starving. What circumstances had forced her to turn away from the respectable venues presented to a young woman in need of funds? There was a story there and it wasn't good. She was fleeing something or someone. Not the law or a husband. Her adamant refusals on these points, along with her indignation at this line of questioning, attested to the truth of her words. It was something else.

A jilted lover? Family? He grunted at the latter and dismissed the former. She had made it clear she was not of mistress stock. Pity there. An image of her blue eyes shooting daggers at him and her thick blonde hair, now hidden under that ridiculous wig, teased him. He recalled the color spotting her cheeks when he'd dropped Kit's name.

No, she was a brave but prissy thing. An innocent. He didn't dally with innocents. Such play led to marriage, and he had no intentions of strolling down that aisle. But this revelation about Miss Daniels confirmed another point; she came from good breeding.

Her speech, poise, and classical beauty attested to it. She was raised to be a lady, thus to adhere to society's strict standards of etiquette. This explained her wariness in flaunting their rules. Yet she did so, again and again. She did what she needed to do to survive. Her words echoed, *some risks are worth taking.*

He noted again what a fine soldier she would have made. However, he had no regrets that Miss Daniels was not in the Crimea *or* a soldier. He flexed his fingers where the touch of her skin lingered. He recalled the swanlike column of her neck, her shallow breathing as he knotted her cravat, and her slim body inches from his. He approved of her trousers, but lamented the length of her jacket that covered pertinent body parts. No, he harbored no regrets. For now, Miss Daniels was just where he wanted her. With him.

All he had to do was learn who the hell she was.

Stepping outside, he stopped short at the sight of Miss Daniels. She appeared rooted to the edge of the lower landing, planted in place. Her attention was riveted to the gleaming black carriage parked in the drive and the emerald green Warren crest sporting the three gold lions.

"Miss Daniels, are you all right?"

"Whose carriage is this?" she asked, not glancing at him.

"It's the Earl of Warren's. As you know, mine is in need of repairs, and this one is safer, not marked for target practice. Wouldn't you agree?" He caught her arm to escort her forward, her steps slow and reluctant.

"Yes, yes. Of course."

Havers circled the carriage to open the door for them. When his gaze narrowed on Garrett's hand on Miss Daniels's arm, Garrett abruptly released her. He needed to clarify Daniels's gender to Havers, but now was not the time. "Havers, we will be traveling to . . . ?" He turned to Daniels, letting his questions trail off expectantly.

"Oh, Chelsea." She supplied the address, still looking distracted.

West of London, Chelsea was not a fashionable area of the city. Then again, any address outside of the West End was dismissed by the ton. Garrett knew the area for the Chelsea Hospital. War veterans, old and without proper means or family, were given beds there. He frowned, unable to picture Alex residing in the area.

Havers turned to climb onto the box. Garrett had no patience for him hovering to close the door behind them. Some niceties made Garrett feel more like an invalid than a gentleman.

Miss Daniels made to step into the carriage but gasped when he gripped her waist and lifted her inside. She glanced back, pink cheeked and flustered, murmuring her thanks before she took her seat. It was the second time he had assisted her into a carriage. He regretted not having appreciated the first, recalling his hand on her buttock.

He vaulted into the carriage, securing the door behind him. He noted she had claimed the seat facing forward as a lady should. Garrett hated riding backward. With a look that dared her to protest, he settled into the seat beside her. She raised a brow but faced the window, not challenging him. There were advantages to this cool, practical side of hers. He settled back in his seat and appreciated this one as he tapped his hand on the back panel, signaling Havers to depart.

For the first few blocks they rode in silence. The only noise was the low rumble of the carriage crossing the paved streets. Garrett studied his companion's profile, noting how she gnawed on her lower lip. He wondered what was on her mind and the tip of her tongue, but he didn't have long to wait.

"I heard a story about the Earl of Warren." She spoke without facing him.

Relaxing, he grinned. "Just one? How disappointing. There are so many."

She glanced over to him and then away.

"Let me guess?" He pursed his lips and discounted most of his and Brandon's earlier escapades and the more risqué ones. She was too young and innocent to have heard those. "The Market Theatre?" At the telltale flush on her cheeks, he nodded. "Yes, that one got the most gossip. What did you hear?"

When she did not respond, he couldn't resist. "You heard he and a friend purchased the theater for the actress Lily Blake so she could star in all the productions. She was—"

"Mistress to *two* earls," she interceded and gave him her full attention. "Warren purchased the theater with *some* friend, a notorious rakehell who was rumored to collect and discard young women with as much frequency as Beau Brummell sailed through cravats." She raised a brow. "The friend was a known debaucher of innocents. Women are warned they risk ruin merely by being in his presence." Her eyes held a hint of challenge as if she dared him to refute the rumors.

His hand covered his mouth as he coughed to hide his surprise. "Excuse me, I, ah . . . that part of the story I hadn't heard." He narrowed his eyes on her, wondering if she played him for a fool.

"What part did you hear?" She tipped her head to the side and regarded him with wide-eyed innocence.

"Ah, something about Lily Blake being Warren's mistress," he offered.

Debaucher of innocents? He had heard the Brummell quote differently, made in reference to married women. Supposedly he ran through them with the same frequency that Brummell changed fashions. At least that one had held a kernel of truth. But he couldn't keep straight what the gossip mill churned out about him. Didn't give a damn. Never had. He found Miss Daniels watching him. Apparently, she had more to add.

"Warren and his friend set up Lily Blake, and each night they escorted a parade of different women to their boxes to watch her performances."

He cocked a brow at her relish in imparting this salacious bit of gossip, an odd gleam lighting her eyes. He sought to steer the conversation in a safer direction. Away from him. "Have you ever seen Lily Blake perform? She is without rival in the theater. It is said that her Juliet brings women to tears."

"Do you think it was her acting or the men's callous use of Miss Blake that brought them to tears?" she asked in all seriousness.

"That would depend on where these women stand in regard to the gossip."

"Where they stand?"

"If they believe the rumors or not."

"It is generally believed most rumors are based in truth," she said.

"Most rumors begin with a kernel of truth," he clarified. "A group of people called gossipmongers nurture its growth. They possess wagging tongues and a desperate need to be heard, but they have nothing of their own import to say. So they steal this kernel of news, water it with their ignorance, and it grows into gossip." He shrugged. "Or if given its proper name, lies, innu-endoes, and slander."

She smiled. "You didn't strike me as the philosophizing type."

Her comment and the smile disarmed him, silencing his retort. It was the first smile she had given him, and it loosened something in his body, a tension he hadn't known he carried. He shifted in his seat. "I have my moments." She had beautiful eyes, a clear, luminous blue with long lashes. When she smiled, they glowed like two full moons.

Good God, he was using trite clichés and pontificating about rumors like a pompous windbag. What had gotten into him? She was lowering a guard he carried like a second skin, a shell honed in life and hardened in battle. He didn't like it.

You lower your guard, you get ambushed.

He needed to move to the other side of the carriage. Put distance between them before he spouted bad poetry in tribute to the sensual curve of her lips. That could get nasty, for he'd never had a way with words or flattery. Besides, she thought he was a philandering rakehell. A debaucher of innocents.

"Are you familiar with Warren's notorious friend?" she asked.

He opened his mouth to respond when something in her tone caught his attention and he paused, his gaze narrowing on her features. Almost immediately, he spotted the sparkle of amusement lighting her eyes and he blinked. By God, she was good. He shook his head, grinning. "I'd say about as well as you are."

She knew damn well he was the friend, had all along. She had played him like an easy target.

"Oh, I doubt that." She grinned.

At his dubious look, she laughed, a lyrical wave washing over him. Light and vibrant, it sent liquid warmth spiraling through his body. Her features softened and for a fleeting moment, she appeared carefree and lovely, delighted with herself. Until that moment and that laugh, he hadn't realized how controlled and guarded she, too, kept herself. They made a pair.

He was unable to tear his eyes from her as he wondered what or who had put up her guard. *Who was she?* Besides being a devious thing, setting him up like that. He couldn't resist his responding smile. "How long have you known?"

"All along, but I had forgotten that particular story until I saw Warren's coach." Laughter laced her words. "I recognized the three lions of Warren's crest, and I remembered he was never without his companion in trouble, the Earl of Kendall."

"A known debaucher of innocents? They risk ruin by being in my mere presence?"

"I debated between that or how they are known to faint at your feet." She peered at him from beneath her lashes, her smile still warming her lips.

"It must have been a difficult decision," he murmured.

"It was indeed." She settled back in her seat and faced him. "So what is the buried kernel of truth in the Market Theatre story?"

He missed her smile. "We bought the theater for Miss Blake because Brandon is a generous patron of the arts, and he asked me to be a partner in a lucrative venture." He tried to keep his expression earnest, but she simply raised a brow and stared him down. He wasn't going to ensnare her that easily.

He shrugged. "Bran was deep in his cups and signed both our names to a promissory note stating we would purchase the dilapidated theater, refurbish it, and promise to give Lily Blake top billing."

"Who placed such a strange wager?"

"Lily's cousin, her big, burly, *I have killed too many men to count* cousin. It would have been fatal for us had Brandon reneged on his signature."

"No," she said, her eyes wide.

She was lovely and enchanting—and as gullible as himself. "No," he agreed.

Laughing, she shook her head. "Mmh, well done."

"I have my moments." The carriage jostled and she slid into him, the warm length of her thigh flush against his until she shifted away. Heat surged low in his body, reminding him of those newly awakened areas that he wished would go back to sleep, particularly while in close quarters. He cleared his throat. "He was a family friend of Brandon's who had been trying to get Bran to invest in the theater for years. Brandon would have backed the venture eventually, but his loss forced his hand. We all made money off it. Lily Blake's Juliet does make women weep."

"So I've heard, *my lord*." She smiled again.

"*My lord?* If you refuse to be my mistress, I'm not really yours, am I?" He couldn't resist the trite quip and watched her blush. Suddenly, he didn't think he'd mind being hers or she being his. *Perhaps when they knew each other better.* He grinned. "But deceiving me so thoroughly should be rewarded. Why don't you call me Garrett."

"Garrett?" she echoed.

"It is my name. Garrett Sinclair. Now that we've clarified my name and title, what about you, Miss Daniels? Don't you think proper introductions are in order?"

She appeared to mull his question over and after a moment, responded. "My name is Alexandra, but most people call me Alex."

Her eyes teased as she silently laughed at him, knowing she had given him no more than he already knew. *Alex Daniels is new to you,* he recalled Richmond's introduction at Hammond's.

Amused, he turned her name over on his tongue. *Alexandra.* He liked the sound of it. Strong-willed and enlightened, a tsarina with whom to be reckoned. He didn't press her for a surname.

He had the first piece to her puzzle. The rest would fall into place.

He would see to it.

Chapter Eight

❧❧

GARRETT watched Alexandra edge forward in her seat as the carriage rolled to a stop. When she bit her lip, he wondered what or who worried her. The idea of it being a *who*, particularly a *male*, had him voicing his concerns out loud. "Will someone be worried over your absence?"

Rather than bluntly ask her if she lived alone, he chose to go with subtlety. When she turned to him, her expression amused, he realized she saw right through him. Hell, he'd never had much use for subtlety. With his men, a direct command, sometimes accompanied by a kick in the arse, worked best.

"They might be, so it is a good thing I have returned unharmed. My, ah . . . *Uncle* Gus is a veteran of the Crimea, fierce, war-trained, and extremely overprotective of me. You'd be wise to remember that." Her smile flashed bright before she turned away.

He blinked at her warning. She dismissed subtlety and went straight for overkill. Recovering, he leaned around her to grasp the door latch before she reached it. "Allow me, I wouldn't want to get on the wrong foot so soon with your . . . ah, uncle, is it?"

He hadn't missed her tripping over the name. If Gus was her uncle, Havers was his.

He opened the door and leapt down, turning to assist Alexandra from the carriage. After a brief hesitation, she allowed him to slide his hands about her waist and lift her out. For a moment, he stood holding her in place, unable to resist grinning down at her.

She was slight of stature, her head barely topping his shoulders. He could almost span her waist with his hands. Too bad they had to leave Brandon's. He'd like to have left her in Molly's care for another week or two, get more meat on her. There would be time to fatten her up later, for he had sent Ned ahead to procure a cook and maids for his country estate.

A deep, throat-clearing cough sliced through his thoughts. He staggered back from Alexandra, cursing himself for not speaking to Havers while cursing the man's hawklike vigilance. Once a valued asset, now Goddamn inconvenient.

Havers stood beside the lead horses. His brawny arms were crossed over his barrel chest and his eyes, hard and inscrutable, shifted between Garrett and Alexandra. Suddenly they narrowed on Alexandra's delicate features, his first view of them in daylight, and then his mouth, pursed in a thin line, relaxed. His gaze met Garrett's and he gave a curt nod before he mounted his perch on top of the box. *Eyes like a damn hawk.*

He glanced over at Alexandra, who watched Havers in confusion. Without responding to her unasked question, Garrett's gaze swept the area, relaxing only when he noted they stood alone. "Shall we go? Your uncle might be worried over your absence."

"Yes, well, he might not be home." She walked ahead of him to the front door of one of the residences in the nondescript line of row houses.

He surveyed the building, its appearance a step above the slum dwellings populating the East End. The lack of gaslights, the broken windowpanes littering the first floor, and the stench that rose from the unswept and unpaved streets betrayed its poor address. It wasn't poverty level, but it struggled to keep its head above it. He clenched his jaw as his hand caught Alexandra's elbow and he escorted her to the front door.

"Sometimes his work keeps him away for days at a time."

"And what work is that?"

They had paused before the door while she withdrew a key from her jacket pocket. At Garrett's query, she fumbled with the lock until he relieved her of the key and opened the door. "After you," he bowed low and extended his arm.

She stepped inside and paused before a flight of stairs. "It's on the third floor."

He nodded and preceded her up the staircase as etiquette dictated. It would not be proper for a gentleman to be staring at a lady's derriere as she climbed. Pity that. With Alexandra attired in her form-fitting breeches, he would have enjoyed the view.

"He was a stable manager, but since returning from the Crimea, it's been hard to find full-time work."

Garrett frowned. He knew that when men who weren't career soldiers sought to return to their places of employment, others had often filled their jobs. If a soldier was maimed or disabled, there was no work to be found for cripples. Disgust curled in Garrett's gut, and he clenched his teeth.

Alexandra caught up with him at the top landing and made her way to the door at the end of the hall. She withdrew a second key and while the door unlocked with ease, she appeared reluctant to venture inside. He stepped behind her and opened his mouth to question her, when she suddenly whirled around and nearly collided with him.

Surprised, she stumbled back. "We should be quiet. When Gus is home, he keeps late hours and often sleeps till noon."

He studied her, aware she hid something, aware of her tension. But he simply nodded, not pressing her. "Of course."

When they entered the apartment, he studied the surroundings. The windows were coated with the city's ever-present layer of coal dust. A threadbare rug covered the floor, a tired sofa lined the back wall, and the lone table was defaced with watermarks. A lone wall hanging consisted of a faded picture of a country cottage. Sparsely furnished and nearly empty of personal effects, the space was clean yet barren. No answers here.

A gasp from Alexandra drew his attention. She had entered the adjacent galley kitchen. She crouched beside the wood-burning stove that dominated the room, leaning over the prostrate form of a bear of a man, sprawled belly up across the floor.

Gus. Her fierce, war-trained uncle.

He moved to Alexandra's side, noting the rise and fall of the man's barrel chest, the discarded bottle in the corner, and the absence of Gus's right leg from the knee-down. Something twisted in Garrett's chest as he knelt beside her. He had seen this scene played out all too often. Christ, he had lived it.

He slid an arm beneath Gus's shoulders and hefted him to a sitting position, propping him against the wall. The man exhaled on a loud snore, and Garrett nearly gagged on the waft of stale gin. The poor man's poison.

"He . . . ah, must have fallen asleep here, not made it to his bed," Alexandra said.

Seeing her flush and avert her face, he simply nodded. "Right. Why don't I assist him while you go collect your things?"

"Oh, no, I should—"

"It's all right." He paused as another snore from Gus interrupted him. "See. He agrees. He'll be fine. I can handle this." When she didn't respond, he added. "You forget, before returning to the ranks of *supercilious imbeciles* in Hammond's card room, I fought in the Crimea." When her eyes met his, he lowered his voice. "I promise you, Gus is not the first soldier whom I have assisted in getting to his bed. Trust me."

Understanding crossed her features. She lifted her hand to sweep Gus's dark hair from his forehead. "Yes, of course." She stood and pointed across the kitchen. "His room is through there." She walked over, peered within, and turned to direct him to a bucket sitting on the stove. "This water will have been boiled. It's probably cold now, but it should do if needed."

"Go. He'll be fine. I'll take care of him."

She hesitated a moment before hurrying from the room.

He waited until he heard the sound of a door open and close. He sat back on his heels and blew out a breath. Unbuttoning his jacket, he shrugged it off and undid the cuffs of his shirt to roll up his sleeves. Standing, he draped his jacket across a nearby chair. He collected the bucket of water and dipped his hand in to test the temperature, grunting at the cold water. It would do.

He hefted the load to carry it into Gus's room, pausing inside the door to give his eyes a minute to adjust to the dim light. No windows back here. He kicked the door wide to let the kitchen's light stream into the room.

Like the rest of the apartment, the furnishings were sparse. A cot, bedside table, bureau, and a single chair filled the space. A wooden leg was propped in the corner, a set of crutches on the floor beside it. The room was a pigsty with clothing strewn over every surface, bureau drawers jutting out, and the bed unmade. He cleared a space to deposit the bucket on the floor beside the cot and went to collect Gus. Ready or not, it was time for the man to wake up. He was going to give Garrett the answers he sought.

Garrett bent over to grab one of Gus's arms and sling it across his shoulder. He leaned lower, pressed his other shoulder into Gus's chest, and hoisted the man over his back. Christ, he was deadweight, and Garrett nearly staggered under the heft of him. Far cry from the slim featherweight of Alexandra.

He gritted his teeth and cursed the man's liquid diet, which had grown the protruding gut pressing into his shoulder. He felt Gus stir.

"What the—"

Before Gus could finish his bark of surprise, Garrett dumped him onto his cot, tugged him to a sitting position, and dragged over the water bucket.

"What the f—"

Garrett dunked Gus's head into the water, drowning out his protests. He counted to four and yanked Gus out, dripping wet and biting mad. "That's to sober you up."

"Christ. Jesus—" Gus exploded before his second dunking.

He counted again, ignoring Gus's thrashing body. On four, he hauled him out. "That's to clean your mouth. Alexandra is in the next room." Gus swatted at Garrett, who lifted his arm in time to block the blow.

Another string of expletives ripped from Gus, his bloodshot eyes blinking wildly. "You bloody jackass, sod off or I'll—"

Back down he went. Garrett shook his head. The man didn't listen. This might take longer than he thought.

"What are you doing?" Alexandra gasped.

He glanced up to see her frozen in the doorway, her expression horrified, her hand covering her mouth. He hoisted Gus up. "Language, soldier. A lady's present."

Gus spat out water, coughing and glaring at Garrett. His face was pale with a yellow sheen coloring it. "Who the hell do you—"

"Language." Down again. "I warned him." Garrett shook his head. "Are you finished packing?"

Speechless, Alexandra's eyes were enormous and riveted on the bucket. When Gus reemerged and blinked his water-clogged eyes balefully at her, she ventured forward, but stopped at Garrett's look.

"You finish there and I'll finish here," he advised her.

"I can't leave him. You're hurting—"

"No. I'm not," he cut her off. "Trust me, Alexandra. I promise you, this is more painful for you than it is for him."

She hesitated, indecision crossing her features and a wet sheen blurring her eyes. After a moment, she gave a jerky nod, whirled around, and left them alone.

"You gonna leave me with this madman?" Gus bellowed after her.

"That's Captain Sinclair to you. Short of black coffee, this is the quickest route to sobriety. Worked for most of my men; worked for me," he muttered the last.

Gus lifted a beefy hand to rub it over his face and shove his hair from his broad forehead. Coal black eyes narrowed speculatively on Garrett before dropping to his neatly tied cravat, his crisp linen shirt, and lifting again to study Garrett.

Garrett read doubt and suspicion on the man's face. "Cavalry, Seventeenth Lancers." He kept his eyes steady on Gus, refusing to say more, but something in his expression must have conveyed the truth.

"Christ almighty," Gus breathed.

He nodded to Gus's leg. "You?"

"Infantry. Fought beside the Turks at the Alma. Leg's rotten luck, courtesy of a friend's ill aim in reloadin' his musket."

"Bad luck was all that was plentiful over there." A moment of silence passed before Garrett spoke. "Alexandra says you work with horses."

Gus's expression darkened, looking defensive. "I did. Ah, I do."

Garrett nodded. "I've sold my commission, demoted from captain back to Lord Kendall. I'm rebuilding the stables on one of my estates. You know good bloodstock?"

Gus grunted. "As well as many, better than most."

"Good, you're hired."

"What? Just like that? Without references? I lost my leg, not my wits." Gus narrowed his eyes. "What do you take me for? What's in it for you? And what the hell you doin' with Alex?" He balled his hands into fists.

"Smart man. You'll do." Garrett stood and crossed to the bureau. He yanked out a dry shirt and tossed it to Gus, who managed to catch it.

Garrett closed the drawer and folded his arms across his chest. "*Alexandra* is fine." He emphasized the name, making it clear he knew of her disguise. "You saw her for yourself. We met at a card game at Hammond's. Next time, you should voice your concern *before* she leaves. After is too late."

Gus glanced away, guilt shadowing his features.

"Considering her actions, she clearly believes her welfare is her own concern, so let's leave her out of this. We were discussing you or rather a job for you, and I did get a reference. Alexandra vouched for you. Now I have need of a stable manager, and you have need of a job." Garrett paused to let his words sink in.

Gus furrowed his brow, clearly struggling to find the snare, to understand him.

Garrett refused to give him the chance. He steered the conversation into the area he had been aiming for all along. "Remind me how long you were at your last employ . . . ?" He let his words trail off, hoping for Gus to fill in some of the pieces of his puzzle.

"I was at Viscount Langdon's estate in Essex for nigh on two decades. And," Gus said defiantly, "I'd have been there still if he hadn't sold off his stables and then died. The old staff left when the viscount's younger brother gained the title." Anger etched his words and his black eyes hardened. "Alex's uncle dismissed the lot, questioned their loyalty. Hmph." He snorted. "More like didn't want to cover their wages." He spat on the ground. "But when the viscount's stables were full, he had the best stock there is, none better than during my time. That I saw to. Ask anyone in the area. You'll get your references."

"I will," Garrett murmured, suppressing his surprise. *Viscount Langdon? She was the daughter of a viscount?* Breeding there indeed. He had pegged her right. *Langdon. Lady Alexandra Langdon.* He ran the name over in his mind, yet it meant nothing to him. But he had been absent from society for over two years. He would have Brandon investigate the family, see what he could learn of them and their circumstances.

Why had the stables been sold? And what of this uncle? Why had Alexandra fled? Gus's answers created more questions, but Garrett didn't dare prod more for fear of rousing Gus's suspicions. Besides, he was pressed for time. Alexandra should be ready any minute, and she wouldn't like him interrogating her *uncle.*

Gus ran a hand through his mop of wet hair and straightened his shoulders. "But I know my stock. Know my job."

"I'm counting on it," Garrett replied. "Give me a day to get a letter of introduction to my secretary. He'll fill you in on what the job entails and give you an advance on your wages to cover transportation and other necessary expenditures." His eyes narrowed. "There will be no drinking on the job. What you do on your own time is your own business. How soon can you be ready to work?"

Stunned, Gus opened his mouth and then closed it. He cleared his throat and swallowed a few times. They both ignored the sheen of moisture clouding his bloodshot eyes before he looked away, blinking furiously. After a moment, he straightened up, squared his sodden shoulders, and faced Garrett with a level stare. "Yesterday, Captain."

Garrett lips twitched. "*Sir* will do. A week should be early enough."

"Right, Captain."

Garrett raised a brow. The man appeared to take orders about as well as Alexandra. No surprise there. He crossed to Gus, offering his hand. Gus stared at it for so long that Garrett wondered if he had sprouted a sixth finger.

Finally Gus wiped his hand along his good leg before planting it firmly in Garrett's and lifting his eyes to meet his gaze.

A glimmer of hope had seeped into his expression like a flicker of light, and Gus gripped his hand like a lifeline. The war had wounded countless soldiers, but the loss of a limb wasn't the worst they had suffered. The loss of dignity was far graver.

The career soldier was dismissed as lower class, little better than an unsavory felon. In the Crimea, those in command also treated the foot soldier as less than human, no more than cannon fodder, sacrificed to the whims of their aristocratic officers. The army was not a lucrative profession, and when soldiers returned home, no responsibility was taken in caring for the veterans, wounded, crippled, or otherwise.

Garrett's lips pressed into a firm line. He couldn't change centuries-old practices or prejudices. However, as an earl he wasn't completely without recourse, nor was he without resources. He had plans, and these plans needed workers to implement them. Recalling his stepfather's lecture at Warren's, his jaw clenched. The business venture did have the additional benefit of driving his stepfather mad. All the more reason to carry it out.

During Garrett's two-year absence, his stepfather had neglected the upkeep of his estates. Tenants weren't properly cared for, rents went uncollected, and positions were vacated when salaries went unpaid.

When not drinking himself into oblivion, Garrett had spent his time traveling between his estates and cleaning up after his stepfather's penny-pinching incompetence. This purpose had provided the tenuous link that had kept him planted on the safe side of the line he had walked between life and death.

He tightened his clasp of Gus's hand. He couldn't save all the veterans who returned to lost lives, but by God, it felt good when he saved one more.

≫≪

ALEX STOOD IN the doorway, unnoticed by both men as she blinked to clear her blurred vision. She had returned to hear Kendall discussing the letter of introduction that he planned to write to his secretary. As he'd spoken, her heart had stopped. Good Lord. He had offered Gus a job.

He didn't know the man, but what he did know of him did not provide a stellar job recommendation. Despite her efforts to mask Gus's condition, the stench of cheap gin betrayed him. When Kendall hadn't contradicted her excuse for Gus's state but rather offered to escort Gus to his room, she had latched onto his offer, ignoring her stab of guilt. But the sight of Gus tore at her, warring with her memories of the boisterous, laughing man she had known.

Gus had taught her to ride her first pony, slipped her sweets for the mares, and hefted her onto his shoulders while he fed the horses. It was difficult to reconcile herself to the loss of this man when she, too, had lost so much. She had also turned her back on Gus because he needed the one thing Alex couldn't provide. He needed a job, a means to earn a decent wage. But with the loss of his leg, no one would hire him.

What made Kendall different?

More important, what did he expect in return?

She glowered at Kendall as he shook Gus's hand, but Kendall's earnest gaze and Gus's stunned expression gave her pause. Something unfurled in her chest, like a bud opening. Fearing it was her traitorous heart, bleating like the proverbial lamb before the slaughter, she pressed her hand to her chest.

Yanking her arm down, she retreated a step. She was not her mother. Gallant gestures and charming words would not lead her astray. She refused to care for a gambling rake who tossed down a fortune with a flip of a card, who seduced young women, dueled with their husbands, cheated on their wives . . . Alex stiffened, aware she had tangled up Kendall with her father. Kendall had no wife to cheat on—yet.

She gave her head a sharp shake. Kendall had a mistress. She didn't wish to remember Kristen, but she did. *She loves me.* She cursed the tight band squeezing her chest each time the words replayed in her mind.

Well, Kristen can have him.

Kendall stepped away from Gus and caught sight of her. When he smiled, she forgot every thought in her head but one.

Good Lord, did the man have to be so handsome?

Kendall had discarded his jacket and rolled up his sleeves. She swallowed at the sight of his bared forearms and the patches of his wet linen shirt that clung to his taut, muscular-toned body. He stood in sharp contrast to Gus and those poor men whom she had read to at the nearby Chelsea Hospital during her visits to Gus while he recuperated, continuing to do so at the request of one of the hospital benefactresses. Kendall's physique was a far cry from the gaunt, battered bodies of those men. Spiraling heat curled around her body.

She might be an innocent, but that didn't mean she was ignorant. This man pulled at her. He had since the first moment she had seen him at Hammond's. It took every muscle in her body for her to resist responding.

Thankfully, she was a practical woman. It was one thing to admit to a physical attraction but another thing altogether to act on these feelings. *That* she would not do.

She deserved better.

Once she fulfilled this bargain with Kendall, she would be able to pursue her own plans—and those plans would enable her to be an independent woman, reliant on no man.

Chapter Nine

◆━◆

A LONG while later, once again settled in Warren's carriage, Alex peered out the carriage window, oblivious to the passing sights. It was impossible to focus on anything when every one of her senses was alive to the man sitting beside her. The scent of his cologne, masculine and subtle, tangled around her. The sight of his strong, firm thigh but a few inches from hers caused her pulse to race. She could reach out and touch him if she dared.

Damn him for taking her appearance as a gentleman for permission to sit beside her. He was too close. Every so often, the carriage hit a bump in the road and she was jostled against his side before she could brace herself or move away. Since admitting her attraction to the man, his proximity was unwanted, unacceptable . . . and . . . well, she didn't like it. She added brazen to his growing list of faults.

As the passing miles grew, so did her annoyance. Her practical side suggested she move, but her stubborn side rejected the notion. Relinquishing her seat would cede an unspoken battle of wills. That she refused to do. Besides, she hated riding backward.

She pressed her lips together and tipped her head to peer at him from beneath her lashes. Then she jerked her head up, her whole body stiffening.

He was laughing at her! She glowered at him. "What exactly do you find so amusing? And please do not tell me it is this situation."

"And what if I do?" His lips curved, laughter brimming in his eyes.

Mentally she scribbled *idiot* to her list of his faults. "Because I really don't want to lose my money. Unlike you, I have need of it."

He cocked a brow. "How does my amusement jeopardize your financial situation?"

"Our agreement was for payment rendered in assisting you with finding the men trying to murder you. It will be difficult for me to collect if I kill you first." She gave him a sweet smile, pleased with the flicker of surprise that crossed his handsome features before he masked it with a grin.

"I see your point."

"I'm glad that you do."

He waited a beat before commenting. "You could move to the other side, you know."

"If you were a gentleman, you would already have done so."

"You forget, *Mr.* Daniels, for today, you're a gentleman as well."

"How am I to remember that with you opening doors, assisting me in and out of the carriage, and carrying my luggage?"

He nodded. "More good points. May I offer my most sincere apologies. Very rude of me to so forget myself." In contrast to his words, he looked totally unrepentant. "I believe this is the first time I've ever had to excuse myself for good manners."

"I'm sure you're better versed in apologies for your breach of them."

"I have a few well polished. About my behavior, from now on I promise to let you open all doors, heft your own luggage, and let you assist *me* in and out of the carriage."

His obvious amusement was infectious, and she smiled in response. "Very funny."

"I'm known to be sometimes," he said.

The timbre of his voice sent shivers down her spine. "I'll

have to take your word for it. Are you also known for your charity?" At his raised brow, she continued. "What you did for Gus, it was very kind. Thank you."

His humor fled. "You mistake charity for business. He needs a job, and I need a stable manager. Similar to the two of us, Gus and I came to a mutually beneficial agreement. No charity taken, none given."

She blinked at his curt response. It was the Kendall of old, the man she had first encountered in Hammond's card room. Hard and inscrutable. She wondered what nerve she had probed. "Most people wouldn't hire Gus because of his leg."

"Most people are idiots." He shrugged. "I'm not most people."

"No, you certainly are not."

"And being in my presence has never ruined anyone, so it's quite all right for you to sit beside me."

His abrupt shift in topic surprised her. While she wanted to view arrogance in his refusal of her gratitude, she admired his astute understanding of Gus. Gus would never have accepted the job if he believed it to be doled out as charity. Such an offer would have insulted him, further crippling the man. Like most people left with nothing but their pride, Gus equated charity with pity.

Clever man, Kendall.

However, he was wrong about the risks of being so near. It *was* dangerous. But she had already acknowledged some risks were worth taking. "Good, because I hate sitting backward, and I have no intention of being ruined."

"Mmh, at least not until we know each other better."

Startled, she shook her head at the wicked gleam in his eyes. "I pity the innocents you and Lord Warren encountered. While I do believe you're above ruining them, I'm certain you broke your share of hearts."

"I'm sure I was forgotten when the next fop dribbled a few pretty words at them. Empty heads have short memories."

Forgotten? She doubted it. He was the very definition of unforgettable. But his words rankled. They were an insult to her sex, and she felt honor bound to protest. "We must run in different crowds. I've found most young women to be immune to insincere flattery from the *empty-headed* rakes who spout it. It's hard to take a man seriously when his cravat is tied so tight that he can't turn his head. It makes him look like a poker-faced stork." She gave him another sweet smile, which belied the cut of anger in her words.

He raised a brow, and once again studied her like some unfamiliar specimen. This habit of his was beginning to irritate her.

"Does this mean no man has ever seduced you with flattery?" His voice had dipped to a low, husky murmur that coursed through her in a warm wave.

She cursed the limited confines of the carriage and her body's reaction. "I didn't realize we were discussing me."

"We are now. No other woman interests me as much."

Disarmed by his answer and the half smile curving his lips, she didn't know how to respond. She refused to believe he spoke in earnest but couldn't fathom what game he played. "I'm no different from most women. A finely tuned compliment is appreciated, but flattery with the aim of seduction is not."

"Are you sure you speak for most women or for yourself?"

She was not sure of the hidden insult, but she feared he'd insinuated she was a frigid prude. She straightened and peered down her nose at him, speaking as if to a child who needed the simplest explanation clarified. "As I said before, perhaps we don't move in the same circles. Perhaps the type of woman you cultivate is more receptive to your games of seduction. But I assure you, a well-bred young woman is not." Her pitch rose at the end, annoying her. She shouldn't let the man know he got under her skin.

He once again gave her that infernal appraisal of his.

"Another good point. But I'm relieved to know, considering our close working relationship, that you are immune to seduction through any flattery on my part." He paused a moment and when he continued, his gaze touched on each body part he referenced. "I'd hate my compliments on the lovely color of your eyes, or the golden hue of your hair, or the softness of your skin to be misinterpreted as a means to seduction."

She blinked, swallowing to put saliva back into her suddenly dry mouth.

What had been her point?

Her body felt lighter and she jerked back when it leaned

toward his. She shifted into the corner of the coach, away from him. "Yes, well, of course not."

Kendall laughed. The sound was rich and appealing and it softened the hard contours of his face, warming them and making him years younger. He sat back. "Good. That should make things so much easier between us."

"Yes, it should," she muttered and turned toward the carriage window, hoping she voiced the truth.

Chapter Ten

❧❧

GARRETT grinned at Alexandra's profile. He'd been dismissed, but he was too intrigued with their discussion to
take offense.

So, the lady believed herself immune to seduction?

He refused to believe she was so innocent as to be blind to
the danger in her words. He had yet to refuse a challenge, and
he had no intentions of ignoring this one.

This was a call to arms with a different set of weapons. In
the art of seduction, he possessed well-honed artillery, a full
arsenal at his disposal. All had been tried in battle and none
found wanting. If memory served him correctly, his conquests
had succumbed with little protest. If memory served him further, his victories had been celebrated to both party's mutual
satisfaction. And he had an excellent memory.

Admittedly, two years had passed since he had utilized his
talents to seduce a woman. He might be a bit rusty, but like
riding a horse, one never forgot how to do so, nor did one
forget its pleasures. The ache in his loins and his growing
awareness of Alexandra made him realize it was time to end

his abstinence. When he had told her that no woman had ever interested him more, he had spoken the truth.

She fascinated him. She was a mixture of innocence and practicality. He didn't usually dally with innocents, but Alexandra might be the exception to his rule. After all, she wasn't a well-cosseted, shy debutante. She was independent and strong-willed. To use her words, she took risks worth taking. She could handle his siege and make her own decision to surrender—or not. If her passion in bed was as strong as that outside of it, her surrender would be sweet indeed.

He settled back in his seat, aware a smug smile curved his lips when he heard the first shouts in the distance. He was instantly on alert, all his senses alive.

Sliding forward, he reached into the pocket of the door to snatch the pistol within. Alexandra jumped when he leaned across her and whipped the window curtain closed after surveying the scene outside. Two men approached on horseback. "Get down," he hissed.

She cried out when he grabbed her arm and dragged her to the carriage floor with him. They were squeezed together, the space coffin sized.

"Stop the carriage! Stop if ye value yer lives!" An explosion of gunshots accompanied the demands.

He heard Alexandra's sharp intake of breath.

He thrust the pistol into her palm, pointing it to the floor, closing her fingers over the butt when she didn't immediately grip the handle. He tossed aside the carriage cushion to retrieve a second gun he had stored in the compartment beneath. Alexandra tugged on his jacket as he checked his weapon.

"I can't. I've never—" She shook her head frantically, trying to hand the pistol back to him.

Her body crushed deeper into his when Havers barked orders at the horses and the carriage rumbled to an abrupt stop. Curses and loud shouts filled the air.

He lifted Alexandra off his lap and with his free hand, covered hers holding the pistol, preventing her from relinquishing it. "You can and you will, for our lives may depend on it." He stared her down as he had with so many men under his command, willing her to obey, willing her to shelve her nerves and act.

Her eyes were two wide blue saucers and riveted to his as her mouth opened and closed.

She radiated fear, but he reminded himself of her mettle. She was strong. She would not fold.

She did not disappoint. Nodding jerkily, she swiped her hand down her trousers. "How . . ." She moistened her lips. "If I need to . . ."

He cocked her gun, careful to keep it aimed at the floor. "Just pull the trigger and brace yourself for the recoil."

"Kendall! We know ye be in there. Get out now, and yer coachman lives."

He met Alexandra's eyes, her gaze devouring his features as if she sought answers from their predicament in his expression. Christ. He should have been more alert. He shouldn't have let her distract him. He shrugged off the recriminations; hopefully there would be time for that later. For now, he needed a plan of attack.

"How do I know you haven't already killed him?" He yelled to the men, buying time. He leaned close to Alexandra, lowering his voice to a barely audible level. "I'm going out the opposite door, but I need a distraction. Fire a shot out the window, then drop down and stay low. The door facing them is locked. They can't get in quickly."

"But what if—"

"Shh." He pressed his fingers to her lips, silencing her. "It's all right. I know what I'm doing. Trust me."

"My lord?"

He clenched his jaw when Havers rapped the front panel of the coach in response to one of the men's orders. There was relief in the knowledge Havers was alive. He intended for all of them to stay that way.

He studied Alexandra. Beneath her fear, he saw resolution in her curt nod and his blood heated. By God, she was brave and beautiful and he wanted her.

He couldn't resist. Depending on the outcome of his actions, there might not be a second chance for them.

Damned if he'd let this one go.

Leaning down, he clasped her neck and covered those soft lips with his. When she gasped and her mouth opened, he drank her in, a sip before a banquet he hoped to savor later. She tasted of honey, tea, and Alexandra. Sweet and explosive. A flavor of heaven, before he met hell. Damned if he didn't want more.

Unable to resist, he took it. Just a little more to quench the burning need that flared within him in a tumultuous rush of sensation. A potent mixture of danger and desire. He plundered her mouth, teasing her into a hesitant response as her tongue tangled and danced with his. He felt her hand clutch his upper arm, her fingers digging deep.

When her body sagged against him in sweet surrender, a deep, throaty growl of masculine satisfaction filled him. She was magnificent. Passionate *and* responsive.

A shout from outside returned him to his senses, and he drew back, cursing under his breath. He sucked in a ragged breath, his blood pounding, his body burning with thwarted desire.

Struggling to compose himself, he studied Alex, who had slid back against the seat in a boneless heap. She blinked up at him, her eyes glazed and unfocused. Resisting the urge to yank her back into his arms, he gave her a gentle prod toward the window.

Christ. There was no more time. Moments had passed since the carriage had stopped. In battle, seconds counted.

Her eyes clearing, Alexandra pressed her swollen lips together and scrambled onto the seat. She lifted the gun, and her hand visibly shook as she aimed it out the window and then glanced back for his directive. When he nodded, she closed her eyes and pulled the trigger.

Garrett vaulted out the door, barely missing Alexandra, who dove back onto the floor as all hell broke loose outside. He clung to the carriage side as the horses leapt up, whinnying and snorting in protest. Havers's voice barked out as he fought to regain control, the highwaymen cursing.

Another shot rang out.

Garrett heard the splintering of wood as the bullet pierced the carriage. He had seen Alexandra's dive to the floor and prayed the shot was high. He added to his prayer the hope that for once in her life, Alexandra took a direct order and stayed low.

He dropped to the ground, lying flat and slithering beneath the undercarriage as the horses settled.

"Bloody Christ, whot the 'ell do ye think ye be doin'?"

One man advanced on the carriage, the other toward Havers and the horses.

Garrett took aim and then fired at the man rushing the door. One bastard down, one to go.

He cursed the seconds it took for him to reload, but before he could get off a second shot, someone else fired. Their second attacker staggered backward and crumpled to the ground, a pool of blood seeping from beneath his still body.

Garrett scrambled from underneath the coach, meeting Havers, who had leapt down from the box, pistol in hand. The stench of gunpowder from Havers's gun mixed with his, and Garrett nodded. "Good cover."

Havers grunted. "Bunch of idiots. Should have killed me straight off."

"Good thing they didn't. I need you around." Garrett walked over to the man he had shot. He lay on the ground, clutching his stomach as he writhed in pain. Havers approached the second man, gave him a prod with his boot and shook his head. Well, one informant was better than none.

Garrett knelt and planted his pistol to the surviving man's head and cocked it. "Who hired you?"

The man's eyes bulged beneath his lanky hair. His face was pale, a mean scar etched into one cheek. "I don't know nothin'." He panted. "I was jist 'elpin' Dickie on a job. Said 'e'd cut me in." He grimaced and fought the rest of his words. "'E would 'ave if ye 'adn't killed the bugger. Christ, I need . . . Oh, sweet Jesus . . ." His voice trailed off as he glanced down and saw his blood-soaked fingers. His eyes rolled back in his head and he passed out.

Garrett pressed his fingers to the man's neck, feeling the pulse weaken and fade. The man's body slumped, his eyes staring out sightless. Garrett straightened, rage coursing through him like molten heat. Christ, he should have shot him in the leg, but then again, the man couldn't give information he didn't have.

"Is . . . is he dead?"

Garrett spun to see Alexandra framed in the door of the carriage. She gripped the coach side with one hand, the other holding her pistol dangling by her side.

Her eyes were locked on the body on the ground, her

features ghost white. "I . . . I killed him?" The pistol fell from her grip as her hands rose to cover her face, and she sagged against the doorframe.

Before she slid to the ground, Garrett reached her side. "No." He lifted her down, grasping her shoulders and giving her a firm shake as he stood her before him. "No, I did. It wasn't you." He willed her to look at him, and she did. "The man's a murderer. He was going to kill us both. God knows how many he's killed."

Eyes wild, she swallowed. "Yes, yes, of course."

He yanked her to him, cradling her close as he felt the tremors rack her body.

"I'm all right. I just need a minute. Just a minute." She burrowed her face into his chest and held on tight, her fingers digging into his back as she fought to steady herself.

Over her head, he nodded to Havers. "Take the blankets from the coach and cover them."

The warmth of her body seeped into his, easing his own tension. He'd hold her a minute. He could hold her forever.

Another shot echoed in the distance.

Their minute was up.

Garrett tossed Alexandra to the ground, lunging over her to protect her from this new threat. One hand pressed her down as he lifted his head to scan the immediate vicinity, hearing shouts in the distance.

Havers dropped to a defensive crouch, his pistol out, but shook his head at Garrett's unspoken question. He didn't see anything, either.

Garrett sprang to his feet and wrenched Alexandra up, his arm around her waist as he half carried her to the carriage and hoisted her inside. "Get down and stay down." He snatched up her pistol and pressed it into her hands. "Lock the door." Slamming it closed, he ignored both her alarmed expression and cry of protest.

The pounding of horses' hooves moved closer. Garrett cursed the lack of time to find cover, but turned and dropped to his knee. He lifted his pistol, thankful for Havers, who braced his legs and took aim beside him. He didn't know the attackers' numbers, feared the odds were against them, but two armed-and-ready men were better than one.

A single horseman rode into view, leisurely leading his

mount into their line of fire. A body was slumped across his saddle. Unruffled by the guns aimed his way, his gaze took in the bodies of the two dead men, before turning to raise a brow at Havers and Garrett. "Kill me and you'll upset Kit. You know what your sister's like when she's in a temper. It's not pretty."

Heart still pounding, Garrett swore under his breath and stood. "Christ, Bran, what the hell are you doing here? I told you to hire some policemen, not to play Lord Gallant yourself."

The wind ruffled Brandon's dark hair as he turned to Havers. "Is he always a thankless ass or it just with me?"

Havers grunted and crossed to Brandon's side. "What ye got?"

"The third musketeer to add to your group." Brandon dismounted. "All dead?" With his riding boot, he prodded the man Garrett had shot and shook his head. "Damn. They could have had information. We should have shot them in the leg."

Garrett ignored Brandon's echo of his own thoughts. "If you're worried about the wrath of Kit, what the hell do you think she'll do if she finds out you're gallivanting about the countryside, covering my arse from a bunch of murderous bastards?"

"Please, since I married your sister, my days of gallivanting are over." Brandon narrowed his eyes on Garrett. "You can't tell her. You want Beau and Will to grow up without a father?"

Garrett shook his head. "You like to live dangerously, don't you?"

Brandon shrugged. "I'm not the one with the bull's-eye on my arse."

Garrett cast a glance at the carriage but saw no sign of Alexandra. He turned to retort, when two more riders trotted out of the copse of trees lining the unpaved road.

"There's the cavalry now," Brandon said. He addressed Garrett. "I did hire some Peelers to further investigate the attacks in the city and to assist me in keeping your arse safe. We had to separate leaving the city but caught up to you just as you dropped the second man. You didn't appear to need our assistance, so we let you handle matters. Good thing we did, or this one would have slipped free." He nodded to the body slumped across his saddle.

"Many thanks for your belated arrival." Garrett eyed the tall policemen, commonly dubbed Peelers after Sir Robert Peel, who while serving as Home Secretary organized the first police force. Havers took charge, directing the men to collect the bodies and load them onto their horses.

"You're welcome."

"Now that you have my thanks, you need to get the hell out of here. It's due to you that I was attacked in the first place."

"Me?" Brandon frowned. "What are you talking about?"

Garrett paced, his hands balling into fists at his side. "They know me, Bran. They know my habits and my haunts. They knew when I didn't go home from Hammond's that I had gone to your place. They knew I'd flee the city, and they were waiting for me. Watching your place. They don't give a damn who they sacrifice in order to get to me, so you need to protect your own. I need you to go home and ensure Kit and the boys are safe."

"Christ," Brandon breathed. They both fell silent for a moment, feeling the weight of this implication. Brandon was the first to speak. "The Peelers haven't dredged up any information from the first attack, but they are investigating a few leads. I also did as you requested and met with Hammond. He will help in any way he can and gave me a copy of his guest list." He withdrew a folded piece of paper from his jacket pocket and handed it to Garrett. "You need to review it and draw up a list of names of those men who want your head on a platter and possess the money to have it delivered."

"Pleasant thought," Garrett muttered, slipping the list into his own pocket.

"Don't forget the women."

Both men turned at Alexandra's words. She had disregarded Garrett's directive, unlocked the door to the coach, and stood in its frame. However, she still clutched the pistol by her side. For someone who was reluctant to pick up arms, she now appeared just as reluctant to relinquish them. "Let's not forget those scorned sisters, mothers, or wives. You might have practiced sainthood recently, but you didn't always."

Brandon glanced at Alexandra and then at Garrett, a delighted grin curving his lips. "Right. Let's not forget, hell has no fury like a woman scorned."

Garrett narrowed his eyes on Alexandra. He should have known she would have listened to every word they'd said. Well, good. It was time they remembered what had brought them together. Forgetting it had nearly killed them both. He clenched his jaw, anger over the recent ambush coursing through him.

"Now then, our manners have been remiss," Brandon said. "You need to introduce me to your companion."

Garrett crossed to the carriage and assisted Alexandra down, hissing in her ear as he did so. "Hold on to your pistol. If he gets out of hand, shoot him." With reluctance, he set her on her feet and faced Brandon. Only after seeing Brandon's expression did he belatedly realize the oddity of his assisting a young man down. "*Miss* Daniels, this is the Earl of Warren."

At the introduction, Brandon's expression cleared and he stepped forward to bow low. "Miss Daniels, the pleasure is mine."

A flush colored Alexandra's fair skin as she transferred her pistol to her left hand in order to offer her right to Brandon, who took it and pressed his lips to her fingers.

Garrett scowled. Brandon was behaving as if they were in a formal drawing room and not surrounded by the dead bodies of the men who moments ago tried to kill them. He was an idiot.

"It took great courage to warn Lord Kendall about the threat to his life," Brandon said. "If he has not voiced his gratitude for doing so, please accept mine on behalf of my wife. She would mourn his loss, for Garrett's her only brother. For Kit's sake, I try to keep him alive."

"I take back my thanks for your help," Garrett muttered. "You should have let them shoot me, then I wouldn't have to listen to you anymore."

Grinning, Brandon lowered his head to speak in her ear. "Keep the pistol close. If he gets out of hand, you have my permission to shoot him. I promise to break you out of Newgate."

Alexandra's gaze swung to Garrett before she replied. "I think I understand why you two are friends," she said dryly.

"It was a mental lapse on my part," Garrett said. "I've been paying for it ever since."

"It's charity on mine." Brandon smiled. "The man has no one else."

"Except for his sister?" Alexandra said, looking at Garrett.

Garrett lifted a brow at the question. She appeared doubtful he had a sister. Did she think he was spawned from the devil?

"I do have one, you know. And unfortunately, she married Warren. Now I'm stuck with him. But now that the immediate danger has passed, I think it's time for him to leave."

Brandon winked at Alexandra. "I've overstayed my welcome. Despite the circumstances, it was nice meeting you, Miss Daniels." He bowed before her and turned to Garrett. "I'll catch up with you in a week."

Garrett walked Brandon to his horse. The other two men moved to mount their own horses where the bodies of Garrett's attackers lay strapped across the front of their saddles.

Brandon would deliver them to the magistrate and see what information they could glean from their family or friends. "This one's name is Dickie." He pointed to the man Havers had shot. "The other one said as much before he died."

Brandon nodded. "Perhaps after this second failed attempt on your life, one of these men's cronies will step forward with some details, for a price."

"Pay it," Garrett said.

"Of course. I've also frequented White's and circulated different addresses for your whereabouts."

"Has anyone asked after me?"

Brandon snorted. "You're a wounded war hero and a survivor of the Charge of the Light Brigade. You make a brief appearance in town after a two-year absence, then abruptly disappear again. You're all anyone speaks of or asks after."

"Bloody hell," Garrett swore.

"Exactly. I will keep an ear open for any persistent inquiries, but"—Brandon shrugged—"I'd start with Hammond's list. It's a lead, the only one we have right now. She saved your life."

Garrett's eyes drifted toward Alexandra, who had wandered back to wait before the carriage. "Yes, she did." And she had agreed to stay with him despite the danger she risked in doing so. He recalled Gus's words and he lowered his voice. "One more thing. Find out all you can about a Viscount Langdon. He holds lands in Essex."

Brandon lifted a brow and following his gaze to Alex, he nodded. "I can do that."

"Good." Garrett faced Brandon. "Then as we discussed, you and Kit will join me at the manor. I think it is the safest place. Only those loyal to me know of its location, and most are my men, veterans, willing to fire a shot on my behalf."

"Kit's been going mad sequestered in the country. She'll be overjoyed to play chaperone, or rather delighted you requested one."

Garrett grimaced, thinking of his half sister and Alexandra together. He then met Brandon's gaze, suddenly serious. "You need to be careful. Stay away if you fear you're being followed and it's not safe."

"I'll keep my eyes open." His gaze leveled on Garrett. "You, too. Watch your back." He clasped Garrett's shoulder again, this time giving it a squeeze.

"I always do," Garrett murmured, stepping away to give Brandon room to mount. He watched his friend ride off. When he disappeared from view, Garrett turned to Alexandra. Now more than ever, he needed to be vigilant.

Today had reminded him of the cost incurred should he let his attention slip. Not only was his life in danger, but Alexandra's as well. He remembered the fear in her eyes, but overriding this memory was the feel of her in his arms and the taste of her on his lips. No, he refused to let anything happen to her.

He ignored the warning that perhaps he spread himself too thin. He was entering battles on three fronts, one against an enemy seeking his murder, another ancient and ongoing with his stepfather, and now this third one. He'd have to review his strategy very carefully, but it couldn't be helped. He wanted Alexandra and was determined to have her. Brave, beautiful, and responsive, she gave him something to live for, and he hadn't had that in a long, long time.

Chapter Eleven

❦❧

THE acrid odor of gunpowder drifted to Alex. Images of their attackers' dead bodies assaulted her. *Murderers*. Men who had no compunction about killing others to line their own pockets.

She felt as if she had stepped into a nightmare in which she was just beginning to comprehend its dangers. In her zeal to agree to Kendall's arrangement, she had forgotten one pertinent fact—someone wanted the man dead.

This nameless adversary also had no compunction about killing anyone else who stood in their way. She pressed a hand to her heart. What good was a monetary reward or independence if she was dead?

She had naïvely assumed her greatest danger lay in her attraction to Kendall.

A noise had her glancing up. A breeze whipped through Kendall's dark hair as he stood watching her. For an endless moment, their eyes locked before his dipped to her mouth. She sucked in a sharp breath.

How could she have forgotten their kiss?

For a fleeting moment, the gun in her hand, the highwaymen

outside, and her escalating fears had all vanished. In the midst of life-threatening danger, nothing had existed but the two of them and the feel of his lips on hers. He had pulled from her feelings she didn't know she possessed, yearnings, aches, and needs. Desire.

She lifted her hand to press them against her swollen lips. She had tasted danger and excitement, the essence of the man himself. Disturbed, she yanked her hand down and gave her head a sharp shake. It was time to recall Kendall's list of faults. Damned if she could remember one.

His heroic actions only compounded the matter. Damn him for his foolhardy courage. It could have gotten them both killed. And damn him for saving her life and his. How was a woman to resist such a man? She condemned Warren as well, cursed him for showing her Kendall's friends were willing to risk their own lives to save his. Only a man worthy of being saved would earn such trust.

She tightened her fingers over the handle of the gun, as if it could offer protection from the man as he approached her. Kendall's long legs made quick work of closing the distance between them. Her heart thundered and unconsciously she moistened her lips. Her problem was formidable and as Kendall neared, it grew larger by the second.

"If I promise to sit across from you, will you relinquish the gun?"

><

GARRETT'S GAZE DIPPED pointedly to Alexandra's white-knuckled grip of the weapon, battling a mixture of amusement and wariness. Amusement at her combative stance and wariness because there was another shot left in her gun. Enemy fire alone hadn't killed or maimed all the soldiers during battle. Gus's lost leg was testament to that.

A flush climbed her cheeks. She pointed the barrel to the ground, gripped it with two fingers and held the weapon out to him as if she offered him a dead sacrifice. "Please, take it before I shoot one of us."

He grinned as he accepted it. "You did fine, but I knew you would. You'd make an excellent soldier."

"Yes, well, not if I had to open my eyes during battle." She glanced away and her voice lowered. "Or if I had to shoot anyone."

He studied the darkness clouding her usually vibrant blue eyes. He followed her gaze and nodded. "I'd be more concerned if that came easily to you or anyone."

He turned from her and walked to the carriage. Lifting his hand to open the door, he paused and dropped his arm, for she deserved more even if his words dug up all he fought to bury. He faced her, meeting her questioning look. "True courage is acting in the face of your fear and conquering it. As I said, you did fine." He watched her eyes widen before he turned back to the carriage, speaking over his shoulder. "We should continue. We have a long ride ahead of us."

She moved to his side. "It's little wonder Tennyson memorialized the fallen soldiers of Balaclava. Courage of that caliber is rare. The men I overheard plotting your murder, they . . . they said you survived the Charge of the Light Brigade."

She studied him as if trying to read his expression, which had closed down the minute she mentioned Balaclava. Every muscle in his body went rigid. Something hard and unpalatable curdled in his gut.

"I don't know how you survived the day, but I thank God you did because I owe you my life. Those men would have killed us both."

For two days since Alexandra had stumbled into his path, he had forgotten the nightmare that had ripped apart his world and plunged him back into the valley of death. Tennyson's words slammed it all back into him.

Tennyson had penned the tribute in the *Examiner* minutes after reading an account of the battle in the *Times*. Once home, Garrett had burned all copies he had received of both papers. Unlike Alexandra and most of its readers, who believed the poem canonized the soldier's heroic bravery, he had found the words a testament to his countrymen's idiocy and pomposity. For Christ's sake, it memorialized the glory of a battle that was a colossal failure.

However, burning the poem could not eradicate its words or the true scope of the tragedy. *Someone had blunder'd: Theirs not to make reply, theirs not to reason why, theirs but to do and die.*

A roaring noise filled his head, pounded his temple.

He fought to yank his thoughts back, but the words combined with the stench of powder from the gun he held brought the nightmare of sights, sounds, and smells that pervaded that day back to life. Mangled corpses, horses plowing over the dead and dying, the writhing screams of the wounded. The stink of gore, rancid fear, and death.

If Lord Cardigan had only clarified Raglan's orders, fathomed he might have misinterpreted them, or . . . Christ, stop!

Don't go there. The warning screamed in his ears.

Garrett whirled around and ripped open the door to the carriage, sweat breaking out on his forehead. He clenched his jaw. He had traveled this road before. It was a dead end, providing no escape from the darkness into which those questions plunged him. He needed to stop asking them. "My Lord . . . ?"

Havers's voice echoed in the deep fog closing in on him. He closed his eyes, drawing steadying breaths.

"My lord?" Alexandra this time. Her hand fell on his shoulder and her voice softened. "Garrett?"

He opened his eyes and worked to regulate his ragged breathing. He needed a minute, just a minute. He had been doing well for so long.

"It's all right," Alexandra murmured. He heard her address Havers. "Why don't you see to the horses. Lord Kendall wants to leave immediately."

The calm in her voice reached through to him, and he grasped on to it as if she could lead him out of the darkness.

Alexandra regarded him with concern as he managed to nod at Havers.

Havers hesitated, his eyes falling on Alexandra for a moment, his features inscrutable, before he turned to follow the directive.

"Are you all right?" she asked.

"Of course." He gave a curt nod. He would be. Someday. He looked off into the distance, not meeting her eyes. "Don't mention . . ." He cleared his throat and tried again, for it needed to be said. "We won't discuss Balaclava. I can't." Without waiting for her reply, he stepped forward to assist her into the carriage.

When he climbed inside and again took the seat beside her, she didn't comment.

Tapping on the back panel, he signaled Havers to depart. It would be a long ride to Kent.

"I'm sorry."

The quietly spoken words drifted to him and he clenched his jaw, staring blindly out the window. His hand fisted on his thigh. Alexandra's hand, soft and comforting, came to rest over his. He momentarily froze, before his breathing evened and he closed his eyes. The tension gripping him eased. For a fleeting moment, he tried to believe that her touch could heal him. After a while, he managed a response. "So am I. Every God-damn day."

He wished that was enough.

⊱⊰

ALEX STUDIED GARRETT'S profile, her heart constricting at the pain in his words, seeing his tortured expression from moments before. The man had appeared strong and brave to the point of recklessness. He had confronted two gunmen, never wavering or faltering—until now.

She didn't fully understand what had transpired, but she recognized the signs of unhealed wounds.

She studied Kendall, who had tipped his head back onto the seat and closed his eyes. Her heart thudded because for the first time, she understood her response to this strong, enigmatic man. She had seen something in his eyes, a darkness when she had first met him. Now she understood. Kendall was no different from the soldiers for whom she had once cared at Chelsea Hospital. He simply hid his wounds beneath a hard, polished veneer. Her mention of Balaclava had unwittingly stripped away this layer and wrenched open old wounds. He didn't want her to see his pain, but she did.

This is what she had sensed in Kendall. What had first drawn her to the man and continued to draw her to him. It was what separated him from the other men at Hammond's.

She wasn't so naïve as to deny her physical attraction, for there was no ignoring the man was striking. But looks alone could not explain the pull she felt. Alex had met many handsome men during her Season, some more handsome than Kendall. Yet none had touched her like this.

She didn't believe in fate, but she had to believe there was a reason she had overheard the plot to murder him. Unlike Kendall, she doubted she would recall any new information to help identify his enemy, but this didn't concern her. Kendall appeared capable of defending himself. Twice he had thwarted his enemy. While Alex couldn't assist him in this fight, she might be able to help him with another battle.

Until he healed his deeper wounds, he would never fully recover. This was a fight she understood and one in which she could aid Kendall. She had learned from her care of other wounded veterans that in order to help Kendall, Alex needed for him to confide in her. This, she conceded, the man had no intention of doing.

We won't discuss Balaclava again.

She gnawed on her lower lip. He sounded quite firm on this subject. She would just have to gain his trust. He had saved her life, and if Kendall could place his trust in her, she could save his.

"Just what is going through that head of yours? I can feel the wheels spinning, kicking up dust. It's keeping me awake."

She snatched back her hand, suddenly aware she had been tightly gripping his. She stared at him and he stared right back. A smile tipped his lips. He leaned close, their shoulders brushing, his hard thigh pressed to hers. She flushed and slid away. "Nothing. Just thinking, that's all. But I'm tired, so I think I'll try to get some rest."

His soft laughter washed over her. "Why don't you do that? We have a few hours ahead of us. Feel free to lean against me."

"That won't be necessary." Her voice sounded prim even to her. Irritated, she cursed the carriage for being hard and uncomfortable as she settled against its side. "I'm quite all right." She closed her eyes and hoped he took the hint and left her alone.

"Perhaps when we know each other better."

The familiar quip was low and husky and sent shivers down

her spine, and she struggled to ignore her body's traitorous reaction. It was difficult with the man's rumble of laughter distracting her. She doubted sleep would offer a safe refuge for her, either. The man and the memory of his damn kiss would undoubtedly invade her dreams.

Chapter Twelve

⤜ ⤛

WHEN the carriage reached the village housing Charlton Manor, Garrett closed his eyes and inhaled deeply. The familiar scent of salt air from the distant sea mixed with the floral scent of the nearby gardens. As an earldom, the Kendall holdings were vast and grand, but for Garrett, his late uncle's residence tucked away in a corner of Kent was home.

His visits to his mother's younger brother, William, had been few and far between. But like water replenishing an empty well, those escapes had filled the empty spaces in Garrett's heart.

His uncle would appear at Eton like an unexpected gift, his booming laugh answering the headmaster's scowl. Winking at Garrett, William would whisk him away for a weekend or during the school breaks his mother had so often neglected. During those magical days at Charlton Manor, Garrett had found the smile he had lost.

He was devastated when William joined the British Indian Army and left the country and Garrett's life. After William's death, when Garrett came of age, he had followed in his uncle's footsteps and purchased his own commission in the Seventeenth

Lancers. Knowing this act would infuriate his stepfather had solidified his decision to do so.

Garrett shook his head to dislodge the memory. Christ. His uncle was dead, he was no longer a boy, and what he had lost in the Crimea was far graver than a smile. In his bleakest moments, he feared it was his soul.

Sweat broke out on his brow, and he rubbed his face but stilled when Alexandra stirred. She had been quiet these final hours as the sun had set and day had drifted into dusk. True to her word, she had fallen asleep after they had changed horses and grabbed a brief bite to eat.

He hadn't lingered long in the tavern, wanting to push forward in order to arrive at their destination before they were waylaid again. He had dropped his vigilance once; he would not do so again.

The carriage turned into Charlton Manor drive, and the movement jostled Alexandra awake. The candlelight bathed her features in a soft glow. Blinking, she pushed away from the window and sat up. Her eyes fluttered closed as the sway of the carriage tipped her body into his. Shifting to get more comfortable, she curled against him, settled her cheek on his shoulder, and drifted back to sleep.

He grinned, not minding his service as a pillow. The heat from her body seeped into his, warming him. No, he didn't mind at all. He resisted the urge to draw her closer. They were nearly home, and he needed to wake her.

In a minute he thought, just a minute.

He leaned down to breathe in her scent, wanting to remove her absurd wig, let her hair tumble free, and bury his fingers in the silken strands.

Her lips parted in her sleep and her hand dropped to his thigh. He sucked in a sharp breath, his groin tightening as a molten wave of lust shot through him.

Charlton House had satisfied a boy's need, but he was a man and it was a woman's touch he now craved. He exhaled. He might not find everything he needed to make him whole, but perhaps with Alexandra, he might salvage a few pieces of his old self and cobble them together. It had been so long since his body had awakened to a woman's touch. It felt good—better than good, and he smiled.

The carriage made another turn and his mood crested. Riding on this wave of exuberance, he leaned down and gently kissed Alexandra on her parted lips. A murmur escaped her and she lifted her hand to cup his cheek. Her fingers slid to the nape of his neck, curling into his hair, and he groaned. God, she felt so good, tasted better. Desire coursed through him, and he wrapped his arms around her body and crushed her to him, deepening the kiss.

Alexandra's eyes flew open and she stared into his, wide-eyed and still.

His lips curved into a smile against hers.

She pushed against his chest, straining away from him. "Stop that," she cried. "You can't keep kissing me."

"But I like kissing you. And your response tells me you liked it, too."

"I was half asleep!" she protested.

He lowered his voice and pulled her back against him, liking the feel of her soft body against his. "Then imagine how much better it will be when you're awake."

She averted her face. "Lord Kendall, I told you—"

"Garrett."

She looked at him, frowning in confusion.

"That's my name. You used it earlier today. And now we've been intimate."

She gasped and shoved against his chest so hard that he released her. "We most certainly have not! A few stolen kisses do not constitute intimacy."

"Good, then let's do it again."

"Absolutely—"

Absolutely worked for him.

He yanked her to him and lowered his head before she could finish her sentence. She stiffened as his lips plundered hers, but it wasn't long before she groaned. God she tasted better than the richest desserts or the finest wines, like a rare delicacy. A starving man, he devoured her. Two years was a long time. His body was fast becoming aware of just how long. He might have to walk to the house with a stooped posture, but by God, it would be worth it. He'd crawl if need be.

When he finally released her, she fell back against the seat.

"Absolutely *not*," she muttered, her faced flushed, her lips swollen as she glowered at him.

He grinned at her expression.

"Lord Kendall—"

"Garrett."

She opened her mouth, closed it, and sighed. "Garrett," she relented. When he beamed at her, she shook her head. "You must stop stealing kisses from me. It is—"

"I agree. Why don't you give them to me freely, then I won't have to steal them."

"Absolutely—"

He reached for her again, but her hands shot up, fending him off as she retreated into the corner of the coach. "Not, absolutely not!"

He laughed. "Perhaps when we know each other better."

"Stop saying that!" She lifted a hand to rub her temple. "This is a business arrangement. Nothing more. I've told you that, and you agreed."

He stared at her flushed features, watching her color deepen to a wine red. He nodded and composed his features into a serious expression. "You're right. I did."

"Good, I'm glad we agree." The coach rolled to a stop and the sudden silence echoed through the carriage. Alexandra sat up, straightened her jacket, and neatened her wig, which had become comically askew during their embrace.

He opened the door. "But you also told me you are immune to seduction. It means we needn't worry about a few stolen kisses." He vaulted from the carriage before she could see his amusement, but he couldn't suppress his laughter when silence greeted his words.

He glanced up to find Havers standing a few yards from him. His eyes were enormous, nearly popping out of his face. His mouth gaped before he shut it. He opened it to speak, closed it, and opened it again, looking like a bird snapping at a worm out of reach.

Garrett paused, baffled by his unflappable manservant's discomposure. What the hell was wrong with the man? He knew Alexandra was a woman. He frowned. "Havers? What is it?" Christ, had they been followed? His amusement fled and he crossed to Havers, his gaze scanning the area, every muscle in his body taut. "Did you see anyone? Did—?"

"No!" Havers said, his expression sobering. He gave his

head a sharp shake and straightened his shoulders. "It were nothing, my lord."

Garrett frowned. But before he could pursue it, Alexandra recovered her voice and bellowed his name. He turned and the sight of her leaning out the carriage door and pointing at him restored his humor.

"Just one minute," she started, "come back here. I don't think—"

"Good, don't."

"Don't what?" She sounded exasperated.

"Think, don't think." He swung her down as her enraged shriek answered him.

On her feet, she slapped his hands away and stepped back. "A thinking woman must be a novelty to you, but you will have to get used to it because we are not finished with this matter. Not at all."

"I quite agree, but we have an audience now, so we'll have to finish it later." He tipped his head toward Havers.

Alexandra whirled to face Havers, who nodded curtly to her before addressing Garrett. "I'll see to the horses and bring up the bags, sir."

Garrett grasped a flushed Alexandra by the elbow and escorted her to the house.

She was right. They were not finished with the matter.

They were just beginning.

❧

Alex's head was spinning. She didn't protest Kendall's, or rather *Garrett's* escort. She feared if he released her, she would stumble, so unsure of her footing was she.

Little wonder there. It wasn't often a woman was awakened from sleep by a mind-numbing sensual kiss. Her world was spiraling out of her control and had been for the past year. At least before Garrett she had been at the helm of her floundering ship. Now she was a mere passenger while Garrett manned the wheel. Worse, she didn't know if she liked the direction he steered her.

But Lord, the man could kiss. She couldn't deny liking that.

She had tasted on his lips the cider he had drunk at the tavern. Like its strong flavor, Garrett's kiss was potent, heady, and it stirred a response deep inside her. She had ached to curl her fingers into the soft strands of his hair and merge her body with his.

Dazed, she touched her fingers to her sore lips, while regarding the manor that loomed before her. She had been so distracted that she had paid little heed to her surroundings. The moon was full and illuminated the house like a bright beacon. Symmetrical in the Elizabethan style, it was an imposing structure of red brick. Matched gables on opposite sides framed the entrance and towering bay windows lined the facade. Ropes of ivy climbed the brick, finding footholds in hidden crevices.

"This is Charlton Manor, my late uncle's former home. It's mine now. The only people who know it is one of my holdings are family and former veterans loyal to me, so we should be safe here for a while."

Garrett's voice startled her, and she choked off her laugh. *Safe?* Was the man serious? He clearly didn't understand the danger *he* presented. She couldn't fathom how he could kiss her blind and not see that he was killing her.

Sighing, she followed Garrett up the stairs to the front entrance. Before Garrett could lift the brass knocker, the door swung open.

A young footman greeted them. "Sir." He nodded to Garrett as he moved aside for them to enter.

They stepped into a spacious foyer. Alex glanced up to see an elegant chandelier dangling from the ceiling of the second story. A polished mahogany staircase with spooled rails curved to a balcony that encircled the second floor.

"Ned, I see you found your way safely. Is all in order?"

Ned bobbed his head. "Yes, sir. I got us a cook and some maids, and they've done started on cleanin' up the place."

Ned was as dark-haired and tall as Garrett, but when he followed Garrett to the foot of the stairs, Alex noticed he walked with a limp, one leg favored over the other.

"Sir, Cook put me to work polishin' some silver and . . . I been thinkin'. I don't think that's a footman's job, sir. And I been thinkin' some more, sir. Perhaps, I'm not cut out to be no footman. I'm better with horses, sir. Perhaps I should be in the stables."

Garrett stopped and turned to Ned.

Alex grinned at the youth's outburst, watching as he shuffled his feet under Garrett's regard. He studied the young man in that infernal silent manner of his. At least she wasn't the only one made to feel like a laboratory specimen.

"It sounds like you've been doing a great deal of thinking, Ned," Garrett said, his expression solemn. "Tell you what, why don't you handle the few horses we do have. I've hired a man to build up the stables and he could use a hand, so if you'd prefer that line of work to being inside, then we'll set you up with him. How does that sound?"

Ned beamed. "Thank you, sir, and you be gettin' a better stable hand out of me than a footman, sir, so 'tis the better deal for both of us."

She stifled her laugh as she observed Garrett tuck his tongue in his cheek and nod, appearing to consider the comment with undue seriousness.

"Thank you, Ned, for bringing this to my attention. A man shouldn't waste his talents in areas unsuited to him. Now then, if that's all, I will show our guest to her room."

"Oh, right, sir." Ned's eyes landed on Alexandra as if aware of her for the first time. He took in her masculine attire and turned to Garrett, baffled. Clearly he had caught the use of the feminine pronoun.

"*Miss* Daniels and I left a masquerade in the city." Garrett delivered the lie with ease, while his closed expression brooked no further inquiries.

Ned's cheeks colored, and he dipped into a short bow. "Thank you, again, sir. I'll head to the stables now." If not for his stiff leg, he would have bolted the distance to the door.

"Think nothing of it," Garrett murmured to Ned's back.

She couldn't resist a comment. "He's charming." After a slight hesitation, she continued. "His leg? Casualty of the Crimea?"

Garrett raised a brow at her question, and then looked amused. "No, that's a casualty of Duke and youthful hubris—or stupidity." At her obvious bafflement, he explained. "Ned's father is the stable manager at another of my estates. Duke is an unbroken stallion that I recently purchased, and Ned thought to break in the horse." He shrugged. "Ned was lucky, for with time, his leg should heal. But in punishment, his father turned him over to me thinking he'd make a better footman than a stable hand. As you can see, Ned has other ideas."

"What do you think?" Alex smiled.

"I think the boy's old enough to make his own decisions and live with the consequences, painful or not." He paused and his eyes darkened. "As do we all." He turned away and strode forward. "I'll show you to your room."

Alex frowned, his last words clearly referring to some decision other than Ned's training of Duke. She wondered what consequences Garrett had to live with that caused his pain? It was more than memories of the war. Of that she was sure.

Disturbed, she followed Garrett upstairs and nearly stumbled into him when he paused in the dimly lit hallway. There were no pictures on the brocade wallpaper and most of the doors were closed.

"This will be your room." Garrett opened a door before him and stepped aside. "I'll have a maid sent to you and see that she brings your valise."

"Thank you," she murmured, aware of the heat of Garrett's body beside her.

"How about a kiss good night?"

Her head snapped up to his, the husky timber of his voice sending shivers through her. Definitely trouble. "I don't think—"

"Good." He crushed her to him and once more, silenced her with a kiss.

She grasped his arms, his embrace forcing her to stand on her toes to reach him. If not for his support, she would have slid to the ground in a boneless heap. In the back recesses of her mind, she knew this would not do. They had a business arrangement, and business partners did not tangle tongues as they were doing, no matter how good he tasted. But Lord, he tasted wonderful. And she wanted more.

Her practical side continued to scream this was a bad idea. She planned to heed its warning . . . in a minute. Desire swept through her in an undulating wave and she yearned to ride it.

When he lifted his head years later, she gasped for breath.

His eyes locked with hers, the steel gray of his warm and amused. "Sometimes not thinking is good," he said. "Sometimes things are best felt."

He released her and she stumbled back against the wall, blinking up at him.

"Good night, Alexandra." His smile was intimate and knowing. He bowed, turned on his heel, and strode away.

Weak-kneed, she stared after him. She needed to call him back. She wasn't finished with him yet. She shook her head. That didn't sound right. Of course, they were finished. He wouldn't . . . she couldn't . . . she refused to venture down that trail of thought. It led to forbidden ground.

She moved into her room and closed the door. Garrett was steering her into dangerous waters. Tomorrow, she would regain the helm. She couldn't think tonight. *Sometimes not thinking is good,* his words echoed. Some things are *best felt.* Lord, did she feel. Hot, prickly, and unsettled. Her arms curled around her waist as her gaze drifted over the bedchamber, seeking to distract her thoughts from Garrett.

The room was decorated in muted shades of rose, green, and blue. The iron bed was ornate, with scrollwork of floral medallions set in the headboard and footboard. An armoire stood in the corner, a vanity with a marble top and an oval mirror hanging above it lined one wall. An Oriental rug covered the hardwood floor. It was lovely. Inviting and . . . feminine. She frowned.

She refused to think about how many other women had stayed here or if Kristen had slept in this room. *Kristen, who loved Garrett.* It was easy to forget Garrett's mistress, particularly when the man was kissing her blind.

So much for distracting herself.

She removed the pins holding her wig in place. Slipping it off, she dispensed with the rest of the clips tying up her hair and threaded her fingers through the freed strands. She untied her cravat and yanked it off as well. When she unbuttoned the top buttons of her shirt, she breathed freely for the first time in hours.

A noise nearby made her jump.

She froze, straining to hear. Another sound carried to her, a dull thud as if something had fallen on the floor. Her eyes searched the room and found a second door beside the armoire. Without thinking, she stormed over to it, yanked it open, and gasped.

Garrett.

He stood in the middle of what appeared to be the spacious

master suite. Her feet sank into a thick Aubusson carpet, and her eyes strayed to the inviting spool bed piled high with pillows. She noticed Garrett's jacket tossed onto the comforter and quickly averted her gaze, her heart thudding.

Garrett grinned. He had removed his boots, thus explaining the noise she had heard earlier. His cravat was untied and the top buttons of his shirt were open, his shirttails untucked and hanging loose. Independent and arrogant, it was so like the man to not wait for a valet to disrobe.

It was of no relevance to her who undressed him. She clenched her jaw. Again, that had not sounded right. She shouldn't be wondering about his valet but more important, she shouldn't be thinking about Garrett undressing.

She needed to focus on his presence in the master suite in the room next to hers. If this door connected his room to hers, that made her bedchamber the . . . She braced a hand against the doorframe and lifted her chin. "Just what do you think you're doing?"

He cocked his brow, leisurely stripping off his cravat and tossing it onto his bed.

After a tantalizing peek at the naked skin through the collar of his unbuttoned shirt, she kept her eyes fastened on his face, which was also a mistake.

He looked amused. "I'm getting undressed. You're welcome to join me."

"This has to stop!" She resisted the urge to stamp her foot. "We had an agreement."

Laughing, he crossed to a side table to lift the crystal decanter sitting there. He filled a glass and crossed to Alex's side. His lips pursed when she pressed back against the doorframe as if seeking refuge.

Without a word, he caught her hand, placed the glass in it, and curled her fingers around its solid surface. "Drink that." He nodded to the swirling liquid. "It's brandy. It will relax you." When she opened her mouth to protest, he pressed his fingers against her lips, silencing her with the intimate gesture.

"I do remember our agreement and I'm sticking to it." His hand dropped. "But part of our arrangement is protecting you. You forget, someone wants me dead. I refuse to let you be a casualty in their plot. As safe as I believe this estate is, I have no guarantees. Your welfare is my concern, so for now, I'm keeping you close." In a quicksilver mood change, his intensity vanished and he grinned, a gleam in his eyes as he leaned close. "If I can't have you in my bed, next door is the safest alternative." He pressed his fingers to the bottom of her glass and lifted it to her. "Drink."

She slapped his hand away and took a sip. Like liquid fire, the brandy burned her throat and made her eyes water. She blinked furiously and coughed, Garrett's laughter rumbling through her.

"And Alexandra," he said, his voice lowered, her name like a whispered endearment on his lips. "I'm not partial to unwilling bedmates. I've never forced a woman. You don't need a house wing separating us, nor this door, locked or otherwise. All you need is one word—'no.'" He flashed a devilish grin and leaned closer still, one hand braced on the doorframe above her head, the other reaching out to capture a lock of her hair.

She caught her breath as his knuckles brushed the pulse beating in her throat before he moved his hand away and the long strand slid through his fingers.

"But I prefer 'absolutely,'" he breathed.

Alex was mesmerized by the slow, seductive smile curving his lips and lighting his eyes. This conversation had not gone in the direction she intended. Once again, Garrett had steered her off course.

But he was right. He had never forced her, and if the man was bent on ravishing her, he could have done it six times over by now. He might be a rake, but he was a gentleman rake. All she had to do was say no. She would do so next time.

And there would be a next time.

A rake, gentleman or not, was still a rake, and stealing kisses is what they did, some better than others. Garrett had perfected the practice.

"Yes, you're right. You're absolut . . ." Her words trailed off. She stepped back into her room and gripped the doorknob. "I just needed that clarified. It's, ah . . . it's good we understand each other." She jumped when Garrett reached toward her.

He removed the glass from her hand.

His fingers were warm, his touch sending a shiver down her body. "Good night, Garrett."

"Alexandra?" She was about to close the door, but Garrett's hand blocked it. "I'll teach you the proper use of a revolver. You need to be comfortable with it."

She moistened her lips to respond. "Yes, that might be wise if I'm going to be near you." She liked his look of surprise. "Good night."

When his hand dropped from the door, she closed it firmly and slumped back against it, her heart galloping.

She heard his laughter through the door and her smile grew. She hadn't fully regained her footing, but she was finding it.

Her parting salvo was a start.

Chapter Thirteen

❧

Garrett leaned forward in his office chair, nodding his head as his secretary reviewed the accounts, updating him on the needs of his tenants and sundry other estate matters.

He listened attentively or rather, presented the appearance of doing so. His secretary, David Stewart, was young and new to the job. In his eagerness, he got bogged down in details. Garrett should have expected it, for Stewart used to be his artillery sergeant. Precision was a valued asset in the man's former profession.

With his secretary's head bent over his papers, Garrett removed his pocket watch under cover of the desk and read the time. Good Lord, they had been at it for over two hours. This would not do. Besides, Garrett needed to assess the grounds for himself and speak to his men about patrolling the area. On Garrett's turf now, the bastard wanting him dead would be trespassing. If he dared to do so, Garrett would be ready. A tic vibrated in his cheek as he clenched his jaw.

His eyes narrowed on Stewart. He'd give him a few more minutes, and then he'd intercede. He had other plans. He also had a woman to seduce, and he had yet to strategize this second, although far more pleasurable, battle plan.

The tension in him eased as his thoughts drifted to Alex, warm and responsive in his arms. Stewart wasn't the only one who had a memory for details. He recalled the taste of her mouth, the pliant arch of her body against his, and the feel of her fingers threading through his hair. He crossed his legs, struggling to maintain an attentive expression. When he felt his lips curve, he knew he was losing the fight.

Before Stewart caught him looking like a besotted fool, Garrett cleared his throat and slid his chair back. "Thank you, Stewart. Clearly, I have the right man in this position." Garrett circled the desk to meet his surprised secretary, who jumped to his feet. He squeezed Stewart's shoulder and steered him to the door.

"Ah, thank you, my lord. But I had a few more matters—"

"I'm sure you do. Why don't we tour the grounds, and you can continue your report along the way."

Stewart nodded, looking chastened. "You're quite right, sir. I should have anticipated you would want to see things for yourself. That was remiss of me."

"On the contrary. I have every confidence that you have missed nothing. Your attention to detail is beyond reproach."

His secretary beamed. "Thank you, sir. The vicar assisted me."

"The vicar?" Garrett raised a brow, his hand on the door.

Stewart shifted his feet, before giving a curt nod.

Garrett studied his secretary, aware for the first time of the shadows underlining the man's blue eyes. "Very wise of you. I'm sure the vicar is a great help in many areas."

Stewart's relief was visible. "Yes, sir. He has been."

"Good." Garrett nodded. After a pause, he added, "And he does have a lovely daughter."

A flush stole over the younger man's fair features. Garrett smiled as he entered the front hallway. But his smile froze and he stopped short at the sight greeting him at the bottom of the stairs. He blinked at the vision standing before him. *Alexandra.*

Her blonde locks were tucked into a neat chignon. She wore a deep, royal blue gown that cinched her slim waist and revealed alluring curves her men's jacket had concealed. Having held her in his arms, Garrett knew her to be a slip of a thing, but still she was round in all the right places and his eyes roamed over them in admiration. She had high, full breasts, another hidden asset. At his side, his fingers flexed and he swallowed. She was beautiful.

Dear lord, he hoped his secretary wasn't the only one to have something of more interest transpire before their next meeting.

The gleam in her eyes snapped Garrett out of his reverie. He'd been caught staring like a boy just out of short trousers, experiencing his first awareness of a woman. There was something to be said for hiding one's light under a bushel.

He cleared his throat and dipped into a shallow bow. "Good morning, *Miss* Daniels. I trust you slept well. You look lovely. After a lengthy business meeting, you are the perfect sight to greet the rest of the day, like a ray of sunshine."

Alexandra looked wary at his trite cliché. Hell, his flattery was rusty. No surprise there. Having no use for it over the past two years, it needed a bit of polish. It was a necessary tool in the art of seduction, and he needed all his weapons precision sharp if he planned an assault.

"I slept fine and have dined as well. Your meeting ran smoothly?" Her eyes drifted between Garrett and his secretary.

"I couldn't have left matters in better hands. This is David Stewart, my secretary and estate manager," he said, not waiting for his secretary's reaction to an unchaperoned woman being his houseguest. "Now we plan to follow up on our discussion with a tour of the grounds, and you have arrived just in time to join us."

Alexandra looked surprised. "Are you sure? I wouldn't want to impose. I—"

"No imposition. In fact, I insist. Your lovely company will brighten our day." Good lord. He sounded like a daft doe-eyed idiot. Feared he looked like one, too. This had to stop. But when Alexandra smiled, her luminous blue eyes sparkling, he found he was smiling back, delighted with himself.

"Thank you, I'd love to join you. It is wise to view things firsthand. On-site inspections often provide the best perspective on how to handle certain matters."

Do they now? Garrett wondered at her response. *Had she assisted her father with the estate? Hadn't they had an estate manager?* More questions, more dreaded puzzle pieces.

"How long has it been since you have visited this estate?"

"A while," he answered. "But Stewart has kept me updated on those issues needing immediate attention, and I trust him implicitly." Garrett addressed his secretary. "Why don't you head down to the stables? See that Ned has our mounts prepared and that Cook has sent food ahead for the saddlebags."

"Certainly, my lord." Stewart bowed his head and turned to follow his directive.

Alexandra watched him stride down the corridor, her eyes dipping to the sleeve his secretary kept tucked inside his jacket pocket. She spoke softly. "His hand—?"

"He was my artillery sergeant. Shall we go?"

"The food sent ahead?" She faced him, raising a brow.

Damn. She was as attuned to details as his secretary. "It could be a long day, and we might not make it back in time for dinner."

"Mmh. You had planned for me to join you all along. What if I hadn't agreed to go?"

He shrugged. "The question is moot as your choice has coincided with mine."

"How convenient for you," she said dryly.

"And the estate," he added. "You speak as if you are familiar with estate management. Did you grow up on a large property? Assist in estate matters in the past?"

He waited for her answer, but relented at the caged look darkening her features. "You don't have to tell me anything you don't wish for me to know."

She looked away, unable to meet his eyes.

He felt a twinge of disappointment; however, he understood he needed to gain her trust. It made seductions run more smoothly. "Shall we go?"

Alexandra started forward, but when he moved to follow, she swung around. "My father owned property and I used to review reports with the estate manager. We often toured the grounds together and met with tenants. My father, unlike Mr. Stewart, he . . . he wasn't a man for details."

He studied her guarded look, wondering how she expected

him to respond. Was she wary of admitting an understanding of men's business? Did she think he gave a damn for such matters? But more important, why did she have to flee when her uncle gained the title?

This was the pertinent piece to completing her puzzle. Anger swarmed him, aimed at her uncle or whoever was responsible for sending her to Hammond's, wearing a masculine disguise and a look of quiet desperation.

As for Alexandra handling estate matters, hell, if during her lifetime, his mother had interceded to rein in his stepfather's incompetent management, it might have saved him a fortune. However, such actions would have required his mother to show strength, and that she would not do.

His admiration for Alexandra grew. The more he learned of her, the more he liked. She attacked life head-on. She was no deserter.

He became aware of Alexandra's eyes on him. Damned if he wasn't grinning like an idiot again. He straightened, for she had shared her first confidence, and it deserved acknowledgment. If nothing else, he had earned an element of her trust. "You are one for details, which is good to know," he said. "It's what I'm counting on, why you are here." He watched her relax and waited a beat before plunging ahead with a question that ventured into grounds Alexandra had thus far avoided. "And the property? Your father no longer owns it?"

Alexandra shook her head. "My parents are no longer alive. The estate went to his younger brother. We had a difference of opinion, and I sought lodging elsewhere." She walked ahead but glanced back when he made no move to follow. "We should start. I'm sure it's been a while since you've toured this estate."

End of discussion.

He had ventured as far as she was willing for him to go. Still, it was progress.

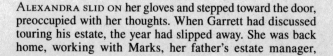

ALEXANDRA SLID ON her gloves and stepped toward the door, preoccupied with her thoughts. When Garrett had discussed touring his estate, the year had slipped away. She was back home, working with Marks, her father's estate manager, scrutinizing accounts her father had squandered and she had salvaged.

Together they had extracted blood from a stone, squeezing out every farthing from the estate to settle her father's debts. It had been a heady time and Alex had reveled in it. Her father had nearly ruined her family. She had saved it all only to lose it to her uncle.

And she wanted it back.

She couldn't reclaim all she had lost, but there was a small family cottage located on the coast of Brighton. She had Marks sell it to a friend of the family, who in turn promised Alex he would hold on to it until Alex could secure the funds to repurchase it. Garrett's money might not be enough to do so, but it was a start.

She was grateful that Garrett had not pressed her for details. She wasn't ready to share the bitterness of all she had lost with another. However, in sharing a few confidences of her own, in exchange, she hoped to receive some of Garrett's. Something for something, or quid pro quo as Marks had explained when loaning money to tenants.

Pleased with herself, she moved to the door and down the front steps. When she turned to wait for Garrett, a gust of wind lifted a lock of his hair and it fluttered in the breeze, mirroring the slow flip in her heart as he closed the distance between them. She swallowed, reminding herself she needed to remember two things for her plan to work.

She held the reins and had the ability to say the word *no*.

Chapter Fourteen

❧❦

GARRETT was in the process of mounting Champion when he glanced over to see Alexandra greeting Autumn, the sleek mare provided for her. Her expression softened and a fleeting look of naked yearning crossed her features.

Why the hell couldn't she look at me like that? With raw, unconcealed desire. As if she saw something she coveted, but couldn't have.

After Ned assisted her to mount, she sat with confidence, keeping Autumn in line. The mare had been spoiled and was hell-bent on eating every leaf within reach. With a gentle hand, Alexandra squelched this inclination, letting Autumn know who was in charge.

Garrett may be out of practice with women, but he did recall most were receptive to gifts. He couldn't fathom his practical Alexandra going soft over sparkling baubles. As much as he'd liked to see them draped over her—preferably wearing nothing but the jewels and her earlier look of desire, Alexandra was a different sort of woman.

Independent, practical, and determined.

His Alexandra would politely thank him for his gift and

then promptly sell it to the first pawnshop in order to put food on the table. She deserved something useful but which she couldn't afford in her present situation. His offer of a horse might catch her off guard. He wanted her off guard, in his arms, and beneath him.

He urged Champion forward to ride abreast of her. She was chatting with Stewart, but when he caught up to them, his secretary rode ahead. Smart man.

He nodded to her seat. "You ride well," he said. "I'll have Gus purchase a mount for you. He should arrive by the week's end with new stock."

Alexandra leaned down and slid her hand over Autumn's sleek coat. "This mount is fine for my use here. I have no need, nor any place to board a horse when I return to town."

Nothing. No flash of raw, naked yearning or flicker of unguarded excitement that lit a woman's eyes when offered a gift. He frowned. Could he have been mistaken in what he saw earlier? No. He recognized a spark of desire when he saw it.

Damn. Alexandra, being unlike most women, forced him to employ a different tactic. "You will be able to afford stabling a horse when you return. I told you I'd pay you for your time spent here. You don't need to worry about finances."

"If I find I need a horse in the city, I will purchase my own."

"I'm happy to give you—"

"Thank you, but no." She straightened. "What's between us is a business arrangement, nothing more. I can't accept gifts from you, nor do I expect you to give me any. That is not our arrangement."

"Arrangements can be changed." Her calm practicality annoyed him. It was a damn irritating trait for a woman to have.

"Not this one." She glanced ahead to Stewart, assessing the distance between them before she lowered her voice and added, "Thank you again for the offer, but no." She gave Autumn a kick and caught up with his secretary.

Garrett scowled. Things were not going well. His flattery was rusty, she refused his gift, and she was using Stewart as a buffer between them.

Time to revise his tactics yet again. He needed to find her weak spot. Hell, he doubted she possessed one—until he recalled their kisses. She had responded to him then. The woman thought too damn much. She needed to feel. He'd take a moment to regroup, deal with some estate matters, dump Stewart, and find a private, secluded glen.

≫≪

When Garrett had first inherited Charlton Manor, its holdings weren't as vast as his other properties. Over the years he had expanded the grounds, purchasing as much of the adjacent land as he could. The once-modest estate now boasted over three hundred acres of fertile ground. And he had plans for all of it. Plans that were finally coming to fruition.

He grinned at Alexandra's gasp of surprise when they crested a hill. The view before them unfurled in an impressive array of undulating brown fields dotted with men. Some trailed behind robust plow horses and raked the ground, and others followed them with cuttings they secured in the deep, sandy soil.

"What are they planting?" Alexandra asked.

"Hops, predominately. Eighty percent hops, some barley, wheat, and rye." He dismounted and crossed to her.

Her expression was puzzled. "Hops? What for?"

"Ale," he said. "Manufacturers of beer use hops as a main ingredient. Kent is renowned for its hop gardens. We'll sell the hops to beer manufacturers and make a fortune."

Her brow furrowed. "But that's . . . you're in trade?"

He nearly laughed at her expression. It mirrored his stepfather's. "Don't worry, I've already met the queen." He couldn't resist the quip, hearing his stepfather's scathing rebuke. *All the more reason to go into trade.*

Her lips curved. "I see that being banned from court would be of grave concern to you."

"Of course. We supercilious imbeciles live for court. That is, when we're not busy tossing our money away on scarlet cravats." He assisted Alex down from Autumn.

"You're not going to let me forget that, are you?"

"Probably not," he teased, pleased to see her smile. It was lovely, and she was beautiful. He felt something release in his chest. He stepped back, dropping his hands from her waist.

"You're not selling directly to people, but rather to manufacturers, so you probably are safe."

"Saved by a clever evasion. Very astute of you."

"Well, you'd be missed at court, at least by the women." She glanced at him from beneath her bonnet rim, her eyes dancing with humor as she added, "But I'm sure your absence would delight their husbands."

He laughed. "Their wives are quite safe from me. I've given up dangerous pursuits. My present interests lie in more lucrative ventures." He leaned close to her. "It's their wallets they should keep an eye on."

She laughed. "A lesson I learned too late."

He lowered the timbre of his voice and his eyes dipped to her lips, which tempted him, being full and ripe and just waiting to be nibbled on. "It's never too late to learn anything." He watched her expression change as his words registered, her cheeks coloring as she stepped away from him.

She tucked a stray strand of hair into her bonnet. "Well, thanks to your generous financial offer, I won't be gambling again."

She refused to rise to his bait. *Pity there.*

Her eyes returned to the fields, narrowing on the workers. "As to this venture, how many of these men are tenants and how many veterans?"

He stilled and his humor fled. "I don't keep count."

"No, you wouldn't. Were these all your men?"

He focused on a field hand, the man's arm draped over his wooden crutch as he conversed with another veteran. Yes, they were his men. Loyal to him. And unlike his would-be murderer, their names were not on the Duke of Hammond's guest list to receive an invite to one of the most coveted balls of the season.

For that reason, he believed he and Alex would be safe at Charlton Manor. However, he didn't want to remind Alex of the danger that threatened them and lose her smile, so he didn't point this out. He planned to speak to Holt, his field manager, and instruct him to set up a defensive perimeter. He turned to answer Alex. "Some are veterans, some tenants. They all need the work, and I need the field hands. I think they've more than earned the right to the jobs, don't you?"

"Yes, yes, I do."

"Many of their former employers refused to hire the men with permanent injuries. Didn't want cripples working for them. Unsightly."

Alex stared at him and turned to gaze over the fields. He watched her blink furiously and wondered if she saw the men or the cripples. Feared she saw the soldiers and him as some Goddamn savior to them. Christ, if she only knew the truth.

A cool breeze fluttered Alex's bonnet and rustled her skirts, and Garrett found his attention drawn to her rather than the men. She was easier on the eyes—and his conscience.

"It's a fine thing you've given these men. And, Garrett"— she paused, surprising him with the use of his name—"it's not just a job that you've provided. You know that, don't you?"

Garrett turned away from her admiring look, unable to respond as she voiced his earlier fear. Hell, he never regretted this venture he had embarked upon, but he was no savior. How could he be when there were too many others that he hadn't been able to save? They'd been his men, too.

He nodded curtly to Alexandra, striding away before he said something he would regret.

He regretted too damn much already.

❧

Alex blinked at Garrett's retreating back. The man revealed so many different facets of himself that she was finding it difficult to remember her list of his faults. She worried that this act of decency eradicated them all. A familiar flutter arose in her chest. If this didn't make the man trouble, she didn't know what did.

However, she was unsettled by the darkness coloring his steel eyes black before he turned away.

Damn the man.

He was like a vault, sealed closed and locked tight. Whatever he hid, it ate at him. And there was something. Something big and boiling inside him. Like those newfangled steam engines that exploded with smoke, Garrett needed a release valve for what churned through him. She feared it was more than tortured memories, more than the death and mayhem of Balaclava. *But what?*

Frowning, she strolled over to stand at the perimeter of the fields. A few of the men tipped their heads to her, those with more visible scars turned away, hiding their features. Her heart constricted, but she maintained a serene expression. She would not cry for these men. They did not need pity. *This* is what they needed. A job. Dignity. What Garrett gave them, but refused to acknowledge. A sigh escaped her.

"You all right, miss?"

She jumped at Stewart's sudden presence beside her. "Yes, of course." She nodded to the fields. "It's impressive. How long before the plants take root and grow?"

"I'm no farmer, but my understanding is that vines or bines, as the hops are called, grow rapidly. Once they do, stakes will be planted for them to be trained up, a few bines to each hill. Holt"—he gestured to the man in conversation with Garrett—"is overseeing the plantings. A latticework structure will be built over the lot to string the bines up to trellises once they grow tall enough."

Stewart explained more of the process, pointing out different plots and the plans for them. He possessed a head for more detail than Alex cared to remember, and she smiled as she listened to him.

"I assumed Charlton Manor had some tenant farmers, perhaps a few kitchen gardens, but never this," she said. "It's quite a large-scale operation."

Stewart beamed. "Holt and Kendall cooked up the scheme in the Crimea. Holt oversaw a property east of here, but they weren't interested in anything more than tenant holdings. Rent to subsidize their life of leisure." He grinned as he added, "But they got into debt and ended up selling half their property to Kendall to subsidize said life of leisure. Luxury is costly."

"Was . . . was the transaction a smooth one?" She innocently posed the question. Garrett had angered someone enough to want him dead. Who better than the owner of a neighboring estate who had lost property to Garrett? Land was power, and no one liked to be stripped of it.

Amusement lit Stewart's eyes. "Things would have gone smoother if Kendall had accepted the hand of Lord Keyes's daughter in the bargain."

"Garrett was not interested in the girl?" Alex kept her tone casual. After all, it was of no import to her where Garrett's interest lay.

"No, he wasn't interested in the girl," Stewart assured her. At her frown, he added, "But you need not worry about her. There are plenty of other blokes in Kent who are. And . . . she's receptive to their attentions. She—" He flushed and cleared his throat. "Well, Lord Kendall has no interest in marriage."

Alexandra dismissed Lord Keyes's wayward daughter, experiencing a pinprick stab to her heart at Stewart's last comment. *Lord Kendall has no interest in marriage.*

It should be no surprise that Garrett was not interested in marriage. He had a mistress and appeared intent on adding another if his attentions toward her were any indication of his plans. Why bother with marriage?

In truth, they held that in common. After witnessing her parents' farce of a union, she was not interested in marriage, either, and had sacrificed much to avoid it. Nor was she interested in dalliances outside of it. She would fulfill their bargain and attempt to heal the man, but that was all she would do. She frowned, acutely aware that she had no idea how to accomplish either goal. She needed help.

Her eyes narrowed on Stewart. "Mr. Stewart, you served under Lord Kendall in the Crimea?"

Surprised at her change of topic, he covered the pocket where he tucked the sleeve of his missing hand. Aware of his actions, he dropped his arm to his side. "Yes, I was his artillery sergeant."

"He was a good officer?"

Stewart stiffened as if she had insulted him by suggesting an idea to the contrary. "He had our backs, unlike some of the other puffed-up . . ." His words trailed off, his expression darkening before he went on. "He used his own money to finagle supplies from the French, who were better prepared with provisions than us poor, forgotten sods. He was one of the few officers who took advice from the career soldiers. One of the few toffs willing to learn what's what." Stewart met her eyes. "And he'd be there still, standing for his men if he hadn't gotten wounded and shipped out." Stewart flushed, looking as if he had said more than he intended. "I should return to Lord Kendall." He bowed stiffly to Alexandra before striding away.

"Stewart?" She waited until he faced her. "He's still standing for his men. He's just doing it here."

Stewart stared at her before replying. "He is indeed."

Alex mulled over Stewart's words, her eyes on Garrett as his secretary joined him and another field hand. The worker gestured at a distant point, while Garrett stood still. He had that quiet strength about him, an ability to listen without moving a muscle. It drove Alex mad. She followed their gazes to focus on the men working and sighed.

He was a good man. A brave man. One with integrity and a bone-deep loyalty.

Taller than both men, his gray jacket molded his shoulders and lean frame. She drew in a breath and her heart flipped over. Good Lord, he was handsome. His classic aristocratic looks belonged in a ballroom, dancing the night away. The man could probably seduce the skirts off the most reluctant bluestocking.

She thought of Kristen and frowned.

He was taken. She cursed a woman she didn't know but suddenly disliked with a vehemence that stunned her.

Alex might not love Garrett, but she felt certain that this Kristen could never fully understand him. Did she see his hidden wounds? Not that Garrett had allowed Alex close enough to see these wounds, but she had worked with soldiers before. She understood these men. Garrett was no different.

"Are you all right? You look a bit flushed."

She blinked, unaware of Garrett's approach. "I'm fine." She stepped back when Garrett offered his arm to escort her. He couldn't touch her. Not now.

"Good." He eyed the patch of dark gray clouds drifting in from the west. "If the weather will hold, there is a bluff that overlooks the ocean that's not too far. I thought we'd stop for a bite to eat. The view there is spectacular."

She needed a spectacular view. Something besides Garrett.

He gave her Autumn's reins and when his hands slid around her waist, her breath caught. She released it with a *woosh* as he set her on her saddle. Lifting her knee, she hooked it around the horn and gripped the reins tightly. She gasped when Garrett's hand slid down to smooth her skirt.

A puzzled expression crossed his features. "Have you grown bumps of late?"

Belatedly she remembered the biscuits she had shoved in her skirt pocket at breakfast. Mortified, she edged Autumn out of Garrett's reach. "They're biscuits," she muttered between clenched teeth, refusing to say more. What did he know of hunger? How it was like a disease that one never fully recovered from, the memory of it a permanent brand in your stomach.

"What?"

"Biscuits. Just biscuits," she snapped. "I might get hungry."

"Good idea. I'm always hungry."

His voice was husky and when his eyes slid over her body meaningfully, she opened her mouth to give him a scathing set down but closed it. He might be a good man, but arrogance still topped his list of faults.

She pressed her heel to Autumn's side and cantered ahead. She didn't know why she cared about helping him. He only wanted one thing, and he was baiting her to get it, knowing how he affected her. *And* he thought he could seduce her with gifts. Offering her a horse earlier. She knew his game. She had learned early not to covet anything for fear of seeing it disappear the next day, sold to cover her father's debts.

Garrett was not like her father, though both were rakes. And once a rake, always a rake.

She paused, her former estate manager's words returning to her. *Quid pro quo. Maybe if she gave him a little of what he wanted, he'd give her what she wanted; he'd talk to her.* Intimacy creates an environment conducive to sharing confidences.

No, she couldn't. She wouldn't. It was dangerous.

She slowed Autumn to a walk, biting her lip as she chewed on the idea, waiting for Garrett to catch up.

She had told Garrett she was immune to seduction, and he had tossed her words back at her. If she'd spoken the truth, she should be able to test it. And she had spoken true.

What harm could come from a few kisses?

For *that* was all she would concede.

It was a perilous game she contemplated. She could get devoured in the process. She took a deep breath and blew it out.

Some risks were worth taking.

Feeling a renewed confidence, she smiled as Garrett caught up to her. She'd handle him. Wait, that hadn't come out right. She'd *help* him.

If things got out of hand, a firm *no* should rein him in. If not, well then, he did promise to teach her how to use a revolver.

Chapter Fifteen

S HE was planning something. Garrett recognized the look
of someone strategizing. Wheels were spinning behind
those enormous blue eyes.

But what? What could a practical, gently bred young woman
be plotting?

He studied her as they rode in silence. He could only hope
her plans coincided with his. He didn't like it, not knowing her
thoughts, but he refused to take a defensive position when he
had already prepared for a full frontal assault.

The bluff was a strategic destination. It was rustic, thus no
prying eyes, and romantic, with its scenic view overlooking a
wide expanse of beach. He had shaken Stewart loose, sending
him to the vicar's to thank him for his assistance with the estate
report. Alexandra had looked wary as she watched Stewart ride
off, but then she had firmed her lips and lifted her chin. God,
he loved practical, independent women.

The area also contained an abandoned hunter's lodge in
which to take refuge should the weather not hold. He squinted
at the threatening, smoky gray clouds. Weather was an unknown

variable in any assault, but he thought they had time yet before the heavens opened.

They rode through a veritable Eden of rolling hills before following a path that cut through a copse of trees. Beyond this wooded stretch lay the bluff. His eyes drifted to Alexandra, as they had throughout their ride. She rivaled the beauty of any natural view.

She had a lovely profile, cameo perfect, and those full lips beckoned to him. Taunting him. He hadn't lied when he had told her he was hungry. He'd been starving ever since his lips had first touched hers. A teasing taste when he wanted the full-course meal. He shifted in his saddle, struggling to suppress his impatience.

An eruption of barking dogs shattered the silence.

"What the . . ." he muttered, struggling to rein in Champion. He glanced ahead to see Alexandra handle Autumn. The horse tossed her head and whinnied before vaulting into a frenzied canter when the barks sounded closer.

Garrett cursed and urged Champion to follow, leaning low over his neck as he cut the distance between them. "You all right?" he called out to Alexandra as she gained control over Autumn, patting the mare's neck and murmuring calming words to her as they slowed their pace.

A shot rang out. Loud and explosive.

What the bloody hell?

Searing pain singed his arm, triggering his defensive instincts. He reached over and swept Alexandra from her side-saddle to sit before him. He curled his arm around her waist and leaned low, digging his heels into Champion's sides and urging him into a gallop.

With one hand on the reins and the other clutching Alexandra close, he was unable to retrieve the revolver in his pocket. He cursed his defenseless position, but protecting Alexandra took precedence over killing the bastard who had fired the shots.

A whistle rent the air, and the baying dogs quieted.

"Good boys, that's fine fellas. What have you got?"

Keyes. The bastard. Garrett gritted his teeth and drew back on Champion's reins. Alexandra gasped and clung to his arm as Garrett whirled them around. The horse was cavalry trained and war honed, quick to obey his command and would not shy from gunshots and cannon fire, let alone a pack of hunting dogs.

"Keyes?" he bellowed, rage vibrating in his voice.

"Hello there! Kendall? That you?"

Garrett reined Champion to a stop, his eyes narrowed on the path in front of him.

A barrel-chested man astride a magnificent bay ambled into view. His riding jacket strained across a bulging gut and thighs the size of tree trunks hugged his mount. Windblown wisps of gray hair failed to cover his balding dome.

He held a hunting rifle, its gleaming barrel pointed to the ground, the stench of powder reaching Garrett. Circling him were four English Pointers, sleek-coated, tautly muscled, and panting with anticipation.

"What the hell do you think you're doing? Are you mad?" Garrett barked, barely refraining from planting his fist in the bastard's florid face.

"Hang on a minute, there. My boys smelled something. I didn't think—"

"You sure as hell didn't! You fired your rifle blind. I ought to report you to the constable. You can't—"

"Excuse me, but the last I heard, hunting is not illegal." Keyes raked him with a contemptuous look. "And this isn't your land, or have you robbed Wharton as well?"

"Christ, if you're still crying robbery, fire your solicitor. He's the one who obtained your signature on the deed of sale. Be grateful the property you're left with is more spacious than a debtor's gaol." At Keyes's sputter of rage, Alexandra's hand squeezed Garrett's and he leashed his temper. "What the hell were you hunting around here? Riders?"

Keyes's expression moved from beet red to pulsing purple. "Are you accusing me of attempted murder?"

"You're holding the smoking gun, and I've got a bullet hole in my jacket. My tailor will send you his bill." Alexandra gasped, twisting to tug at his sleeve and assess the damage. He tightened his arm around her waist to still her movements.

Keyes's eyes narrowed on Alexandra, but his expression held no remorse. "My finger must have jerked on the trigger. My mistake." He shrugged. "My apologies to your tailor.

However, you look none the worse from your mishap, and you appear to be in good hands now." His eyes dipped meaningfully to Alexandra. His smile was slow and insinuating. "I don't believe I've been introduced to your . . . ah, friend?"

Alexandra stiffened and Garrett surmised her expression shot daggers, for he had the satisfaction of watching Keyes squirm under her regard. "Lady Daniels, Lord Keyes," he spoke curtly. "The lady is a guest of Charlton Manor, along with Lord and Lady Warren." It was a partial truth, for they should arrive by week's end.

"The pleasure is mine," Keyes drawled. "Or perhaps all yours."

Alexandra's sharp intake of breath filled the silence. Garrett nearly launched himself at the lout but refrained. The ass wasn't worth it. "I might not be able to hang you for murder, Keyes—at least not yet—but I can drag you in for trespassing and poaching. This is Wharton's land and under my estate manager's care while Wharton resides in town. I suggest you get the hell off it." He withdrew his revolver from his jacket pocket. "I'd hate for *my* finger to jerk on the trigger."

Keyes drew himself up. "Are you threatening me?"

"I am. Do you wish to call me out? Name the time and place." He ignored Alexandra's fingers digging into his forearm. There would be no duel. The man was a coward, preferring to shoot at unsuspecting targets.

Keyes paled. "And have you kill me? I'm not an idiot, Kendall, contrary to your belief otherwise. I'll leave. But you don't control all the land in this region, and hunting *is* legal. You'd be wise to remember that." He nodded to Alexandra. "*Lady* Daniels." He sneered her title, the derision in his tone conveying his opinion of her dubious status.

"Are *you* threatening *me*?" Garrett demanded.

"Consider it words of advice as you're new to the area and unfamiliar with our ways." Keyes steered his bay around and whistled to his dogs. With a brusque hand gesture, he brought them in line as he kicked his horse and trotted off.

The silence stretched as they watched him depart. Garrett blew out a breath and slipped his revolver back into his jacket pocket. "The man is an ass."

Alexandra spun around to scowl at him. "You still need to

speak to the constable and report this incident. He could have killed you. Who's to say he didn't attempt it?"

He snorted. "He couldn't hit a target if he tripped over it. He's a coward."

"Cowards kill, too."

"They do," he conceded. "But this one didn't receive an invitation to the Duke of Hammond's ball."

"What are you talking about?"

"Unless something about Keyes has sparked your memory, he wasn't at Hammond's plotting my demise but here whining about his lost land, loose daughter, and growing debts. Stewart confirmed his whereabouts, which does eliminate one suspect. The man's an idiot, not a cold-blooded killer."

"It must be nice to be confident of your immunity from idiots, but blind arrogance can't stop bullets." She yanked at his sleeve. "Let me see to your arm. There is blood on your jacket. He grazed you, and I should bandage the wound before we continue." She ducked her head and tugged on his arm, leaning over to assess the damage.

He shrugged off her efforts. "It's just a scratch. You can check on it after we round up Autumn." He settled Alexandra back in front of him and pressed his knees into Champion's side, urging him forward.

His tension eased at the feel of Alexandra's slim body close to his, the warmth of her back against his chest, her thighs flush against his. She smelled good, too. Honeysuckle and something else he couldn't put his finger on.

Perhaps the day was not a total loss.

The first drops of rain fell and he gritted his teeth. His thought was premature. The day was starting to get on his nerves. Where the hell was the mare?

"Would Autumn return home on her own?" Alexandra said, hunching her shoulders against the wind, which had picked up along with the spitting rain.

He drew her closer, leaning low to shield her body with his. No hardship there. "Probably. She's no fool. There's food there, and it's dry."

"Smart horse. Let's follow her lead."

"Right," he muttered, his mood souring as the rain pelted his back. He started to urge Champion faster, but instead drew back on the reins. It was a long ride back to the house while the old hunting lodge was much closer. They could wait out the storm there. And he had food. They needn't rush home immediately.

He circled Champion around, feeling his dark mood lighten.

He might salvage the day along with his plans—or drown in the process.

Chapter Sixteen

※

ALEX wrapped her arms around her waist in an effort to get warm. Unlike Garrett, she wasn't soaked through. His body curled over hers had taken the brunt of the deluge. Other than her skirts, she had stayed relatively dry.

She stood in an old weather-beaten hunting lodge, the rain pounding the roof like a herd of thundering elephants. She glanced at the ceiling, half expecting the water to leak through any minute.

Garrett was seeing to Champion, hitching him to the posts under the eaves in the back. He said they could wait out the storm here, convinced it was a passing front. Alex believed otherwise, but was too cold and hungry to argue.

Her eyes drifted over the room. There was a sofa, a scarred table, a few scattered chairs, and blankets draped here and there. The hearth held kindling and half-burned wood stacked in the fireplace. Evidence suggested the place wasn't as abandoned as she had first surmised. It clearly was still used as a rustic refuge, perhaps providing succor for other riders caught in a storm. Eyeing the cozy throw blankets, she refused to consider the trysts the lodge may have hosted. She swallowed. This was a bad idea. She needed to leave before it got worse.

Picking up her damp skirts, she hurried to the door, but a crack of thunder stopped her short. Leaving was not an option. Balefully, she scowled at the buck head mounted above the front door. Beneath an impressive array of antlers, coal black eyes stared straight ahead. As if amused at her predicament, a sparkling gleam lit the dark orbs. At least *she* hadn't been stalked, stuffed, and mounted . . . she paused. That hadn't come out right. Cheeks burning, she closed her eyes. This was ridiculous. Her nerves were running rampant, and she was not a hysterical female.

If she were such a female, she would have panicked earlier. The dogs, the gunshots, and Garrett's self-proclaimed "scratch" were enough to send most women into hysterics. While those incidents had her heart pounding like an orchestra in full concert, she had remained levelheaded enough to control Autumn. After that, Garrett had taken charge. She bit her lip as she recalled him whisking her onto his saddle, his arm curled around her as they raced along the wooded path. Her heart had played a different tune then, and opening her eyes, she sighed.

He certainly had a commanding way about him. She didn't mind his take-charge, protective manner. After her father's lackadaisical care, she found she rather liked it. It was his arrogance that worried her. His dismissal of Keyes as an incompetent idiot, incapable of engineering Garrett's murder, was ludicrous. Did the man truly believe the mastermind behind this deadly plot to be an intelligent man? Or a sane one? Contrary to Garrett, she believed the man behind these attacks to be a coward and an idiot.

A man like Keyes.

She jumped, barely stifling her cry when the front door banged open. Garrett staggered in, his hair dripping wet, his arms loaded with a stack of wood, a saddlebag dangling from one arm. "Thought we could build a fire. I found a dry cord of wood stacked out back under cover of the porch."

She rushed to shut the door behind him, securing the bolt. She was glad for his interruption, not ready to further contemplate that a neighboring estate might harbor a cold-blooded killer.

Garrett unloaded the wood before the fireplace. "Storm moved in fast. We made it here just in time." Straightening, he shoved his wet hair from his forehead as he looked around. "Looks like we aren't the only guests who've sought refuge here. And they left some towels." He grinned at her as he crossed to the sofa.

Alex bit her lip as his thoughts echoed hers.

He dumped the saddlebag on the nearby table, and then snatched up one of the smaller blankets from the sofa to dry his face. When he lowered the blanket, his hair was askew, his jacket soaked and plastered to his tall frame, and his eyes were alight with humor. "Not the view I planned to show you, but it's dry, and we have food." He nodded to the saddlebag. "Same plans, different venue."

Alex sighed as she approached him. "Here, you need to take off your jacket before you catch a chill. It's soaked through."

"Just the jacket?" he teased. "My shirt is also wet. And my trousers."

Alex quirked a brow, not deigning to respond.

He laughed. "Fine, but I thought you wanted to tend to my arm."

"Your scratch, that is?" She met his eyes. "I believe I can do that with your trousers on. Wet or not."

"Pity that," he murmured.

"The fire will dry them. Why don't you light it?"

His eyes darkened. "Why don't I?" When she stepped back from him, he chuckled and shrugged out of his jacket.

Before she could voice a protest, he dispensed with his cravat as well. He undid the top two buttons of his linen shirt, revealing a teasing triangle of skin. She exhaled. Why bother with the fire? One sultry look from the man, and she was burning up.

Garrett turned to the hearth, collected matches from a metal box on the mantel, and bent to gather some wood.

She caught her breath. He needn't be worried about her missing the view. No scenic vista could rival the sight of Garrett bent over, his wet shirt stretched taut across his broad shoulders, its damp patches plastered to his golden skin. Her eyes drifted lower, sliding over his fitted trousers to his buttocks, and she sighed again.

This was a very bad idea.

She jumped when a violent gush of wind rattled the windowpanes, reminding her she was trapped. Well, she was a practical woman, and it was time she made the best of a bad situation.

Her eyes moved back to Garrett. The fire caught on the pieces of kindling he had stuffed beneath wood stacked like a pyramid. When he leaned over to blow the flames higher, she caught her breath. There was no denying that the best of her situation stood yards away from her.

Straightening, Garrett planted his hands on his hips as he watched the flames climb.

Drawn to both the man and the warmth of the fire, she crossed to his side. She noticed for the first time the red streak staining his torn sleeve below his shoulder. The sight sobered her and she grasped his arm. "Just a scratch?"

He jerked when she started to pry his sleeve away, the material stuck to the blood. "It's fine. I'll take care of it later." He walked to the table where he had dumped the saddlebag. "Are you hungry?"

She was determined to stay focused on his wound. "You are no coward, so why won't you let me tend to your arm?"

Surprised, he looked at her and after a moment, shrugged. "Fine." He unbuckled the saddlebag and withdrew a silver flask and a cloth packet. Untying the packet, he slid out a small serrated knife. Collecting both items, he grabbed a chair and dragged it before the fire. Dropping onto it, he slipped his hand into his sleeve, grunted once as he yanked it free of the blood-encrusted wound. He looked over at her. "Well, come on, Nurse Nightingale, don't let the patient do all the work."

When she moved to his side, he handed her the knife. Amused, she turned it over in her hand, the firelight dancing over its blade. "Is this to keep you in line?"

His eyes met hers. A gleam flickered in the gray depths. The moment dragged on long enough to ratchet up her pulse. "Let's stick to 'no' for that." He grinned at her dubious look and lifted his torn sleeve free of his arm and nodded to where he pulled the material taut. "Slash it here, and I can rip the sleeve off. It will do for a makeshift bandage."

She leaned over with the knife and cut the area he indicated. When she finished, he tore the sleeve free.

"See, just a scratch." He grabbed the flask, unscrewed the top, and poured some of its content over the wound. A sharp intake of his breath was his only reaction to what must have been a burning sting.

The liquid washed the dried blood away to reveal a two-inch gash that could be defined as a scratch, but a mean one. He handed her the bandage. "Supplies were low in the Crimea. We learned to make do."

"So I see." She accepted the swath of linen and slipped it under his arm. Her heart thudded as her fingers brushed his bare skin, the taut muscle of his bicep warm beneath her hand. The view was getting harder to ignore. Along with the burn . . . of the fire. She knotted the bandage and stepped back. "Did you ever meet Miss Nightingale?"

He twisted his arm to view her handiwork, but he stilled at her words. "No. No, I didn't." He didn't glance up but continued after a pause. "In the beginning there were no nurses. The wounded were left unattended and piled up in filthy corridors lining this dilapidated building rank with sewage, vermin, and disease." His eyes lifted to hers. "More men died from disease than from their wounds." He fell silent, his expression brooding as he stared into the fire.

Upset by the bitterness darkening his words and his eyes, she moistened her lips. "Then Miss Nightingale arrived with her mission, her nurses, and a whole lot of gumption . . . or so I heard." She shrugged.

He looked up and stared at her with his usual quiet intensity. After another drawn-out moment, his features relaxed. "Sounds like someone else I know."

A flush warmed her cheeks, but his shared confidence warmed her heart. She held still, hoping he'd continue. When he didn't, she took a deep breath and ventured into forbidden ground. "And you? Did her nurses treat you?"

His hand tightened its grip on the knife, the other around the flask he still held. "No. I didn't need them. I had Havers."

His words were final. Subject closed.

Abruptly he stood and turned to face her. "And here I have

you." He smiled down at her, a familiar sparkle returning to his eyes. "And you are much prettier than Havers." He leaned close. "Don't tell him I said so. He'd be crushed."

She grinned and a warm glow spiraled through her.

"But you must be hungry. Shall we see what Cook has packed for us? Something to go with your biscuits?"

Baffled, she stared at him, unable to keep up with the man's transitions. *What biscuits?* Her eyes widened and her hand slid to her skirt pocket, Garrett's laughter rumbling through her as he crossed to the table. He set the flask and the knife upon it and proceeded to rummage through the saddlebag.

As Garrett unpacked, Alex struggled to suppress her irritation over his reticence. Damn the man. She could help him if he would only let her, if he would only talk to her. She blew out a frustrated breath and went to assist him, but her eyes fell to his bandaged arm and another more pressing matter distracted her. She might not be able to heal old wounds, but if they worked together, they might be able to protect him from new ones and, more important, save his life.

Keyes's attack was a stark reminder of why she was here. Someone wanted Garrett dead, and she and Garrett were here to strategize a plan to prevent that. It was what he was paying her for, and it was time for her to uphold her end of their bargain.

Garrett lifted his head, his hands full of wrapped parcels, a loaf of bread tucked under his arm. "We'll make a picnic before the fire. Grab those blankets from the sofa and spread them over the floor."

She moved to do his bidding and once the blankets were laid out, she assisted him with the food. It was a veritable feast with sundry meats, cheeses, and the aroma of fresh, homemade bread wafting up to engulf them. Alex sat down and tucked her skirts around her, waiting until they both were settled before she ventured to speak.

"Your bandaged arm reminded me that I am here for a reason. I can't accept any payment for services I have not rendered, so . . ."

Garrett's spasm of coughs interrupted her. His eyes watered as he slapped his chest and struggled to catch his breath. At her raised brow, he shook his head. "My apologies." He cleared his throat. "Just an interesting choice of words." Amusement danced in his eyes, and he lifted his hand to cover his mouth as he coughed again.

Understanding dawned, and she scowled at him. "Oh, for goodness sake." Clearly the man considered only one type of services to be rendered by a woman. Annoyed, she thrust a flagon of water at him and continued on, refusing to traverse *that* path. "Look, you brought me here in the hopes that I could assist you in apprehending these men plotting your murder. I think it's time we devise some sort of plan."

He grinned. "Having the company of a beautiful woman to share my exile with me is payment enough."

"That's a lovely compliment. However, this is a business arrangement, and I suggest we take it seriously and figure out how to save your life, because I can't collect payment if you're dead." He choked again, and she reached over and slapped him on the back.

He shoved his plate of food away. "Point taken, but we're not going to need any plans if I choke to death, nor is killing me going to help you get your monies."

"Point taken." She grinned back at him. "Now about a plan . . ."

"I have one."

"What?" She blinked at him, pausing as she lifted a piece of bread to her mouth.

He wagged his finger at her. "At least I made sure you're mouth wasn't full first. I have a care for *your* life."

She shook her head. "I'm trying to have one for yours, but you do make it difficult."

He raised the flagon in a toast. "So I've been told."

"I'm sure you have. About this plan, were you intending to share it with me?"

"I was waiting until my sister arrived, as we will need her and Brandon's assistance. However, as you appear to be in a rush to earn your keep, we could do without them and proceed in another manner. You've been quite clear about your thoughts on being my mistress, but are you equally averse to the idea of *pretending* to be my mistress . . . ?"

She simply raised a brow and stared at him, her expression cool.

"I take it that is a yes." Amused, he shrugged, unrepentant. "A man can hope. Perhaps when we know each other better."

"I know you just fine now," she drawled. "About Brandon and your sister and this plan . . . ?"

"Right. We're going to return to the scene of the crime. Brandon is working with Hammond to orchestrate another event to which the same list of guests as the party where you over-heard the plot against me will be invited. The killer's name is on that list, and we hope he'll accept the invitation, particularly if he knows that I'm there. As we've discussed, once you're in the same room with the bastard, you might recognize his voice or observe some mannerism or gesture that might trigger your memory and help you identify him.

"Kit is bringing gowns for you to wear, and she and Brandon will play chaperone so that your reputation is safeguarded. After all, we wouldn't want you to risk ruin by being in my presence. However, you do look none the worse for wear so far." He tossed her long-ago words back at her, a teasing light entering his eyes.

After the initial surprise at his plan wore off, she smiled at his last quip. "It's still early yet, but I think I shall survive." Her eyes strayed to the fire, and she frowned because Garrett's words of ruination had unwittingly stoked the embers of old fears.

It was ironic, but despite the danger threatening Garrett, since she had come under his protection, Alex had felt safe for the first time in over a year. Lulled into this sense of false security, she had forgotten her own plight.

Garrett could never ruin her because her uncle had already orchestrated that, enabling Lord Cheaver to savage her reputation beyond repair. Should her uncle find her or learn that she had sought protection from another man, he would make sure all knew of her disgrace. It would all come out, everything but the truth, and damn the consequences to those innocents who would be ensnared in his web of deceit. Should she attend a ball with Garrett and be seen in so public a forum, her uncle could very well find her. She swallowed the bile that rose to her throat.

But how could she not assist Garrett?

Surreptitiously she studied him as he stared into the fire, a companionable silence having settled between them. His black hair was damp and disheveled, a rakish lock sweeping his forehead. Her eyes dipped to his bandaged arm and she stifled the urge to reach out and, like the dancing light from the fire, let her fingers skim across his bare skin.

How could she stand by and let him be murdered by some nameless coward?

She closed her eyes and blew out a breath.

She could not. She would not. She couldn't do it when she had first overheard the insidious plot, and she couldn't do it now.

Some risks were worth taking, and Garrett's life was worth her risking her own. Resolute, she opened her eyes, drew a deep breath, and turned to Garrett. "Do you think he will accept the invitation? That the assassin will dare to return to Hammond's?"

Garrett shrugged. "Let's hope that he does. I'd like to finish this. I don't like living with a guillotine's blade hanging over my head."

She blanched, and he relented.

"Look, it's a plan, and that's a start. We'll find the bastard, and we're safe here until we do so. That is, if we can avoid trigger-happy Keyes," he added dryly. Standing, he reached over to grab the fire stoker. Looking back at her, he nodded to the food. "Why don't you eat something? You need to keep up your strength. Besides, one can't survive on biscuits alone." With a wink, he turned to tend the fire.

Alex shook her head and stared blankly at the food before her, aware of the bitter irony that for the first time in over a year, she had no appetite.

≈

GARRETT FINISHED A last bite of cheese and eyed the remains of their repast, marveling over Cook's ability to pack so economically as to fit it all into the saddlebag. They could have used her in the Crimea, or perhaps not, as they never had enough food to fill a thimble anyway. Garrett leaned back on his elbows, stretched his legs before him, and crossed them at his ankles.

Earlier, his wet trousers had tightened over a growing need that had made them more uncomfortable than their dampness.

As much as he wished to cool down, his need to dry off became greater. Now relatively dry and full, there was only one more need to be satisfied. He studied Alexandra.

She sat with her legs drawn up before her, her arms circling her knees as she stared into the fire. Orange flames cast shadows over her hair, making some strands appear golden, while darkening others.

He longed to unpin her hair and bury his hands in the thick locks. Itched to run his finger over a curved cheek to those full, beckoning lips. Yearned to unbutton her dress. Very, very slowly. One button at a time, tormenting himself with peeks of soft, satin skin. To press his lips to the hum of her pulse at the slim column of her neck and feel its rhythm skip in response. He'd lay her down and cover her body with his, her breasts flush against him, and then . . . then he'd lick . . .

"Garrett?"

What? Where? He blinked at Alexandra, who clearly had been speaking. Her narrow-eyed expression made him feel like a boy caught looking at portraits of Rubens's nudes. He sat up and cleared his throat, finding it spit dry. "Yes?"

"I was asking about your sister. I was surprised to hear Lord Warren had married. I mean, his reputation as a rake has preceded him, and I was curious as to what sort of woman he had married."

Brandon and his sister? That slammed shut the book on his nudes with a finality that annoyed him. He sighed. "Once a rake, always a rake? So you're wondering how big a fool is my sister?"

She flushed. "No, of course not."

"Yes, you are. Don't worry, I won't tell her. Don't they say reformed rakes make the best husbands?"

"They also say love is blind." She smiled sweetly at him.

"So she's a blind idiot?" He grinned. "My sister will like you."

"I never said . . . what?"

He laughed. "She will adore you."

"You haven't answered my question."

"What is she like?" He furrowed his brow and sought to explain his half sister. "She's a sweet, docile, biddable thing."

He nearly laughed when he saw an expression of distaste flicker across Alexandra's features before she could suppress it.

"I look forward to meeting her."

He looked forward to their meeting, too, considering Alexandra believed Kristen to be his mistress.

"Are you two close?"

"Very."

"I suppose it helps that she's a docile, biddable thing. Considering you are so domineering."

"Domineering?" He frowned. "I prefer decisive. But yes, my sister always did what I told her to." Except when she didn't want to. She really could be an opinionated pain in the backside, and he was done discussing her. "Have your skirts dried?" He fingered the material, but she slapped his hand aside.

"They are fine."

"No, they're not. You need to move closer to the fire. You are going to catch a chill if you don't. I promise you, you won't get burned."

She raised a brow at that but refrained from commenting.

He sighed and pressed the flask upon her. "At least take a sip of this. This is the one with brandy, and it will warm you."

"Domineering," she muttered but took a sip.

They needed more heat. Lots of it. Things were cooling down. He sprang to his feet and laid another log on the fire. He used the fire poker to once again jab at the burned embers, teasing the flames to catch on the fresh wood.

"You were speaking of Florence Nightingale earlier. You know, she helped me, too."

Startled, he glanced back at her, waiting for her explanation. She had lowered her legs and tucked her skirts around her. She caught him watching her and took another sip of the brandy, as if she needed fortification. Something prickled at the back of his neck. It was similar to the feeling he got before an ambush. He shouldn't have spoken of the wounded men, feared he had opened a door he kept bolted shut.

"I used to visit Gus during his recovery at Chelsea Hospital and I would read to him. I read to other soldiers as well, and it drew the attention of one of the hospital benefactresses. She was an admirer of Florence Nightingale's work with the men, and she arranged for me to get a small stipend to read and write letters for other wounded veterans."

He nodded, surprised she had been permitted to work so closely with the men. It was little wonder why she had neither flinched nor retreated at the sight of the men working in the hops field.

Alexandra rose to her feet and returned the flask to him, holding her hands out to the fire. "Some of the men talked to me, sharing some of their experiences."

Every muscle in his body tensed. He set aside the fire poker and flexed his hand.

"It helped—"

"Did it?" He cut her off, his words cold.

"Yes, it did. The nurses told me it lessened their night-mares."

Sweat pooled between his shoulders, and it wasn't from the fire. Enough. He had heard enough. "I told you I—"

"And I heard you," she cut him off. Her eyes sought his, wide and imploring. "But you need to talk to someone. I could help you. You can't bottle up everything inside you. It's not—"

"Can't I?" He stared her down, his jaw hard, one hand fisted at his side, the other nearly crushing the brandy flask.

He spun back to the fire. The flames licked at the wood, eating away at it just as his guilt ate at him. He swiped a hand down his face, lifted the flask, and then froze with it halfway to his mouth. Christ. What was he thinking? There was no escape for him. His eyes locked on the flask and a raw, visceral rage ripped through him. Riding it, he hurled the drink into the fire, ignoring Alexandra's gasp at the explosion of sparks.

He whipped around to face her, causing her to back away, her eyes wide. God, she was an innocent. Did these men really share anything with her and be healed?

Did they truly think they could be?

"What do you want me to talk about? The dead and wounded strewn across a field that looked like a blood-soaked carpet? Our gallant cavalry plowing over them like discarded rubbish, desperate to save their own skin? Tennyson neglected that detail in his tribute to the brave six hundred. Doesn't make for pretty poetry or heroic men."

He pressed a hand to his temple as if to stem the flood of

memories. "Christ, I still smell it. The stench of rotting flesh and raw sewage. I hear it. The screams of the dying. Their cries for water, their mothers, and death." He spat the words out, like a vat of poison leaking out of him. A roaring filled his head. He needed to make it stop. Push it back before it was too late.

Before he was lost.

"You think you can erase such memories?" He advanced on her and she backed away. "You can't. And because I'm not wounded, you can't heal me."

"Garrett, I can—"

She caught his bandaged arm and her hand connected with bare skin. His passion flared. He grasped her arms and yanked her close, his eyes on her startled features. "Do you really want to help me?"

She swallowed, her breathing quickened, and her hands planted on his chest. "Yes, I do, but—"

"Then help me to forget." His head lowered to hers haltingly, waiting for her rejection, waiting for her *no* to slice through him. He'd give her a moment . . . just a moment.

Time was up.

He crushed her to him, his mouth plundering, drinking deeply, forcing her lips to open and savoring the taste. Tongues dancing, he wanted to consume her. She was sweet and clean and innocent. He wanted her taste to wash through his body and cleanse him. To push back the darkness.

He drew her body closer and still closer until he could feel her breasts crushed against him and the beat of her heart pound against his. He threaded his fingers through her hair, pulling the pins free. A yearning fulfilled, he fisted his hands into the loose strands, while Alex's hands splayed across his back. He moaned, his linen shirt an irritating barrier to her touch. He tore it free from his trousers, nearly ripping the buttons apart, so desperate to feel her touch on his bare skin, on him.

He lifted his head and dropped to his knees, catching her hands and pulling her down with him. He sat back on his haunches and shucked off his shirt. Her lips parted, but unwilling to hear her protest, he crushed her close again, silencing her response with his mouth. It was only a moment before her hands returned to his bare shoulders, tentative at first before sliding over them. Her touch on his naked skin was ecstasy.

Slowly, his lips never leaving hers, he lowered her down to the blanket. The heat of the fire merged with the flames of passion igniting between them. His breathing quickened and his blood heated to boiling point. He ran a hand along her back and over a round buttock, but her skirts hindered his explorations. He captured a full breast and despite her pleasurable groan in response, he cursed. There was too much material separating them. The dress had to go.

He gritted his teeth at the prolonged agony of taking the time to dispense with the endless strip of buttons from her neck to her waist. She gasped when he parted her gown and tugged it off her arms. He stared at the lace edging of her chemise, her breathing rapid and the round curve of her breasts rising above it. She was beautiful. Perfect. His head lowered and his lips touched the teasing mounds, satin soft and glorious.

She arched under him, her hands threading through his hair. He wanted to get closer, but she still had too many damned clothes. He untied her chemise and yanked it down, freeing her breasts for his eyes, hands, and lips to feast upon. And he did. He drew a hard nipple into his mouth, while he cupped her other breast. He was rewarded with another gasp and her body arching beneath him. Her hands returned to his back, her fingers dug into his shoulders, clutching him to her.

He felt her shiver and writhe beneath him, and her passionate response urged him on. Burning with desire, his body pulsating with it, he moved to lavish her other breast with his mouth, while his hand lowered to find the hem of her skirt. He slid beneath yards of petticoats. He cursed the frigid old maid who must have designed the current fashion. The style of layered skirts made it damn near impossible to get close to a woman. When his hand finally touched her bare calf, he groaned. He skimmed his palm up her leg over sleek, toned muscle, her skin warm against his hand.

His loins throbbing, he lifted his head and moved up to capture her mouth. He devoured her lips again and again, his hips pressing into hers, his hand grasping her thigh and lifting it against his waist. He wanted to merge his body with hers, to plant himself deep within her soft, moist flesh.

To forget.

His body ached for it. He was rock hard and damn near bursting for release, and if her response was any indication, she was, too. He slid his hand from her thigh and moved between her legs, cupping her, and feeling her moist, wet, and ready. For him. Groaning, his fingers stroked her sensitive folds.

Alexandra's body bucked at the intimate invasion, her hands freezing in his hair. He waited for her to move again, to respond. His body was strung tight as a bow, an arrow ready to fire, to pierce its target.

"*Stop!* I can't. I . . . you must stop. *No!*" Then louder still. "No!" She planted her hands against his chest and pushed, shoving him away.

It took him a moment to respond, to douse the flames licking at him. Finally, he rolled onto his back with a frustrated groan. He lifted an arm to cover his eyes as he fought to catch his breath and let the blood pounding in his loins recede. After a moment, he felt Alexandra sit up. He lowered his arm to watch her yank her chemise over her breasts, her hair a golden curtain veiling her flushed features. She pulled her gown up to cover herself. Pity that.

Sighing, he turned his head and stared into the leaping flames of the fire, its heat no match for the inferno smoldering inside him.

A while later, he jerked at the unexpected feel of a tentative brush of fingers along the jagged scar crossing his abdomen. It was like being prodded by the fire poker, and he shot to a sitting position.

Alexandra's hand froze in midair. She was kneeling beside him, her hair a wild cascade about her, her features flushed, her lips swollen.

Good Lord, she was beautiful. An angel delivered to save him. Pluck him from his private hell and into heaven.

Her eyes dipped to his waist, and he swore again.

What the bloody hell was he thinking?

He swept to his feet. She thought she could save a damned man, and for a fleeting moment, he believed he could be saved. She was an innocent and he was an idiot.

He snatched up his shirt and shrugged into it, hiding the scar that sliced across his left side like a venomous snake.

He finished buttoning his shirt and stared down at Alexandra. "You see. You can't heal me because I have no wounds. Only scars. And you can't get rid of those."

He watched her flinch but turned his back on her to brace his hands on the mantelpiece. Leaning against it, he closed his eyes and blew out a breath.

If Balaclava was hell, he was in purgatory.

Chapter Seventeen

>⃪≪

LATER that evening, back at the manor and settled in her own bedchamber, Alex listened to the return of the storm as it raged outside. It matched the one unfurling inside her as she tossed and punched her pillow, sleep eluding her. No surprise there. Strong arms and sultry kisses stole into her dreams and had her writhing until her sheets tangled around her sweat-drenched body. There would be no sleep tonight.

Not when Garrett lay in bed with her.

Damn him. Damn him for stoking the embers of her desire into a passion she couldn't bury or worse deny.

Thunder exploded outside, an unleashed beast roaring God's rage. *You can't heal me.* Garrett's tortured words cried out to her, his pain-ravaged features haunting her.

She *could* help him. If he'd only let her.

She pictured the raw-edged, puckered scar that branded his beautiful body. The scar, while jagged and mean, didn't concern her. It was the other wound that worried her. The one that had cut a deeper swath. The one that had sliced into Garrett's soul and broken him.

Sighing, she rolled onto her back.

A flash of lightning lit the room, followed by another rumble of window-rattling thunder. A raw, guttural yell accompanied the storm.

Alexandra bolted up in bed. Eyes wide, she clutched the sheet close. The cry sounded as if it was torn from a tortured man strung on the rack.

Garrett? Her heart beat in rhythm to the pounding rain.

A moment later, a door slammed open and closed. The low murmur of voices carried to her. She leapt off the bed and snatched up her robe, dashing to the door leading to Garrett's room. Biting her lip, she eased it open and peered within.

Havers leaned over Garrett, who lay in the bed, both arms flung over his face, the sheet twisted across his waist. Firelight lit his sweat-slicked chest, his back arched while his mouth clenched into a tight line.

Havers held a tray with a mug on it. He reached out to Garrett, barely touching his shoulder, but at the movement, Garrett lurched up as if burned. His arm shot out and sent tray, mug, and liquid crashing to the floor.

"No!" The word exploded from him as if extracted from the darkest corners of his pain.

Alexandra rushed over to the commode and snatched up the pitcher to pour water into the porcelain bowl. Grabbing a cloth from the towel rack, she dipped it into the cool liquid, rang it out, and crossed to Garrett's bedside.

"Let me, it's all right," she said.

Havers jerked at her approach, but ignoring his reaction, she circled around him to ease herself onto Garrett's bed. "Shh," she murmured as if settling a skittish child, or in this case, a wild animal. "It's all right. Lie back."

Unfocused, bloodshot eyes impaled her, staring at her blankly.

"Shh," she whispered. His pale, ravaged features broke her heart. She placed her hand on his shoulder and slowly urged him back into the pillows.

As he settled, his eyes darted between her and Havers, his breathing fast and furious. She pressed the cloth to his brow, dabbing at the sweat beading his temple, dampening his hair. "Shh," she repeated the calming sound, dropping her voice to a soothing cadence. "You're home. You're safe." His eyes bored into hers, as though he desperately searched for something beyond his reach.

After an interminable period of time, his breathing leveled and his eyes slid closed. She lay the cloth over his forehead and threaded her fingers through his hair, brushing the disheveled strands back from his temple.

When she felt he had settled enough to leave him, she eased to her feet and turned to Havers, who stood rooted beside the bed. He had recovered the tray and mug and held them in his hand. She lowered her voice. "Why don't you see if you can get a hot toddy from Cook? I'll sit with him for a while."

Havers looked at Garrett, his expression a picture of indecision.

"Havers, I promise, I will not leave him. He will be all right."

He studied Garrett before he gave a curt nod and dropped his voice to a barely audible murmur. "Talk to him. Talk him through it. It don't usually last long, but the storm . . . the noise." His words trailed off as his eyes drifted to the window, his brow furrowed. "It brings it back. It's—"

"I understand," she said.

When the door closed behind Havers, Garrett sprang up, whipping the cloth off his forehead, his eyes darting around the room.

Alex sat back on the bed, refusing to recoil from the wild look in his eyes. When they landed on her, he stared at her without recognition. Enormous pupils colored the steel gray black. She cautiously rested her hand on his shoulder, his skin clammy beneath her fingers as she eased him back. "Shh, it's all right. I'm here. Lie back. You're all right."

At first, he resisted until his unfocused eyes settled on her and he swallowed, allowing her to push him down.

She reclaimed the cloth from where he had flung it across the bed and again pressed it to his forehead.

"Don't leave me." His words wrenched from a hoarse throat. His fingers curled around her wrist. "Stay."

"Of course." Alex blinked away the moisture blurring her gaze. "I'm here. I won't leave you. It's all—"

A crack of thunder cut short her words and Garrett's hands shoved hers away to clasp his head, holding it as if in a vice.

"Christ." His back arched, his eyes closed and then opened, dark and wild. "We're surrounded . . . Christ, ride!"

"You're safe! Look at me!" She leaned forward and cupped her hands over his. She stared into his eyes and forced them to meet hers, as if through sheer willpower she could tame his madness.

"Listen to me! Garrett, you're safe." She raised her voice and repeated the words, watching as his eyes clung to hers. When she felt he had returned from his battlefield, she lowered his hands to his sides and threaded her fingers through his hair, sweeping it off his brow. She dropped her voice to dulcet tones and as Havers advised, she began to talk.

"When I was a girl and the thunder roared, my father told me the angels of music had heard me practicing on my mother's piano. He said I had offended their sensibilities, not to mention deafened them with my pounding."

Garrett's eyes became less vacant, his panic receding and his breathing leveling off as her words pulled him back from the darkness gripping him. She dabbed the cloth over his forehead, his cheeks, and his neck until finally, his eyes drifted shut. But still, she talked. Her words low and soothing.

"My father would beg me to have a care for his head and of those in heaven, and refrain from practicing unless old man Bates came for a visit. Then I was given free rein to pound away. If Lady Bates arrived, I was also to sing. My father compared the woman to a magpie. Like a magpie, Lady Bates was a scavenger who enjoyed foraging in other people's nests and devouring everything she thought edible." She grinned at the memory.

"He told my mother my playing was a foolproof plan to not only clear a room but stop all guests from dropping in uninvited. He wanted to loan my talents out to friends who complained of their relatives overstaying their welcome. He planned to charge them for my services, convinced he'd make a fortune. My father was always in need of a fortune."

"Did . . . did it work?"

She froze. The words were music to her ears, more beautiful than anything she could produce, for she had spoken the truth. To her musical mother's despair, she couldn't sing a note.

She swallowed back her tears. "Of course it worked. That's

why I'm confiding this pathetic story to you rather than singing a lullaby. I do have a care for your head."

His eyes opened, and the familiar glint lit the gray depths. "Thank you."

Her breath caught and her heart flipped over. She blinked to clear her blurred vision before she managed a small smile. "You are welcome."

She couldn't drag her eyes from his, so delighted to see the sanity returned to them. To have him back. She might not be able to carry a tune, but her heart played a joyous, pulsating song.

"You'll have to sing for Keyes should he ever dare to visit."

His words shattered the moment, but when their meaning registered, she grinned. "He would fare better in a duel with you. Less pain and suffering."

"And the piano playing? As bad as the singing?"

"Of course not." She beamed. "That's much, much worse."

He laughed. "Accompany your song with the piano, and the combination will be so lethal, Keyes won't feel a thing. He'll drop dead on the spot."

"You might have something there."

Another moment passed and his gaze drifted to the window. The storm had tapered off to a persistent patter, the wind whistling and the raindrops dancing over the roof. "The noise . . . it's . . . well, the angel of music is no longer angry."

"No, he's settled for now," she murmured.

"But . . ."

"I'm here." She assured him, unwilling to let the shadows cloud his eyes again. "I'll stay with you." She shrugged. "You never know when a poor child might butcher a tune on their piano."

Garrett's gaze swung back to hers. Finally, he nodded. "You are probably right. I've heard many bad singers in my day."

"I commiserate with them." Suddenly she became aware that his sheet was tangled about his hips and his chest was naked and inches from her.

The firelight flickered over the broad expanse, and she drew in a sharp breath, wondering how she could have been oblivious to it. To him. "Ah . . . ah, where is your nightshirt?"

He laughed.

"Do you have one?" she persisted.

"No." He sat up and arranged his pillows behind him before settling back into them. "Can't abide them. In fact, the one you are wearing looks like an old maid's castoff. Wherever did you get it?" He fingered the collar of her white linen robe and grimaced.

Slapping his hand away, she sat up poker straight. She narrowed her eyes at him. "I didn't think you would recover if I wore my silk nightgown, the whisper-thin one with the slit up the side and the drooping lace décolletage. The shock alone would have killed you."

He closed his eyes and groaned. "I'm a weak man, and you have no mercy. Wait—" He held up his hand. After a moment, he opened his eyes. "Right. I have the image down." He smiled. "I feel better now. Much, much better."

She stared at his smug expression, torn between offense and laughter. Her amusement won, and her laugh slipped loose. "You are incorrigible."

When he smiled, she shook her head. She never would have thought she would miss this arrogant side of him.

He furrowed his brow. "But I need more details to get a clearer picture of matters."

"What matters?"

"Exactly how low does the neckline to this gown plunge?"

Her laugh was rich and sultry, stunning even her. She leaned close and opened her mouth to respond when a throat cleared. It was like being doused with a bucket of ice water. When she recovered her ability to move, she did so quickly, jumping to her feet and whirling around.

Havers stood framed in the door, his expression carefully blank. He held a mug in one hand, the other clutching a stack of books. "I have what you asked for. And . . ." He glanced down as if he needed a visual reminder of what he held. "Ned gave me these books that Kit left last time she were here."

"Thank you, Havers," Garrett said. "I appreciate it."

Havers handed the items to her, eyeing her as if she were an apparition from the underworld who had bewitched Garrett.

"That will be all, Havers."

Havers bobbed his head and shuffled backward. "Right, sir." He turned, gave his head a sharp shake, and departed.

Alex stared at the closed door. She should follow the man

out. She didn't know what had gotten into her earlier, but it wasn't good. It veered into that boggy ground that she had been struggling to avoid.

"What did he bring?"

She jumped at the words and spun to face Garrett.

"What books?" He nodded his head to the stack in her arms.

She stared at the bare expanse of his chest, his naked shoulders, and his handsome features. When a loud flood of rain thrashed the roof, she jumped and dropped her eyes to the books.

"Bring them over here," Garrett said.

She crossed to the bed and dropped the volumes beside him.

"What's that?"

She followed his eyes to the mug she held. Remembering her request for the rum drink, she handed it to him. "It's for you."

He peered into it and frowned. "What is it? Poison eye of newt?" He tried to return it to her. "It's not necessary. I promise to forget about the images of you in the satin nothing. And the one of you naked in my arms. Poof. Gone."

He was becoming more himself by the minute. And Garrett Sinclair in his full faculties and bare-chested was a lethal combination. "Very funny. It's a rum toddy."

As if she had taken a candlesnuffer to the flame burning in his eyes, the light died, and his amused expression vanished.

"No." The mug slid from his fingers onto the floor. He never glanced to the spill pooling over the carpet.

"Garrett!" She snatched the towel she had used to swipe his brow and knelt to soak up the mess. "What is wrong with you?" She set the mug onto the bedside table, hurried to the commode to wring out the cloth, and dumped it into the porcelain bowl.

When she returned to the bed, Garrett had his arms crossed over his chest. "Havers knows this. No spirits. No laudanum. Never again. He must have brought the toddy for you."

She stilled at his words and his truculent expression. "All right."

After a moment, he swiped a hand down his face and exhaled. "I can't." He looked at her and then away. "I can get back faster if I'm not . . . if . . . I need to be in control. That day during the charge . . ." He swallowed, but forced himself to continue. "I had no control. I couldn't stop it. Then I was wounded and the nightmares began. They toss me back into the battle. Over and over again.

"They came all the time, day or night. I couldn't escape them. I turned to drink. A lot. First to dull the edges and then to blur the rest. It worked for a while, but then it . . . it didn't. So I stopped." His voice fell. "They don't come that often anymore. Only sneak up on me when I'm not in control of a situation. And certain triggers set them off."

An image of him at Hammond's came to mind, when he had shoved the brandy glass away from him. Then another of him at the hunting lodge, whipping the flask into the fire. She recalled the thunderstorm and her heart constricted. "The storm?"

"Some loud noises. The storm. The name of a battlefield. So you see why I don't talk about it. It's not a pretty sight."

"Garrett, I—"

"Don't." He met her eyes. "I wanted you to understand, to explain tonight. You were kind to me, even after my behavior today. The things I said. You could have left me alone, but you didn't. This is all I can give you." He swallowed. "Let it be enough for now."

The shadows had returned to his eyes and they seeped into her heart, but she raised her chin and grasped on to his last words—*for now*. That meant there would be a later. It was a small breach in his wall. "Of course." She hesitated before continuing, compelled to respond as honestly as he. "This afternoon, it's all right. We both got carried away."

Her words restored his humor, for he grinned. "Is that what happened?"

"Yes. The storm, the secluded lodge, the fire . . ." His plea to her. *Make me forget.* "But it won't happen again."

"Pity," he murmured. He studied her in his infuriating manner. "At my home, when I can't sleep, I read. It keeps the worst of the images at bay. So I'll be all right with these." He glanced at the books and then to the window. "And the worst of the storm has died down. Thank you."

She shook her head. "Slide over."

"What?"

"Come on, move. I haven't read a novel in years."

Garrett stared at her and then slid over. "Damn bossy woman."

She climbed onto the bed. "Have you hoarded all the pillows?"

Grinning, he leaned forward, snatched one from the stack behind him and tossed it to her.

It still held the warm heat of Garrett's body. If she hadn't killed her reputation already, sharing a bed with a man shredded it to pieces even without more sultry kisses and naked tussles and . . . "What book did you choose?"

"This has potential."

"*Tom Jones*?" She read the title. "By Henry Fielding."

"Have you heard of it?"

She glanced up and saw a gleam in his eyes. A warning bell rang in the back of her mind. "No, is it any good?"

"It's entertaining."

"Why don't I read a chapter, and you read the next. Shall we begin?"

He smiled at her. "I'm looking forward to it."

He certainly seemed pleased about something. But feeling pleased herself, she shrugged off her misgivings. Tonight they had won a battle.

Later, she planned to win the war.

And so she began.

Chapter Eighteen

GARRETT watched Alexandra sleep. She lay on top of the covers, her body aligned with his. Sighing, she snuggled closer, rolling to her side and flinging her arm over the quilt across his waist. Her cheek rested on his bare chest. He sucked in a sharp breath as his body responded with a powerful surge of heat to his groin.

Dear God, she was killing him.

Usually after one of his episodes he awoke with a throbbing headache. It was a novel change to feel the throbbing farther south. It was . . . normal. He hadn't experienced normal in a long time. Not until Alexandra's arrival.

She had seen a side of him that he had dared show no one. *I won't leave you.* And she hadn't.

You're safe. And he was.

He had been stripped bare before Alexandra, both literally and figuratively, and yet when he awoke this morning, the anger and shame he expected to feel wasn't present.

Ever since he had looked up from his cards at Hammond's and met those enormous pools of blue across the table,

Alexandra had been tipping his world onto an angle. Perhaps such a drastic action was what he had needed to shake the dirt and blood of Balaclava free.

His eyes dropped to Alexandra's parted lips, feeling her breath stir against his chest, warm and intimate. She was magnificent. He desired her, but now he wanted so much more than her body.

He feared he wanted her heart and soul as well.

She was already stealing pieces of his, but she wanted to force him back onto the battlefield to fight his demons. He closed his eyes. He couldn't go back. Refused to do so.

She had seen how it tore him apart, so she should understand. As he had told her the prior evening, what he had given her had to be enough for now. He needed time to regain his footing. And lest he forget, he needed to find the bastard who was trying to kill him. They might have a plan to do so, but until it succeeded, there was no point in contemplating a future when he might not have one. His eyes opened and he frowned, wondering why choosing to confront a killer rather than his past made him feel like a coward?

He had no answers for himself. However, before tomorrow arrived, he had today. And Alexandra was beside him . . . in his bed. Warm, and with a bit of gentle persuasion, perhaps willing.

⋟⋞

ALEXANDRA ROLLED ONTO her back in the bed. Lifting her arms over her head, she stretched as she blinked to clear her befuddled thoughts about food and Garrett. And not necessarily in that order. Before she could untangle her thoughts, her gaze fastened on Garrett. He leaned over her with a devastating smile on his lips and his black hair deliciously sleep-disheveled. His gray eyes stared knowingly into hers.

Good Lord, she was still in bed with Garrett!

She scrambled to a sitting position and yanked her robe closed around her throat. She must have fallen asleep while he was reading the end of the chapter. It was scandalous. She was a wanton hussy.

She recoiled when he sat up as well, the sheet slipping to

his waist and baring his naked chest. She needed to leave. And she would. She would flee just as soon as the blood restored to her limbs and her legs could support her.

"Good morning," Garrett drawled, flashing that slow, lethal smile.

"What time is it?" She gasped, shifting her attention to focus on anything but on him. Naked. In bed with her.

"It's late, very late. Do you know what you whispered in your sleep?"

That brought her attention back to him. "Nothing. I said nothing!"

He simply cocked a brow. "How would you know? You were asleep, so you wouldn't hear it. But I did."

She clutched her nightgown tighter together and stared at him balefully. He was teasing her. Had to be. She did *not* talk in her sleep. Or did she? Would she betray herself so?

He leaned close and dropped his voice to a murmur. "You said my name. You sighed it twice."

Her cheeks flamed. "I most certainly did not!"

"You did, too!"

"I don't believe you," she protested.

"That's your choice." He shrugged, lifting a bare shoulder and sitting back.

She scowled at him, and seeing the teasing gleam in his eyes she paused, for two could play at this game. "I think I heard you as well."

"Oh? What did I say? Your name?"

She pursed her lips and looked thoughtful as if trying to recall his words. "It wasn't very clear the first time, but then you said it again. You said, 'Champion.' Clear as day. Is that not the name of your horse?" She gave him an innocent look.

He laughed. "It is indeed, but a cavalry soldier and his horse become like one. My life depended upon him." His eyes roved over her. "It's little surprise that we call out to the one we feel closest to or need."

"So you say."

"I do."

"Mmh. As edifying as this has been, I find that it is late and I'm rather hungry. So, if you'll excuse me."

"That's Mr. Fielding's doing."

"Mr. Fielding?" Confused, she stared at him.

"The author of *Tom Jones*. Remember? The narrator was a restaurateur who called his work a feast and the reader a patron to dine on the cuisine of human nature. It makes one hungry." His eyes roamed over her. "Very hungry."

The husky timbre of his voice sent shivers spiraling throughout her body. He was very close. Crowding her. She leaned back. Clearly, he was feeling much better this morning. "His squire, Allworthy, also spoke of virtue," she primly replied.

"Yes, he was a bit longwinded about that. But I liked his point about lust."

"Lust?" Her voice squeaked, mortifying her.

"Don't you remember?"

She shook her head, leaning close to him as he lowered his voice.

"He compared lust to a person's appetite for a good chunk of white flesh."

Her mouth dropped into a round *O*. She felt it do so, for how was one to respond to *that*? And Garrett's naked flesh within a finger's reach.

She now understood the wicked gleam in Garrett's eyes the prior evening when he had chosen Mr. Fielding's wretched book.

"Don't you have any biscuits hidden away in that god-awful nightgown of yours?" Garrett teased.

Her eyes flew open when she felt Garrett's hand prodding at the fabric of her gown.

"Stop that!" She slapped at him, but he leaned over her, forcing her back into the pillows. His eyes locked on hers and her pulse skipped in response.

His hand slid up from her waist, and she caught his wrist as he cupped her breast. But she didn't push him away, wanton hussy that she was.

"No, biscuits. But there is some fruit." He opened her gown, lowered his head and pressed his lips to her bared nipple, his tongue stroking her, arousing her. "Apples complete with stem." He lifted his head, "or perhaps peaches. Very nice, ripe peaches."

He slid his arms around her, flattening his body to hers. His mouth moved over her lips, devouring them. She should have pushed him away, but she opened her mouth and groaned, for that was what wanton hussies did.

For the second time in her life, she caressed the smooth, warm skin of a man. Not just any man, but Garrett. Her heart thudded and her pulse raced in anticipation, for it was what she had secretly yearned for ever since their tryst at the hunting lodge and Garrett had awakened her to the passion that slumbered within her.

With a mixture of wonder and solemn reverence, her hands moved over him, her pulse skipping. She slid them over his strong back, liking the feel of his bare skin, liking the feel of his body, hard and pressed to hers. It felt decadent. Delicious. She dared to slide her hands over his bare buttocks, eliciting a masculine groan.

Her robe parted, so the thin layer of her linen gown provided the only barrier between them. And it was an old, flimsy, weathered gown.

He lifted his head and smiled into her eyes. He grasped the collar of her nightgown. Before she could decipher the gleam in his eyes, he ripped the gown in two, rendering her speechless.

"I owe you a nightgown. This one has to go." He swallowed her protests in a demanding kiss.

He was a feast for her senses. He tasted so good as his tongue thrust and parried with hers. Her hands slid into his hair and she arched against him, an intoxicating heat building to a fervent pitch. His hands touched her everywhere, leaving tingling heat in their wake as they caressed and kneaded her breasts, her abdomen, and slid to her thighs. When his head lowered to draw her nipple into his mouth, she closed her eyes and arched, yearning to get closer, to merge her body with his.

In a haze of delirium, she felt his hands urging her thighs to part, and his hips press intimately against her. She gasped at the feel of his erection, hard and dangerous against her. A molten wave of desire coursed through her. When Garrett's hand slid between them to cup her, the protest she had lodged the other day stuck in her throat. A growing need she could no longer deny silenced it.

When no denial came, he moved his fingers, increasing their

pressure and pleasuring her as they found her most sensitive spot, the key to her passion. As his fingers worked their magic, she writhed and gasped, yearning to reach something that was just beyond her grasp.

"Shh, relax. It will come," he breathed against her lips. "Trust me."

And she did. Trusting in his words, his touch, and him, she let her body open to the emotions flooding her. His fingers slid inside her and her hips bucked against the invasion, a whimper escaping as his fingers moved, tipping her into a wild frenzy. Oh, God. His touch did things to her that should be forbidden.

She grasped his wrist, wanting to stop him, but then just . . . wanting.

Anticipation exploded within her, building until she felt her body erupt in an explosion of sensation. Like smoldering embers of a fire bursting into flame. She cried out with the force of it, digging her nails into Garrett's sweat-slicked back as her body bucked and arched against his hand.

Good Lord. She didn't think she had ever felt anything like it. It was like a taste of heaven, but better. Like the richest brandy coursing through her body in a hot, liquid warmth. After a few more spasms, she collapsed beneath Garrett. She savored the feel of his hard body pressed to hers, his ragged breathing matching hers, and his heart pounding wildly against her ear. It wasn't until she felt the twitch of his manhood, still large and very much alive against her thigh, that awareness returned and her eyes flew open.

Good Lord, what had she done?

This was not good. Well, it had been good, better than good, but they couldn't finish it. She was not this type of woman. She did not . . . She froze.

There was someone at the door.

Panic-stricken, Alex sprung into action, moving as if the hounds of hell were biting at her heels. She shoved Garrett from her, scrambled to sit up and yanked the two sides of her torn gown together. One handed, she struggled to pull her robe on, keeping her head lowered to hide her mortification.

"My lord? Sir? Lord Warren has arrived with your sister. They are—"

"Just a minute," Garrett barked. He blew out a breath and sat up, dragging his hand through his tousled hair.

With shaking fingers, she belted her robe closed.

"Are they downstairs?" Garrett called out.

"Yes, my lord."

Her eyes widened. It must be far later than she thought. They had been up very late last night, reading that blasted book. Flushing, she eased from the bed, swatting at Garrett's hand when his fingers curled over her wrist. "No," she hissed, frantically shaking her head. She needed to escape.

Havers's voice said something else, but she didn't hear it. She dashed across the carpet and escaped to her room.

≫≪

GARRETT FROWNED AT the closed door and slammed his fist into his pillow, cursing Havers's untimely arrival and Alexandra's more untimely departure. His desire ebbed from him and he collapsed back into his bed, a mixture of pain and sexual frustration warring within his body.

"Sir, Lord Warren said to tell you, and I quote—"

Another voice cut Havers off and the door flung open.

"I know you're a good-for-nothing wastrel, but company has arrived, so you need to get your scrawny arse out of bed before I come in there and haul it out." Brandon stood scowling in the door. "Do you know what time it is? It's nearly past dinner and I'm hungry." His eyes narrowed on him. "Damn it, man, are you sober?"

Resigned, Garrett sat up, wiped his hands down his face, and addressed his brother-in-law in a near growl. "First of all, my arse is not scrawny. Secondly, obnoxious family relations do not constitute company. Thirdly, not that it is any of your bloody business, I *am* sober but waking to your ugly mug makes one crave a drink. Perhaps you should leave."

Brandon raised a brow. "You look like hell." He paused and his voice lowered. "Are you all right?"

Worry darkened his friend's eyes. Garrett sighed. "I'm fine. Or was until your arrival. What the hell are you doing here? This is midweek. You weren't due until the end of it."

Brandon strolled into the room, closed the door behind him, and lowered himself into the easy chair across the room. "What do you think happened? Kit happened. She discovered you were traveling here with a young woman, unchaperoned. You calculate the rest. As far as she's concerned, you've had more than enough time to enter into a bacchanalian orgy of ruination. I held her off as long as I could. But"—he blew out a breath—"one can't stem a tidal wave once it starts rolling."

Damn Kit for being an all-knowing busybody. And a correct one. He *was* on the road to ruination. What was he doing tangling the sheets with Alexandra? She deserved better than him. But he wanted her like he wanted no other woman. And her body's passionate response told him that she wanted him, too, whole or not. The knowledge of this revived his spirits, and he flung off his covers and came to his feet. "Where is Kit? Downstairs pacing a hole in the carpet?"

"Of course." Brandon paused, before adding in a more serious tone. "She was worried when you weren't awake. She sent me up here to check on you."

He paused in the midst of yanking on his trousers to glance over at Brandon, who shrugged apologetically. Well, he deserved that. His past behavior had not been exemplary. He clenched his jaw as he turned to the commode and scooped a handful of water over his face, scrubbing hard. Straightening, he grabbed a towel and eyed Brandon. "And the boys?" he asked as he dried his face and then crossed to his wardrobe and selected a crisp white linen shirt.

"They're in the stables. Your tomcat has found a mate, and she had a litter of kittens. I couldn't drag them away. I'll collect them after I retrieve you. I am under direct order to bring you downstairs, willingly or not."

"You mean sober or not," he muttered, shrugging into his shirt.

"You still don't have a valet?" Brandon frowned.

"Unlike you, I'm quite capable of getting myself dressed or undressed as the case may be." He moved to the mirror to tie his cravat.

"The truth is that Havers is the only man who'd put up with you."

"Havers is a smart man. One of a kind. Except for Poole, whose misplaced loyalty is to be commended."

Brandon smiled. "He always saw right through your antics."

"Yes, and my not-so-scrawny arse has the scars to prove it."

Brandon laughed. "Yet you still turned out to be a wastrel."

"Kept bad company." He turned from the mirror to grin at his friend. "But since I'm stuck with you, let's hope you've been useful. What about this Viscount Langdon?"

"I thought Alexandra's name is Daniels."

"You thought wrong, but continue to address her as Miss Daniels. Did you learn anything?"

"A Viscount Phillip Langdon owns a modest estate in Essex. He has three young daughters, none of whom have come out yet. He is new to the title, being the younger son and having inherited it upon the death of his elder brother. The elder Langdon and his wife died of the influenza two years ago while traveling in Italy."

Garrett leaned against his bureau, folding his arms over his chest. "What do you know of the elder Langdon?"

Brandon sat back, stretched his legs out before him and crossed them at the ankles. "Paul Langdon was a notorious philanderer and gambler. He had a reputation for investing in disreputable business ventures, often authoring many of his own schemes while finagling others to finance them. He ran through fortunes as frequently as he did his mistresses, stripping his estate and selling it piecemeal to stay out of debtor's gaol."

Garrett frowned as he recalled Alexandra's story about her father's plans to sell her abysmal singing voice to neighbors to scare off potential houseguests. *My father was always in need of a fortune.* Her words sent a cold chill through him. "Anything else?"

"He had a child, a daughter," Brandon said.

He waited for Brandon to continue, refusing to shift under his knowing gaze.

"Your Alexandra had one Season and made quite a splash, garnering a dozen or so offers for her hand. She refused them all."

Garrett frowned at the thought of a bevy of fops salivating over his Alex. "What else?"

He shrugged. "She disappeared. Dropped out of school to take a grand tour. No one's heard from her since. That is with the exception of you, if I'm to understand she is *your* Miss Daniels?"

Garrett ignored the query. "What about the estate? Is it debt ridden or solvent?"

"A year before the elder brother's death, the estate turned around. Word is the late viscount had hired a new manager who took a firmer hand on his finances. He put him on a strict budget, reined in all excess expenditures, while working more closely with the tenants to turn a neat profit."

My father owned some property, and I used to review the reports with the estate manager.

"I'll just bet she did," he muttered, his lips curving.

He'd gamble his last pence there had been no grand tour with her parents. Alexandra had returned home to salvage her father's floundering estate. Probably was withdrawn from school when her father couldn't foot her tuition. Christ, what a way to live.

It was little wonder she had agreed to his financial proposal.

"And the new viscount?" Garrett asked. Though he feared he already knew the answer. "The younger brother? How is the estate managing under him?"

"I don't know. He stays in the country and doesn't venture to town much, but he has to finance three dowries, which won't come cheap."

"No, it won't." Another thought struck him. There was money to be had in a lucrative marital agreement. But Alexandra had refused all proposals. He'd place another bet that her uncle didn't admire her independence as much as he did.

These provided more answers to the puzzle that comprised Alex. When he put all the pieces together, the finished picture of her life wasn't pretty. The only remaining question was whether or not Alex had fled of her own accord or her uncle had forced her out.

Alex's history only furthered his admiration of her. By God, it had taken a great deal of courage to salvage her father's estate and forge her own path.

Some risks are worth taking, she'd said.

He knew she was different. Had known it from the first moment he'd laid eyes on her. Admittedly, he hadn't known she was a woman then, but the discovery only enhanced her appeal. And his desire. She was magnificent.

A gruff cough made him jerk his attention back to Brandon, and he realized he stood grinning like a demented fool. He felt a warm flush steal up his neck and straightened. "Yes, well, that explains—" He got no further.

"Bloody hell." Brandon jerked up. "You slept with her."

"What?" he sputtered. "Why—"

"Don't deny it, man." Brandon shot to his feet. "Kit is going to kill us both, and I am not deflecting any hits for you because you deserve every shot she aims." He stormed to the door. "Miss Daniels seemed like such an intelligent young woman when I met her. What the hell do you do to these women?" He shook his head. "I thought you had changed since your return."

"I have," he protested, hearing the disgust and disappointment in Brandon's voice. A few months ago, he wouldn't have given a damn if Brandon thought he had slid back into his old philandering ways. But today he did. Things were different today, and he liked those differences. "There have been no women. No other women. It's not like that."

At Brandon's dubious look, he raised his voice. "I didn't sleep with her!" he barked. When Brandon merely cocked a brow, he hissed, "All right, I did, but it's not what you think."

"I'm not thinking about it. And don't put visuals in my mind." He held up his hands. "Please. Spare me the details."

"Shut up, for Christ's sake. She was in here last night, but not tangling the sheets with me." They performed that dance this morning, but he refrained from clarifying this discrepancy. Splitting hairs and all that. "She helped me."

Brandon paused, waiting for him to continue.

"There was a storm, and I had . . . I had—"

"I understand," Brandon rescued him. "Miss Daniels, she helped you through it?"

He exhaled. "She did. It's the only reason she stayed with me last night. And the reason I was late to rise."

Brandon studied him for a moment, before his hard expression softened. "Perhaps I wasn't mistaken about her." He waited for Garrett to add something more, but when he didn't, he continued. "However, there is still the lesser charge of the two of you being here alone and unchaperoned. I'll collect the boys and meet you downstairs with them in tow. Kit wouldn't dare kill you before the children."

"You're too kind," Garrett said dryly.

"I got your information for you, didn't I? And I spoke to Hammond, and he will send out the invitations as soon as we confirm a date. By the way, what have you done with mine? Any progress?"

"Yours?" Garrett paused in collecting his waistcoat from the wardrobe and glanced over at Brandon.

"Hammond's guest list that I passed on to you?" His eyes narrowed at Garrett's obvious blank look. "You were to review it to see if any names raised a red flag? Cut it down to a handful of would-be potential killers? We were going to have the police investigate the names you've flagged." When he didn't respond, Brandon frowned. "I know the list of men wanting your head on a platter, preferably with a roasted apple stuffed in your mouth, is extensive, but I had hoped you might have succeeded in slicing it down to a manageable group. It appears you had other matters more important than finding your would-be murderer. My mistake."

Garrett held up his hands. "Point taken. I understand."

"Do you? *Do you really?*" Brandon's eyes were once again hard and leveled on him. "I'd hate to think you forgot why you are here. If so, forgive me for reminding you of those pesky facts. Someone wants you dead. Has made two attempts on your life. You'd be wise to remember that." He turned to go, speaking over his shoulder. "You need to go downstairs. Your sister is worried about you. God knows why when you can't be bothered to do the same."

The door opened and slammed closed with a finality that shamed Garrett. He sagged back against his bureau and blew out a breath. Christ.

The morning had started off so well. He didn't know how it had spiraled south so quickly. He had managed to anger both his sister and Brandon, and Alexandra was none too pleased with him, either. He might not have reviewed Hammond's damn list yet, but he did have a plan. And he knew damn well why he was here. A man didn't forget that he was a walking target. Christ. He cursed the fact that he had forsaken drink because he was in dire need of a shot. Hell, forget the shot, he could swallow the whole decanter. He raked his hands through his hair and swore. It was going to be a hell of a long day.

Chapter Nineteen

❧❧

ALEX waited for Jemma, the lady's maid assisting her, to finish buttoning the back of her light green day dress. She straightened her bodice as she reviewed her plans for the day. After this morning, she had concluded that she needed to revise her strategies for dealing with Garrett.

The morning had taught her that she could not let Garrett touch her. Once the man got a hold of her, she was no longer the practical, intelligent woman she considered herself to be. In his arms, she became someone altogether different. Cheeks burning, she gritted her teeth and ignored the voice inside her head hissing about wanton hussies. There would be no more name-calling.

Garrett was a charming and attractive man. Her reactions to him were no different than any other woman's would be when confronted with the full power of his seduction.

Admittedly, she had not reacted to any other dashing rake in the same manner. But no man was as handsome as Garrett, nor were they as brave . . . and they didn't touch her like . . . She closed her eyes and pressed her hand to her forehead. She had lost her point. What was it? Touching. It was about how there would be no more of it. Theirs was a business arrangement. Nothing more could ever come of it, so embarking on these illicit detours was dangerous and decadent and . . . Well, they needed to stop. She opened her eyes and relaxed, feeling more in charge of herself.

Alex's mind was made up, her new course of action laid before her, and there was nothing left to do but test the waters. She couldn't wade in too deep now that Lord Warren and Garrett's sister had arrived. Frowning, she followed Jemma to the door, unable to explain the sudden heaviness dragging her steps.

She was fiddling with the lace on her cuffs when she exited her room. She did not see Garrett coming down the hall, so gasped when he caught her arms to prevent her from barreling straight into him. Staggering, she slapped at his hands while backing away.

His eyes did not meet hers, but rather dipped to her mouth and slowly lowered to drift over her body. A ball of heat exploded deep in her belly. Images of their hot, sultry kisses, his hand cupping her breast, and his fingers working their magic assaulted her. She lifted her hand to cover her pounding heart.

Maybe he should neither touch nor even look at her.

Or at least look at her *like that*. Like if given a spoon, he would dig in and then lick her clean.

"Good morning, oh, wait, it's afternoon. Good afternoon." He grinned. "It looks like we are heading in the same direction. After you." Bowing low, he held out his hand for her to precede him. When she did not move, he raised a brow. "Or we could remain here until you are ready or our hunger gets the better of us, for we did miss breakfast. I don't know about you, but I'm starving—"

"Don't!" She came alive at his words. "Don't you dare start on hunger and appetites and all that."

He laughed. "Fair enough."

She gave him a wary glance, but when he did not speak again, she continued down the hall, aware of him falling into step beside her. As they walked, she cast suspicious glances his way. For one who never resisted a retort, Garrett was quiet. Too quiet. And behaving himself.

He looked good. He was wearing a dark gray morning suit,

his cravat neatly tied, his jacket fitting over his shoulders like a second skin, his trousers snug over muscular thighs. She yanked her eyes from him, nearly tripping on the first step.

His arm slid her around her waist, catching her before she tumbled headfirst down the stairs. "Whoa, there. Are you all right?"

Cheeks flaming, she shoved his arm from her and muttered under her breath. "I will be if you'd keep your hands to yourself."

His lips twitched. "My apologies. I didn't know you preferred to go down the stairs headfirst, but next time you start to do so, I promise not to intercede."

"You know exactly what I mean. Please keep your hands to yourself." She whirled around and stomped down the stairs, the low rumble of his laughter carrying to her.

That was more like him.

She refused to give him another thought. She needed to focus her attention on meeting his sister, the docile mouse.

She plastered a smile on her face and entered the front parlor, braced to meet the Lord and Lady Warren. When she stepped into the room, it was empty. Puzzled, she turned to Garrett.

He surveyed the room as well, a frown on his lips.

"I thought Havers said Lord Warren and your sister had arrived."

"He did and they are here. Just not at the moment." He shrugged. "You should know, Brandon has explained to my sister what you overheard at Hammond's and why you are here. Kit admires your courage in coming forward and for providing me with whatever assistance you can."

Alex had wondered how he had explained her presence to his sister. It didn't alleviate her nerves, but she was grateful Garrett had said something. One could get ideas. She gnawed on her bottom lip, worrying over those ideas and how perilously close they were to being true.

Garrett's expression turned pensive.

"You have a lot of rules this morning. No talking about appetites or hunger. No touching." He tucked his hands into his trouser pockets. "I want to make sure I get them all straight. I don't want to upset you in front of Warren or my sister."

She frowned, not knowing where he was heading with this.

He studied her in his usual quiet, drive-her-mad manner of his. That irritating trait now topped her lists of his faults.

"What about food? Can I mention food?"

"Of course."

"That's good because you know how I love apples and small, ripe peaches and—"

"Stop!" She gasped. She advanced on him. "No apples, and certainly not peaches."

He laughed. "Since you didn't mention kissing, I assume that's permitted?"

Before she realized his intent, he slid his arms around her waist and yanked her to him. "That's touching! That's against the rules." She pushed ineffectively at his chest.

He smiled, a slow, sultry smile as he lowered his face to hers. "You're right. But, my dear Alex, you should know by now, I've never been one for rules. Never liked them. Broke them all." His mouth captured hers in a deeply thorough kiss. Taking, teasing, and torturing her as the familiar flash of desire ignited within her.

She groaned against his lips, struggling to draw breath as his arms crushed her close and his kiss damn near devoured her.

Her lips opened under his and she sighed.

"I knew I should have come earlier! I just knew it. I'm too late, aren't I?"

Alex's eyes shot open and she wrenched free from Garrett. Mortified, she braced herself to face Garrett's sister, wondering how she could have forgotten her. That wasn't completely true, for Garrett's kiss made her forget everything, including to say no.

She squared her shoulders and plastered a smile on her face, hoping to salvage a remnant of her shredded reputation. But when she turned and her gaze landed on the woman framed in the doorway, the blood drained from her head. It wasn't his sister. It was worse. Much, much worse.

It was the portrait of Garrett's mistress come to life.

Kristen.

She was beautiful. Thick auburn hair framed a porcelain face, with full lips pressed into a disapproving frown and golden catlike eyes blazing at Garrett.

How could she have forgotten Garrett's mistress?

It was as if her body had turned to stone, her humiliation so complete it had immobilized her. Her eyes dropped to the woman's stomach, her very pregnant, bulging stomach, and the last drop of blood left her head.

Before she could recover from this added shock, Kristen spoke.

"Decadence appears to agree with you." She eyed Garrett. "You may be an incorrigible rake, but it is good to see you looking so damn well." Her voice broke on her last words and she stepped forward to fling herself into Garrett's arms.

"You're a bit high in the instep and a meddlesome do-gooder, but I'm glad you've come." Garrett buried his face in Kristen's hair and lowered his voice. "I'm fine. You need to stop worrying about me."

"It's a lifetime habit, curse of loving you," Kristen murmured, accepting a handkerchief from Garrett as she drew away and dabbed at her eyes.

Like a sledgehammer, Kristen's words shattered Alex's immobility. *The woman loved him.*

Garrett had told her that. Kristen was everything to him, while she was what? A country distraction? Dessert before the main banquet? She satisfied a lustful craving, while Kristen satisfied . . . she refused to think of what he received from Kristen.

She whirled on Garrett, fisting her hands at her sides. The man had survived two attacks on his life. But this time, this time he would die.

And she would not weep for him, she vowed as she furiously blinked back her tears. "You are despicable. How could you?" she hissed.

Surprised, Kristen turned to her and raised a brow. "You are quite right, my dear. Let us not be distracted." She also whirled on Garrett, planted her hands on her no-longer-slim hips, and glowered at him. "What were you and Brandon thinking with this idiotic plan? Dragging this young woman out here all alone and with no chaperones?"

"There wasn't time," Garrett protested. "I needed to leave town, to relocate to a safe place to strategize an offensive plan." He turned to Alex and, seeing her expression matched Kristen's, his hands shot up before him. "Wait, it's not what you think. We're not what you think."

"Do you take me for a fool? She's having a baby! *Your* baby!"

"What?" Kristen gasped, stumbling back from Garrett.

"No, she's not!" Garrett protested. "We're not. You don't understand."

"I understand that!"

"No. This is my sister! *My sister!*"

"And I am most certainly not having my brother's baby!" Kristen pressed a hand to her forehead and gave her head a firm shake. "Dear Lord, please tell me those words did not leave my mouth."

"More important, promise me they won't leave this room," Garrett muttered. "Kit, this is Alexandra Daniels. Alexandra, this is my sister and Brandon's wife, Lady Kristen Warren."

Stunned, it took Alex a moment to recover. *Kristen . . . Kit.* Of course. She was an idiot, and Garrett was a deceitful ass. She gave him a fulminating look. She'd refrain from killing him over his clever lack of clarification, but he should suffer. He had made her think she was a damn dessert. Worse, he had let her believe he had a mistress. Made her think that every kiss they had shared was a betrayal of another woman. Made her think she couldn't have him. Not that she wanted him or could ever have him, of course. But . . . well, he deserved to suffer. She had.

"Please, forgive my misunderstanding. I saw a portrait of you in Garrett's London residence, but I don't know why I presumed—"

"Oh, I have an idea," Kristen drawled, her eyes narrowing on Garrett. She squeezed Alex's hand reassuringly and smiled. "In my condition, I'm flattered." She lifted a hand to pat her hair. "Of course, I would make an excellent courtesan, but I draw the line at having my brother as my benefactor."

"Ah, those words remain here as well," Garrett said, blanching.

"I would have to agree with that."

The words came from behind Alex and she spun to see Brandon standing in the door, a cherubic, fair-haired toddler in his arms. He blinked at Alex with Brandon's green eyes, plugged his mouth with his thumb, and buried his face in his father's shoulder. "The portrait you saw was in my house," Brandon explained. "I had it commissioned of my wife, Kit." Brandon turned to Garrett. "Sorry, I had trouble collecting the reinforcements. Fear I lost one. But you look none too bruised and battered."

"Yet," Alex hissed under her breath. To her mortification, Kristen heard her and gave her an all-too-familiar, slow appraisal. Clearly that look was a family trait.

"I think we shall get along very well indeed," Kit said, beaming.

"This is *not* good," Garrett muttered to Brandon.

Kit raised an imperious brow. "My dear brother, women are not horses. We do not like to be led or misled, as the case may be. You'd be wise to remember that."

Alex blinked at Kit. Garrett might be a deceiving, good-for-nothing ass, but she liked his sister. The mouse had claws and roared. She watched Garrett glower at his sister, who smiled sweetly back at him.

"Mama!"

Kit turned to the little boy squirming in Brandon's arms. She crossed to him and stretched up on tiptoes to kiss his plump cheek. "You'd be wise to remember that as well, little one." She faced Alex as she made the introductions. "This angel is William. His older brother is the one we have lost. He's the little devil of our family. He takes after his uncle."

"Very funny," Garrett said.

"He was right behind me when I headed up to the house." Brandon frowned.

"And Gus said he had behaved himself. I should have guessed it wouldn't last."

"Gus?" Alex perked up at the name, turning to stare at Garrett in surprise.

"I did hire him to manage the stables, remember?" Garrett cocked a brow at her.

She did remember, but it never occurred to her that Gus would be working at the same manor as them. Would be reunited with her. Damn Garrett. It was hard to hold on to her anger when he continued to do things like this.

"He traveled with us," Brandon said. "You'll have to go and

say hello. And perhaps locate our eldest son. He's about so high"—he held his hand to waist level—"and usually knee-deep in trouble."

"I'm right here," an amused voice piped up from the door.

A young boy of about six or seven years stood just inside the room. His hands were folded around his waist, his ink black hair windblown and in dark contrast to his bright pink cheeks.

"So you are. Where have you been?" Brandon's eyes narrowed.

"Leave off, Bran, he looks fine." Garrett bent to give the boy a hug but was stopped by a firm hand thrust out to him. Grinning, Garrett clutched it in his and shook it firmly, bending into a shallow bow. "Aren't you mature."

"I'm almost seven. You can hug Will, but don't shake his hand. You'd get slobber from his thumb all over you."

Brandon's raised a brow. "Yes, Beau, but . . ."

"Papa, it's not Beau, it's Nelson. I've told you again and again." Impatience flashed in his eyes. "I've changed my name to Nelson," he explained to Garrett. "Poole told me I got saddled with Beauregard because it was the first Earl of Warren and every other Warren is stuck with the name. But I don't like it, so I've tossed it over for Nelson. It's a dapper name, and Admiral Nelson trounced the French."

"Apt choice, Nelson," Garrett said, clearly fighting to keep his expression somber.

Alex lifted her hand to suppress her smile. The boy was charming. She feared he did take after his uncle.

"Beau . . . I mean, Nelson," Brandon corrected himself after a disgruntled look from his son. "About your jacket—"

"My jacket?" Beau opened his eyes wide, giving them a look of guileless innocence.

"Yes. It is moving."

Beau waved a hand dismissively. "That's my stomach. Hunger pains and all that. Perhaps I should change for dinner? I'm ravenous." He started to back out of the room.

"One moment, Nelson. Your stomach appears to be sprouting a tail." Kit's amused gaze dropped to his waist where the furry appendage protruded.

Beau flushed and shoved the tail underneath his jacket hem just as a paw slipped up between the lapels of his coat.

"Beau, rather, Nelson, I told you to leave the kittens in the stables with their mother. They are too young to be weaned yet," Brandon said, setting Will on his feet when he squirmed for release.

"He didn't want to stay with his mother. He followed me. He was crying when I put him down."

"Will cries to follow you sometimes, but then he wants his mother," Brandon explained. "Like Will, this kitten is not ready to be separated yet."

"Why don't I help Nelson return the kitten to his mother," Alex offered. "I know you two would like to catch up with Garrett, and I would like a chance to greet Gus."

Garrett knelt beside Beau to help Will pet the kitten. "Nelson, this is Miss Daniels, and she is a friend of mine and Gus's. Why don't you show her where the kitten's mother is? She likes kittens, too," Garrett explained, making the introductions.

Watching Garrett with the boys, Alex felt the rest of her chill toward him melt. Of all the facets to Garrett's personality, this could prove his most dangerous, for she had a weakness for children.

"I come." Will toddled over to Alex and raised his hands to be lifted.

Charmed, Alex laughed and bent to scoop up the little boy. "Of course. We wouldn't leave you with the boring adults when there are kittens to be seen."

"I am this many," Will thrust two fingers into her face.

"Gus brought a pony," Beau said. "He's going to let me ride him."

"Lucky you. Gus taught me to ride when I was a girl." She followed Beau to the door, turning back to smile at Kit and Brandon. "I promise to return quickly, as dinner is already abysmally late, and I'm sure you're all . . . ah, ready to eat." Her eyes snapped to Garrett's and a flush stole up her cheeks at the knowing gleam in his eyes. She spun around and hastened from the room.

She had meant to say they were all *hungry*, but the word had stuck in her throat. Damn Garrett for making her trip over a simple word that now harbored a whole new wealth of meaning. It was bad enough that she couldn't think around Garrett; now she couldn't talk.

The man was turning her into a mute idiot. There would have to be a new set of rules, which of course, Garrett would break. She huffed out a breath, but seeing Beau skipping ahead of her, she paused. What she needed were reinforcements, someone else to enforce the rules. She had the perfect pair to do so. And the plan required little thinking and no words. Perfect for a mute idiot.

Chapter Twenty

❧

"S HE'LL do," Kit said when Alexandra and the boys had
disappeared.

Garrett had been admiring the tantalizing sway of Alexandra's skirts and the way Will's arm slipped so naturally around her neck. Lucky boy. At his sister's words, he turned and narrowed his eyes. "Dare I ask what you mean by that?"

Kit lowered herself down on the sofa, neatened her skirts, and rested her hands on her extended stomach. "What do you think, Garrett? You're an intelligent man when sober, which thankfully you are." Kit was unmoved by his warning look. "You've been sequestered here, all alone with a young woman, without chaperones, and what do you expect me to say? You are lucky she appears to be a lovely, intelligent, and *forgiving* young woman. You could do much worse."

"Much worse for *what*?" he asked exasperated.

"For a wife," Kit said, raising her voice to match his.

Stunned, he gaped at her. *A wife?* He was not getting married, not now, not ever. "What are you talking about? She is here to assist me with finding out who the hell is trying to murder me. She is the only link to this plot. I thought Brandon explained the situation to you." He wasn't about to admit to his sister that he had other motives for keeping Alex, not when they could force him to the very altar to which Kit appeared intent on directing him.

"I see," Kit said. "Do you kiss all your assistants? How does that go with Stewart?"

Brandon coughed and strode over to the decanter when Garrett shot him a dirty look.

"It's not like that."

"Oh, then what is it like? Why were you kissing her?"

"Because . . . because I like kissing her!" Hell and damnation that was the wrong answer.

Brandon rolled his eyes and poured himself a drink. He lifted it in a toast to Garrett. "To a man with a death wish."

"Will you shut up?" he barked.

"What did you expect would come of this?" Kit asked. "Your reputation is black as sin. Hers will be darkened by mere proximity. The poor girl won't weather the siege of wagging tongues. That's if the tongues have not started flapping already. What have you said to the neighbors?"

"Nothing. I've said nothing," he muttered, Kit's words falling like hail stones, bruising him with the hard, cold truth.

"You've seen no one?"

Garrett opened his mouth and then closed it. *Keyes.* Damn the man.

"That would be a . . . ?"

"We might have run into Keyes," he admitted with reluctance.

"Might have?" Kit raised a delicate brow.

"All right. We did." He sighed. "We ran into him while he was out hunting. At the time, I thought I was his target."

A stunned silence met his words. Brandon lowered his drink and narrowed his eyes. "Do you think he might be behind the attacks on you? He'd have cause, being angry over your purchasing his land."

"He's still hot under the collar about that. But he's not our man." He waved his hand dismissively. "He's a coward and an idiot. It would take bravery, brains, and the wherewithal to get off his backside long enough to engineer the plan. Keyes is not our man."

"At least there's one name to cross off your list of enemies." Kit said dryly. "If you had kept your trousers buttoned, that list would be considerably shorter. I warned you—"

"Bran, can't you do something with your wife? As usual, she's venturing into areas that are none of her damn business."

Brandon laughed. "When she speaks the truth, my hands are tied."

"Keyes may not have brains, but he does possess a tongue," Kit went on. "I'm sure he has wasted no time wagging it to further blacken your name and Alexandra's along with it."

"Oh, Christ." Garrett dropped onto the sofa beside Kit. "Will you stop quaffing that brandy," he snapped at Brandon. "I'm the one trying to salvage my neck here." He planted his elbows on his knees and cradled his head in his hands.

He knew Alexandra was an innocent. Knew he should have kept his hands off her. But he had convinced himself otherwise. That she was different. A woman who made her own choices and damned the consequences. *Some risks are worth taking.* But she was the daughter of a viscount and that stamped her marriage material—never mistress potential, pretend or otherwise. *I won't be your mistress.* The finality of her words reverberated and Garrett cursed.

What the hell was wrong with him?

He jerked at the feel of a hand rubbing his back. He lifted his head and turned a baleful look on Kit. He was surprised to find her eyes warm with sympathy.

"I think you already have," she murmured.

"What? I have what?" He raised his hands in supplication.

"Saved your neck," she said and smiled. After a moment, she continued. "And as you say, Lady Alexandra will help you once we return to London. I have brought gowns for her to choose from, and I have arranged for a seamstress to come here to make the necessary alterations. I know it is safe here, but you can't hole up here forever. We need to catch this man before it is too late."

"What's to guarantee the bastard will accept Hammond's invitation?" Garrett said, echoing Alex's concern with their plan. "He's probably hiding in his lair, waiting to receive news of my untimely demise."

"He has a point there." Brandon nodded. "That's what I would be doing."

Kit glared at Brandon. "We'll have to bait him, make the invitation too tantalizing for him to refuse. We'll also hire men to provide protection for Garrett while he's in town. And the bastard wouldn't dare commit murder at a ball before three hundred witnesses."

"I thought I was the bait?" Garrett said.

"No, you're the target," Brandon replied.

"Can I hit him if he speaks again?" Garrett turned to Kit.

"Please do." She narrowed her eyes on her husband. "The invitation should be to a coveted event. An engagement ball should do it. One announcing your betrothal to Lady Alexandra."

"What? We're back to that?" Garrett stood up. "I should have—"

"It's the only way you can squire Lady Alexandra anywhere without tongues wagging and brows raised." Kit cut him off. "Don't think Keyes hasn't already started them flapping. You're a bachelor, not to mention a rake with a reputation black as sin and—"

"Stop!" Garrett held up his hand. "You're treading on ground you've already stomped on earlier."

"This is a good plan. And she's perfect for you. Aside from this nasty plot on your life, you look the best I've seen you in two years. You're sober, more handsome than ever, and barking at me and snarling at Brandon. You're kissing a woman and, to use your words, liking it." She grinned. "She's doing something right if she's dragged you back from the brink of self-destruction. From your indulgent ritual of suicidal inebriation, from—"

"Point taken. Stop hammering it home; the pounding is killing my head."

"It took a great deal of courage for her to confront you about the plot on your life. She also agreed to help in finding these men, even after she believed she had given you all the information she had. And, she didn't strangle you when she clearly had a right to after you led her to believe I was your mistress, of all the deceitful—"

"All right!" Garrett rubbed his temple. "I understand. I'm a bloody scoundrel, responsible for ruining the reputation of an innocent paragon of virtue."

"The former sounds right, but considering she was kissing you back, I'll allow the latter point to be moot."

Surprised, Garrett stared at Kit and seeing her eyes light with a teasing sparkle, he grinned. He had forgotten that part. Alex *was* kissing him back, even after she laid out her list of infernal rules. He hated rules. Not touching her? It was like holding the tide from the shore.

Kit was right, but what she didn't know, couldn't know, was Alex's incredible passion and her response to him. She came alive in his arms. And when he held her close, he felt complete. He didn't deserve her, but he wanted her . . . and she wanted him. Perhaps it wouldn't be so bad if they got married. Then she would be legally his.

To touch, to kiss, to have.

Forever.

He chewed on the idea and found it didn't choke him. He was still breathing, and he felt . . . good.

He eyed his friend. Brandon had years of this marriage business under him and he looked none the worse for wear. Come to think of it, the man walked around with a smug look on his face, like he knew the secret to a life worth living. Hell, Garrett deserved to know that secret.

He looked up to see Brandon and Kit watching him with knowing amusement. When he realized he had been pacing a wide swath in the carpet, he stopped. "All right, I'll do it. So what's next? Posting the banns and whatnot?"

Kit blinked and Brandon paused in lifting his brandy snifter to his lips.

"I'm glad you've arrived at a sensible a decision, but haven't you forgotten something?" Kit said wryly.

"What? What now?" He glanced between them, baffled. He had the woman, he had the will, he had Kit's approval, and to hell with his stepfather's. And they had a plan to identify his would-be murderer so he might have a future.

What else was there?

Brandon coughed, and this time it was Kit who glared at him. She then spoke to Garrett as if he were a child who had forgotten rudimentary mathematics. "My dear brother, there is one small but rather pertinent detail you need to consider. To men, it may be a pesky inconvenience, but to women, it is the first step toward winning their hand." When he still looked blank, she threw up her arms in disgust. "You have to propose first, you idiot!"

Hell. He had forgotten about proposing. He frowned as he contemplated asking Alexandra for her hand. That could be a problem. Brandon had said Alexandra had already turned down several proposals during her Season. Well, Garrett's mind was made up.

Alex was marrying him.

He looked at Kit. "What do I have to do to get her to say yes?"

Brandon exploded. "Christ. Once upon a time, you were en route to seducing half the women of London. Have two years of celibacy truly rendered you a damn eunuch?" He shook his head. "I tried to talk you out of buying that commission. I tried."

"Ignore my idiot husband. There will be no seducing of anyone. Do you understand me?" Kit's eyes narrowed on Garrett. "This is about courtship, not seduction."

"What's the difference?" Garrett asked.

Brandon laughed.

"Brandon, my love," Kit spoke through gritted teeth. "Will you collect Alexandra and the boys? I fear I'm getting weak with hunger, and when that happens, I lose all patience."

Concerned, Brandon set his glass down. "Do . . . do you want me to get you some bread or something?"

"No, just the boys. I'll be fine. Thank you."

"Are you sure?"

"Yes, quite. Thank you, just go." She smiled sweetly at him.

Brandon eyed her warily, his eyes dipping to her bulging stomach before he departed, glancing back once or twice in indecision.

Garrett frowned. If marriage could reduce him to that sort of puddle of water, he might have to reconsider matters.

Kit placed her hands over her stomach and drew a deep breath. "Garrett, listen to me. Courtship is about taking the time to get to know one another better. Considering you've progressed to the kissing stage, you must be making strides in that area. Continue to be your charming self, treat her with decency and respect, stay sober, and of course, forsake all other women. And Garrett, can you refrain from taking her to bed before you've—"

"Kit, have a care for my head. You're hammering your point home again. Your first line was enough. I can handle the rest."

"It's the handling part I'm worried about," Kit said dryly.

"Don't give it a thought," he said. "I mean that literally, Kit. You need to let me take care of matters from here on."

"You'll do fine," Kit said. "Now help me up. Once I plant myself, I'm stuck."

Garrett grinned and walked over to link hands with her. With a quick tug, he hauled her to her feet. "We wouldn't want you growing roots."

"Very funny." She pressed her hands to her back. "However, you do need to feed me now or I won't remain as pleasant and understanding as I have been."

"You've been the soul of understanding."

"Yes, well, I did have Brandon pack his pistols. My brother taught me when negotiating any transaction, one needs to plan for all possible contingencies."

"That's my girl." He smiled. She reminded him of another formidable young woman. He offered his arm to escort her out, his mind already drifting to Alexandra. To courting Alexandra.

He frowned. His flattery was rusty, she had tossed his offer of a new mount back in his face, and she had refused all her other suitors. If he continued down the same path, he really would be whispering Champion's name in his sleep.

However, as Kit had reminded him, when negotiating any transaction, one needed to plan for all contingencies. Should Alex refuse him, he'd simply kiss her senseless, toss her over Champion's saddle, and they could be at Gretna Green in no time.

Chapter Twenty-one

❦❧

THAT evening Alex sat before the dressing table in her bed-chamber, staring into the mirror as she drew her brush through her hair. Her thoughts shifted back and forth between her reunion with Gus and meeting Garrett's sister. Both made her smile.

Gus had never looked better. He was healthy, robust, and . . . sober. When she had spotted him framed in the stable door, time had traveled backward. Before she knew her feet were moving, she had launched herself into his open-armed embrace. Returning Gus to his old self was the greatest gift Garrett could have given her. This gift was priceless, or it had been until Gus had opened his mouth.

He had wasted little time in telling her she was still too damn scrawny and what the bloody hell had she been thinking to travel here alone with Kendall without waiting for the War-rens' arrival. He had more to say, but it had faded to background chatter, her resentment drowning it out. She had forgotten how often his thick head had butted up against hers.

While Gus appeared to be her outspoken cross to bear, Kris-ten appeared to be Garrett's. *A docile, biddable thing.* She scoffed at the image, for it was the antithesis of the woman, and Alex thanked God for it. However, Garrett had been honest about one thing in regard to his sister. Kristen loved him. It was another mark in Garrett's favor. For only a man deserving of it would gain this woman's affections.

The man certainly had a way about him. And he had behaved the perfect gentleman tonight.

Gone was the teasing rake who flirted with her and stole kisses. Not that she missed those, she hastily added, but she couldn't help but cast suspicious glances his way. Under the watchful eye of his sister and Brandon, he behaved impeccably, and like his nephews, she found herself falling under his spell.

She planted her elbows on the dressing table, dropped her head into her hands, and sighed.

She was in trouble.

Her heart was pulling her in a direction she wasn't free to go.

Her uncle had seen to that.

She lifted her head, and her reflection swam in her blurry-eyed gaze. Gus was right. What had she been thinking traveling here alone with Garrett? She was not free to follow her heart or her passions, for nothing serious could ever come of them. She tossed her brush onto the table and sat back with a sigh. A knock on the door had her jumping. She whirled to stare at the door separating her room from Garrett's. He wouldn't dare enter. Not since his sister and Brandon's arrival.

The knock came again. She gnawed on her lower lip. This was ridiculous. She could handle him. She closed her eyes. No touching. There would be no handling of anyone. She opened her eyes, swept to her feet, and crossed the room.

In one smooth motion, she flung open the door. "What do you want?"

Garrett smiled, ignoring the bite in her tone. He had discarded his jacket and stood in his linen shirt, minus cravat. The top buttons gaped open. She stared at the bare expanse of his throat and cursed the leap in her pulse. He looked so casual and unbearably handsome, a curl of black hair falling over his forehead and his gray eyes bright with amusement. Heart thundering, she drank him in, until his smile turned into a frown.

"What? What is it?" she blurted.

"That nightgown is as hideous as the last. Wherever do you get these things? A monastery? I thought we got rid of those, thanks to Henry the Eighth and his lust for Anne Boleyn." He fingered the collar of her gown.

She swatted his hand away and snatched her robe closed, belting it together with irate jerks. "Stop that."

"Forgive me. I suppose *lust* is another one of those unmentionable words on your list. However, if used in a historical reference, doesn't that render it harmless? A passive verb, rather than active." He leaned against the doorframe and crossed his arms over his chest, his expression pensive. "Perhaps you should make a note by those words that can be rendered harmless when used in certain context. Like peaches and apples." His eyes dropped to her breasts.

"Will you stop!" she hissed. "I knew it couldn't last. I just knew it!"

"What couldn't last?" he asked, laughing.

"Your behaving like a gentleman. It's just an act for you, a role to be played for the benefit of Brandon and your sister. And thank you very much for making me look like a complete fool in letting me believe Kit was your mistress."

"I did no such thing," he protested. "You did that all on your own."

"What?" she cried.

"It was you who assumed Kit's nightgown was a castoff from one of my mistresses," he pointed out. "And I did clarify by asking if you referred to the mistress of the house. I might have neglected to explain that Montclair wasn't my home, but that of my sister, who *does* love me. You appeared to have already made up your mind about the matter. Far be it for me to correct your misinterpretation." He shrugged. "I've learned women don't like to be told they are in the wrong." Amusement danced in his eyes.

"They don't like to be humiliated, either. I looked like a fool in front of your sweet, docile, biddable sister." She narrowed her eyes.

"I confess to that one." He grinned. "Kit's about as biddable as an ornery mule. But I was right. She does like you." He beamed at her.

"With no help from you," she retorted. She sounded like a

petulant child. "Look, why are you here? I can't believe it was to insult my nightgown or to remind me that I thought your sister was your mistress."

"You're right, we digress." He leaned forward. "I came to kiss you good night."

She blinked at him. The man was mad. When he moved toward her, she held her hands up. "No, you can't!"

He paused and studied her for a moment. "Fine then," he nodded. "Why don't *you* kiss *me* good night."

"I don't think so," she said, shaking her head. "It would not be wise."

"You're right. One kiss usually leads to another. The next thing you know, we are naked on the ground with your hand on my—"

He got no further. Desperate to shut him up, she leapt up, her arms circling his neck, and planted her mouth firmly on his.

The touch of his lips on her was as explosive as ever, sending a blast of fiery heat through her body. When his arms curled around her waist and crushed her close, her mouth opened under his. He always tasted so good. Rich and masculine. She drank him in like a sweet sherry that whet her taste for more. Damn him for being right. One kiss was not enough. She arched her back, merging her body to his.

She wanted more. So much more.

When his hands slid low to cup her bottom, her senses returned. She pushed him away and stepped back. "Good night." She couldn't suppress her smug smile as a dazed-looking Garrett struggled to compose himself.

He had to clear his throat to respond. "Ah, good night, Alex."

She turned to close the door.

"One last thing."

She peered back at him and raised a brow.

He nodded toward her gown. "Next time, wear your other nightgown. The whisper-thin one with the plunging neckline."

After a speechless moment, she slammed the door in his face.

"Sweet dreams," he called through the door, his laughter following.

She wrenched off her robe and stomped over to the bed. Flinging the garment over the nearest chair, she climbed under the covers, yanking them up to her chin. Sweet dreams indeed. He knew damn well what she would be dreaming about, and the adjectives used to describe them would be far from sweet.

Her body quivering with her unfulfilled desire, she rolled on her side and sighed. It wasn't the adjectives in her dreams she worried about, but rather the proper noun that served as the subject for them.

Garrett Sinclair.

She whispered his name, and it echoed in the silence of the room and filled the empty chambers of her heart.

>=<

THE NEXT MORNING Alex was given a reprieve from the unsettled feelings Garrett evoked. He had taken Brandon to view the hops fields, and under the watchful eyes of one of the maids, the boys had disappeared to visit the kittens in the stables.

Settled in the back gardens with Kit, she kept glancing toward the entrance of the garden. Every sound had her expecting to see Garrett's handsome figure. Annoyed at her behavior, she vowed to forget the man for one damn minute. Difficult, but not impossible.

Kit, despite her bulging stomach, had lowered herself to a blanket on the ground. Wearing a pair of old garden gloves, she was busy rooting out weeds and debris from neglected flower beds. Spring wildflowers covered the grounds in a riotous jumble of colors. The look was chaotic and unkempt compared to most well-tended English gardens, but Alex thought it suited the rustic manor and its compelling owner.

She slipped on the extra pair of gloves Kit had brought for her and knelt. Her gardening skills were on par with her musical talents, but the task was mindless and comforting and the May day was bright and beautiful.

After a pleasant interlude of chatting and gardening, Alex realized that she did not know if Kit was Garrett's step or half sister. She posed the question to Kit, who looked surprised.

"My father married our mother when Garrett was seven, and I arrived a year later. Garrett is my half brother, but he is eight years older than I am."

"But you are very close."

"Of course. When Garrett was home from school, I trailed him like his shadow." Kit laughed ruefully.

"He didn't mind?" Alex asked. "Don't most older brothers find their little sister following them around to be annoying?"

A sheepish look crossed Kit's features. "Truth be told, I was a bit of a wild thing when I was young. I suppose Garrett took me under his wing because no one else would. I went through nursemaids as quickly as Beau outgrows his trousers."

"What about your parents? Where was your mother or father?" She and her mother were very different, but her mother had strived to teach her stronger-willed daughter to be a lady. And her father had glibly joked that she was the one asset he had refused to sell, making her priceless.

"My father wanted nothing to do with me. I was a constant reminder of his failure to sire a son." Kit leaned forward to brush the weeds she had uprooted into a pile.

"No! But didn't he already have a son in Garrett?"

"No, he never did. Garrett is the spitting image of his late father. In my father's eyes that made Garrett like me, another symbol of his failures. You see, Garrett's father had been the love of my mother's life, so Garrett was a constant reminder to my father that he was second choice. Garrett and my father never got along." She sighed. "Garrett tried for a while, but then he stopped. I think he realized that to my father, he would always be another man's child."

"That is sad," Alex murmured.

"No, that's my father, Arthur Brown." Kit wrinkled her nose and yanked out a stubborn weed. "He is not an admirable man, nor a kind one. Once I asked him to open his shirt. Garrett had told me there was a black hole in the place where his heart should be, and I wanted to see it." She gave a rueful smile.

A chill seized Alex at the heartless description. Another thought struck her and she turned to Kit. "But what about your mother?"

"She tried, but the more attention she paid to Garrett, the more it disturbed my father. Forced to take sides, she chose the wrong one. Garrett deserved her; my father didn't."

"That's sacrificing her child for her own happiness." Alex blurted before she could restrain the comment.

"Or sacrificing her child for her marriage." Kit's smile was sad. "My mother needed to be taken care of, and Arthur lived on the neighboring estate. When Garrett's father died, he swept in and took charge." She shrugged. "Garrett was sent away to school, so he couldn't be what my mother needed."

"She couldn't be what *Garrett* needed, and her failure is the greater one," Alex said, her words heated. Aware of her outspoken condemnation of Kit's mother, she turned to apologize, but found Kit smiling at her.

"I don't like to speak ill of the dead, but being a mother myself, I agree. That is why my mother and I were not close. It's difficult to admire someone you don't respect."

Unwittingly, Kit's words mirrored Alex's relationship with her own mother.

Her mother had served as the living embodiment to the adage *love is blind*. In her devotion to Alex's father, she had overlooked his women, debts, and failed investment schemes. She had loved her father for better or worse. Not until death did they part.

Alex vowed to belong to no man but rather to make her own fortunes. Financially secure, she'd never have to marry so no man could cheat on her or gamble with her livelihood, counting on legendary luck to replenish their fortunes. No child of hers would be given a gift of a horse, only to go to ride him and find he had been sold to pay off a debt. Nor should they have to hide their jewelry, for fear of needing to pawn it later to pay the servant's wages.

Alex studied Kit, who was clipping dead heads from a wild rosebush. Her eyes drifted to Kit's stomach, and she frowned. There was one hitch in her plans.

Children.

Her heart twisted. Alone was alone. No kitten-smuggling Beaus or thumb-sucking Wills to brighten her day or her heart. It was a weak point in her plan, for she wanted children. Very much. There also would be no more hot, torrid kisses or tangling sheets with naked men, or one man in particular. She straightened abruptly. "Are you happily married?" Her question had escaped before she realized she had spoken aloud.

Surprised, Kit glanced at her stomach and back up, laughter

dancing in her eyes. "I should hope so. No turning back now." She laughed. "And what about you and my brother?"

Alex stiffened. "Nothing, there is nothing between us."

"That kiss didn't look like nothing to me."

Alex's face heated, and she glanced away from the teasing light in Kit's eyes. She had forgotten about Kit seeing them. She jumped when she felt a hand on her arm.

Kit's expression was apologetic. "I'm sorry. I'm too outspoken at times. Bran reminds me of it often enough. It is just that since Garrett's return from the Crimea, he . . . Well, when he returned, he wasn't the same. He—"

"I know." Alex covered Kit's hand with her own and gave it a gentle squeeze. "I understand."

"Well, there haven't been any women since his return. Not that I condoned his chasing every silly skirt that twitched, but I understood it was another one of his ploys to drive my father mad." Her eyes lifted to Alex's. "What I mean to say is, he looks the best I've seen since his return, and I don't think the country air is responsible for his improvement."

She smiled at Kit. How could she not? She had wanted to help Garrett and hearing she had warmed her heart. It was what she had hoped to do for him. All she could do for him.

She sat back on her heels and mulled over Kit's words about Garrett's women being mere pawns in his feud with his father. And Garrett had had no women since his return from the war. No women before *her*.

She pressed her hand to her heart, feeling it pound beneath her palm. There was an irony in this, and the bitterness of it sliced clear through her. She had fought her feelings for Garrett, thinking him not worthy of them and believing him not free to receive them. Now when she feared she was losing her battle, the point was irrelevant. Gus's arrival reminded her of this, bringing her past back with him.

It had never mattered whether Garrett was free or not.

It had never mattered, because she wasn't free.

While Alex Daniels might be able to follow the yearnings of her heart, Alexandra Langdon could not.

Thanks to her uncle, Alex Langdon could never be free.

Chapter Twenty-two

❧❦

G ARRETT tossed his quill pen down and leaned back in his chair. This was absurd. He should be courting Alexandra, not locked in his office staring at a list of over three hundred names. But Kit was right. While they were safe at Charlton Manor, they couldn't hole up here forever.

And there could be no wedding bells if he was dead.

However, Brandon was wrong about one thing. He hadn't been without recourses here. He had sent two of his own men into the city to see what they could ferret out about the attacks on his carriage. Since Peel's policemen had discovered nothing, Garrett had decided it was time to employ a different caliber of investigator.

Alex had said the man who was disguised as one of Hammond's footmen spoke with an East End dialect. Garrett needed someone who knew that area, one of their ilk to question their own. His men were former East Enders, grew up around the rookeries. They knew the back alleys and hidden haunts of pawnbrokers, thieves, and murderers. They spoke their language and would know whose palms to grease to extract information. They would track down this man and root him out like the rat he was.

They would also find out what the hell had been tossed for final payment at Hammond's. Odds are it rested in some pawnbroker's hands by now. Once located, it could be linked back to the assassin, and this payment rendered would provide further evidence to implicate the man.

They would catch the bastard. It was just a matter of time. By reviewing Hammond's guest list, the list holding his killer's name, Garrett hoped to cut this time short.

Newly resolved, he straightened, leaned forward, and returned to the task.

A while later, he paused on one of the names—Mr. Alex Daniels. He grinned, intrigued as to how Alex had finagled an invitation to one of the most exclusive balls of the Season for a man who didn't exist. Another puzzle, but he was finding he enjoyed unraveling them more than he thought.

He gave his head a sharp shake. *Focus.*

Brandon had jotted down notes beside a few who might harbor motives for his murder. He reminded Garrett that he had mistaken Lady Weatherbee's pint-size poodle for a hairy hand muff and sat on him. Garrett had asked Lord Ashton if he was playing Puck in *A Midsummer Night's Dream*. Garrett snorted, for the man had looked like a bloody fairy in his puce-colored jacket and lime green shirt.

Brandon went on to recount Garrett's planned tryst with Lady Brisbane in her gardens at midnight. Garrett had never appeared. The irate lady had blamed him for her having caught a chill waiting all night in the altogether.

Garrett blew out a breath and rubbed his face. Enough. He knew he had been an ass because it had amused him to be so, aware that stories of his behavior would be repeated to his stepfather. But that was before the war.

Before Alexandra.

While thoughts of Alex usually improved his mood, he found his disposition souring. And he knew why.

It was the damn courtship.

It was a failure.

Why? *Three kisses.* Three kisses in three days. It was a

paltry showing for a man with his history. And the third one didn't count, for he had held Will in his arms.

He felt like a powder keg ready to explode. If the assassin didn't kill him, Alex would. He shoved his chair back, circled his desk, and stormed down the hall. He marched into the living room where Kit sat on the settee, knitting, and Brandon stood by the mantel, Garrett's interruption cutting short their conversation.

"It's not working. She's more interested in the children than me unless I'm kissing her. How the hell can I kiss her with the boys always underfoot? I need to be alone with Alex and properly seduce her. Then I will kiss her senseless, ask her to marry me, and get all this dithering over with."

"Dithering?" Brandon cocked a brow, amused.

"I believe he means indecision," Kit said. "Garrett, my love, stop thinking about kisses and concentrate on enjoying Alex's company." She brandished her knitting needle. "Focus on courtship, not seduction."

Garrett stared at her as if she were mad. His patience snapped. "What the hell do you think I've been doing for the past week?" He swiped his hands through his hair. "With most women, all it takes is a pretty bauble, some poetic dribble, and a bit of flirtation, right?

"Well, I—"

"Don't stop him," Brandon interceded. "This could be good."

"You listen to them prattle on about their newest bonnet or Lady What's-her-name's garden party, and congratulate her friend on some forgettable piece she's pounded out on the piano. But not with Alex." Garrett sliced his hand through the air. "The woman is an anomaly. She's a puzzle, and you know how I feel about puzzles."

"I do," Brandon said. "Bane of his existence." He winked at Kit.

"You don't understand," Garrett said. "She collects biscuits, for God's sake."

"Biscuits?" Brandon looked confused.

"Biscuits," Garrett repeated. "Hides them in her skirt pocket like a damn squirrel storing nuts for winter." He paced the room. "Her father's estate manager took her under his wing, explaining the running of the property, so she peppers me with questions about mine. And she can't sing or play the piano. She is polite but keeps a safe distance from me while she jabbers on to Beau and Will.

"She doesn't want to be alone with me. And I know why. She knows if I get her alone, I'll kiss her, and she'll stop her infernal thinking and respond like a normal woman for once. Well . . ." He froze and his eyes whipped to his sister.

"Well, indeed." Kit smiled.

Heat rushed to his face and he shot a daggered glare at Brandon, whose eyes danced with laughter. He dropped onto the settee beside Kit and cradled his head in his hands. "Fine, go ahead. Laugh. I'm not deaf. I hear myself. I sound like the court jester, here to amuse your peasant husband."

He felt a hand on his shoulder. "What you are my obtuse brother, is a man who has fallen in love but is too stupid to realize it. And you wouldn't be the first."

He lifted a brow. "So I'm stupid rather than the court jester?"

"You're the fool," Brandon said. "The one who wears the pointed dunce cap and sits in the corner."

"Explain to me again why you married him?"

"It was a weak moment," Kit said, brushing a lock of Garrett's hair back.

"Warn me when you have another one. I—" He stopped cold, staring at Kit. "Wait a minute. I never said anything about falling in love. I was babbling—"

"About how painful it is to be madly in love with someone and not sure that your feelings are reciprocated," Kit said. "I know the feeling, suffered it for years until Brandon came to his senses after I told him I was marrying Ned."

"Well, I couldn't let you make a misery of your life, now could I?" Brandon winked at Kit, who laughed.

"Maybe I should tell her I'm marrying Keyes's daughter," Garrett muttered bleakly. He stood and crossed the room to stare out the window. Kit's words could not be ignored.

He had convinced himself marrying Alex was a practical decision because he wanted her like he wanted no other woman. She had awakened a part of him he had thought had died with so many others on the blood-soaked battlefield at

Balaclava. He was scarred and broken, but she made him feel whole.

Kit was right.

He was madly, irrevocably in love with Alex.

He had started falling from the first moment she had opened her eyes and demanded her clothes. He had recognized her intelligence when she derided the London fops as supercilious imbeciles. He had admired her practicality when she agreed to their unusual collaboration. But he hadn't known she was his until he kissed her. She had touched him as no other, and her response to him had sealed his fate.

She was perfect. And he was keeping her.

"And Garrett, whatever you're doing, it is working," Kit added.

Surprised, he turned to look at his sister.

"You're playing to all her weaknesses," she explained.

He frowned. "Considering I have no idea what they are, I'll have to trust you on that. Perhaps if you enlightened me I can sharpen my tactics. Speed matters up."

"Good point." Brandon turned to his wife, his brows furrowed. "What are they?"

Kit tossed up her hands. "Children, you idiots. She adores the boys. Seeing you with them is enough to weaken any woman's resolve. And she can't stop looking at you, so you are doing something right."

Children. He hadn't considered that. It made sense. Alex wouldn't get attached to a pricey gift when she had watched them all disappear to pay her father's debt. But children, children were permanent. He had wanted children, but never considered he'd have any after his return from the Crimea. Now with Alex, things were different. By God, he'd give her a whole brood of them. His eyes strayed to Kit's bulging belly, and he swallowed. Perhaps a few would do, for they did stick to you like burrs until they grew their own roots.

"You're right." He made to leave the room, when another thought gave him pause. He faced Kit as uncertainty filled him. "Do you think . . . do you think she loves me, too?"

"Oh, Garrett, how can she not?" Kit shoved herself to her feet, crossed the room and yanked his head down to kiss him on the cheek. "I do."

He grinned. "I love you, too."

"Don't look at me," Brandon drawled. "I only tolerate you because you've been useful in extricating me from a scrape or two."

"The feeling is mutual," Garrett said. "I'll make you god-father to our firstborn. Don't push him into the lake until *after* you teach him to swim." He left the room, grinning as Brandon's retort carried to him.

"What? No kiss for me? That was years ago! You need to get over it. And how was I to know you would sink like a rock?"

≫≪

THE FOLLOWING AFTERNOON, Alex found herself walking beside Garrett to the barn. Her eyes drifted to him as he held Will in his arms and strolled with long, sure strides. He wore a blue tailored suit and his lethal smile, the one that wreaked havoc with her pulse rate. When those gray eyes fastened on her, she sought to convince herself that he was less dangerous than the seamstress who had arrived early that morning to tailor Kit's gowns to Alex's figure. She had suffered through the woman's poking, prodding, and pinning for hours.

While the gowns were exquisite, Alex was wary of this plan's success. More so, for the first time in a year, her fears weren't for herself or her uncle's reprisals. Her heart thundered as she thought of Garrett leaving the safety of the manor and stepping back into the killer's path. Kit had promised to see about getting proper chaperonage and protection for him. However, after her loss at Hammond's, Alex was hesitant to wager on the success of this venture when once again, the odds seemed stacked against them.

However, it was the best idea they had at the moment. Once the dresses were altered, they would return to town and wager on its success. Garrett had saved her from her debacle; she vowed to do the best she could to return the favor for him. She swallowed, refusing to contemplate the cost of failure.

Forcing her thoughts away from this dark cloud that hovered at the periphery of her mind, she turned to happier memories of the past few days.

She recalled Garrett's attempts at seduction. The memory alone stirred her desire. He was clever. Like an expert crafts-man, he whittled his way through all her defenses.

No surprise there, for the man had been a soldier, and he knew how to fight for what he wanted.

He wanted her.

She was under siege.

Worse, she wanted nothing more than to wave a white flag and surrender.

More disturbing thoughts.

Frowning, she sought another distraction and her eyes locked on Will, who had located Garrett's pocket watch, the item having become a coveted toy. She watched his face screw up while he worked to snap open its cover. Beaming in delight when he triumphed, he showed Garrett his success, snapped the cover closed, and worked to open it again. Each triumph brought that look of pure, childish pleasure to his face.

Alex wondered if anyone had ever praised Garrett's childish triumphs. He'd had his father for the first six years, but six was still a baby. At least he hadn't been alone. He'd had Kit, and then Brandon. The thought gave her comfort and she smiled. "Kit said she was your shadow when you were young?"

Garrett glanced over at her and grinned. "Only until I brought Brandon home. Then she only had eyes for him. No loyalty." He shook his head. "I remember when Brandon first met her. She had run away from home and had succeeded in disappearing for a few hours until we tracked her down."

"She must have had a good hiding place. Wherever did you find her?"

"Up a tree," he said, laughing at her expression.

"Did you climb up after her?"

"Unfortunately," he muttered. "The branch holding her couldn't support both our weight, so it snapped and down we tumbled. Damned near broke my neck."

She covered her mouth to hide her smile. "But you were both all right?"

"Brandon caught Kit, which started her tailspin into starry-eyed hero worship. One of these days, she's going to wake up and realize it was the shock of the fall that addled her wits for all these years."

"A man can dream," she said. "And you? Were you all right?"

He shrugged. "The break healed after two months of being

trussed up like a turkey, but my left arm still doesn't bend all the way. Perhaps you can look at it later? You did such a fine job with my scratch."

"It's a little late for bandaging."

"Who said anything about bandaging? I was hoping you'd kiss it and make it better."

"And shock poor Will here?"

"You're right." His eyes locked with hers. "Our kisses are combustible. We'll wait for Beau to chaperone us. With his thick hide, he'd get singed, but I doubt he'd burn."

Seeing the teasing gleam in his eyes, she laughed.

A gentle breeze brushed over her, and she lifted her hand to brush a lock of hair from her cheek. She had forgotten her bonnet on the bench in the garden, so instead of a hat, along with her sun-warmed cheeks, she wore a pink rose that Garrett had plucked from the garden and tucked behind her ear. The gift touched her as no priceless gem ever could. It was far better than his earlier offer of a horse. She smiled, the rose and her present company lightening her troubled thoughts and her heart.

Nearing the barn and excited to see the kittens, Will squirmed for release. In his distraction, he lost his grip on Garrett's pocket watch, and it tumbled to the ground.

Alex bent to retrieve it. When she picked it up, she noticed an engraving on the back cover. *To Arthur, love Garrett.* She caught her breath and looked to Garrett, who was watching Will toddle toward the barn.

When his attention returned to her, his smile froze. "What is it?" His gaze dropped to her hand and his mouth pressed into a firm line. He removed the watch from her grasp and casually returned it to his jacket pocket. "Shall we catch up with Will?"

She fell into step beside him, struggling to hold her silence and respect his privacy.

The hell with it.

"I understand it's none of my business, but I was curious as to why you carry around a watch that is a gift from yourself to your stepfather. Did he return it to you?"

"No. I won it from the footman in a game of cards. As you know, I'm good at cards." He winked at her. "I had purchased it with my last winnings."

She shook her head, baffled. "And the footman, did he win it from your stepfather in a game of cards?" She tried to match his light tone, well aware she ventured onto dodgy ground.

"No. I believe it was given to him as thanks for polishing a pair of boots."

Alex stopped. "Garrett?" He paused at her rare use of his name. "Why do you carry this watch around with you like a treasured keepsake?"

Garrett cocked an eyebrow. "Treasured keepsake? No. It's a reminder."

She tossed up her hands. "What can it possibly remind you of that it warrants a special place on your person when it didn't merit any consideration by the very person to whom it was gifted? He couldn't even deign to keep it!"

"That's exactly what it is a reminder of." His voice became cold and his eyes hard. "That my stepfather is an ass, and I was an idiot to think otherwise." He located Will and watched as Gus emerged from the barn to collect the boy. He waited until they had disappeared inside before he spoke again. "It took me months to save up to buy that bloody watch. Months! I fought to master the cards. At first I lost more than I ever won, including the shirt off my back, for I was too young to be playing, was but a few years older than Beau is now. But I did it. I learned so well that it ceased to matter that no one remembered to send my allowance to school. To remember me, period. I didn't need it or them.

"But I shouldn't have had to learn. I shouldn't have had to buy anyone's favors, especially those of a cold-hearted bastard whose affections should have been freely given. He was my stepfather, but I was never his son. I was nothing to him. This bloody watch reminds me of what kind of man Arthur Brown is. It was a hard lesson to learn, but you can be damn sure I'll never forget it." He spun away from her and stormed into the barn, not looking back.

Alex wrapped her arms around her waist. She yearned to turn back time and gather that brave, lost little boy into her arms. A parent's rejection digs deep wounds, and she had just poured salt over Garrett's. She should have left it alone.

She ached to steal that damn watch and pulverize it with the heel of her boot. Half of her understood Garrett's reasons for keeping it, the other half viewed it as more salt being crushed into raw heartbreak. She remembered the scar traversing Garrett's abdomen and wondered how many blows a man could sustain before he broke. Garrett believed himself broken, but he was not.

He was a survivor.

She lifted a hand to shade her eyes, seeing Gus emerge from the barn. She met him outside.

"That Beau, he's got the makings of a top rider," Gus boasted, thrusting out his belly as he hooked his thumbs in his trousers.

Smiling, Alex looped her arm through his as they walked. "Under your tutelage he can't be anything but. Look at me."

Gus snorted and tipped his head toward the barn. "The captain has a fine seat as well. Handles the reins like he was born to them. Then again, he's a take-charge sort of bloke. Look what he has done in the hops fields. Blimey, I ain't seen nothin' like it." His bark of a voice softened. "He's a decent bloke, your captain."

Alex opened her mouth to protest his use of the possessive before Captain, but then closed it. He only stated what her heart already knew. Garrett wasn't hers, but she wished it otherwise.

Garrett was a decent bloke, and she was head-over-heels in love with him.

Despite her valiant attempts to draft a growing list of Garrett's faults, she had worked in vain. She had dismissed Garrett as a philandering rake, with his mistress and dispensable women. She had believed him a gambler who had stolen her fortune, another member of the spoiled aristocracy who cared little for the welfare of others.

She had wanted to believe these things of Garrett because it made him into a man like her father, a man whom she could not respect. More important, one she could dismiss and forget. Garrett used his watch to remind him that his stepfather was not the man he wished him to be, and she had drafted her list to protect herself from seeing Garrett for the man he was. This had enabled her to ignore the inexorable tug of her heart toward this brave, wounded, enigmatic man. She blinked at the moisture filming her eyes. She had been a fool and a coward, but no more.

It was time to lift that white flag and surrender.

She lifted her face to the afternoon sun. She may not have forever with him, but she could enjoy today. She remembered Garrett's words about dealing with his nightmares.

Let it be enough for now.

She turned to smile at Gus. "Yes, he is a decent bloke, and so are you." She stood on her tiptoes and kissed his cheek.

Chapter Twenty-three

❦

Aᴼᴳᴬᴵ after checking on Will with the kittens, Garrett went to locate Beau. He found his nephew set up in an empty stall beside his pony. Beau had cleared the straw from a space on the ground and lined up a battalion of his toy soldiers. Kneeling before them, Beau recited aloud.

"Cannon to right of them, Cannon to left of them, Cannon in front of them. Volley'd and thunder'd; Storm'd at with shot and shell."

A roaring exploded in Garrett's head, and he lifted his hand to grip the stall's railing.

He'd be all right. He just needed a minute.

He closed his eyes against the images assaulting him, giving his head a hard shake to shrug them loose.

He had been caught off guard. Alex's questions about Arthur's bloody watch had thrown him off balance.

Arthur and now this.

Bloody hell. The walls of the barn were closing in on him. He needed air. He shoved away from the stall and staggered out the back exit, trying to put distance between himself and the darkness reaching for him. He had come so far. He would not retreat.

He drew a deep breath and released it, recalling another veteran's advice on the calming effects of doing so. The roaring in his ears receded, and he lifted his eyes to drink in his surroundings. The warmth of the breeze and what remained of the afternoon's waning light soothed him.

His breathing regulated.

He felt his shoulders loosen, and his tension gradually eased.

≳≪

ALEX LOCATED WILL with the kittens and Beau with his soldiers, but no Garrett. She turned to Gus, who shrugged at her unspoken question. She moved to join Beau but froze when fragments of Tennyson's poem drifted to her.

"*They that had fought so well came through the jaws of Death, back from the mouth of Hell.*"

Had Garrett heard?

She spun around, a sense of urgency propelling her search. Finding the last stall empty, she stepped outside and shaded her eyes to scan the paddocks. Garrett stood at the farthest end of the field. His hands were thrust into his trouser pockets, his head tipped back, and the wind combed through his hair. He looked so alone, like the lost boy he had once been, and her heart pinched at the sight.

She hurried toward him but stopped a few yards away, unsure of her approach. Unsure of him. "Garrett?"

"Did you know Lord Raglan had never commanded men in battle?" He spoke with his back to her.

Lord Raglan was the commander of the British army in the Crimea. "No, I didn't."

He turned to her. "He saw action, serving as an aide to Wellington for forty years, but he never commanded men in battle. Most of the officers in the Crimea had no battle experience or training. They knew nothing of military tactics, strategy, or organization. When Raglan landed in the Crimea, he didn't even own a map of the peninsula." He paused and his gaze roamed over the horses grazing inside the fence.

Alex stepped closer as he continued speaking. His voice was quiet.

"There were more qualified men to lead, career soldiers who had served in India, but they weren't given command because they weren't of aristocratic birth." His attention returned to her and his smile was like his words, bitter and rueful. "The English aristocracy believe bravery and chivalry are the only qualities needed to lead men in battle. Through our blood, our noble birth, we possess the innate ability to command."

He snorted. "I knew damn well my birth wasn't providing me with any courage or leadership, and I knew if I wanted to live, I had best listen to my men with military experience. In those early days, I wanted to live. I was responsible for the lives of the men under my command." He crossed to the fence.

"It took me a while to gain my men's trust and eventually respect, but by God I fought to do so. If I was leading them into battle, I wanted to make damn sure I was worthy to do so and not from the rights garnered through the purchase of my commission, but by rights of my own merit.

"But it didn't matter what I did or any of the junior officers did because they placed Lord Lucan and his brother-in-law Lord Cardigan in charge of the cavalry brigades, and our fates were sealed."

Alex moved to stand beside him, wanting to reach out and touch him, to offer comfort, but he held himself with such a detached stillness that it frightened her. She feared that like fragile glass, he might shatter if she stepped too close. So she did what she had done time and again for each of the wounded men who had been under her care. She listened. It was all she could do.

The wind whistling through the trees was the only noise to break the silence. After a few minutes, he continued. "To say my horse had more intelligence than Lucan and Cardigan combined is an insult to Champion. But they were placed in command of two cavalry battalions, a total of twelve hundred men. I served under Cardigan in the Seventeenth Lancers. Neither possessed much battlefield experience or any training but they were *earls*. If that's not perverse enough, they detested each other, fought like rabid dogs, and more often than not, weren't on speaking terms."

He wiped a hand down his face. "Lucan didn't know the proper military commands to lead our men, while Cardigan held nothing but contempt for those who earned a living as a career soldier. His men suffered in horrific camp conditions, while he slept on his yacht with a French cook on board. My men called Lucan the 'cautious ass' for his inability to commit his troops to battle, while Cardigan was the 'dangerous ass' because he'd commit his men under any circumstances."

His voice became harsher. "By God they lived up to their names. Cardigan sent more than six hundred men riding to certain death in the wrong direction because he and Lucan were too arrogant to clarify Raglan's orders or ask a subordinate to do so. Afterward, Cardigan retired to his yacht to have a champagne dinner. Lucan provided no backup to the charge, and whether it was due to his enmity toward his brother-in-law or not, we'll never know."

Silence fell again, the only sound the furious pounding of Alex's heart. Garrett turned his back on the horses and faced her, and she bit her lip at the despair in his expression.

"The guns Raglan wanted captured to prevent them falling into the hands of the Russians weren't at the farthest end of the North Valley, but on the left side of Causeway Heights. Lucan and Cardigan argued about the order, but neither man deigned to ask Captain Nolan, Raglan's quartermaster general who had delivered it, to clarify which guns Raglan meant. You see, Nolan was one of the men Lucan and Cardigan scorned for earning a living as a professional soldier.

"So blind, unmitigated arrogance sent over six hundred men and horses on that suicidal charge. The Russians had a battery of guns at the end of the valley before us with batteries and riflemen flanking both our sides. If you survived the three-fronted barrage, you then had to turn around and ride back to our lines. One hundred forty-seven of my men rode into battle, thirty-eight made roll call the next day."

Garrett took a deep breath and blew it out; he lifted his eyes to the distant horizon as if he could no longer meet her gaze. "I saw a horse carry one of my men's headless body down the length of the valley and back. I went to assist another of my wounded men, but he lost his seat and like so many others, tumbled to his death in the stampede of riders coming from behind.

"My men rode with arms and legs being shot off until they

fell to their deaths. Others used their swords like a sickle to carve a path through our own soldiers in their flight."

Alex struggled to suppress her horror, knowing he needed to get it all out.

"In the midst of that madness, I no longer cared about living because I thought I had already died and gone to hell. I don't remember my injury or Champion carrying me back to our lines. I awoke in Havers's care, and later Brandon arrived and transported me home."

Alex yearned to wrap her arms around him, but seeing him swallow as he fought for control, she held back. She understood he needed to unleash these festering memories. She had heard similar tales from the soldiers, and the *London Gazette* had published Raglan's dispatches as well as his blame of Lord Lucan for the whole debacle. But it did not compare to witnessing the raw pain the story in all its horror inflicted on Garrett.

He rubbed his forehead, dropped his hand, and continued in a resigned voice. "Do you know Cardigan's main concern after the battle was not over the bloody carnage or the loss of his men but to lodge a complaint against Nolan for trying to ride in front of him? Nolan had ridden out in vain, brandishing his sword toward the correct guns we were to take, but we were already under siege and he was killed."

He looked at her then, his features haunted. "The charge down the valley and back took less than twenty minutes. But for every man who participated, it will never be over because each one of us has to live with the question of our survival. They were my men, and I couldn't save them, so why did *I* live?" He lifted his arms as in supplication, then dropped them to his side and straightened.

"That question hangs over me like a guillotine, and I'll never escape it because every breath I draw serves to remind me. And so I drank. I drank not just to forget the carnage, but to forget I lived when so many other men under my care had died." He turned and walked away, wiping unsteady hands down his trousers legs.

His body was strung so taut Alex feared a strong breeze could snap him in two. Garrett's words had chilled her to the bone, the horror of them, of what he had carried all these months. Of the guilt he wore like the Grim Reaper's bloody cloak of death.

But he was wrong.

By God, she'd be damned if she would let this wretched battle continue to bleed him. Unlike Garrett, she spoke distinctly, hoping her words would reach him.

"I can answer that," she said, struggling to suppress the tears that choked her. She waited until he turned to face her before she went on. "I know damn well why you lived. For them." She gestured to the hops fields. "For Stewart and Gus and every single one of those wounded men who would have no place to go if not for you. For those veterans who gave everything to England but received nothing in return. You stand for them. Had you died, where would they be? And for Kit and Brandon. You are the only family they have.

"You couldn't save your men, but you didn't kill them. Their fate was sealed when the English nobility chose blood lineage over military competence and put Cardigan and Lucan in commands they never should have held. You listened to your men, provided for them out of your own pocket, and rode beside them into hell. They could ask no more of you.

"There are horrors from that day that will never be forgotten, but time should dull some of the sharper edges of their pain. You need no longer question your right to survive. You survived because it was meant to be."

Finished, she drew a deep breath and saw he watched her silently, his hands thrust into his trouser pockets, his eyes dark and troubled.

She waited for him to respond, not certain he would. He studied her in that heart-wrenchingly familiar silence of his. She didn't believe her words would miraculously heal him; she wasn't that naïve. She simply hoped for them to begin chipping away at the guilt-ridden fortress he had locked himself inside.

She wished he would stop standing there and *do* something.

"So it wasn't my time?" He cocked a brow at her, a strange light in his eyes.

"No, it damn well wasn't," she exclaimed and then nearly slapped her hand to her mouth. "I mean—"

"I understand."

She blinked when she saw the barest hint of a smile. Her heart took flight. "Well, then."

"Well, then," he echoed. He stared out past the paddock fences toward the distant hops fields. "I think I'll take a walk and mull that over."

"I will come with you." She refused to leave him alone with those horrid images.

"No." He held up his hand. "Thank you, but I'm all right. I need to walk some things off alone. Can you take the boys up to the house so Kit won't worry?"

"Are you sure? I can—"

"I'm sure. Really. I'm all right. Or, thanks in part to you, I will be."

His smile was slow and gentle and twined around her heart. Undecided, she gnawed on her lower lip. If he wanted to walk and think, well, she'd give him something to think about.

Before he turned to go, she raced over to him, jumped up, and flung her arms around his neck. She planted her mouth on his and kissed him with all the desire he ignited within her. She kissed him as he had taught her. Thoroughly. Deeply. Expertly. Her heart pounded fit to burst and her pulse rate skipped. And still she kissed him. She threaded her fingers into his hair and arched her body into his.

After he recovered from his surprise, a groan escaped him and his arms snaked around her like welcomed steel bands. They molded her close, lifting her feet off the ground as he met her ardor with his own.

She moaned as the familiar heat spiraled through her. Damn, but the man knew how to kiss. He wasn't completely broken. Parts of him were very much alive.

A long while later, she broke off the kiss and loosened her grip so she slid to her feet and stepped away. She smiled smugly at his expression. His hair was mussed and his eyes dazed. He held up his hands as if he didn't know what to do without her in his arms.

Good.

"I thought you needed something else to think about." She spun away. "Enjoy your walk."

She had almost reached the barn but couldn't resist the urge to turn back. He stood where she had left him, a bemused expression on his face. Tall, heart-stoppingly handsome, and staring at her as if he waited for something.

It took all her willpower to not race back, fling herself into his arms, and whisper what her heart had answered when he asked why he had survived.

For me.

Chapter Twenty-four

❧❦

LATER that evening, Alex paced a hole in her bedroom carpet.

Where the hell was he?

Damn him. He might have escaped the valley of death and two attacks on his life, but he would not survive her wrath. Garrett had never returned for dinner. Kit and Brandon kept the conversation going, but the strain of his absence had stretched taut.

She understood Garrett had things to think about and he carried baggage no man should have to tote, but damn it, he was not alone. He needed to toss off some of those burdens from his arrogant shoulders and let others help.

She didn't know how a man could be strong yet at the same time be cobbled together by so many broken pieces that given a good shove, he'd fall apart. And she had shoved him today. Pushed him to change his perspective. Sometimes a person stood in the same place for so long, they were blind to any other views. Garrett had been rotting in place. No, she didn't regret uprooting him. She just wanted to assure herself that he was able to pick up his broken pieces and string them back together much stronger.

To make sure he was whole.

She gnawed on her lower lip as her eyes strayed to the wall clock. It was nearing midnight.

Where the hell could he be?

A noise caused her to jump and she stared at the door separating their chambers. She heard a bang, and her breath caught. After a moment, flickering light seeped under the door.

Was he all right? Was he sober? Unbidden the question rose, but she squelched the thought. He had said his drinking had not helped him to forget. She had to trust that he spoke true.

It was late and she should retire. Her eyes drifted to her bed and back to the glow of light beneath the door. She would wait for Garrett to do so. Time dragged on and yet the light beckoned her close, like a moth to fire.

Her feet moved of their own volition to the door. She wasn't thinking straight, but Garrett's husky words from ages ago resonated in the silence.

Sometimes not thinking is good. Sometimes things are best felt.

Her heart thundered, a wealth of feelings assaulting her. Concern. Desire. Need. Heat cascaded through her body and she closed her eyes. After a beat, she opened them and lifted her chin.

By God, after this afternoon she was done thinking.

Light was the sign she needed, not darkness. It meant Garrett remained awake. And alone. And thinking when he shouldn't be.

Today she had admitted her love for him. Tonight she refused to hide from it. Nothing mattered but that Garrett needed her.

Her hand closed over the doorknob and she drew a deep breath. She opened the door.

The room was bathed in dim candlelight. After her eyes adjusted to the ambience, she located Garrett lying in bed. His covers were draped over his waist, his chest bare, his eyes open and fastened on hers. The candlelight cast alluring shadows over him and her breathing became shallow. He didn't move, and that patient stillness that so defined him excited her. It was too dark to gauge his expression, but not dark enough to dull the impact of those steel gray eyes.

This heady rush must be what Garrett had felt before he'd ridden into battle. The warring emotions of excitement and fear. Like Garrett, she refused to retreat, but there would be no fight, for she planned to surrender everything.

She glided across the carpet as her hands lifted to her night-gown. She wore no robe, had no need of one. Stopping, she undid the buttons to the front of her gown and when it gaped open, she gave a shrug and let it fall from her shoulders to pool at her feet. For the moment, she simply stood there, feeling Garrett's eyes sweep over her naked body like a warm caress. A shiver swept through her.

Garrett lifted the covers in silent invitation, moving over to make room for her.

She stepped forward and slid into the welcoming warmth. A gasp escaped her, for she had anticipated him gently drawing her close, but there was nothing gentle about Garrett's reaction. Before she could digest the shock of his beautiful body, long, lithe, and bare beneath the sheets, he crushed her to him and his mouth captured hers, hard and demanding. She arched against him, her tongue tangling with his in an erotic dance. Teasing and tasting.

Thinking was the first thing she surrendered.

He pulled back to draw breath, and his gaze, heavy-lidded and smoldering, met hers.

She swallowed. "You're beautiful." Her words escaped her in a breathless murmur. His lips curved in that lethal smile that pierced her heart, had done so since he had first wielded it.

"That's my line for you," he whispered and captured a long strand of her hair and watched as it slid through his fingers. "When you left the card table at Hammond's, I told myself not to follow you. To let you go and perhaps learn from your loss." His eyes met hers. "Thank God, I didn't listen."

She ran her thumb along his bottom lip, soft and full. "At the time, I wished you had. You thought I was a spoiled, irre-sponsible boy! And you were quite horrible, swearing at me and shoving me toward the window."

"Perhaps I should make amends for my boorish behavior.

After all, I have since learned the error of my judgment." She drew in her breath as his hand slid down to cup a full breast. "No boy here."

"Very perceptive of you," she said dryly. "But about making those amends for your boorish behavior . . . I rather like that idea. How do you propose to do so?"

He grinned. "Did you have something in mind?"

"I can think of something. Why don't you place yourself in my hands, and I will tell you what I'd like you to do." She leaned over and kissed him quite thoroughly, her tongue dancing and parrying with his.

When she drew back, she was pleased to see his gaze was unfocused and he had to blink to clear it. She dropped her voice to a husky murmur. "That is . . . ah . . . that is until it gets to a point where I need *you* to tell *me* what to do." His eyes flared, but when he leaned forward to kiss her again, she planted her hand on his chest to stop him. "After all, you've also said that you could teach me things when we knew each other better."

"I, ah . . ." He had to clear his throat before he could continue, "I did, didn't I?"

"Yes, you did," she confirmed.

"Well, then." He again caught a lock of her hair, and winding it around his fist, he drew her close. "Perhaps you should put yourself entirely in *my hands*." Releasing her hair, he slid his hands down to cup her breasts as she leaned over him, his thumbs brushing over heightened peaks.

"Perhaps that might be a better idea." She gasped. After all, he did have fabulous hands, rough and calloused from his years in the cavalry. They kneaded and molded her breasts, and she squirmed in response. Her groans were swallowed up when his mouth plundered hers, kissing her senseless. He caressed her ribs and the curve of her hips, raising a trail of goose bumps along her flesh. When his hands squeezed her thighs, she drew back to gasp for breath. A soldier knew how to strategically stake out his ground, and Garrett did so with a finesse that left her panting. She collapsed on the bed beside him.

Her body was the second thing she surrendered.

"You need to tell me if I do anything you don't like. More

important, you need to tell me what you *do* like, what you want."

In the back recesses of what was left of her mind, she heard Garrett speaking. However, as he spoke, his mouth trailed molten kisses down the nape of her neck and distracted her, his breath hot and moist on her flushed skin. His lips drew a pliant peak into his mouth and she arched her back as his tongue lavished her breasts. She moaned out loud, her breathing quickened. Shivers spiraled down her body, bringing to life yearnings she had never felt before.

It was as if he had opened her private Pandora's box and instead of curiosity, he unleashed more volatile emotions. *Passion. Desire. Lust.*

Feeling was good.

"Alex?"

She shook her head, unable to respond. She couldn't think, only feel.

"Alex?"

"What? What is it?" She blinked up at Garrett, nearly crying out in protest at the absence of his hands on her body. Gradually, she realized he was sitting up and the candlelight bathed him in a flickering halo of light. His hair was disheveled, his chest bronzed and beautiful before her, and she reached out, needing to touch his warm skin, but he caught her hand in his and kissed each of her fingers and then her palm.

"I want you, Alex."

He could have her. If he would just stop talking and continue to touch her like he had been, she would give him anything he wanted. Her body was a tightly coiled spring, ready to snap.

"What do you want?"

"What?" Her heart raced as she watched Garrett smile at her.

He leaned down and pressed his mouth to her temple in a featherlight kiss. "I want to know what you want." He moved to her cheeks, his lips skimming her flushed skin with gentle kisses. "What you need." His mouth hovered near her ear. "I want to hear you say it." His tone was husky and the whisper of his breath brushed her feverishly hot skin.

"Say what?" She gasped, closing her eyes and lifting her chin as his lips nuzzled the curve of her neck and the now-skipping beat of her pulse.

His laugh was low and husky, sending shivers down her spine. "Do you want me to touch you here?" His hands spread out over her shoulders and down her arms. "Or here?" He cupped her breasts, his thumb drawing delicious, provocative circles around her nipples.

"Garrett," she breathed.

"So you like this?"

Her eyes flew open and seeing the smoldering intensity in his eyes, her languid, dazed delirium gradually cleared. He was teasing her, taunting her, knowing exactly what she liked. What she wanted and how she wanted it. After all, he was a rake.

Well, two could play at this game.

She might not know all the rules, but Garrett had taught her some and she had always been a fast learner. Emitting an almost feline purr, she sat up and twined her arms around Garrett's neck. She touched her lips to his ear and dropped her voice to a low, sultry tone. "Do you want to know what I really want? What I really need?"

"Ah . . ." Garrett cleared his throat. "Yes."

She felt her cheeks burn at her daring, but hearing Garrett's stuttering response emboldened her. It was almost as arousing as his touch . . . almost.

"I want your hands on me. I want them to touch and caress me everywhere. My arms, my breasts, my stomach, my thighs. I want you to kiss me so deeply and so thoroughly that I can't hold a coherent thought." She threaded her fingers through his hair, thick and soft to the touch. "You see, you have taught me well, for I have learned the pleasures of just feeling. And tonight . . ." She moved her mouth from his ear to let her words fall in a breathless whisper against his parted lips. "Above all else, I want to feel you making love to me and you letting me love you back."

Delighted with Garrett's stunned expression, she locked her arms around his neck, planted her lips firmly on his, and with the weight of her body pressing into his, she eased him back into the pillows. She slid her hands over his hips, buttocks, and then his firm thighs. He was hard, all angles and sleek, well-toned muscle. Her battle-hardened soldier. His abdomen against hers was flat and taut. His body fascinated her.

Sleek and beautiful and . . . wounded.

Her fingers flitted over his smooth skin until she reached his jagged scar. At her touch, his body finally came alive with a jerk and he emitted a grunt of protest. Shushing him, she slid her body down his and pressed her lips to the puckered skin that snaked along the curve of his hip.

She heard his sharp indrawn breath as her tongue reached out to skim the mean scar. He could have been killed, but he had survived. After a minute, she felt him exhale and his body relax. "Thank God, you lived," she breathed. "Thank God you lived for me." She kissed his healed skin, and then lifted her head to press her lips to the pulsating beat of his heart.

≈≤

"Alex." Garrett growled her name, yanked her to him, and devoured her mouth with his.

An experienced lover, he had satisfied and been satisfied by many women. It was a carnal itch scratched, mutual desires satisfied. Nothing more. He thought it was enough. Thought he was incapable of feeling more.

Alex was teaching him otherwise.

"Good Lord," he breathed when she broke the kiss to draw breath. His gaze drifted over her soft features and kiss-swollen lips, the golden strands of her hair cascading in an intimate canopy around them. He noted the bright flush staining her cheeks, but noticed no more when her hand reached between them and closed over him.

He bucked at her touch on his aroused shaft. The tentative feel and sight of her delicate fingers sliding along his burning erection nearly drove him mad. Sweat broke out on his forehead, and he gritted his teeth as his body hardened and tightened. He needed to stop her before he made a fool of himself.

"My turn," he grunted. He cradled her close and twisted her around so that she lay beneath him. Braced on one arm, he lowered his free hand and slipped it between her legs to cup her moist center. She gasped and her body shivered.

His forehead dipped to hers. "Are you all right?" Silence answered him, and he paused until he heard Alex's barely audible response.

"Don't I feel all right?"

He blinked, not sure he had heard her correctly, but when he lifted his head to cock a brow and saw her cheeks burning brighter than the candle flame, he grinned. "You feel perfect."

He slid his fingers inside her wet folds, stroking her as his mouth swallowed up her responding whimpers. Her knees rose, her heels dug into the mattress, and her hands fisted in the sheets.

"Oh, God, I don't think I . . ."

"I must be doing something wrong if you're thinking, perhaps I should . . ."

"No!" Alex cried and grabbed his hand.

Obliging her, he found the most sensitive spot between her legs and let his thumb move over it, smiling when Alex gasped and bucked beneath his hand. "Easy," he murmured. A sheen of sweat broke out on her body and, unable to resist, he dipped his head to press his lips to the soft, delicate skin of her inner thigh.

Gasping, Alex grabbed his hair and pulled him back up. Laughing, he relented, moving away but keeping up the assaulting thrust of his fingers inside her, his own breathing becoming as ragged as hers. She was so damn responsive. Wet and ready. He gritted his teeth, struggling to draw deep breaths and cool his own rising sexual tension. Not yet.

Moments later, he watched Alex's back arch and she grabbed his forearms as her release exploded from her. Spasms shook her and she clung to him. "Garrett!"

The combination of his name on her lips and the feel of her nails digging into his arms as she climaxed was like tossing a match onto his smoldering desire. He was on fire. His pulse spiked and his heart thundered fit to explode. He grasped her knee and urged her leg to his hip, needing to be with her, be inside her.

It took him a moment before he noticed Alex's sudden stillness and that her hands had moved from his forearms to vise around his wrists. When he lifted his head, he saw her bite her lip, her eyes two wide blue pools of uncertainty, a clear sign of belated nerves kicking in.

Dear God, *she was an innocent*. She might be vocal about her wants and open in her passionate response to him, but she was still inexperienced and forgetting so made him an ass.

With an iron will, he stamped down the fire raging in him and ignored the growing, taut pressure in his loins. He braced himself on his hands and leaned low to press his lips to her forehead and then each cheek, kissing her with featherlight brushes. She closed her eyes and her hand on his wrist loosened.

"It's all right, Alex. We can stop."

Her eyes flew open. "No!"

"No?" He teased, for she had blurted the one word he had advised her to use to stop him.

"No, don't stop. I'm all right. I want . . ." Her voice trailed off. As she met his knowing gaze, a pink flush seeped down her neck.

"What do you want?" he breathed. Needing to hear her say it.

Her gaze drifted over his features and her eyes softened as she lifted her hand to cup his cheek. "You. All of you."

Heart pounding, his eyes met hers in the dim light and he rested his forehead against hers. "Finally," he breathed, "because I've wanted you damn near forever."

When he lowered his mouth to hers, he kissed her softly at first, only deepening the kiss with her response. She removed her hand from his cheek and slid her fingers into the hair curling around the nape of her neck. Drawing back, she sighed his name in a breathless whisper as her eyes drifted closed.

With his name warm on her lips, he haltingly settled his hips between her thighs. He watched her face as he positioned himself and slowly entered her. She was so damn wet and he was desperate for her. His arms nearly shook from bracing himself above her as he slid home, thrusting deep inside her. She cried out at his initial penetration, her hips instinctively bucking up, and her eyes flew open to stare into his, unsure.

"Shh, relax." His voice was hoarse as he struggled to reassure her, but she felt so good and he had waited so long. It took all his control to hold still and let her body become accustomed to the size and feel of him. He moved slowly, sweat breaking on his brow, as he watched her lips part. "Are you all right?"

She shifted her body slightly, stilling at his deep groan. "Do I feel all right?" she murmured, her fingers again gripping his arms as she echoed her earlier words.

She was killing him. "If you felt any better than you do, this would end before we've even started." He burst out in a half laugh, half growl.

"There's more?" Her eyes widened.

He was definitely dying. "Perhaps I should show you."

"Mmh, perhaps you should."

He moved his hips, thrusting gently, distracting her with his words and kisses. "God, you feel too good." His heart raced and his breathing labored as he tried to rein in his stampeding need. "I've waited for this for damn near forever."

After a few moments, a frown furrowed her brow. Garrett recognized that look, and thanked God for it. She was thinking again, wondering, and attuned to her needs, he vowed to dispense with that.

He quickened his pace, moving in rhythmic strokes, creating a moist, sliding friction that tore whimpers from her as he embedded himself deeply within her. He withdrew only to torture her again in quick thrusts and retreats that had her hips reaching up to meet him after each withdrawal. It was a sensual dance, a merging of bodies that teased and tortured and brought him to a near boiling point. He didn't think he could hold back much longer.

"God, I need you, you are incredible," he rasped.

"Garrett, I feel . . . I feel . . ."

"I know!" he cried out as her nails dug into his shoulders. His rhythm increased with each thrust. Heat fused between them, and his breathing quickened to match hers. Her legs tightened their grip around him, her ankles digging into his sweat-slicked back as she lifted her hips to meet his when he moved faster and deeper. He lowered his body and his arms tightened around her, drawing her into him as their bodies merged again and again, drawing out her pleasure. Her moaning whimpers ratcheted up his already skipping pulse rate, and he lifted his head to kiss her fiercely.

"Garrett!" Alex's eyes opened and she bucked beneath him, her release exploding from her, her body gripping him tight. She shivered as spasms gripped her. Garrett leaned down and devoured her mouth with his, kissing her again and again, her climax pushing him to the edge, arousing him to a fevered pitch, and he gritted his teeth to hold on to the moment.

When he lifted his head and saw her languid smile, his breath caught. Wearing that smile, her lips swollen, cheeks flushed, and her hair in golden disarray, she had never looked more desirable.

He swallowed, sweat breaking out over him. He wanted to savor the moment before he joined her in his own surrender, but when she slid her hands over his buttocks and clenched them tight, his control snapped. Emitting a guttural growl, he embedded himself deeply within her. She was so hot and wet. His own release rolled over him again and again in a fierce, pulsating wave that shook his body. His back arched and Alex curled her arms around his waist, holding him close as the spasms shuddered through him.

A long time later, he collapsed on top of her.

Together they lay entwined, spent, dazed, and exhausted.

It seemed an eternity had passed before Garrett grunted and somehow summoned the energy to lift himself off her. Alex sighed but smiled when he gathered her into his arms and lay beside her, cradling her against him.

She pressed her cheek to his shoulder and lifted her hand to his chest.

Garrett watched her eyes close and her breathing level as she drifted to sleep. He drew her closer, his arm draped around her waist. He closed his eyes and rested his chin on the top of her head, inhaling the subtle fragrance of lavender that rose from her hair.

He smiled at the memory of her coming into his chamber. His heart had pounded so loud he was certain it echoed in the room, yet he hadn't been able to draw a breath when she'd reached up and let that god-awful nightgown pool at her feet. Bathed in the glow of candlelight, she was breathtakingly lovely. High-breasted, slim-waisted, and long-legged, her hair a soft, golden cascade down her back. His angel.

Alex's words resonated with him.

Thank God he had lived. For her. For this.

He would ask her to marry him in the morning. But the morning was a long time away, and he had plans for tonight.

≫≪

ALEX STRETCHED, GRIMACING at the unfamiliar burn of muscles she had never felt before. The sound of masculine laughter brought her fully awake.

Garrett was propped on his elbow. His hair was deliciously mussed, a strand falling over his forehead, and his eyes sparkled.

Her cheeks flamed. After all they had done she shouldn't be embarrassed. But it was disconcerting to awake to a naked, gorgeous man in bed with her. He watched her with a knowing look and for the first time in her life, Alex understood what that look meant.

She had surrendered everything.

They had made love not once, but twice. She had awakened earlier to the feel of his hands roaming over her body and his mouth cajoling her response. Her heart had taken flight and her body soon followed. Garrett made her feel more alive than she had ever been. Her body had been asleep, and Garrett's touch had awakened it, turning her body into an instrument that only his touch knew the notes to make sing.

She would never be the same.

A shiver of fear slid over her. She had lost her head, her heart, and her innocence to this man. What more could he take from her that she could give?

She feared it was her soul.

"Good morning." He brushed a strand of hair from her face and leaned over to kiss her cheek.

She caught sight of the bedside clock. The hour was early, near dawn. Relief flooded her. Once she garnered her courage, she could escape to her bedchamber without anyone knowing what had transpired. Except for she and Garrett. She would never forget. His touch was branded on her body. She would always relive the way his lips . . .

Her eyes snapped to Garrett's when she heard his rumble of laughter.

"You're thinking again." Grinning, he shook his head. "I don't approve of it so early in the morning, but if it's a habit of yours, we'll have to ensure your thoughts are about me."

His hand cupping the back of her head, he leaned forward and thoroughly kissed her. She laid her hand against his bare chest but hadn't the strength to push him away. The morning had yet to fully awaken, so why rush the day?

He drew back and scattered featherlight kisses along her cheeks, lowering his head to press his lips to a sensitive spot on her neck. Tipping her head back, she sighed.

Garrett smiled against her skin. "That's better. We'll have to make sure we wake up every morning like this. I don't know if we'll ever leave this room because I can't get enough of you. Cook can send up our meals. I'll make sure she sends peaches, lots of peaches because you know they are my favorite."

His mouth slid down to the curve of her breast and her breath caught as he aroused a pliant peak.

"Kit and Brandon might worry." She finally managed to find her voice in a halfhearted protest.

"I'll have Stewart get rid of them and the boys. They were useful during the courtship, but now we'll lock ourselves in here and make our own babies. You like children, so we'll have a couple. A girl and a boy. One of each."

"What?" Alex's eyes flew open.

"All right, four, but no more." His lips slid down her stomach and he spoke between kisses. "We'll name our firstborn Arundel. He'll demand to be called Wellington. Our next child will be a girl who is a practical, independent blue-eyed beauty who will climb trees and keep Wellington in line. She'll be—"

Alex came alive and frantically shoved at Garrett, scrambling from his arms to flee the bed, nearly tripping in her flight. She scooped up her nightgown and held it to her, a cold chill seizing her.

Courtship? Babies? He was talking madness. Talking about a future that could never be.

Garrett sat up, swung his legs over the bed, and started to rise. "Alex, what—"

"Stop!" A hand shot out to ward him off. "Don't come any closer. You don't understand." She blinked at the rush of tears blurring her vision, struggling to hold herself together. "I can't. We can't." She shook her head frantically, her unbound hair hiding her face as she edged to the door. "You don't understand."

Garrett stared at her in his quiet manner. His lips pressed into a firm line and his eyes hardened. After a moment, he slowly rose to his feet.

She averted her gaze from his naked body, but her heart thundered. She never should have touched him.

He deserved more than what she could offer.

"What don't I understand? Why don't you explain? What exactly does all *this*"—his hand shot to the bed—"mean to you?"

"Everything! It means everything to me and let that be enough!" The tears she fought streamed down her cheeks and she swiped at them. "It's not about us. It's about me. I've given you all I can. There is no future for us because I can't be what you want. What you deserve. I'm not free to be so. I . . . I belong to another."

"What? Like hell you do!" Garrett exploded. "You belong to me!"

A cry escaped Alex and she backed away as he advanced on her, his expression thunderous. She sucked in a ragged breath and struggled to explain. "My uncle betrothed me to another. He made sure to give the illusion of it being consummated—"

"It damn well wasn't," Garrett swore. "Don't take me for a fool. I know a virgin when I lie with one. You—"

"It doesn't matter!" she cried, her eyes beseeching him to listen to her, to understand. "My uncle ensured I'd be ruined if I refused his betrothal agreement. And he succeeded. It wasn't consummated, but the man spent the night in my room. Should I break my betrothal for another, my uncle vowed to spread word of my ruin."

"Alex, it doesn't matter. I love you, and I don't give a damn what your uncle has done."

She blinked at his words, her heart near bursting with the joy of them before the burdens she carried snuffed out the spark of light. She looked away, shaking her head. "You don't understand. It's too late. My uncle has other men to testify that they lay with me as well. And . . . I can't . . ." She closed her eyes.

"They lie!" Garrett barked. "I know it and you know it, so nothing they say can touch us. Alex, you—"

"No! I can't! You still don't understand." Sobs broke from her.

"Then by God make me!" He held up his hands. "For I'll be damned if I'll give you up based on the lies and slanders of another!"

"You have to!" She cried and recoiled at the stricken look on his face. She needed to be merciful and end this for both their sakes. Clutching her nightgown, she pressed her fists to her heart to hold its broken pieces together. Exhausted, it took all her strength to speak. "I'm not like you, Garrett. You're a soldier. You're used to having shots taken at you. I'm not. And . . . my father, he . . . he was a notorious philanderer."

She forced herself to finish, blinking furiously at the tears streaming down her cheeks. "And I hated him for it. I abhorred the parade of ladies, maids, and governesses whom he used and discarded like worn cravats. His reputation cut a wide swath and was hard earned, but by God, it won't be mine! I won't let it be. I can't! You can't ask that of me. No one can." Her voice shook on her words.

She sighed and softened her tone as she beseeched Garrett to understand the finality of their situation. "More important, it's not just me who will be ruined by my uncle's accusations. My scandal touches my cousins. My ruin is their ruin. I can't do that to them. My parents neglected to think of the conse-quences their behavior had on my life, forcing me to leave my school, friends I loved, and forfeit any thoughts of a Season. I won't do that to my cousins. I won't link their ruin to mine. Don't ask me to."

She blindly groped for the door behind her, whipped it open, and fled.

She locked the door behind her, collapsed against it, and crumpled to a boneless heap on the floor. Her cries tore from her as Garrett pounded the door, bellowing her name. She couldn't open it. She hadn't the strength.

It was too late for them.

It had always been too late.

≫≪

"ALEX! DAMN IT, open this bloody door!" Garrett hurled his body at the cursed barrier, but the thick oak would not give. He slammed his fist against it. He wanted to kill someone and he knew damn well who. Alex's conniving, manipulative bastard of an uncle.

He would die.

And it wouldn't be pretty. Alex's sobs drifting through the door were like added punctures to his already bleeding heart. He yanked at the doorknob, cursing it and his bruised fists.

Stepping away, he dragged his hands through his hair, pacing the room. This was not over. Alex was his and she damn well knew it. She wouldn't be crying her heart out for a loss she didn't mourn. She loved him even though she hadn't said the words that he had bellowed like an idiot in the midst of his world crashing down around him. He closed his eyes, blew out a breath, and stood still.

This courtship had wreaked havoc on his sanity. Christ. But he had spoken true.

He loved Alex and he refused to give her up.

Alex did not believe she had the strength to fight for what she wanted, but he believed otherwise. She had mettle. He wouldn't have fallen in love with her if she weren't a fighter.

But she was afraid. Her uncle had threatened her, and her father had humiliated her. It was a formidable combination. Together he and Alex could overcome both. Once he killed her uncle, the odds were on their side.

He stomped to his wardrobe and began yanking out clothes. He needed to get dressed, pack a few items, and drag Brandon's lazy arse out of bed. The man could make himself useful by helping bury the body. He'd take a few men with him for his protection, but with murder on his mind, anyone daring to confront him now wouldn't survive the day.

When he returned, he'd tell Alex he loved her in normal decibels, get her to admit she loved him, inform her they were marrying, and then they'd start making those damn babies.

He stormed from the room and down the hall. It was a good thing a man only got married once in his life, for he didn't think he could go through this again.

But Alex was worth it.

She was worth everything.

Chapter Twenty-five

≫≈≪

A LEX grabbed a fresh nightgown and tossed it on, dragging herself into bed. She curled into a ball until she drifted into an exhausted sleep. A persistent banging had her jerking awake and blinking in confusion. She thought the noise was the pulsating throb in her head until she realized someone was knocking on her door and heard Kit calling her name. Sitting up, she pulled the sheets to her and answered. Despite her fervent desire to disappear, she felt compelled to face Kit and explain herself. She was done running and hiding.

Kit entered, took one look at her, crossed to the windows, and threw open the curtains.

Alex recoiled from the sunlight that streamed into the room. Groaning, she slid back under the covers and shielded her face beneath her arm.

"Here's a sight. What in the world happened last night? I awoke to Garrett bellowing Brandon's name. The next thing I know, the two idiots have packed their bags and ridden off to murder your uncle."

Alex shot up in bed, horrified.

Kit waved her concerns away. "They won't be killing anyone.

I warned them I refused to raise my boys under the shadow of their father and uncle swinging from nooses at Newgate."

Alex collapsed back into her pillows and closed her eyes. She felt the bed dip as Kit sat beside her.

"Alex, honey, what is it?" She asked gently, all levity gone. What on earth happened last night that has Garrett swearing murder and my normally rational husband vowing to dispense with the body?"

Alex flung her arms around Kit, burying her face in her shoulder. She thought she had cried herself dry, but there were more tears to be wrung from her yet.

After a few minutes, Kit eased back and handed her a handkerchief. She waited for her to dry her eyes before she prodded. "Alex, talk to me; perhaps I can help."

Alex brushed a strand of hair from her face and struggled to decide where to begin. She supposed it began with her father, so she started there. Sighing, she told Kit of her father's philandering ways, his gambling debts, and her mother's devotion to her father in spite of all his faults. Lastly, she confided her determination to never be beholden to another.

It was this goal that had led her to rejecting all offers for her hand and had motivated her to accept Garrett's mercenary arrangement. Then her voice broke. "It was easy for me to dismiss my suitors, for none of them were like Garrett."

"Of course they weren't. No one is like him," Kit murmured.

"It's easy to reject men for whom you don't care."

"You didn't love them. But why would you? You love Garrett," Kit said.

"Yes, well, the trouble began when my parents died and my uncle took over my father's estate. He was adamant to see me wed despite my objections. I didn't understand what I do now. You see, my uncle has three daughters. A betrothal contract to a wealthy suitor would finance the dowries my uncle couldn't provide."

Alex laid the handkerchief she had twisted into a soggy mess on the bedcovers. "My uncle led a parade of suitors before me. But none of them . . . I didn't feel any of the things Garrett makes me feel. Didn't believe I was capable of it."

"Of course you didn't, because you hadn't met the right man," Kit offered.

"I thought I was different from other women, of harder stock. The word my uncle used was *frigid*." Her breath hitched at the insult.

"Garrett was right." Kit slapped her hand on the bed. "The man deserves to die. That will teach me to meddle."

The small bubble of laughter that slipped from Alex stunned her. She shook her head. "It didn't matter. I was intent on my independence and believed no man could change my mind."

"Independence is highly overrated. It doesn't warm your bed at night and it can't give you children."

"Yes." Alex smiled wistfully. She thought of her plans to purchase her family cottage. There was no Garrett and no children in that picture. They were a girl's dreams. Garrett had offered her children and together they'd nearly set the bed on fire. She couldn't go there. Not now. "Eventually my uncle lost patience with me and took matters into his own hands. After a dinner party abetted by liberal drink, I escaped to retire early for the night. I was finishing my toilette when my door was opened, closed, and locked.

"It was an older gentleman, a more persistent suitor. He informed me that he and my uncle had reached an agreement and we were formally betrothed. He had come to claim his reward for payment rendered. I had cost him a fortune and he looked forward to my paying it back."

"Dear God." Kit gasped. "He and your uncle should be put on the rack and stretched. There must be one of those medieval contraptions tucked away in a dungeon somewhere. Brandon has connections. He loves me, he'll locate one." Kit closed her hand over Alex's, her expression anguished. "I'm sorry, so very sorry."

Alex squeezed Kit's hand. "You need not be as sorry as you are thinking. He didn't hurt me. A bit of pawing, but I was able to get away."

Kit closed her eyes and exhaled. "Thank God."

"Does he still get the rack?"

Kit's eyes opened and narrowed. "Perhaps we'll tease him with it, not stretch it so taut."

Alex smiled. "He had drunk a lot, so it was easy to make him believe that if he but waited a few minutes, his patience would be rewarded. I told him I needed to dress more appropriately and would soon return. There was another door to my room that led to my old nurse's chamber and I fled through there. Her room contained a hidden back staircase. My father's paramours used this entrance, my father liking the clandestine nature to it all."

Heat burned her cheeks and she hastened to continue. "But for the first time in my life, I was indebted to my father's rakish life. Due to his penchant for pawning my jewelry, I had taken to stashing my valuables in a secret alcove in this back staircase.

"I knew I wouldn't get far in the dead of night in winter, so I hid in one of our maid's rooms for over a week. She was eager to assist me, not being an admirer of my uncle. I knew it would never occur to my uncle that I would remain on the grounds and not take flight."

"I'll have to remember that should I ever decide to flee Brandon. Garrett always tells me to have a contingency plan, particularly in regard to my marriage." Kit rolled her eyes, and then ruefully regarded her bulging belly. "But I doubt I'd get far."

"The maids kept me updated on my uncle's plans." Alex went on to recount his threats should she try to break the betrothal contract.

"No!" Kit stood and began to pace the room. "The rack is too good for your uncle. He needs to be drawn and quartered. A few bribes in the right pockets and I'm sure it can be arranged."

"I like that picture myself. Eventually, the maid pawned a piece of my jewelry and I made my way to Gus's wife, Meg, my old nurse in London, and found refuge with her." She told Kit about inheriting her father's luck at cards and taking the name Daniels. She explained how she had solicited the assistance of Lady Olivia, the Duke of Hammond's daughter, with getting coveted invitations for her family friend, Alex Daniels. Thus Daniels had been introduced to the ton.

Kit beamed at her. "What an odd twist of fate. Your father served you well in the end. The Langdon luck won out because here you are."

"Yes, here I am." She nodded as the tears she held at bay blurred her eyes. She hadn't cried so much in years. "Kit, I hurt Garrett. He talked of being together and having babies and he said he loved me and I couldn't let him go on. I couldn't."

"You told him of your betrothal?" At Alex's bleak expression,

Kit nodded. "I now understand his motive for murder, and it's a good one. But, Alex, why the tears? Don't you believe Garrett can resolve this matter?"

"How can he? My uncle has made sure my name will be ruined should I break the contract. He's only kept silent thus far because he is still searching for me. That is why I changed my name." She shrugged. "When my uncle does speak, people will believe his slander because of my father's notoriety. And it's not just my name and reputation that is ruined, but my cousins' as well. They are the true innocents in my uncle's machinations. So there's nothing to be done because if Garrett does murder my uncle, he'll hang for it!"

"Do you really believe that your uncle would ruin his daughters' chances of a marriage when he was fighting for them to gain a dowry in the first place?" Kit frowned.

Alex shook her head. "I don't know. But I do know that he'll do anything to get what he wants and is capable of sacrificing anyone who stands in his way. He fired everyone loyal to my father when he gained the estate. Kit, he sent a man into my bedroom when I defied him." She turned her face to the window and bit her lip. "I couldn't go back. And when Meg died, I couldn't leave Gus."

"I understand, but, Alex, you have to trust in Garrett to help you through this. That's what loving someone is about. He's trusting you to help him; it's time you trust in him to do the same for you. You don't really believe Garrett would abandon you now, not when he has vowed his love for you."

Alex drew a ragged breath, struggling to digest Kit's words. It had been so long since she had leaned on anyone, but Garrett was different.

If she could trust Garrett now, he could give her everything.

She lifted hopeful eyes to Kit, then stilled. "I've never even confided my real name to him. He doesn't know what uncle to kill."

"Oh, honey, he's known since meeting Gus." At her surprise, Kit spoke gently. "Gus didn't betray your secrets, but he did mention working for a Viscount Langdon, and it was enough for Garrett to go on. It was never important to Garrett. He wanted you to tell him when you were ready. He was willing to wait."

"I was afraid," Alex murmured.

"Of course you were. Your uncle made sure of that. Now then." Kit stood, straightening her skirts. "Dry those tears, have a good soak in a tub, and then we shall face the day. To get our minds off matters, we'll search for a torture device for your uncle around here." Kit crossed to the door but turned back. "Alex, in all of Garrett's plans for your future, did he ever actually propose?"

Alex frowned. "No. I don't believe he did."

"I knew it!" Kit slapped her hand on the door. "My brother takes too much for granted. Don't let him get away with it. Next time he talks about making babies, you make sure he gets down on bended knee and begs for your hand!"

Alex couldn't picture Garrett so humbled. "He did say we would name our firstborn Arundel, but he will demand to be called Wellington."

Kit laughed. "He does have a charming way about him. I'm so very glad you stumbled into his life. He needs you very much."

Alex's tears returned. "I need him, too."

"Then you make a pair." Kit smiled and slipped from the room.

Alex plopped back on her pillow, feeling lighter than she had in hours. She didn't know how things would resolve, but at least there was some hope.

While the future was uncertain, she knew one fact. No son of hers would be named Arundel.

Chapter Twenty-six

◦❦◦

Five days had passed since Garrett had left and Alex started at every sound, half expecting to turn and see him scowling at her. Irritated, she flipped the page of her book, nearly ripping it from the seam. Her patience was a strained and frayed cord, ready to snap.

Where the hell was he?

Sighing, she slammed her book closed and stood. She would have Cook prepare tea, for Kit and Will would awaken shortly from their afternoon nap. Beau had accompanied Stewart to the hops fields. She set her book on the table, smiling as her eyes fastened on the title. Garrett was a wily one, for *Tom Jones* had been a clever choice. Its lusty hero Tom further reminded her of Kendall. Like Garrett, Tom was a notorious rakehell who proved more noble than those whose pompous moralizing hid false virtues.

She swept her fingers over the leather-bound cover, then jumped at the sound of ferocious pounding on the front door.

The noise continued, shattering her immobility and reminding her that Garrett had no butler. However, he had assured her that he had men guarding the manor and property. She neatened the skirts of her peach day dress, squared her shoulders, and opened the door.

A stranger stood before her. He was Garrett's height, but thinner, and his auburn hair was peppered with streaks of gray. Hawkish features carved with age lines glowered, and golden eyes locked on hers. A chill swept over her, which was odd because she was certain she had never met the man before.

"No butler," he muttered. "Typical. Lady Daniels, I presume?"

"Yes, can I help—?"

"Keyes was right!"

"I beg your pardon—"

"And well you should! I've thought many things of Kendall, most well earned, but this sinks below even his level of degradation."

Stunned, Alex opened her mouth to respond when the man stormed past her, giving her no choice but to move aside or be plowed down.

He paced the foyer. "Where is my daughter? Where is Kristen?" he demanded.

Alex's eyes widened. *This* was Kit's father and Garrett's nemesis? *Arthur*. She now understood her instinctual reaction to him upon opening the door.

Arthur didn't wait for her reply. "Keyes said she and Warren were here and don't deny it, for I saw Beau in the fields digging like a common laborer. I'm aware Kendall has no respect for his name, dragging it through the gutter with his scandalous ways and now this venture into . . . into *trade* for God's sake!" He spat the word out as if he could barely stomach it.

"I thought better of Warren. Lord knows why, considering the two of them were troublemakers as boys and rakehells as young men. I thought Warren had settled into his seat when he'd married Kristen. Clearly, I thought wrong." He shook his head. "But this is unacceptable. It is one thing for Kendall to drink himself into a stupor or switch his women as often as he changes his mounts, but to indulge in his sordid proclivities when innocents are on the premises is beneath contempt."

Having been rendered momentarily speechless, Alex now

recovered her voice. "Sir, you have said quite enough, and all at grievous insult to Lord Kendall, your daughter, and her husband, the Earl of Warren. Perhaps you should leave." Her tone dropped to frigid levels and she whirled to retrace her steps to the front door and swing it open. "Short of a butler, allow me to show you out."

Ignoring the open door, he cocked a brow and studied her with renewed interest. "Do you think I don't know what you are doing here? Keyes wrote to me and told me all about you and Kendall. More important, I *know* Kendall. From your indignant expression, perhaps you don't."

She lifted her chin and looked him dead in the eye. "I know exactly who and what kind of man Garrett is. It is you who are mistaken about him as well as my position here." She deliberately employed Garrett's Christian name, having noted his stepfather's refusal to do so.

Taken aback, Arthur studied her, recognizing the battle line her words had drawn. "I see. So Kendall has made clear his intentions toward you? And they are honorable?" He waited a beat before adding, "As honorable as they have been toward the rest of his women?"

Her cheeks burned. She had wasted time in mourning Garrett's loss of Arthur as a father. Garrett was better off without the arrogant, insufferable prig.

It took all of her control to remain civil. "I won't deign to speak for other women or presume to discuss Garrett's past. For myself, Garrett has told me *exactly* what his intentions are and left no doubt as to his honor."

Surprise lit his eyes. "I don't know what he has told you or rather given you, but he is incapable of—"

"He's told me all I need to know, and given me everything any woman could ever want."

"Just who do you think you are?" He advanced on her. "You are nothing but—"

"I know exactly who I am. It is you who are confused or rather misinformed." Her voice rose to silence him. "As we have not been properly introduced and Lord Keyes has clearly drawn a grossly inaccurate picture of the situation here, it is understandable. Allow me to introduce myself."

He sneered at her audacity.

"Daniels is a name I choose to use when traveling anonymously." She lied without compunction. "My family name is Langdon, and I am Lady Alexandra. If I accept Garrett's proposal, I will be the next Countess of Kendall." Unable to resist, she released the door she still held and let it slam shut, adding a dramatic flourish to her words. Guilt at her premature announcement pricked her, but she ignored it. Garrett had named their firstborn without her consent, so she felt comfortable in announcing their betrothal without his.

She was appreciating the color draining from Arthur's face when a trill of laughter broke the silence. She turned to see Kit poised at the top of the stairs, her golden eyes shining.

Kit swept down the stairs and walked over to loop her arm through Alex's. "Hello, Father, this is a surprise. Had I known you planned to visit us to deliver another of your lectures on our scandalous behavior, I would have had a room prepared for you . . . or not." She shrugged. "You do know how I feel about your lectures."

His attention shifted with visible reluctance to Kit. "I see you still retain your arsenal of double-edged greetings, Kristen. However, you need not worry over my accommodations. Lord Keyes has put me up." He addressed Kit, but his gaze returned to Alex and he furrowed his brow.

"Yes, well, Lord Keyes should consider penning a novel since he has such a clever hand at fiction. But that would be embarking on a career in trade and the horror of it just couldn't be born." Kit shuddered.

"Your sharp wit has not dulled with marriage, but you're Warren's problem now, not mine. Lord Keyes simply wrote to voice his concern over the status of Kendall's company because there are impressionable children on the premises."

"*And* responsible chaperones," Kit returned. "Keyes must have forgotten that detail, but facts do tend to bog down a good yarn. However, I find it odd that Keyes should concern himself over the company my children keep when he pays little heed to those whom his own daughter entertains."

"By God, you haven't changed. You—" Arthur closed his eyes and blew out a breath. "As usual in discussions with you, we digress. You are late in your condemnation of Lord Keyes and my response to his missive. Kendall's guest has made it clear that Keyes's concern was premature, my judgments erroneous and offensive, and that my congratulations and most sincere apologies are in order."

He bowed low and the smile he turned on Alex was so brittle that she believed if touched, it would crack. She still seethed over his slanderous words but was forced to retreat from full battle mode.

"Langdon?" He murmured, his eyes narrowing. "Any relation to a Viscount Langdon?"

"My late father." Alex smiled sweetly, praying he did not pursue the matter further. "Are you acquainted with my family?"

"Mmh. I have heard of your father." He regained some of his composure, and a gleam entered his eyes. "He and Kendall have much in common. Their reputations precede them."

Alex forced out a gay laugh. "They do. In fact, I met Garrett over cards at the Duke of Hammond's. He won some coin from me, so what could I do but marry him to retrieve it?" She grinned at Kit. "Luckily I fell in love with him, so my winnings were twofold."

"Very smart of you." Kit laughed. "Why don't we continue this conversation in the parlor. Father, you will stay for tea?"

"I have some time. And where are Kendall and Warren? I should offer my felicitations to Kendall."

"Not burning anything down, I assure you," Kit turned to Alex. "Father's new carriage caught fire in Garrett and Brandon's ill-fated attempt to light some cigars they had pilfered from him. Father's never forgiven them for it."

"Cost me a fortune. Both the carriage and the cigars." His voice was gruff, disgust coloring it.

Kit settled on the sofa, Alex beside her. Arthur sat in one of the easy chairs across the table from them, crossed his legs, and leaned back. His smile did not reach his eyes. "Now then, you say you met at the Duke of Hammond's?" He shifted in his seat and addressed Alex. "Was this recently?"

Alex smiled. "Very, only a few weeks ago. He literally swept me off my feet, giving me little choice in the matter of accompanying him here and meeting his family. My head is still spinning." She spoke the truth.

Straightening, Arthur uncrossed his legs and his fingers

curled around his thighs. "That must have been Hammond's ball on the fifth. I made a brief appearance but was unable to stay."

"Perhaps you learned Kendall was attending?" Kit spoke dryly.

"And why would I hear that?" His words were sharp, and Kit looked surprised. "You of all people should know I give little heed to Kendall's schedule."

"On that we agree," Kit said. Her hard expression softened when the maid carrying a tray laden with teacups and saucers paused at the entrance to the room. Kit smiled and waved her forward.

"I'm surprised Kendall made an appearance. Since his return from the Crimea, word was that he avoided town, seeking his *pleasure* elsewhere." He deliberately drew out the word. "However, as I said, I'm not privy to his activities. Your courtship was certainly quick. Hammond's was three weeks ago."

"Mmh, it was." Alex smiled, but said no more, refusing to defend what was none of the man's business. She accepted the cup Kit prepared and took a sip.

"I shall speak to Hammond about hosting an engagement ball for them," Kit said and ruefully eyed her large belly. "I'm not in a position to do so, and Brandon is being dictatorial about my avoiding town until after the baby's birth." She frowned, then addressed Alex. "I shall make the wedding, and I insist on helping with all preparations."

Alex felt another prick of guilt at planning a wedding for which she had yet to receive a formal proposal.

"If given advance notice of dates, perhaps you can find time in your busy schedule to attend an event." Kit eyed her father. "If not for Garrett, for appearance's sake."

"Since when has Kendall ever cared for appearances?" Arthur grunted. Before Kit could retort, he went on. "Perhaps he's changed because I couldn't fathom checking my calendar for Kendall's nuptials a few months ago. Frankly, I thought it would need to be cleared for another less celebratory event."

"Oh, please, had Garrett drunk himself into his grave, you would have been the first to raise a toast in celebration," Kit snapped, and then pressed her hand to her temple. "I apologize, that was uncalled for."

"Yes, well, I'd like to think that despite our differences, we can welcome Kendall's new wife into our family, as humble as it is. Hopefully you can give Kendall the happiness he seeks through a more respectable venue."

Alex caught Kit's surprised look at his words, and she hastened to respond before Kit rejected this dubious olive branch. "I love him very much and will do all in my power to ensure his happiness. After all, it is now tied to my own."

"Well said." Kit lifted her cup in a mock toast.

"Mum!"

Kit turned to see Will toddling her way, a maid hovering behind.

When Will neared her seat, he spotted Arthur and altered course, delight lighting his features. "Grapa," he cried. "Up."

"There's my little man." Arthur hoisted Will to his lap with a grunt. "You are getting so big."

Arthur's broad smile softened his austere features, and Alex blinked at the transformation.

"I this many now." Will thrust his two fingers before Arthur's face.

"That explains why you are so big. Pretty soon you'll outgrow Grandpa's lap."

"I too big for Mum," Will boasted.

"Mum can only carry one child at a time," Kit murmured to Alex.

"Of course you are," Arthur said. "Soon you'll be as big as Beau." He smiled as Will popped his thumb into his mouth and, with his free hand, patted Arthur's jacket and reached inside to extract his watch. Arthur's booming laugh rang out. "Clever boy, aren't you? You remember Grandpa's toys, don't you?"

Will extracted his thumb to turn his find over between his pudgy hands. "Bird?" He looked at Arthur.

"Why, you are smart indeed. You'll find the falcon engraved on the inside cover."

Will caught his tongue between his lips as he struggled to pry open the watch lid.

"On family crests, the falcon stands for one who does not rest until his objective is achieved." Arthur explained. "Here, let me." He flipped open the lid for Will.

Triumphant, Will smiled and held up the watch face for Alex and Kit. "I keep?" Will cocked his head to peer up at Arthur.

"Will, that's—" Kit began, but Arthur interceded.

"It's all right," he assured her. "You keep." He smiled at Will. "Consider it a present for a big boy. Perhaps someday it will give you the correct time. It refuses to do so for me. It's a poor replacement for another I recently lost, and I won't miss it."

"That's very generous of you," Kit said. "Will, my love, can you thank Grandpa for his gift?"

"Tank you, Grapa." He smiled. "Mine."

"Yours." Arthur laughed. "Speaking of time, I better heed it and not overstay my welcome. Considering I got off on the wrong foot, let me depart on the right one." As he stood, he set Will on his feet.

"Did you want to say hello to Beau?" Kit rose from her seat.

"No, another time. Lord Keyes has guests arriving. Do you expect Kendall's return soon?"

Alex stood as well. "He's been gone for nearly a week, so I expect he should return any day now."

"All the more reason for me to make my departure. You'll have to pass on my best wishes on his news and do keep me apprised of matters. Despite Kendall's belief to the contrary, I've always hoped he would settle down and find himself a lovely bride, someone who might understand him. I see he has found that as well as a protector in you, Lady Alexandra."

"Thank you," Alex murmured, wary of this conciliatory man who embraced his grandchild, yet rejected his stepson. A man who could hurl insults as effortlessly as he could wield charm. One who had callously rejected Garrett's gift of a watch, yet generously gifted Will with his own. She didn't understand him but neither did she care to. In her eyes, he would always be guilty for his treatment of Garrett as a boy.

Arthur swept his hand over Will's blond locks and moved to the front foyer to make his departure.

Once the door closed behind him, Kit blew out a breath. "I'd say that was well executed on both sides. A few thrusts, some parries, even a retreat or two but no serious wounds. He really wasn't himself. Must be the news of Garrett's betrothal."

"I will leave it to you to make the final tally. Lord Keyes's slander had him at a disadvantage and the betrothal is a surprise."

Kit waved her hand dismissively. "It's still Arthur's decision what he chooses to believe. With Garrett, it's always the worst. It's probably good that Garrett wasn't here. Less blood. In fact"—Kit looped her arm through Alex's—"why don't we keep this little visit to ourselves?"

"I don't think that's a good idea. I don't want—"

"We'll eventually mention it, but not until after you and he have ironed out all your differences. We don't want to overload his plate. This manor has always been a safe haven for Garrett. I worry he won't feel the same about it knowing Arthur was here. Damn Keyes and his wagging tongue. I'd like to slice it off."

"You and me both," Alex muttered, then sobered. "I can give you time, Kit, but I'm not comfortable keeping Arthur's visit from Garrett. He has a right to know, but I will defer to you as to when we tell him—as long as it's not too late."

"Fair enough," Kit agreed and led them back into the parlor.

Chapter Twenty-seven

※≪≫

GARRETT dismounted on a swath of grass overlooking a wide expanse of beach. He tossed his reins to Marcus, one of his men whom Holt had directed to guard the area, and followed a windswept path leading to the water. His steps slowed, and he paused a moment to survey the scene before him.

Alex stood silhouetted before the ocean, and his eyes feasted on her like a prisoner tasting his first meal in freedom. She lifted her hands to secure the ribbons beneath her chin as a gust of wind threatened to strip her bonnet from her head. The breeze plastered her blue gown to her body and caused his loins to ache and his pounding heart to fight for release.

Bathed in a halo of sunlight and with a gentle smile curling her lips, Alex tilted her face up to the bright rays. Tall and slim, she was picture-perfect lovely. And she was his. Forever.

Or would be as soon as he proposed. But first things were first.

He needed her in his arms, preferably naked and preferably alone. His eyes shifted to Beau, who was running in circles around a sand castle.

"Bang, you're dead."

Garrett froze and his heart stopped cold.

After what felt like an interminable amount of time, he managed to feel his blood still flowed and slowly he lifted his hands to turn and face his adversary.

Christ. Deacon, one of his own men. Noting the man's wide-eyed look of surprise, he frowned. *What the . . . ?*

Deacon stumbled back and lowered the gun he held, his apologies spewing forth in a panicked rush. "Christ. So sorry, Captain. I thought ye was Ned. I was funnin' Ned. I mean, I knew Marcus wouldn't let anyone through on his watch 'cept for Ned, so I thought . . . From the back you and Ned . . ."

"I understand." Garrett had to swallow, his mouth spit dry, his heart only now settling into a smooth rhythm. "And where is our good man Ned?"

"He went to take a piss. That is, he went . . ."

Garrett held up his hand. "Again, I understand."

Deacon shifted his feet, his cheeks flaming. "Again, me apologies, Captain."

"It's all right." For he was alive—this time. His eyes strayed back to Alexandra and he swallowed. They were on borrowed time. He'd steal a little more of it because after the last few days they had earned it, but then they had to return to the city and find his killer. It's what brought Alex and him together, and he'd be damned if it was what tore them apart. Not now. Not after she was his.

He turned to address Deacon. "Keep an eye on Beau till Ned returns. Lady Alexandra and I have somewhere to go." Lady Alexandra. He liked the ring of it, but Lady Kendall sounded much better.

With purposeful strides he walked down to the beach, his eyes fixated on Alexandra, who was bending down to lift a shell from the sand. She lifted her head as his shadow fell across her, raising her hand to shield her eyes. A gasp escaped her and she sought to stand, staggering back from him.

He curled his hands around her upper arms and yanked her to him. He hauled her to her toes, crushed his mouth to hers, and all but inhaled her. His arms snaked around her, molding her body to his while his lips plundered hers as if he could swallow her whole. He tasted chocolate on her tongue. The potent mixture of the confection and Alex was incredibly arousing and he deepened the kiss, his mouth devouring. He couldn't get enough of her. His hand slid into the hair at the base of her neck and held her to him as his mouth drank from hers. God, she felt good. She was all he had ever dreamed of the past week.

It felt like an eternity had passed before Beau's gagging noises separated them.

Alex recoiled from Garrett, her face burning as she stumbled away.

"You looked like you were eating her." Beau made a face.

Garrett's eyes roved over Alex's beet-red face and he smiled, wanting to lift her in his arms and spin her around. Wanting to, as Beau said, devour her whole. "Brilliant idea, Nelson, because I happen to be starving." Acting on his earlier impulse, he lunged forward and swept Alexandra into his arms. He swung her over his shoulder, his hand firm on her buttock, securing her in place. His laughter drowned out her shriek of indignation.

"Deacon will help you build a moat for your castle until Ned returns. Don't drown all the knights." Garrett spoke over his shoulder as he strolled up the beach, Alex right where he wanted her. She pounded his back and he grunted. Well, not quite yet, but soon. "Put me down! Put me down this instant!" Alex pummeled him and raged in his ear.

"What do you think you're doing acting like an apeman buffoon?"

An apeman buffoon? She certainly had a way with words.

"What are you doing? Garrett, stop!" She punched his back. "Listen to me!"

His beautiful English rose with sharp thorns. He adored her. He nodded to Marcus, who held Champion's reins. They hadn't covered too much ground, so a few more miles wouldn't hurt the tireless horse.

"Garrett!" Alex gasped when he lifted her and set her on the saddle. Luckily, she wore a simple blue day dress. The fewer clothes, the better. Once they reached the lodge, they wouldn't need any. Havers would deliver some food, and that was *all* they would need.

"Garrett, wait!" The plaintive tone in her cry stopped him. He paused and lifted his gaze to hers. "My uncle. Does he still live?"

He clenched his jaw and swung up behind her. After a minute, he managed a terse reply. "Unfortunately."

"What happened? Was he very angry?"

Garrett frowned. "We'll get to all that later. Trust me."

"Garrett, I—"

"Not now, Alex. I mean it." His words were final. He'd be damned if her uncle ruined their plans. He'd done enough damage to their relationship.

"I do. I do trust you."

He paused at the barely audible words and then kicked Champion into a canter. Alex's responding cry restored his smile. When she clung to him and called him an obtuse, domineering, arrogant ass, his laughter rang out his joy.

He wasn't domineering but decisive. There was a difference. He was a man who knew what he wanted. Once they reached the lodge and he rid Alex of her clothes, he'd see to it that she wanted the same thing. He grunted when she elbowed him in the gut.

By God, she was a magnificent fighter and he adored her. Thorns and all.

≈❤≈

ALEX CLUNG TO Garrett's arm circling her waist and silently seethed. He had no right to sweep her onto Champion without explanation or word of greeting and . . . and abduct her! Unless he had news to the contrary, they were not a properly betrothed couple. He didn't own her. She gritted her teeth. There would be no discussion of marriage until certain questions were asked and answered.

Like what *did* happen at her uncle's?

Why hadn't Garrett killed him?

Not that she wanted her uncle dead, but she wouldn't mind torturing him with Kit's rack. And if Garrett wasn't burying a body, what took him so damn long? She would stand strong and speak her mind because if Garrett thought there would be any more kisses or . . .

Her thoughts trailed off when Garrett reined Champion to

a stop and she recognized the hunting lodge that had sheltered them all those weeks ago. "Oh," she breathed, snapping her mouth closed at Garrett's rumble of laughter. Her heart thudded in her chest and she bit her lip, feeling her traitorous body respond to the memories.

She wasn't that strong after all. She was a weak, pitiful thing.

Garrett dismounted and assisted her down, but before she could gain her footing, he crushed her to him, his mouth swooping down and covering hers. His large hand cradled her head, his free arm circling her waist and bending her body into his. An almost savage desperation filled his kiss, erasing all thoughts of her uncle or explanations from Alex's mind. Surrendering to the intensity of his ardor, she became pliant, her knees weakening and a delicious shudder ripping through her body.

She didn't regret her capitulation, for Garrett was right. They should not let her uncle come between them again. Garrett might have foiled her uncle's machinations, but the far graver matter of the murderous plot against Garrett remained unresolved. This threat shadowed their time together and made it all the more precious.

It was time they stopped wasting it.

Garrett's desperation now gripped Alex, and she locked her arms around his neck and breathed him in. The feel of him, vibrantly alive, safe, and in her arms, forced the black thoughts to the back recesses of her mind.

Heart pounding, she reveled in the sensory overload that comprised Garrett. His body, hard and firm against hers, was sun-warmed from his ride and radiated a burning heat. She tasted cider and cinnamon as her tongue danced with his. He must have washed recently for the hair curling over the nape of his neck was still damp and curled around her fingers. He smelled of a mixture of sandalwood soap, fresh air, and needy male. She drank it all in, before she moved away to draw a ragged breath, closing her eyes as his lips traveled over her flushed features. He kissed her temple, her hot cheeks, and moved down to press his lips to the rapidly beating pulse at her neck.

She felt her knees buckle and tightened her grip on Garrett, who released a triumphant laugh and swung her into his arms. He carried her to the door, fumbling to unlatch it, his efforts assisted with a solid kick that sent the weather-beaten barrier crashing open. He crossed the threshold, shouldered the door closed behind him, and gave her a look rich with question and smoldering with desire. Her answer was to reach up and secure the latch, locking them within. His head lowered and again their lips met.

As he kissed her, he withdrew his arm from beneath her legs and let them slide intimately down his body. She felt the taut hardness of his flat stomach, the strength of his muscular thighs and through his trousers, the bulge of his arousal pressed against the juncture of her thighs. Her breath quickened, and she was surprised when her legs supported her weight.

His hands threaded through her hair, undoing her combs. Freed strands tumbled down her back, his fingers sliding through the thick locks.

He lifted his head and gazed into her eyes, the compelling gray of them silver bright and intense. "Stay with me. Be with me. Love me."

Poetry. She smiled. "When my father had a winning streak, he attributed it to 'Langdon luck,' which he promised me I would inherit. When I lost to you at Hammond's, I thought he was wrong." Her voice lowered. "But he wasn't. I believed I had lost everything that day, but I hadn't. I had won more than I had ever dreamed."

And by God, she refused to lose it.

Silently she vowed to keep Garrett safe. To fight for him as he fought her uncle. *Whatever it takes.*

She ignored the lurch of her heart and forced herself to steady her tremulous smile as she met Garrett's heated gaze.

Garrett dipped his head. His kiss was deep and sweet, his tongue stroking lightly over her lips. When he drew away, he grinned. "Best hand I ever won." He gripped her hips and nudged her back, turning toward a closet in the corner of the room.

Bemused, she watched him open the door, her eyes widening when he withdrew a stack of what appeared to be clean blankets from a shelf. Two pillows were piled on top. She raised a brow. "Yours?"

"Yes." Garrett's eyes sparkled. He dropped the stack on the hearth and knelt to spread a blanket on the floor.

Her eyes fastened on his jacket as it tightened over his shoulders, and she swallowed. "Were you expecting company? You appear prepared."

"Soldiers learn to be prepared for every contingency." His gaze swept her body in a slow, hot perusal that stripped her naked.

Her breath caught and she lifted a hand to her heart.

Garrett emitted a low, husky laugh and grabbed another blanket to flatten it on top of the first. "I had hopes of abducting you earlier but was having difficulties prying the boys from your side. Then this business with your uncle interrupted us." He tossed the pillows onto the makeshift bed and stood. A predatory gleam entered his eyes as he stalked her. "So we're a bit off schedule, which means we have catching up to do." His eyes fastened on her lips, dropped to the rise and fall of her breasts, slid down her thighs, and then slowly and insolently traveled back up. Meeting her gaze, he lifted a cocky brow in challenge.

Every place his eyes touched burned, heat spiraling through her, but she lifted her chin and met his dare. More than ready for him. "Mmh, so where do we begin?"

A spark of appreciation lit his eyes. "First, we take up where we left off in my bedroom before you ran out." He held up his finger and wagged it at her. "And this time, there'll be no escaping."

She felt a warm, moistening pool at the juncture of her thighs and had to swallow before she could respond. "I see. And second?"

He captured a strand of hair where it curled against her chest. Her breath caught as his fingers brushed her breast. Gently tugging on her hair, he drew her to him. "Second, we need to get rid of all these cumbersome clothes. They are *not* part of my plans."

His eyes were heavy-lidded and darkened with a fiery passion that had her mouth going dry. She wished he would stop talking and rid her of her clothes. As if he could read her mind, he released her hair and slowly began to undo the pearl buttons lining the bodice of her gown. She was grateful he hadn't lit a fire. His touch and burning looks were combustible. She shivered when his hands brushed her gown from her shoulders and it pooled at her feet.

"Now what?" she breathed.

A wicked light flared in his eyes and he lifted his hand to gently, slowly, tortuously trace one finger over the round curves of her breasts, bared above her chemise.

"Now? Why now, I caress every inch of your delectable body, bathe you with hot, wet kisses, and thoroughly, completely seduce you. But to be done right, we must move slowly . . . very slowly."

Her breath quickened when his thumb brushed her nipple, circling the sensitive peak and sending ripples of pleasure throughout her limbs. She nearly joined her gown in a limp heap on the floor. Slowly? Dear God, didn't he know their time was precious? Her desire funneled, pouring more moisture between her legs, and she shifted her stance. Slowly? She couldn't wait. She wanted him now.

His eyes watched her as his fingers teased and tormented, cupping a full breast. "And when you are a whimpering, desperate pool of need, begging me to make you mine, I promise to thoroughly, expertly ravish you!" His hand slid lower, a smile curving his lips as he molded the thin linen of her chemise to the wet juncture between her thighs. When she gasped, he laughed and stepped away.

"Does that meet with your approval?"

She stumbled back, blinking up at him. When her dazed delirium cleared, and she saw his amused expression, her eyes narrowed. He was teasing her, playing her like some marionette doll, pulling the strings of her desire. Well, she was no longer the innocent. He had turned her into a wanton hussy, and she reveled in it.

She tipped her head, lowered her lashes, and gave him a scorching perusal that dropped to his full, sensual lips quirked in amusement, down over his shoulders, his taut stomach, and settled on the growing bulge in his trousers. "Mmh, this ravishing? Will it be done slowly as well?"

"Ah . . ." Garrett's voice was hoarse, and he had to clear his throat before he could respond. "I might be able to manage that."

"See that you do." Emboldened, she slipped her chemise over her head and tossed the undergarment onto the couch. Naked from the waist up, she shook her hair back as she slid off her petticoats and brushed them aside. Wearing only the pink flush that suffused her body, she brazenly lifted her chin.

"Oh, dear Lord," he breathed, his gaze like a sensual caress over her naked body, roaming over every inch of her. When his eyes lifted to hers, all humor was gone. "I want you. I need you. I love you."

She thought she was strong, but his words had reduced her legs to jelly and her body to one quivering mass of desire. "I think . . ."

"Shh." He pressed his fingers to her lips. "No thinking, only feeling."

She shifted his hand to her cheek and amended her words. "I *feel* that I'm at a disadvantage. You have too many clothes on while I have none." She fingered the lapel of his jacket. "Maybe I should assist you with that?"

His smile flashed, and the heavy-lidded look he gave her sent shivers down her spine. "Maybe you should."

Returning his smile, she unbuttoned his jacket. She moistened her lips as she slid her hands inside, gliding them slowly up over his strong chest, around his broad shoulders, and finally slipping the jacket down his arms, feeling the heat of his body through his linen shirt. When it landed on the ground, she brushed it aside with her foot. She started to work on the buttons of his shirt, but his hands were there.

He stripped it from his trousers, whipped it over his head, and flung it to the floor. Patience was not one of Garrett's virtues—thank God. She reveled in the sight of his muscle-toned body half clothed before her, tall, lean, and strong. Her beautiful soldier.

Her love.

She closed the distance between them, standing on tiptoes to spread a trail of kisses over his shoulders. Planting her hands on his chest, she lowered them to splay over his taut abdomen and curl her fingers around his lean hips, pulling him to her. He felt so good, all satiny smooth muscle and hard planes.

Her touch again encountered the puckered scar curving over his hip. She flattened her palm over the healed skin and lifted her eyes to his. Her heart fluttered as she cupped his smooth, shaved cheeks. "I need you. I want you. Be mine." She knew poetry, too. He was teaching it to her. "I love you, Garrett."

She leaned into him, crushing her breasts against his chest and pulling him down for another kiss. Her hands curled over his shoulders, her fingers digging into them as she sought to merge her body with his. To hold him to her.

Safe. Alive. Hers.

She closed her eyes against the words and tightened her grip.

A guttural groan tore from him, and his hands cupped her buttocks, urging her closer, his erection pressing against her, firm, hard, and fully aroused. His lips were no longer gentle but persistent, drinking her in, his passion matching hers as their tongues and bodies tangled. He tugged her down to the blankets, laying her on her back. He knelt poised over her, his hands braced on either side of her, his hair in disarray.

Her beautiful, battered, but unbroken soldier.

She would not lose him. Would not let him go.

Whatever it takes.

Closing her eyes, her heart thundered as a mixture of desperation and desire coursed through her in a crushing wave. Riding it, she opened her eyes and pulled Garrett to her, gasping when he twisted so that she lay sprawled on top of him. He grinned at her surprise.

"Finally, I have you right where I want you," he murmured.

She settled herself more comfortably on top of him, reveling in the feel of his heart pounding against her, his hot skin, satiny smooth beneath her. The light covering of chest hair tickling her breasts. "Maybe I have you where I want you." She leaned over and nipped his ear, drawing a grunt from him. Laughing, she tickled the curve of his ear with her tongue, feeling him jerk beneath her.

He pushed her back and lifted his head to let his tongue stroke along her lips, his breath warm against her mouth. "Isn't it nice to know that for once our wants finally coincide," he teased, dropping his head back to the pillows and brushing her hair from her forehead. Grabbing a large strand, he pulled her head back. "What else do you want?" His voice was low and husky, his eyes locked on hers.

"For you to be mine, for you to love me forevermore," she responded, leaning down to press her lips to his heart and hide the sheen of tears that pooled in her eyes.

Don't leave me.

"Done," he growled. With one quick motion, he rolled over so she was beneath him. She sighed at the delicious weight of his body, crushing into hers, his arousal hard and firm against her thigh. She lifted a knee, settling him more comfortably between her legs, feeling wet and more than ready for him. His hands, rough and calloused, stroked the soft skin of her inner thighs, and her breathing turned to fast and shallow gulps. "Garrett," she breathed his name.

His lips sank into the curve of her neck, kissing the sensitive skin. He weaved a path of kisses along the hollow dip of her collarbone. His hands cupped and molded her breasts, tormenting the pliant peaks until she writhed and moaned in delicious agony. His mouth was hot and wet as he teased one breast, suckled her thoroughly before moving over to lavish the other with his attention. She arched, small moans escaping her as her hands clutched his head to her.

She caressed the curve of his back, sweat slicked and smooth beneath her palms and . . . a frown creased her brow. His trousers barred further exploration of his glorious skin. This would not do. The trousers had to go. She tugged on a strand of his hair, pulling his head back until he looked at her with passion-glazed eyes.

"What? What is it?" He struggled to focus, his breathing rapid, his voice hoarse.

"I think . . . I *feel*," she hastened to clarify, "too many clothes. I *feel*"—she shifted her hips suggestively against his hard erection and lifted her leg to run her foot down his trousers leg—"that is a problem. And I *want*," she emphasized, "them off. Now." She slid her hand beneath his trousers, sliding it over his buttock and pinching him.

He jerked, then flashed her a wicked grin. When she removed her hand, he caught it and pressed a quick kiss to her palm. "Done." He rolled to the side and shed his trousers so quickly she barely had time to draw breath before he yanked her back to him. The feel of his hot erection, hard and pulsing against her thigh, had her pulse racing.

He slid his hand over the curve of her hip, her belly, and then lower, slipping between her legs and drawing a gasp from her as his fingers stroked the moist folds between her legs. "Garrett." She sighed again, her cheeks burning.

"Is this what you want?" His fingers moved with more deliberation, and she groaned, digging her nails into his arms.

"Yes, oh, God, yes."

Just when she thought she would tumble over the precipice and fall, he removed his hand. She cried out in protest. When his guttural laugh answered her, she opened her eyes, frowning as he lowered his head and rained a trail of wet kisses over her belly, moving lower and lower.

She gasped and grabbed his hair, tugging him up as she squirmed to close her legs. No, he couldn't, he wouldn't. It was indecent. A hot, mortified flush suffused her body. "No! I can't!"

Garrett lifted his head and braced himself on his arms. His gaze met hers and he lifted his finger to press it against her lips, silencing her denial. "Shh. It's all right. Trust me. You said you did." He lowered his mouth to hers and his kiss was soft and gentle. "You're safe with me. You'll always be safe with me. I love you, Alex."

She looked into his eyes and felt herself surrendering to him—again. "I do. I do trust you. Only you."

He smiled and his head dipped. She gasped when his mouth closed over her moist center, her most private part, nearly bringing her bucking off the bed. Her hands fell limply to her sides, her fingers twisting into the bed linens. An intoxicating heat flooded her as he worked his magic on her, his tongue tasting, coaxing, and torturing her, his strong hands parting her thighs. Good Lord, it still couldn't be decent . . . It wasn't . . . Well, she didn't know what it was. Could no longer think. Could only feel and trust in Garrett to catch her when she collapsed.

And wasn't that the point?

She tossed her head back and forth, biting her lips as a molten heat climbed within her.

"Let go, Alex. Trust me." Garrett's breath was warm and teasing against her thigh. Suddenly he moved his hand and his fingers found the most sensitive tip of her feminine folds and he worked more magic, sending ripples of pleasure exploding throughout her body. "Oh, dear Lord." She gasped.

The combined assault of his mouth and his fingers pushed her to the brink. She could only do as he requested and trust in him to catch her when she let go. Her breathing quickened and a while later, she cried out as her body jerked, and she tumbled off that precipice. Garrett lifted his head and moved up to snake his arms around her, holding tight to her limp, pliant body as she tumbled. The welcome weight of his body against hers, his smooth skin scalding hot, added to her pleasure, and her smile was drowsy.

"So much for slowly," Garrett's voice was a hoarse croak. "I can't . . . I can't wait."

When she opened her eyes and collected her scattered thoughts, she noted the intensity of his expression, the sweat beading his temple. It took all her strength to lift her hand and cup his cheek. "Then don't," she whispered and ran her thumb over his full bottom lip.

His eyes flashed, and he caught her hand, linked their fingers together, and stretched her arms high above her head, causing her to arch into him. His eyes locked with hers, and she felt the warmth of his pulsing shaft, hard and powerful, probing against her slick, wet folds. Moistening her lips, she lifted her hips in invitation. With one smooth thrust, he slid home, embedding himself deeply within her body. His hands squeezed hers, and her heart thundered.

"Oh, God, you feel so good. Better than good." He gasped, moving his hips slowly, his gray eyes almost black. "I love you, Alex."

"I love you, too." She gasped.

He kissed her, and she tasted herself as his tongue parried with hers. His hips lifted and sank as he thrust into her, deep and hard. She found herself straining upward, reaching again for the climax of moments before. He lifted his head, and the bright, feral look in his eyes as he watched her writhe against him was as erotic as his movements.

A guttural groan emerged from deep within him when she

wrapped her legs around his hips, his fingers squeezing her hands tighter as she arched against him, meeting his deep, powerful thrust. He fully withdrew from her and then slid deep, repeating the movements again and again in a slow, delicious rhythm. She was not surprised when the first whimper escaped her, for he had said he would turn her into a whimpering pool of need. "Please." He had reduced her to begging.

He released her hands and slid them beneath her to cup her buttocks, burying himself deeper within her as the heat climbed between them. His movements and thrusts became deeper, swifter, and more savage. His breathing quickened and his back arched. "Garrett!" His name ripped from her and she tightened her muscles to hold him inside as her climax exploded from her.

"Oh, God, I can't . . . I . . ." He gasped. He closed his eyes as his body shuddered again and again with the force of his release, triggering another response from her. She felt the warm liquid of his climax explode through her, his hips pressed to hers as his body sagged, small spasms still shaking him.

A while later, he drew an unsteady breath. Folding her body into his, he gathered her close and collapsed beside her.

She curled her fingers into his damp hair, his head cradled against her breast, his mouth pressed to her pounding heart. "Actually, I think you can," she whispered, once she recovered her voice. "And very well indeed."

He emitted a sound that was more grunt than laugh. "Always thinking."

"Not always." She smiled. "I've learned the pleasures of just feeling." His lips curved against her breast as a companionable silence settled between them. She played with his hair, lifting a black, silken strand and sliding it around her fingers.

She stretched beneath him, utterly content with her abduction, her seduction, and her captor. "I'm sorry your plans were slowed down, but catching up does have its merits."

"So does ravishment." He lifted his head and leered at her.

She laughed. "So it does. Another lesson learned. Pity it took us so long."

"Actually, the timing worked beautifully because you had me puzzled, and I've never been good at puzzles." Garrett shifted onto his side next to her, propping his head on his elbow, a teasing glint in his eyes.

"I was a puzzle?" She frowned. "How so?"

"You had rejected my offer of a horse and made it clear you would not accept any gifts from me. Then you kept reminding me of our blasted business arrangement. I feared you didn't want anything from me, while I had decided I craved everything from you." His voice lowered and he ran his finger down her cheek and over her now-tender lips.

"I finally understood what you needed from me. It wasn't something I could put a price on or gamble away or sell. It took me a while to realize it because they were things I never thought I'd give to anyone. As of a few months ago, I believed they had no value. That no one would want them . . . until you."

"What?" she whispered, mesmerized by the husky timbre of his voice.

He lay down and gathered her into his arms, cradling her against his chest. "My heart. My soul. My love."

She sighed, her body warming at his words. They were better than poetry. Blinking at the moisture in her eyes, she had to swallow before she could respond. "It's a fair exchange, considering you have mine." Against her ear, she listened to the beat of his heart. "Gifts from the heart are the most valuable. Much better than a horse." She smiled at his rumble of laughter, closing her eyes as his hand swept through her hair.

For the first time in her life, she understood why her mother never cared when cherished possessions disappeared to pay a debt, a favorite horse was sold, or rooms were emptied of furniture. For should fate again steal her fortune, she'd still be rich. As long as she held Garrett's heart, she was in possession of all she ever needed to secure her happiness. After a year of hunger, she was full. After months of fear and uncertainty, she felt safe. After so much poverty, she was rich. For tonight, she possessed everything she could ever want.

Her arms lifted to encircle his neck, and Garrett gasped when she nearly strangled him in her hold. Untangling her arms, he pressed a kiss into each of her palms, and lowered her arms to encircle his waist. Once again, she clung tight, desperately seeking to hold him to her, to push away the blackness hovering over their happily-ever-after and threatening to take Garrett away from her.

She'd think about it tomorrow.

Tonight was theirs, and she was taking it.

It was a long while later that her eyes fluttered closed and she fell asleep to the slow, even beat of Garrett's heart against her cheek.

Chapter Twenty-eight

❧

FOUR sharp knocks on the door in rapid succession had Garrett jerking awake. The war had trained him to be a light sleeper, ever on alert. Upon his return home . . . well, there wasn't much sleep to be had then, either. He bolted up, tense and disoriented, disturbed at how deeply he had slept and how erotic his dreams had been. A curse at Havers and his signature knock formed on Garrett's lips, but the sudden awareness of warmth against his side distracted him. Relief flooded him and he relaxed. He knew exactly where he was and for the first time since his return home, it was right where he wished to be.

Memories swarmed over him, supplanting his dream, the images vivid and all involving Alex. His eyes dropped to her sleeping beside him and his heart skipped. It wasn't often a man awoke to paradise, complete with his own angel, so he took a moment to savor it. The supplies Havers had left for him would still be sitting outside the door when he was ready to collect them.

He propped his head on his hand and watched her. Her lips were parted and her cheek rested on her hand. Romeo's words drifted to him, *O, that I were a glove upon that hand, That I might touch—* He blinked. Christ, he was getting soft and it wouldn't do. His eyes fastened on a bare breast and his body stirred, aroused.

Not all of him was soft.

Grinning, he leaned over and kissed her, gently at first and then with purpose, coaxing her into wakefulness, wanting her again with a desperation that surprised him. He feared he'd never get enough of her, would crave her in his grave. He heard her sigh as her fingers slid into the hair at his nape. She was so damn responsive. Her surrender to him so sweet.

She loved him. No one, with the exception of Kit, had ever loved him as honestly as Alex. When women had declared their love for him, it had amused him, for the man they claimed to love was but an illusion he had made of himself. Only Alex had he trusted enough to reveal all his broken pieces. She knew his nightmares and hadn't turned away, but rather took him into her heart and claimed him for her own.

Closing his eyes, he lowered his mouth to the slim column of her neck, burying his face in her soft skin and breathing her in. He needed a moment, just a moment.

A sharp tug on his hair had him lifting his head in protest.

"What happened at my uncle's? What did he say? Did you see my cousins?"

Damn. His moment was up.

He had wanted Alex to waken, but this was not the response he had desired. He groaned. She never stopped her infernal thinking unless he kissed her senseless. *There's a thought.* He dipped his face to hers, but she yanked harder on his hair.

"Oh, no, you don't. I want answers."

"What about what I want?" He wiggled his hips against her.

Her eyes widened. "Mmh, I feel your want."

"Well?"

"We'll take care of it later." She shoved his shoulder and scrambled out from beneath him.

Growling, he rolled onto his back and swore under his breath when she scooped up his shirt and slipped it over her head. She turned and knelt before him expectantly. Her hair was disheveled, her lips swollen, and her cheeks flushed pink. She had never looked more delectable. Or more determined.

He flung an arm over his eyes and blew out a breath. He had forgotten about that irritating mettle of hers. He admired it, but there was a time and place for one to exert their steely resolve. Once they were married, he'd make damn clear it wasn't when they were naked and he was fully aroused.

"Ouch!" He jerked at the hard poke to his ribs and lowered his arm to glower at her.

"Well?" She glowered back.

Muttering about bossy, ornery females under his breath, he sat up and rolled to his feet, searching for his trousers. Locating them, he snatched them up and yanked them on. "If I'm discussing your uncle, I'm not doing it on an empty stomach. I'm having trouble swallowing the fact that he lives."

He buttoned his trousers and planted his hands on his hips, regarding Alex as she peered up at him. He studied his shirt, the sleeves rolled up, the tails covering her bare thighs. Unable to resist, he crouched before her. "It's chilly; perhaps I should put on my shirt?" He laughed when she slapped his roving hand away. "Fine, I'll light the fire." He stood, but looking back, he narrowed his eyes and lifted a finger to wag it at her, his expression one of mock severity. "Don't try escaping. You have my shirt and my heart, and I will come after both."

She rolled her eyes. "I'm not leaving until I get answers."

"You're a relentless woman," he muttered as he retrieved the basket from outside. He carried it over to Alex, answering her unasked question. "Havers delivered it. He also advised Brandon and Kit not to worry about us. I had him explain that I was abducting you, and we wouldn't be returning until you were thoroughly compromised."

"You didn't!" She gasped.

"I did!" He laughed at her expression. "Perhaps not in those exact words, but I had to forestall Kit sending out a search party. So now we are at liberty to remain here indefinitely."

"I see. So I've been indefinitely abducted?"

"*And* thoroughly compromised. Don't forget that. It's the best part. Now you have to marry me. You yourself stated that you refused to be my mistress."

She shook her head. "However, we're prevaricating. My uncle?" She cocked an imperious brow.

Smiling, he turned to the hearth. *Indefinitely abducted.* He liked the ring of it. He'd have to do it more often. The compromising part was pleasant, too.

His mood improved as he worked to build a fire. He blew on the smoldering embers, coaxing them to catch on the logs, the old editions of the *Times* crumpling as they ignited. He sat back on his heels and watched the fire lick the wood until it eventually caught and climbed in an undulating dance of flames. At the touch on his shoulder, he turned to accept the mug Alex handed him. "Cider?"

"Cider," she confirmed. "I've made up a plate for you."

He nodded and stood to follow Alex to sit beside her on the sofa. While he had made the fire, she had dragged the table before it and prepared two plates of food. She handed him one, piled high with bread, meats, and cheeses. While his appetite craved something more carnal, this would have to suffice. For now.

"So my uncle?" Alex prodded.

There went his appetite. He struggled not to choke on his bite of bread, taking a swig of his cider to wash it down.

"You were gone over a week. What took you so long?"

His light mood darkened at the memory of his confrontation with her uncle. The combed-over strands of her uncle's hair had done little to hide his gleaming scalp. The man's head was as round as the rest of him. Garrett could not fathom his relation to Alex until he looked into the bastard's vivid blue eyes, magnified behind his wire-rimmed spectacles. He had Alex's eyes and Garrett damned him for it.

He shifted, shaking off the disconcerting portrait. "Murdering him would have been faster, but Brandon had another plan. His plan took longer because we had to track down your former estate manager, Edward Marks, prior tenants of the estate, various merchants, as well as your uncle's banker."

"Marks! However did you find him?" she exclaimed. "And what did you want with all these people?"

"To have leverage in our negotiations. We knew your uncle would bargain over the betrothal contract." Rather, gouge him for coin to silence her uncle's slander. "We anticipated his settlement price would be steep."

He studied Alex's expression, waiting for her reaction as he continued. "We met with *Viscount Langdon* to negotiate a betrothal agreement between myself and his niece, Alexandra Langdon." Her eyes shot to his. "Don't blame Gus; he didn't know you hadn't given me your true identity when he let it slip who your uncle was."

"I was going to tell you, but I was afraid," she murmured.

"I love you, Alexandra *Daniels* Langdon. Your surname changes nothing for me." His shoulder nudged hers. "As Juliet said, *What's in a name? that which we call a rose . . .*" Appalled, his voice trailed off and he snapped his mouth closed. He was spouting Shakespeare. *Again.* Is this what love did to a man? Little wonder Brandon walked around looking like an idiot.

Disgusted with himself, he gave his head a sharp shake.

"That which we call a rose by any other name would smell as sweet," Alex finished. She lifted their joined hands to her lips and pressed a kiss to his knuckles. "That's for the poetry."

He forgot his concerns over Shakespeare as his body warmed under her adoring gaze.

"The negotiations?" Alex prodded. "How did they proceed? Was Brandon with you?"

He blinked. "Yes. He played the haughty, intimidating earl while I was the handsome, charming suitor. We both excelled at our parts, but then again, I didn't have to act."

She smiled. "And?"

He needed to get this over with or he was never getting her out of that shirt. Resigned, he leaned back and raked a hand through his hair. "Your uncle isn't a gambler, but he found other venues in which to run through the estate's profits and climb into the same hole of debt that your father had." His eyes met Alex's. "What you didn't know when you fled is that he didn't need you to make a lucrative marriage to provide dowries for his daughters, but rather to save himself from debtor's gaol."

"No! The estate was profitable. Marks and I—"

"It was profitable when your father lived and you worked with Marks. Your uncle fired Marks, raised the rent on his tenants until most followed the manager's departure. Fields went fallow because there weren't workers to farm them. Without crops or tenants to pay rent, there was no income." He shrugged. "It's a vicious cycle and your uncle was spinning in it. He needed a lucrative betrothal agreement. So when I arrived, he offered me your hand in return for my paying him a small fortune."

Eyes wide, she stared at him. "What did you do?"

He grinned. "I made him a counter offer, one lucrative for both of us. He retained his life and his freedom, while I married his niece and refrained from killing him."

"You didn't!" A choked laugh escaped Alex.

"I did. I told your uncle I believed he'd agree to the terms once he understood I was in possession of all his outstanding notes, having paid off his creditors to gain them. I intended to call them in, but gave him a choice of payments. He could pay me the monies owed, or if he signed his niece's betrothal agreement, I'd cancel his outstanding debts.

"Your uncle quickly understood the benefits to my offer, especially when Brandon advised him that should he decline my terms and continue to spread lies about you, Brandon would kill him if I didn't get to him first. So I got you and he got to live—and of course, stay out of debtor's gaol. Both parties were satisfied and negotiations proceeded amicably from then on."

"Oh, Garrett," Alex breathed. "And Lord Cheaver?" she murmured, her eyes downcast, her thumb moving over his hand.

He frowned at the mention of the old lecher who had tried to buy Alex from her uncle. The man still lived only because he hadn't touched her. "Apparently, he got caught in a compromising position with another man's wife and hasn't been seen since. Rumor has it that he's recovering from a rather delicate wound and won't be playing Lothario for a while, if ever again. And as you once so sagely advised me, there is usually truth in rumors." He grinned.

"Oh, dear." Humor danced in Alex's eyes.

"What it cost him was dear indeed." His lips twitched. "And the other men who would slander your name were empty threats. But no one will dare come forward now that you are mine. They'd know if I don't kill them, Brandon would." He squeezed her hand. "On another matter, your uncle also agreed to rehire Marks, be allotted an allowance, and leave estate management in Marks's more capable hands."

"Why on earth would he agree to that?" She frowned.

"Because if he did, I promised to provide his daughters with full dowries when they marry."

"You offered dowries for the girls?" Alex looked stunned.

He shrugged. "They are your cousins, and as you said, innocent of your uncle's mendacity. Also, one of the girls was peering between the railings of the upstairs banister when we arrived. She had to be no more than ten or twelve and had these enormous blue eyes and a wild mane of blonde hair." He grinned. "She reminded me of someone I had met over a hand of cards and who stole my heart."

"That must have been Prudence," Alex murmured.

"No, that would be you," he teased.

"I meant peering through the banister," Alex clarified with a smile. With a glad cry, she threw her arms around his neck and spread eager kisses over his face. "That is wonderful! You are wonderful! I adore you!"

He smiled and wrapped his arms around her. "So now we can get started on making those babies . . ."

The light in Alex's eyes suddenly dimmed, and she pushed away from him, evading his arms when he would have pulled her back into his embrace. He frowned. What now? Was there someone else he had to kill? Was he ever going to get her out of his shirt? "No, Garrett, we can't."

"Why? What now?"

She lifted her hands and dropped them in a plaintive gesture. "Garrett, how can we sit here and discuss our future when we might not have one?"

Christ. That was what truly kept them apart. A smoldering ember ready to ignite, or rather a loaded gun aimed and ready to fire. He blew out a breath and closed his eyes.

He felt Alex shift on the couch, and her forehead pressed to his, her breath warm on his lips as she spoke. "We need to return to London and resolve this murderous plot." She drew back and stared into his eyes. "We can't forget why I am here, why I agreed to come with you in the first place."

"You're right." He nodded. "There is our bargain to consider, and your need to uphold your side of it. Should I pay you for services rendered to date, *services rendered* being your choice of words, not mine, well then, one can construe that as payment rendered for—"

"Don't even go there." Her eyes narrowed in warning. "Not while we are discussing needing my help in saving your life. It could be dangerous."

He laughed and held up his hands defensively. "I'm in full retreat."

"Good." Her smile dimmed and her words were soft. "It is time, Garrett. I want those babies, but I refuse to raise Romeo and Juliet alone."

He gave her a dubious look. "Romeo and Juliet?"

"It's in tribute to your poetry."

He laughed and then became serious. "Fine. We'll head for London at the week's end and catch the bastard."

"Good." She smiled. "I trust you to do so."

Silence settled between them, laden with the unspoken knowledge of the high cost of failure. So they wouldn't fail. There was a reason he had survived Balaclava, and she sat beside him. "Let's not let your uncle or other worries steal any more of our time when God knows how much we have left of it."

"Don't say that!" Alex flung her arms around his neck. "Don't even think it. I can't bear it."

Sighing, he closed his eyes and crushed her close. "I'm sorry. I didn't mean it, it's just this morning did not go in the direction I had planned when I woke up with you naked in my arms. Too many distractions rudely interrupted us. Let's put them aside and discuss a far more lucrative negotiation." He removed her arms from around his neck and set her away from him. "Something mutually rewarding."

"What can you possibly want from me?" Alex moistened her lips and cocked her head to the side, batting her eyelashes at him.

He laughed at her coy look, but then slid his gaze meaningfully over her body. "I want to know what it will take for you to get naked?"

Alex pursed her lips and looked as if she were seriously pondering his question. She lifted her hands to her collar, sliding them down to undo the top button, teasing him with the curve of her breast. "Well, you'd have to get me out of your shirt." She eased off the sofa and stood, slowly backing away from him.

He frowned, not sure of her game, but appreciating the

challenging gleam in her eyes and the sudden surge of heat spiraling through his body.

"In order to do that," she said as she moved farther from him. "You'll have to catch me first." She tossed her words over her shoulder as she turned and fled.

Instantly, he was on his feet and had rounded the sofa before Alex had gained a few yards, had nearly caught her when she squealed and ducked behind an old rocking chair. He dodged one way and she the opposite, laughing as she kept the barrier between them. He planted his hands on his hips and assessed her bright, blue-eyed gaze.

"You are lovely."

"But still wearing your shirt," she countered, laughing.

He shrugged. "For the moment." He watched her, waiting as her eyes narrowed in suspicion. She had never liked it when he fell silent. Her unease had amused him. When it suited his mood to unnerve her, he had simply remained quiet and watched her and waited. His calm, composed Alex would get flustered and color a delightful shade of pink.

She studied him, trying to gauge his intent. Then she made her mistake, her eyes straying from his momentarily to seek an escape route.

In her one unguarded moment, he whipped the chair out of the way and his arm snaked around her waist, yanking her to him.

She squealed, shoving at his bare chest before her foot caught in a rug. She cried out as she stumbled, and he scooped her into his arms.

Triumphant, he laughed and spun her around, her arms clinging to his neck. He pressed his forehead to hers. "I have you now."

"No, I have you." Alex smiled and added, "And your shirt."

"So another mutually beneficial resolution has been found," he murmured as he carried her over to the blankets before the fire. "But about that shirt . . ."

Chapter Twenty-nine

THEY had allowed themselves one night at the lodge. A long, languid night of talking, laughing, and making love before the fire. Garrett found he had an aversion to clothes on Alex. While she looked lovely in anything she wore, he preferred her wearing nothing but the pink afterglow from their lovemaking, a dazed expression, and a satisfied smile.

One night wasn't enough. He wanted forever. For that reason, as soon as they returned home, he had sequestered himself in his office and took another look at Hammond's damn guest list.

He had isolated a few murderous contenders, and something nagged at him when he looked at the list, but he couldn't jog it loose. It was like a hook snagged on the clutter of his thoughts. Perhaps if he stopped pushing at it, it would shake free.

He stood and rounded his desk, recalling that Alex and Kit were in the back garden. Kit was never happier than when she had her fingers in a pile of dirt. With luck she'd convert Alex to the pastime and keep her out of Stewart's hair. When his estate manager and Alex got their heads together, it was difficult to pry Alex away, but the garden . . . well, Alex gardened as well as she sang. There was hope she'd be willing to abandon her task for a more intimate respite.

He strode through the back doors and down the steps, his mood lifting at the sight of Alex. She was kneeling beside Kit and jabbing at the dirt with a trowel. She was lovely. Furrowed brow and all. At his laugh, she stood, brushed her skirts, and smiled at him.

As he started forward, his name was called in a high-pitched squeal. He turned to see Will scramble through the doors, his nursemaid struggling to catch him. His sights set on Garrett, Will tripped on the last step and went sprawling to the ground. The item clutched in his hand spiraled through the air and landed with a clatter at Garrett's feet. He scooped it up as Will's howls pierced his ears.

"All right, little man, a bit of a spill is all." He lifted Will into his arms. With his nephew's face buried in his shoulder, Garrett turned to see Alex assist Kit to her feet. "Here, let's feel for broken bones." He gently probed Will's arms, legs, and then poked at his stomach, tugged on his ear, and squeezed his neck, transforming the boy's distress into squirming giggles of delight.

"He's in one piece," he reported to Kit. "No broken bones, no missing pieces on the ground. Oh, wait, we did find one thing." Smiling, he lifted the pocket watch that Will had dropped and brandished it just out of reach.

"Mine!" Will cried out, straining for the watch.

"Is it now?" Garrett teased. "I don't know. I have one just like it. Maybe we should take a closer look." Evading Will's grasping hands, he snapped open the cover and froze. His smile faded as he stared at the bird engraved on the inside. *A falcon.*

The Brown family crest.

The falcon stands for one who does not rest until his objective is achieved, his stepfather's pompous words reverberated. Garrett wouldn't forget them, for the damn bird was branded on the watch burning a hole in his own pocket.

The Browns had been a titled aristocratic family, but they had taken umbrage at Henry VIII's courtship of Anne Boleyn. Due to their lack of allegiance, they had been stripped of their title and banned from court. Garrett recalled Arthur's bitterness over his ancestry, had been reminded of it every time Garrett had sullied his own title and Arthur had lectured him on being undeserving of an earldom.

"Mine!" Will cried. "Grapa give me! Mine. I have."

Will's words chilled Garrett. He returned the item to Will and set him on his feet. Straightening, he regarded Kit and Alex. Will did not have this watch before he left, always coveting Garrett's. It was a recent acquisition. His jaw clenched.

"He was here. When? When the hell was he here?" He struggled to keep his voice level for Will's sake, but his bile rose at the knowledge of his stepfather invading his home. But how? How had he bypassed the men he had patrolling his property? But he knew. Arthur was family, regardless of whether or not either of them chose to acknowledge that fact. He doubted any of his men would believe his directive about no trespassing applied to his stepfather.

"Garrett, I can explain," Kit started.

His gaze locked on Alex. Kit's loyalty was to Brandon; Alex's should be to him. "You said you trusted me. Is this how you show it? You know how I feel about him."

"No!" Alex gasped, blanching at his attack.

Kit stepped in front of Alex. "The decision wasn't Alex's but mine. She wanted to tell you, but I asked her to wait. Garrett, you need to listen to me. I can—"

"How the hell did he know I was here?"

"Keyes wrote to him. Garrett—"

"I can imagine what he wrote." He snorted. The sudden image of the watch flying through the air flashed before Garrett, and his blood ran cold. The debris cluttering his mind cleared, the hook unsnagged, and the thought that had pestered him earlier bobbed to the surface. "And the watch? Why the hell would Arthur part with his treasured family heirloom? Didn't he tout it as his only fortune?" It was why as a naïve boy he had sought to buy the bastard another.

Kit looked taken aback by his question. "This isn't what you think. It's a cheap replacement that doesn't even keep the time. Arthur said he had lost the other one. He'd never have willingly parted with the original. Not even for Will."

No, Arthur hadn't willingly parted with the watch. He'd had no choice. Payment was due.

"Garrett, about Arthur's visit, let us explain." Alex spoke for the first time, her tone beseeching.

"Not now." His eyes locked on Alex. "But later. Later we will have lots to discuss." His thoughts spiraling, he turned his back on her and retraced his steps to the house.

"Garrett, wait!" Alex's cry bounced off him as he dashed through the French doors, his mind racing.

He knew the identity of his would-be murderer.

Arthur.

⇒⇐

GARRETT RODE AS if the beasts of hell were on his heels, needing to race off the rage boiling inside him. If the truth were told, he hadn't learned anything new. When Brandon had first given him Hammond's guest list and his eyes had lit on his stepfather's name, he had paused and considered, but he had rejected the thought. He had done so for Kit's sake and because he had refused to lend credence to his darkest suspicions. But slowly, inexorably, like a pulsing tide wears down the most impermeable surface, the truth wore at him until he could no longer reject it.

His stepfather wanted him dead. Had hired assassins to murder him.

It was a truth he ignored at his own peril.

He had fought in the Crimea for two years, but he and Arthur had been at war his whole life. It had begun when he was six years old and Garrett had sought to console his newly widowed mother. Arthur, their closest neighbor, had physically dragged Garrett from her side and coldly explained that he would be taking care of Garrett's mother from then on. Garrett was not needed.

He didn't know what had changed or why, but Arthur must have decided the time had come for one of them to be declared a winner. The Browns' damn falcon might stand for achieving their objective, but the Kendall coat of arms had two crossed swords that stood for justice and military honor. Garrett had earned the latter and he would achieve the former.

He reined in before the periphery of the hops fields, searching out Brandon, who had ridden down earlier with Beau. He dismounted and handed Champion off to one of the workers who stepped forward to assist him. He nodded a curt greeting to those who recognized him. However, intent on his purposes, as soon as he located his quarry, he made his way to where Brandon stood conversing with Holt. When Brandon noticed his approach and his black expression, he excused himself and met Garrett halfway.

"What is it? Is it Kit?" Brandon's face was etched with worry, and he caught Garrett's arm in a painful vice.

"Kit's fine. Everyone is fine. Where is Beau?"

Brandon raised a brow, but dropped his hand. "He's riding with Ned." His brow furrowed as he waited for Garrett to speak.

Garrett nodded. "Good, that's good."

"Christ man, what the hell is it?" Brandon studied him. "You're sheet white. Look like you've seen Lazarus rise from the grave. You haven't, have you?"

"It's Arthur, Brandon. Arthur is behind the attacks on my life."

Brandon recoiled at Garrett's words. He opened and closed his mouth, eyeing Garrett as if he had spouted two heads. When he recovered his voice, his words shot out in a heated tone. "Are you certain? Do you understand what you're saying? We're talking murder here!" he hissed, his gaze hard and sharp. "Your stepfather, for God's sake! Kit's father! My father-in-law plotting your murder!"

"I know what the hell I'm saying and what it means, how it touches us all. But this is Arthur's doing, not mine. Denying his guilt could cost me my life. I choose me over Arthur."

Brandon raked a hand through his hair and looked around, assessing who could overhear their conversation. He blew out a breath. "I saw his name on the list. And . . . and it crossed my mind. He's been talking strangely of late, things about Will, about Beau inheriting my title and Will your fortunes."

"Not so strange. I don't have an heir, didn't plan to have one until recently."

"Yes, but Arthur talked about things changing soon. How Will won't stand in Beau's shadow. The boys are Warrens, but Brown is in them as well. He finally has his boys. What made you realize it was Arthur? What happened?"

"It was the watch." At Brandon's confusion, Garrett recounted his belief that the flash of gold tossed for payment at Hammond's ball was Arthur's lost watch. "But deep down, I knew, and that's why I was dragging my feet about pursuing the matter. I can't fathom a madman's reasoning, but Arthur always said I wasn't worthy of my title and should be divested of it as well as control of the Kendall estates. My death certainly takes care of that. And you know how he rants about the Browns' fall from grace. Perhaps he refuses to stand by and watch Will's fortunes fall. My death protects Will's inheritance, which I'm jeopardizing with this new venture into trade."

Brandon looked at him and his expression hardened. "It makes sense in a madman's perverse reasoning. But we'll need proof. Evidence implicating him. We need that watch."

"We'll get it. Once we find the man hired to pull the trigger. Once he's in custody, he'll squeal like the rat he is."

"I take it you have a plan?" Brandon cocked a brow. "One that will keep us out of Newgate?"

"I do. Let's collect Holt and I'll go over it with you. But there's something else. We followed your plan with Alex's uncle, but we're using mine this time. I need you to back me up, but I can't have you in the forward guard. This is my fight, not yours."

Brandon met his eyes. "Fine. What do you want me to do?"

Garrett released his breath. He'd known Brandon would have his back with no questions asked. He always had, always would. Garrett hoped this was the last battle he and Brandon would wage together.

He was looking forward to spending the rest of his life sparring with Alex instead.

≈≈

Alex paced in the front parlor, seething. Damn Garrett. Damn him for storming off and refusing to listen to a word of explanation. To upset Kit like that. Poor Kit had gone to bed complaining of a headache. When Garrett returned and Alex had said her piece to him, his head would hurt, too. If it didn't, she'd pound on it herself. However, considering how thick it was, she doubted she'd make a dent.

If Garrett continued with this behavior, she might have to

reconsider her answer to any proposal of his. And he could forget making those babies. The world didn't need any more replicas of Garrett Melrose Sinclair. There would be . . . She paused, a sudden knocking on the front door interrupting her tirade.

Stewart was visiting the vicar, Ned had moved to work in the stables, and still short of a butler, which Garrett appeared in no rush to hire, Alex blew out a frustrated breath and changed course.

Pausing a moment to collect herself, she swept her hand over her hair, neatened her skirts, and opened the door. Surprised, she blinked at the unexpected sight of Garrett's stepfather, Arthur Brown, standing on the front landing.

He looked a far cry from the angry, confrontational man who had stormed inside during their last encounter. His clothes were dusted with dirt, his golden eyes anxious. Concern filled her. "Mr. Brown? Are you all right?"

"It's Beau . . . it's . . ."

"What?" She gasped, rushing outside and grasping his sleeve, the door slamming closed behind her. "What has happened?"

"He's all right," he hastened to clarify. He patted her hand reassuringly as he tucked it around his arm. "My apologies. I should have said that first."

"Thank God," she exhaled in relief. "Then what is it?"

"I'll explain along the way."

As they spoke, Arthur led her down the front steps. They stood before his carriage, her arm still looped through Arthur's. "But I need to get Kit," she protested, moving to disengage her hand. "If something has happened to Beau, she needs to know. Beau will want his mother."

"But it's you that I need."

Alex frowned at his enigmatic reply. "I don't understand."

"Please, if you'll come with me, I can explain." He opened the carriage door and withdrew the steps. "I must insist."

Despite her concern for Beau, Alex found her hackles rising at Arthur's officious manner. "Mr. Brown, I'm not going anywhere without speaking to Kit first. She needs—" She sucked in a sharp breath when something jabbed into her side. Hard.

She looked down to see Arthur's hand curled around a revolver, its menacing barrel lodged firmly in her waist.

"As I said, I must insist."

Her eyes shot to his face, her heart thundering. She knew that voice, its furious whisper. His lean, hawkish features, aquiline nose and thin lips, and his golden eyes now dark with a hard, feral gleam all came into sharp focus.

It was as if she was seeing him for the first time, recognizing him in all his evil duplicity.

When Arthur had visited previously, she had felt as if she had known him. She had been right. She had first encountered Arthur that fateful night on Hammond's patio when he had orchestrated the murder of his stepson.

However, she had seen him from a distance and could never identify him again with complete confidence, so it was not surprising that when she met him a second time with Kit, she didn't recognize him. His voice had also been different, not as nasally as it had been before, as if he had a cold.

"Move," Arthur barked, prodding her with the gun.

Damn Garrett for his abrupt departure and damn him for not hiring a big, burly butler because she really had need of both of them right now.

She gritted her teeth. If Arthur thought she would docilely climb into his carriage, he thought wrong. Arthur would have to drag her kicking and screaming into the carriage. Her eyes searched out the man on the box, but seeing his averted face, she knew he was Arthur's man and he would be of no help to her.

"If you value Beau's safety, you need to come quietly. His life depends upon it."

Damn it. For Beau's sake, she had to go. She had to make sure he was all right.

She cast a helpless glance over her shoulder before lifting her skirts to move toward the carriage.

She needed a plan of action and she needed it fast. Nothing came to her. Fear, cold and numbing, clouded her thinking.

"For Christ's sake, hurry up," Arthur hissed, giving her a shove.

She stumbled. Anger replaced fear and she vowed to muster a plan. If not, Garrett would find her.

She just needed to stay alive until he did so.

It was her last coherent thought before Arthur vaulted in behind her. As she turned to face him, a searing pain exploded across her temple.

She cried out as her knees buckled and her world went black.

Chapter Thirty

≫≪

W HAT do you mean you thought she was with me?" Garrett exploded when Kit informed him that Alex was not in the house and she hadn't been seen for a few hours.

Kit's eyes widened at his temper, her gaze shifting to Brandon as if seeking an explanation. "I thought she had gone to find you after you had stormed off so abruptly. Really, Garrett, I didn't tell you about Arthur because I knew you'd act like this, and he's just not worth—"

"Have you looked for her?" Garrett cut her off, a chill sweeping him.

She raised a brow. "Of course, and no one has seen her. She's not here."

Brandon held up his hands when Garrett cursed and began to pace the foyer. "Let's not jump to conclusions. We'll divide up and search the estate. She could still be here."

"I'll look outside," Garrett said, whirling on his heel. Two years in the Crimea had taught him to heed his gut instincts. His gut told him Alex was not inside and her disappearance was not good.

"Garrett—"

He heard Kit start, but Brandon must have silenced her because she quieted and let him go. He needed to go. He'd speak with Gus first, determine if Alex's mount was missing.

Quickening his pace, he covered the ground to the stables and burst inside at a near run, startling Gus, who was rubbing down Champion. The chill sweeping Garrett plummeted a few degrees at the sight of Autumn in her stall. "Have you seen Alex?" He stormed over to Gus. "Has she been here? Is Ned back yet?"

Gus frowned. "No, I haven't. I don't think she's been here. Least if she was, she didn't speak to me. But I was out repairin' fence in the back paddocks and Ned's ridin' with Beau."

"When you were out, did you see anyone near the house or riding this way?" Damn Keyes for his big mouth in informing Arthur about Garrett's location. If anything happened to Alex, Garrett vowed the man wouldn't survive the day.

Gus shook his head. "Can't say I did."

Garrett swore. "I need Champion, and I need you to keep an eye open for anything unusual—and for Alex. I fear she may be missing."

Gus's expression hardened as he clenched his jaw before collecting Champion's saddle. He worked with quick efficiency as he spoke. "Do you think she's all right? Is it her uncle?"

"No, it's not her uncle." Garrett's eyes met Gus's and he vaulted onto Champion. "As to her being in danger, I plan to find her before it comes to that." He spoke to himself as much as Gus as he urged Champion out of the barn and into a gallop.

A litany of recriminations spiraled through Garrett. He shouldn't have been distracted by Alex. Why didn't he listen to her explanation about Arthur's visit so that his last words to her would not have been spoken in anger? He should have hired a Goddamn butler and more house staff who would have witnessed Alex's departure and, more important, with whom she had left. He should have asked her to Goddamn marry him.

Such thinking did him little good, so he concentrated on what helped—vowing to locate Alex and kill Arthur.

He searched the adjacent fields, tenants' dwellings, and the hunting lodge, despite knowing that absent a mount, Alex could never have covered so much ground. But he couldn't face returning to the house. Not alone. Not yet.

He alerted Holt to Alex's absence, instructing him to advise the men to keep watch for any strangers or carriages in the near vicinity. He directed a group to search the area, scouring the grounds for foot tracks or recent carriage ruts. Some of these veterans were expert trackers from the war. Others could pry information from a statue, and two were sharpshooters, trained to spot the enemy before he knew they were upon him. He'd use them all. They were loyal to him and battle trained. He was back at war.

New enemy. Same rules, different engagement.

It wasn't until he had covered every trail or shelter that he finally conceded Alex had not ventured out on her own.

Reluctantly, he returned home. Brandon walked down the front steps to meet him. His grim expression answered Garrett's unasked question, and he swore. He needed another strategy, a new plan of attack.

"Look, if Arthur has her, he won't harm her." Brandon spoke quickly, keeping his voice level. "He wants you, not Alex. If your reasoning for Arthur's motive is right, he's protecting his grandchild's inheritance that *you're* threatening, not Alex. She's simply the bait. He'll get in touch with us because you're the ransom he wants in exchange for Alex."

Brandon might be right, but he couldn't wait. "I'm going after him."

Brandon lunged forward and snatched his reins. "Wait! You don't know where the hell he is, nor can you be certain if Arthur is behind this. Don't be daft—"

"But I do! I know Arthur!" He snapped back, yanking against Brandon's grip. "And he doesn't know we are onto him, so he can return home and hide there. He's arrogant enough to do so. I'll ride to his country estate; he wouldn't dare try to hide her in London and take the risk of being recognized or seen. I'll kill him if he's touched her, Brandon. I swear, I will." He leaned down to Brandon. "And this time, I won't be stopped. Don't even try."

"For God's sake, this is Kit's father we're talking about!" Brandon lowered his voice and cast a glance behind him before he continued, holding up his hand. "I can't save Arthur if he's taken Alex or harmed her. But until you are certain he has done so, you have to back off, Garrett! You have to. This is Kit's

father you plan to murder. Her blood. I'm not asking you to
have a care for Arthur, but I am asking you to have a care
for Kit."

The repetition of Kit's name managed to breach Garrett's
rage. He paused, his grip on the reins slacking. Christ. What a
coiled, incestuous mess.

Arthur was his half sister's father—bloody, murderous bastard or not.

Therein lay the difference between Arthur and himself.
Arthur never thought of Kit; Garrett could not forget her.

"We need you here coordinating a plan of action," Brandon
pressed. "You understand how to launch this kind of offensive,
and the men are loyal only to you."

"Fine." He blew out a breath. "But I'll be damned if I'll play
defense to his offense. If Alex is anywhere in the vicinity, I'll
find her or some bloody scrap of evidence leading to her whereabouts. I'm sending Stewart into town to collect some policemen, men to each of Arthur's properties, and a scout to ferret
the bastard out. *They will* have orders to shoot Arthur if Alex's
life is in danger." Garrett dismounted and slapped Champion's
rump, prodding him toward the stables. "Arthur's arrogant and
has no idea we know about him, so that might make him
careless."

Brandon fell into step beside him. "Let me break the news
to Kit. I can do that much for you."

Garrett clasped Brandon's shoulder. "She's strong. She'll
weather it."

"Yes, but she shouldn't have to." Anger laced Brandon's
words. Silence fell as they reached the front door. Stopping,
Brandon faced Garrett. "Alex is strong, too. Don't forget that."

"She is. She'll be all right."

"And we'll be ready."

Garrett nodded. "Damn right."

≻≺

ALEX WOKE UP with a pounding headache. The pain was remi-
niscent of the time she'd cracked her head on the door of Garrett's carriage. She searched the room, taking in the sheets
draped over every item of furniture and the curtains pulled
across the windows of a large, spacious bedroom. Shimmering

candlelight illuminated the area and she sought its source, her eyes widening at the sight of Arthur.

He sat on a sheet-covered chair in the corner, a candle sconce in one hand, the revolver in his other, casually propped against his thigh.

She jerked to a sitting position and grimaced at the bolt of pain that blazed across her head. Groaning, she pressed her hand to her temple, feeling the egglike swelling.

"You might have a bit of a bump. My apologies, but I didn't trust you to behave."

She shifted back on the bed, retreating from him. "Where . . . where are we?"

"Keyes's estate. He is away for a few days. This wing of the house has been closed off." Arthur waved a hand over their surroundings and wrinkled his nose. "Keyes is in debt. He thinks to save a few farthings by closing off rooms, reducing his staff and his stables, and of course, selling off parcels of his property. I believe Kendall—"

"Where's Beau?" She cut him off. She searched the room for Beau's small figure. Seeing the darkness behind the curtains, she gauged it to be evening, and the passage of time ratcheted up her fears for the child's safety.

Arthur's brow rose. "At this time of night, he should be safe at home with his mother." At her obvious surprise, he simply smiled. "It wasn't the boy I wanted, but rather his usefulness to you. Using his name served my purposes well enough."

He had played her expertly. She cursed him to hell and back before another thought struck her. "Is Keyes working with you?"

"No. The man hasn't the stomach for murder. While he is not a partner in my plans, he, like Beau, is useful to me."

"I don't understand."

"It's rather simple. He will hang for murdering you and Kendall at the hunting lodge. I heard about Kendall accusing him of trying to kill you both when Keyes's shot went wild during his hunt. I have no doubt the authorities will revisit Keyes once they find your bodies. Do you recall the incident?"

Alex nodded and slumped back into the pillows, her stomach roiling at Arthur's smirk and calm, conversational tone. The man could be discussing his gardening plans rather than cold-blooded murder. He was mad. Poised, collected, but stark-raving mad. Due to its throbbing pain, she refrained from giving her head a shake to clear it. Arthur's sanity or madness was irrelevant; the important point was his proximity to her. She needed to get far away from him. To escape.

"The man does have motive," Arthur continued. "He hates Kendall. Never forgave him for snatching up the property around here, including half of Keyes's land. Keyes has also complained about Kendall's plans to manufacture ale. We do agree on that issue. Engaging in trade is beneath the dignity of an earl, but Kendall never showed any deference for his title."

"Why?" Alex breathed. "Garrett is your stepson, Kit's half brother."

"He's not a Brown. And I refuse to let him risk Will's inheritance." His lips curled and with those cryptic words, he stood, ending the conversation. "It is you who are the real victim. I thought Kendall was too busy digging his own grave to find time to marry. My mistake. However, knowing my stepson, I can't take the chance that you aren't breeding."

Alex gasped, recoiling from his blunt crudity.

Ignoring her response, he spoke in a flat, instructional tone. "The door is heavy oak, two inches thick, and will be securely locked. This wing is on the second floor, over a twenty-foot drop to the ground. It is isolated and closed off from the other floors, so your screams will only earn you a sore throat. Keyes's staff has been slashed to three who inhabit the opposite end of the house. My man is well paid to not heed your cries. I'll bring your meals, but you have bread and water until I do so." He waved a hand toward her bedside table. "I suggest you eat, as you may be here a few days."

"Why?" she blurted. "I mean, why the wait?"

He paused with his hands on the door handle. "I have my reasons, and I don't give a damn if Kendall suffers over your disappearance while he waits." He stalked out, and the sound of the key turning in the lock echoed in the silence of the chamber.

Alex swung her legs over the side of the bed and stood, only to drop back onto the mattress and clutch her head. She lay down. Escape would have to wait until she could stand without the room pitching beneath her.

Tears leaked beneath the corners of her eyes. She swiped at them, refusing to cry. She would escape. Arthur's need to finalize his plans gave her the time she needed to recover and thwart them. Once the pounding receded in her head, she vowed to do so.

Arthur had found her an easy target once; he would not do so again.

≈≼

GARRETT SUFFERED TWO tortuous days and endless nights in a living purgatory. Having resided there during Balaclava and after his return home, he should have been accustomed to its tribulations. However, unable to seek oblivion in liquid solace, nothing prepared him for the slow, inexorable creep of time or the sense of helplessness he felt.

Each day was like awakening to an impenetrable blanket of darkness. Rather than having his hollow emptiness filled with the horror of his war nightmares, this time a bleak, unrelenting despair gripped him.

Then there was the fear. Fear that as each hour passed, each minute, each second, not only did he not know where Alex was but what torments she suffered. He could do little to help her but scour the vicinity, questioning the villagers and searching neighboring estates looking for any signs of recent flight, only to be forced to return home when exhaustion broke him.

It wasn't until the morning of the third day that Garrett received word of Arthur's first mistake, and a sliver of light seeped into the darkness engulfing him.

Garrett stood beside Havers before the hearth in the front parlor, his arm braced against the mantel as he surveyed the men before him. Gus, Holt, and a handful of his men from the hops field were clustered in one half of the room. Brandon and Stewart stood on the other half, flanking the three Peelers dressed in their familiar blue tailcoats and top hats, their wooden truncheons jutting out of the long pockets in their coats.

The two East Enders whom Garrett had sent to London, Booker and Haverill, had returned and had recounted their success in collecting the evidence needed to implicate Arthur. Once caught, Arthur would not be escaping the imprisoning bars of the law.

However, justice was taking too damn long for Garrett, so he was changing tactics. "We need to broaden our search, speak to the neighbors again, question the servants."

"Keyes is away," Stewart spoke up. "The vicar told me he had departed last week to visit his wife's family."

"There are still servants to question," Brandon said. "Gardeners, we can—"

"Not at Keyes's. He dismissed the lot before he left," Stewart interjected, disgust lacing his tone. "Gave them no notice or references. The vicar knew you were looking for staff and had talked to me about hiring some of them. I was going to speak to you about it, but in the wake of recent events, I forgot."

"Ah, that be strange." Holt cleared his voice and scratched his head. "The men said a carriage was seen on the day of Lady Alexandra's disappearance, but it was tracked to Keyes's estate. Assumed it was his." He shrugged.

Garrett straightened. "Keyes has sold most of his stables off, his land, and reduced his staff. He'd have taken his own carriage, and it's doubtful he'd finance the keeping of another." He and Brandon exchanged a look.

"Then whose carriage was it?" Brandon voiced the unasked question.

"Arthur has been there once before," Garrett said, thinking out loud. "Keyes not being in residence would suit Arthur's plans if he's traveling with a reluctant companion, and no servants means no spies if he is holding a captive. Arthur only had to drive to the neighboring estate, so this explains why nobody saw any carriages on the road. Clever bastard had probably already sought refuge at Keyes's long before we began our search."

"Keyes's place provides a good location to scout this area, find a window of opportunity when Alex was left alone," Brandon added.

"I believe we've located the devil's lair, and here's how we're going to trap the bastard. Listen carefully."

Garrett laid out his strategy in precise, military terms. Finished, he dismissed the group and turned to Brandon. "Let's end this. I want it over." As they left the room, he added. "Don't get too close. He's mad, Bran."

"Therefore, unpredictable. You need to remember that as well."

Their eyes met and Garrett gave a curt nod.

Once Alex returned to his side, he would do what he had failed to do earlier. He would get down on bended knee and ask the woman he loved to spend the rest of her life with him.

Chapter Thirty-one

❦

GARRETT'S suspicions were confirmed the moment Keyes's door swung open to reveal Arthur's man. This same door had failed to open to any of his men on previous visits in their search for Alex. Arthur was waiting for him.

He left the drawing room where he had been instructed to wait and retraced his steps to the front door, waving Ned inside. Ned was dressed in a suit similar to the one Garrett wore.

In the drawing room, Garrett directed Ned to stand before the back window. Ned clasped his hands behind him, tilted his head back, and appeared to be intently studying something outside. Garrett positioned himself behind the door.

He heard footsteps on the stairs, and then Arthur was there, within arm's reach. It took all of Garrett's will not to pounce on the bastard and demand Alex's whereabouts.

Arthur stormed into the room, his strides long, his purpose sure. "So, Kendall," he addressed Ned's back. "I knew if I waited long enough, you would come to me." He slid his hand into the pocket of his jacket and withdrew a gun. "However, I should have taken matters into my own hands months ago. Ended this all much sooner."

Slowly, Ned turned to face Arthur.

Arthur recoiled, the gun in his hand wavering. "You're not Kendall! Where the hell is Kendall? I was told he was here."

Ned's eyes lifted to a spot beyond Arthur.

Arthur whirled, but Garrett was ready, had been ready since Alex's disappearance. He sliced his hand into Arthur's arm, sending the gun flying.

It fell to the ground and skittered to land at Ned's feet, who bent to retrieve it.

"Kendall! I should have known!" Arthur stumbled back, rubbing his arm. "Christ! You have an uncanny ability to escape death." He glared at Garrett with unmitigated hatred. "For someone bent on his own destruction, I find it ironic that you still live. And a pity."

Garrett stared at Arthur's blazing eyes, their catlike slant and deep gold a disturbing mirror image of Kit's. This family resemblance stopped him from bashing the man's head into the stone hearth and being done with the matter. He showed mercy for Kit, not Arthur.

Garrett didn't deign to reply. "Watch him. If he moves, shoot him." He delivered the cold directive to Ned and crossed to the door, but stopped and spoke over his shoulder. "I find her alive, you live, hurt or worse, you die."

Without a backward glance, he strode to the front door, swung it open, and motioned his men inside. Brandon entered first, Havers, Booker, and Haverill following. He instructed the policemen to keep watch for anyone exiting the estate without Garrett's consent. Holt and Stewart had remained at the manor to provide protection for Kit and the boys.

Garrett watched Brandon's gaze stray to the drawing room. "Alex first." Garrett answered his unasked question. "He's not going anywhere."

They would locate Alex and afterward, he would deal with Arthur. End one chapter of his life and begin another.

≈≈

ALEX HEARD POUNDING footsteps. The noise broke the silence that was driving her to madness faster than her captivity, her three-day-old dress, and her ill-fated escape attempts. The latter had been such good ideas. Pity they all had failed.

First, she had planned to tie the sheets together into a make-shift ladder to climb to the ground. However, the old window frames were swollen shut and she had been unable to pry them open. Arthur had noticed the sheets missing from the furniture, located the knotted mass in the closet, and confiscated the lot.

Plan two had involved using a painting of those ubiquitous red-coated riders chasing the fox. Once again feeling a kinship with the endangered fox, Alex had slammed the frame into the window to shatter the glass. She had Kit to thank for plan two, recalling her tree-climbing escape that had delivered her to Brandon. Eyeing the tree branch jutting just out of her reach from the window, Alex's plan had failed when her gaze had dropped the two stories to the distant ground far, far below. Her knees had trembled and her breath hitched. She hadn't been able to do it.

Arthur had noted the broken window and simply smirked. His man arrived soon after to clean up the shards of broken glass.

If Arthur thought she would give up, he thought wrong.

She now stood poised for plan three as she listened to the rumble of voices increase in volume as they neared her room. She had drawn a chair up beside the door and stood on top of it. She had requisitioned the picture frame and clutched it in a white-fisted grip above her head. Her heart thundered in her chest as a masculine voice commented on the locked door.

"It's locked. No worries, guv'nor. I can pick it right quick."

She sucked in her breath. The man on Hammond's patio had spoken with the same coarse dialect. Arthur's hired assassin. *Hired to murder Garrett.* She tightened her grip on the frame and gritted her teeth. She was ready.

For Garrett's sake, plan three would not fail.

"Sees, I tell ye, I's knows me locks." The door swung open and the man speaking stepped inside. "'Tis a handy—"

Alex didn't hesitate. She swung with all her might and brought the frame crashing down on the man's head, silencing him. She didn't wait to see him drop to his knees as she jumped down and turned to flee—straight into another man's rock-solid chest.

Her heart stopped beating. Simply sputtered and died.

The scream that ripped from her reminded her that she still

lived, and with every fiber in her body, she fought the arms closing around her, thwarting her escape.

"Alex!"

A steel vice gripped her and gently shook her. "You're safe. Alex, my love, it's all right. I have you now. You're safe."

She was crushed so close to the man's body that she felt the beating of his heart against her cheek, breathed in his familiar scent. His voice, soft, gentle, and reassuring, reached out to curl around her. Her three-day nightmare ended. "Garrett!" She gasped, sagging against him.

"I'm here, my love. You're safe. It's over."

The tears she had fought streamed from her eyes as she clung to Garrett, burying her face in his chest.

Eventually, she drew away and lifted her face to bask in the warmth of his gaze. Her heart pounded, another reminder that she was alive and safe and madly in love with this wonderful man. "You rescued me. Again. I knew you would."

He smiled, his eyes drinking her in as he tucked an errant curl behind her ear. "It's good to know that had I not found you, you would have escaped on your own. That's my brave, resourceful Alex, and why I adore you."

Her eyes flooded again and she slipped back into his arms. "I would have gotten free sooner but the window was stuck and he took my sheets, and I'm afraid of heights and you weren't there to catch me and I must look a mess. I . . ."

"Shh," Garrett's words and the tender press of his lips against her temple soothed her as her voice hitched. "I have you now."

Her eyes drifted to the two men leaving the room, the smaller of them clutching his head and being supported by his larger companion. She drew away, feeling contrite. "I thought they were Arthur's men."

"And well you should have." His eyes darkened as he gently probed her bruised temple. "Are you all right?" He studied her features, giving each careful scrutiny.

She closed her eyes, savoring his touch. "Yes, he . . . he didn't hurt me." Her eyes opened and she looked rueful. "Oh, Garrett, I'm so sorry. I understand now why we shouldn't have kept Arthur's visit from you, but I—"

"Shh." Garrett's fingers pressed to her lips, silencing her. "It's all right."

Alex's eyes lifted to his. "He's mad, Garrett."

"He is." He tucked another errant curl behind her ear and let his fingers brush over her cheek. "For that reason, I need to make sure he is taken care of." He drew away and nodded to someone behind her. "I need you to stay with Brandon while I finish this."

Alex frowned, turning to see Brandon, who was eyeing the broken picture frame.

"Looks like the cavalry is redundant," he dryly commented. "You didn't need us after all."

"I did. I always will." Alex stood on her tiptoes and kissed Brandon's cheek.

When she stepped back, Garrett grabbed her arm and slammed her against him. His mouth swooped down on hers in a kiss that swallowed her gasp, her words, and all thoughts of protest. It scorched her body, warmed her heart, and branded her soul. When he released her, Brandon slid a supportive arm around her or she would have slid to the ground.

She simply smiled, happy to be alive and rescued.

❧

GARRETT RETRACED HIS steps into the drawing room, savoring Alex's taste on his lips. She looked a bit bedraggled and had lacked color until he had kissed her, but all in all, none the worse for wear. The image of her crashing the frame down on poor Booker had him grinning. She was perfect. *Brave, brilliant, and beautiful.* He cursed having to leave her to deal with Arthur.

His stepfather stood where he had left him. In vain, Garrett sought to understand the depths of the man's hatred, believing it to have sprung from a well so deep, the man now drowned in it.

"Who is your friend? Why have him stand in for you?" Arthur nodded toward Ned.

"Strategy. Decoys are often employed when planning an ambush." Garrett shrugged. "I'm surprised you had the guts to carry out what you hired another to do. Guess you have a spine after all." Garrett leaned against the doorframe and folded his arms across his chest.

Arthur eyed Garrett's casual pose, which bordered on insolence, and tightened his jaw, speaking through clenched teeth. "Be careful of what allegations you dare to make against me. You have no proof to back them up, other than your word, which lately hasn't stood for much."

"Oh, but I do, thanks to your incompetence. We have Nobbs in custody." Garrett enjoyed Arthur's surprise at his mention of the hired assassin's name. "We have your watch, which you tossed to Nobbs to meet his demand for more money. The watch engraved with your initials and the falcon, the Brown family crest. The symbol for one who does not rest until his objective is achieved. See, I did listen to your pompous lectures on your Brown ancestry."

Angry red blotches stained Arthur's cheeks.

"Nobbs, seeking to spare his head the gallows versus deportation, betrayed you like the rat he is."

"You're mad. You forget, my illustrious family name means something, perhaps not to you, but to a magistrate. They'll never take the word of a cretin like Nobbs over a Brown. My ancestors helped Henry the Seventh gain the throne. It wasn't until that Boleyn whore seduced Henry the Eighth that the Brown fortunes fell. I have plans to replenish those fortunes so the Browns can rise again."

"No, Arthur. I'm not mad. But you are. I have evidence and witnesses. *I have Alex*. Battle won."

"I should have killed you years ago," Arthur spoke softly.

"Why the hell didn't you?" Garrett demanded, his composure slipping.

"Because you appeared hell-bent on doing it for me!" Arthur snapped, then pressed his hand to his temple.

Garrett fell silent. Shaking his head, he straightened and moved from the doorway. He gestured to Ned. "Take him away."

Ned grasped Arthur's arm but was shrugged off.

"I'm a Brown. Browns stand on their own." He straightened his jacket and walked forward, his head held high, refusing to look at Garrett as he strode from the room.

Then all hell broke loose.

Garrett stumbled back under the weight of Ned's body shoved into his.

Alex's screams rent the air, piercing Garrett's heart.

Shoving Ned aside, Garrett regained his balance and bolted into the foyer, only to stop short at the sight greeting him.

Once again, Arthur held Alex captive.

His arm encircled her neck, cutting off her scream, the other cinched around her waist. Arthur yanked her tightly to him, a feral gleam in his eyes. "Stay back!" he barked.

It wasn't the directive, but the flash of the silver knife pressed to Alex's throat that stilled Garrett's hand and chilled his blood.

Christ. She must have been waiting with Brandon in the foyer. He held up his hands, giving a warning shake of his head to Brandon, who advanced on Arthur. "It's all right. No one needs to get hurt here. Not you, not Alex. Put the knife down and let her go. It's over."

He kept his voice level as he had when confronting the distraught boys under his command. His heart twisted at the sight of Alex's pale features.

"It's not over; you're still alive!"

Garrett's hand shot up to stop another movement from Ned, but he kept his eyes locked on Arthur. "And so are you. For Kit's sake, I didn't kill you as I wished to."

Ned lifted the revolver and pointed it at Arthur. "Just tell me when."

Christ, two madmen. "Put down the gun, Ned. We're still talking. Arthur mentioned his plans to replenish his family fortunes." He circled back to his stepfather's enigmatic comment as he followed Arthur, who edged toward the front door, dragging Alex with him. "With my death, Will gains my fortunes, not you, the title going to a distant cousin. How does that replenish the Brown coffers?"

"Because I finally have my boys! Boys who carry the Brown family blood. Boys of my ancestry. You weren't mine! You were never mine!"

"I could have been, but for the first time in my life, I thank God you thought otherwise."

Arthur stared at him, the knife's blade pressing into Alex's neck. She cried out, her fingers digging into his arm to pry it free, her eyes riveted on Garrett.

Her cry sliced through Garrett and every muscle in his body tightened, desperate to act. He looked at Alex, fighting to convey a reassuring calm. Some of the terror left her eyes, but her face remained deathly pale. For that alone, he could kill Arthur.

"No, you were always *his*. Kendall's. I could never look at you without seeing him. And Kit was a *girl*," he sneered the word. "What good is a girl but to breed me sons."

Disgust filled Garrett. Out of the corner of his eye, he saw Brandon stiffen. "Christ, you're madder than I thought," Garrett breathed.

Arthur ignored his words. "And she finally did! She had Beau, who belongs to Brandon, but then she had Will. Will is mine! The son I never had. Loyal to me, of my blood. With your fortune, he can purchase his own title. He wouldn't sully it as you are hell-bent on doing, dragging your name through the mud so it's black as sin and now this risky venture into trade. Don't deny it, man. Those rumors about your plans for Kendall Ale are true. I couldn't stand by and watch you bring this family down again, watch you squander Will's inheritance. I needed to protect my boys before your fortunes fell and your tarnished name stained theirs."

Garrett studied Arthur's wild expression. His eyes strayed to Alex, who looked as stunned as he. What a bloody waste. Years of anger expended at this pathetic man who wasn't worth a moment of his time.

Arthur turned his head, seeking the door behind him. He forced Alex backward, his eyes darting between Garrett and the exit, all the while keeping his choke hold on Alex. "Open the door!"

"Arthur, listen to me. You have two choices. Let Alex go and you live. Hurt her and you die."

"Open the door!" Arthur bellowed.

Garrett nodded to Brandon, who moved to obey Arthur's directive.

Arthur's lips curled into a snarl as he looked at Brandon. "You always stuck with Kendall. Never saw how he was destroying the family."

"Release her, Arthur. It's over," Garrett repeated, his voice cold.

Arthur stared wildly at Garrett and then Brandon. Emitting a savage yell, he shoved Alex from him, hurled the knife at Garrett, and whirled to flee.

Garrett easily deflected the blade, his arm swiping it harmlessly aside. He turned to Alex, drinking her in as Brandon caught her. Seeing she was safe, Garrett pursued his stepfather outside.

Havers stood with the two policemen flanking Arthur, holding him captive between them. One of the men lifted a pair of handcuffs and proceeded to secure Arthur's arms behind his back.

Arthur's earlier bravado had burned out. He slumped in the arms gripping him, looking like the pathetic, old man that he was.

Garrett studied his lifelong nemesis and felt nothing. "I'm not going to kill you as I'd like to. I said you'd live if you didn't hurt Alex, and she's alive. I don't want the blood of Kit's father on my hands. For those reasons, you live, and you'll live a long, long time remembering all you could have had and all you have lost. There's an asylum in York, far away from all my estates. Far away from me and mine."

"You don't understand! You—"

"No, you don't!" Garrett cut him off. "You already had replenished your family fortunes. You had a wife who loved you, a young boy who could have, and a daughter who tried to. But you rejected them all to fulfill some perverted delusion. And for what? The legacy you now leave your ancestry, as the last surviving member of the illustrious Brown family, is the stain of madness."

"You've always had it easy. Never had to fight for your birthright. You—"

"I fought for everything! Every scrap you'd toss my way until I realized you didn't have anything to give. That you are a bitter, empty shell of a man."

Mouth pursed, Arthur glowered at Garrett, before finally looking away. Defeated.

"Take him away," Garrett instructed the policemen.

They led Arthur down to where Stewart had arranged for a carriage to take custody of Arthur.

Ned came forward, nodding to Garrett before joining the

police. Garrett had asked him if he would accompany Arthur on his journey, knowing Kit would not want her father to be alone. Brandon and Alex stepped forward, and Brandon gave Garrett's shoulder a squeeze before walking ahead.

The police had protested Garrett's refusal to bring charges against Arthur, who would have hung for the attempted murder of a member of the peerage. With the clout of two earldoms between them, Brandon and Garrett had managed to save Arthur's neck from the noose. It was the best Garrett could do for Kit, and all he would do for Arthur.

Evening had settled, and Garrett watched the police and Arthur disappear into the darkness. He turned in time to catch Alex as she launched herself into his arms. He crushed her close, buried his face in her neck. "I love you."

She drew back and her hand cupped his cheek. "And I love you." She kissed him. "Let's go home."

"My thoughts exactly." He pressed his forehead to hers, the image of Arthur's knife against her soft skin a fresh nightmare to plague him. He leaned back from her and became serious. "However, before we return, there is a loose end that needs to be secured." At her puzzled expression, he went on. "I'd like to renegotiate the terms of our agreement."

"Oh?" Alex cocked a brow.

"Yes. You see, it appears that I no longer need your services in apprehending my murderer. However, I have little doubt that you would have single-handedly and heroically accomplished that feat had not my inopportune rescue thwarted your plans. But about our alliance, I'd like to change our arrangement into something more permanent and mutually rewarding to us both."

"Oh, what did you have in mind? As you know, I'm always open to new negotiations." She smiled up at him and then lowered her voice so that only he could hear her soft words. "And of late, those that are mutually rewarding to both of us are my favorite kind."

"My thoughts exactly," he murmured. Ignoring the remainder of his men standing but yards away, Garrett stepped back, knelt on one knee, and grinned into Alex's suddenly watery gaze. "Alexandra Langdon, will you marry me?"

Alex's smile wavered and she blinked back her tears, her

response almost drowned out by the animated hollers of his men. "Yes, yes, I will."

"Buss her a good one, Capt'n, an' seal the deal!"

Grinning, Garrett stood. He heard Brandon's laughter and his men's hoots of encouragement, but he didn't need any prodding. To the delight of their audience, he snatched Alex off her feet and swung her in a circle. His kiss was filled with the joy that exploded within him. When he drew back, he set her on her feet and let his eyes rove over her beloved features. "Now let's go home."

She was his and no one could ever take her away from him again.

"My thoughts exactly." Laughing, she echoed his earlier response and looped her arm through his as they began walking. "And since I no longer have to focus on escaping, or upholding my part of our bargain, I can concentrate on tying up my own loose ends."

"Oh, and what are those?"

"Well, when I wasn't cursing Arthur, planning my escape, or waiting for you to rescue me, I had a lot of time to think these last few days. And I was wondering about something."

"Oh?" Amused, he grinned. "And what is that?"

"Why did you follow me from the card table at Hammond's after I lost to you?"

Surprised, his smile disappeared and he stopped. He lifted his gaze to his men behind them and then returned it to rest on her. "It was your panicked expression when you realized you had lost."

She stared at him.

"It reminded me of the boys under my command before they rode into battle. I couldn't save them, but I thought I'd be damned if I'd be the ruination of another innocent." He shrugged. "I didn't need the money, and you looked as if you did."

"So once again, you were saving me?"

"I was." He grinned. "Little did I know that saving you would save me."

"Oh, Garrett." She rested her hand on his heart. "We were fated to be together."

He caught her hand and pressed a kiss into her palm. "Looks like." He brushed a stray wisp of hair back from her temple and let his fingers linger. "If we hurry, we could get started on making a tribe of boys. I've heard practice makes perfect."

Smiling, she slid her arms around his waist. "I might have heard that somewhere as well. There is only one problem."

"What is that?"

"I refuse to have three boys named Rogue, Rake, and Debaucher."

He pursed his lips. "Fine. We'll have twins, a girl named Verity and a boy named Trouble."

She shook her head with a laugh and slipped her arm through his as they started walking. "Let's start with one at a time. I'd like a little boy with raven black hair and slate gray eyes and we'll name him Garrett Melrose Brandon Sinclair."

He stopped dead. "Brandon? Absolutely—" He got no further.

Alex flung her arms around him, stood on tiptoes, and planted her mouth firmly on his, kissing the rest of his denial from him.

He momentarily resisted her embrace before his arms tightened around her. Groaning, he crushed her to him, his complaint forgotten in the pure joy of once again holding Alex right where she belonged—close to his heart.

Sometimes thinking was not good.

Feeling was best.

Turn the page for a preview of
the next historical romance from

VICTORIA MORGAN

Coming in Fall 2013 from Berkley Sensation!

S HE knew what they said about her.
Dumped by a duke. Bedford's forgotten fiancée. The hushed murmurs circulated in a widening pool of ripples. The betrothal contract was still good, just yet to be honored. If the man hadn't wedded and bedded her yet, he never would—or so pledged some of the wagers filling White's infamous betting book. Others proved more generous, wagering on the year, or decade, of the pending nuptials.

Long after the news should no longer have been grist for the gossip mill, it still managed to turn the wheel. After all, she was Lady Julia Chandler, the daughter of an earl, an heiress and renowned beauty. But that was yesterday. Today, she was a fading flower, waiting and wilting at the ancient age of three-and-twenty.

She knew what they asked about her, too. The question circulated in the same hushed stage whispers. *What is wrong with her?*

Of course, the fault had to lie with *her*. After all, Bedford was a duke, practically anointed royalty, perched at the pinnacle of the revered aristocratic pyramid. Toss in young, handsome, and rich, and who dared to question such sterling credentials? No one.

Except Julia.

And she knew the answers—or at least most of them.

Today she vowed to get the rest.

Julia tightened her hands on the reins and dug her heel into Constance's flank, leaning low over her sidesaddle and streaking across the field. She relished the bite of the wind against her cheeks, the whip of it through her riding habit, the feel of freedom it gave her. The sense of purpose, for today she had a purpose.

Edmund was back in Hertfordshire. Spotted in town. Her damn duke, for that was her name for him these days. Still evoked with affection, but lacking the reverence she had used when he had been her Beautiful Bedford or her Earnest Edmund. After all, there was a price to pay for his paucity of visits, letters, and of course, those nasty rumors he never deigned to squelch. "Damn duke," she muttered. But he was still *her* damn duke, and today, she vowed to remind him of it.

Julia didn't know what made her take the shortcut through Lakeside Manor, which abutted her father's estate. Despite the scenic views overlooking the lake, the charred, skeletal remains of the burned-out manor house were haunting. Black timbers rose up like a plaintive plea to the heavens to rebuild. A riotous mass of untamed weeds, ferns, and brambles snaked, weaved, and climbed over the sandstone foundation and crumbling brick walls like wild decorations breathing life into the desolate landscape.

She didn't understand why Edmund hadn't razed the estate to the ground. The property had come from his mother's side of the family and had only been inhabited a few weeks each summer. Edmund had never cared for it, so why let it sit and rot over the past decade, a morose symbol of loss?

She shuddered and reined in Constance, coming to a halt on a bluff overlooking the remains. The site held a macabre fascination for her. How could it not, tangled up in so many childhood memories? Those were the days when Edmund had been beautiful. And she had been happy.

She shook her head, bemused. *Had been happy?* One would think she heeded the rumors about her. Well, she was not quite ready for a silver-tipped walking cane, and she *was* happy. Planned to be happier if her courage didn't desert her. But still, her gaze drifted back to those stark, bleak, ghostly timbers, and she frowned.

"Bleak, but still beautiful."

Julia started at the words, her sudden movement irritating Constance, who grunted, tossed her mane, and danced back a step. Julia leaned over to rest a calming hand on the mare's neck as she turned to confront the intruder. Her heart thudded and her mouth went bone dry.

Edmund.

Her damn duke.

Tall and lean, he stood in the shadows of the copse of trees framing the back perimeter of the manor house. As she straightened, he moved forward and into the sunlight. A few months had passed since she had last seen him, and she drank in the changes to his appearance.

He looked thinner, his hair unfashionably longer and lighter than she remembered. Thick, wavy, and golden brown, it curled over the collar of his crisp, white shirt. His black riding jacket hugged his lean frame, the tight fit of his buff-colored trousers accentuating his muscular thighs and long legs as he strode toward her with an easy grace.

A gust of wind lifted a stray lock of hair from his forehead, and her gaze roved over his handsome features, the strong jaw, the sharp cheekbones and that enigmatic cleft denting his chin. But it was his eyes that were so arresting, being a rich, deep moss green. Edmund was vain and clever enough to appreciate their asset, spearing many a maiden's heart with a well-aimed look.

He stopped a few feet away, and Julia found her own heart endangered when those eyes locked on her. Her breath caught at his expression. Never before had he studied her with such intensity, looking at her as if she were some ghostly apparition or as if he were seeing her for the first time. She squelched the urge to shift in her saddle, like so many giggling, twittering maids did under his regard. There were advantages to being older. She rarely giggled and had never twittered.

"Julia." His lips curved into a slow, devastating smile.

She blinked. What game was he playing now? Edmund

liked his games. More so, he liked to win. Well, today she refused to play—or at least by his rules.

"You're beautiful. I knew you would be," he said.

She stared at him, bemused at his words, wondering if he was seeking to undermine her with that dangerous charm of his. When he chose to wield it, it was lethal. She cursed the heat climbing her neck and the traitorous leap of her pulse. Today, he'd need more than charm to derail her. "We need to talk."

He paused and raised a brow at her words, but then nodded. "That we do." He strode forward, "May I?" He lifted his hands, but waited for her to acquiesce before moving closer to assist her in her dismount.

She unhooked her knee from the pommel and nearly gasped at the touch of his hands on her waist, the cotton fabric of her burgundy riding jacket but a thin barrier between them. Her gloved fingers curled over his sturdy shoulders, bracing herself as he easily lifted and set her on her feet before him. Rather than step back as a gentleman should, he stood inches away, staring down at her with a rather odd and un-Edmund-like smile curving those sensuous lips.

Her body temperature, already elevated from his earlier scrutiny, climbed another degree. She had forgotten how tall he was, almost a foot taller than she. She had to tip her head back to meet that mesmerizing smile of his. When she did, her heart took another leap.

Good lord, he was beautiful.

He stood so close that she could smell sandalwood soap and a hint of some musky, masculine cologne. She blinked. This would not do. Betrothed or not, they were not married and they were unchaperoned, for she had refused a companion for this private affair.

She retreated a few steps, putting distance between them. "I will start."

He looked surprised and then amused. "You always did like to go first."

The comment, delivered with warm amusement, further disconcerted her. He really was not behaving like himself. "Yes, well, they do say ladies first."

He grinned. "So they do."

She paused at his manner. Charming and impatient were

Edmund's usual postures toward her, confounding traits, as they compelled or repelled her depending on which mood she confronted at the time. She was not as familiar with this Edmund and hoped this would not complicate matters. However, things needed to be said and as her damn duke had the uncanny habit of disappearing for long periods of time, she was determined to seize the moment. Enough time had been lost.

"You do know that my father is no longer grieving the loss of my mother, Jonathan has turned a robust five, and Emily is doing much, much better, so I think—"

"I'm glad."

At his interruption, she paused.

"I'm glad to hear about your father and Emily. I didn't know her fiancé, but grieving over the loss of a loved one is always a difficult journey."

She frowned. *Difficult?* The word was too tame a description for her sister's bedridden breakdown after Jason's death at Waterloo. However, that *was* so like Edmund. He had never liked to discuss Emily's "illness," as he referred to it. Back on familiar footing, she continued. "Yes, well, now that my family's concerns and my obligations have lightened, I think we are finally . . ." She paused to swallow, her words caught in her throat. "What I mean to say is . . ." She trailed off, and heat climbed her neck.

She might have acted impetuously upon hearing Edmund was in town. She should have taken time to collect her thoughts and prepare a proper speech. Usually the man took the lead in such matters, so she was at a loss as to how to proceed. And her damn duke appeared to have no intentions of rescuing her.

He watched her with a slightly amused expression on his handsome features, looking as if he enjoyed her discomfiture. Maybe she should have left this meeting to her father. She gritted her teeth. No, because by the time he got around to addressing the matter, she would need that silver-tipped cane to assist her to hobble to the altar.

She began to pace as she groped for a proper lead-in, well aware of Edmund's eyes trailing her, not making matters easy for her. "I just thought it is only reasonable that after so many years of waiting, we now—"

"Waiting? I'm not sure I—"

She stopped and frowned at his furrowed brow. Edmund was not obtuse, so she couldn't fathom what he gained in pretending to be so. Irritation spiked within her. "For goodness sake, it's been five years! Bets are being wagered at White's as we speak. I think it's time."

"Time?" He echoed. Suddenly his eyes widened and he retreated a step. "I'm beginning to understand." He lifted his hand to rub his neck, a tinge of color spotting his cheeks.

Julia's lips parted at the unusual reaction.

What was wrong with the man?

A rueful smile curved his lips. "However, there is something I need to clarify before you continue." He held up his hands. "You see, I'm not who—"

"No, it's not necessary," she broke in, cursing her earlier outburst and seeking to avoid the tired explanations over what the two of them had long understood. "I have always appreciated and been grateful for your patience and discretion while my family worked through these travails. But it's our time now. I want to honor the betrothal contract. I couldn't before, but now I can. I—"

"Julia, wait, stop! I do need to explain—"

"You don't need to explain anything to me." Before her flagging courage abandoned her, she stepped closer to him, lifted her chin, and took a deep breath, gazing straight into his eyes. "All I need you to do is kiss me and tell me that everything is going to be all right. That *we* will be all right."

"You don't understand. I'm . . . what?" His hands dropped, and he had to clear his throat before he could continue. "Ah, what was that about kissing?"

Feminine satisfaction filled her, helping her to regain her lost footing. Emboldened, she decided that if Edmund could behave un-Edmund-like, then for once, she could abandon the calm, collected, and responsible Julia. Tired of being trapped by her responsibilities, she wanted to feel young and reckless. More so, she wanted to relish the thud of her heart in her chest and the heat spiraling through her body as Edmund fastened his beautiful eyes on her.

Shoring up her courage, she lifted her arms and slid her hands up his chest, marveling at the feel of the warm, hard strength of him through his jacket and wondering why she had never dared do this before. Why had she waited so long, particularly as she felt his heart thud against her palms. It felt good. *He* felt good.

His fingers curled over her forearms. "Julia—"

"Edmund." She cocked her head to the side. "Aren't betrothals sealed with a kiss? Considering ours was penned when I was in the cradle, I appreciate your waiting." Freeing her arms, she slid her hands around his neck, sliding her fingers into the soft curls teasing his cravat and smiling at the flare of light in his eyes. "But as you can see, I'm all grown up now."

She watched him swallow, felt his hands lower to her waist, but frowned when he held her away from him.

"You certainly are." He grinned. "That I noticed straightaway. But you see—"

"I do see. I see that you are wasting more of our time. I also see that you're stammering when you could be kissing me. Don't you want to kiss me?" Before she lost her nerve, she moistened her lips as Emily had once showed her to do to make them more alluring.

He expelled a choked laugh and shook his head. "Of course, I want to kiss you! A man would have to be lacking a pulse to reject such an offer. But Jules—"

She paused at the old childhood nickname. He hadn't used it in years. But his hands had drawn her back to him, which bolstered her courage—and her daring.

"You do have a pulse, don't you?" she whispered. She was standing so close to him that she could see his long eyelashes, and admire his lovely moss green eyes, and how they warmed at her question.

"For the moment," he quipped. "However, I'd prefer to retain it, and should we proceed further with this, that could be dangerous for both of us."

He had a point, and the old Julia would have heeded it, considering how the warmth of his gaze sent her pulse skipping into a treacherous rhythm. However, his look and the grip of his hands on her waist made the new Julia feel young, beautiful, and desired, something Edmund had not made her feel in years. "Really, Edmund, it's one kiss. How dangerous could it be?"

She raised a brow, knowing Edmund never could refuse a challenge.

He sucked in a sharp breath and stared at her. After a beat, he exhaled and swore softly. "Hell, I've been living dangerously my whole life." His eyes dipped to her parted lips. "Why stop now?" He yanked her to him, his arms a vise around her waist, crushing her tight to him.

She gasped at the explosive heat of his body against hers. Her eyes widened when his head lowered, and inches away, the warmth of his breath whispered into her parted lips, "Forgive me." His mouth closed over hers and he kissed her as she had never been kissed before. Kissed her as if he had waited as long as she had and was desperate to catch up.

His lips were warm, soft, and sensual. She clung to him, her arms circling his neck, and was dimly aware of his grip tightening on her when her legs turned to liquid jelly and were unable to support her. And still he kissed her. Deeply, erotically, and expertly.

Better yet, she kissed him back!

She savored the taste of him as her mouth surrendered to his. He was a mixture of ale and cider. The sensual assault of taste, touch, and scent overwhelmed her. She loved the feel of his body, hard, warm, and muscular, crushed against her softer contours, and when he broke away for a moment to draw breath, she inhaled the rich masculine scent of him, and felt a wave of molten heat cascade through her limbs.

When she felt his tongue run along her lips, she gasped and drew back. She needed to breathe, to pause and gather her thoughts that had scattered like leaves to the winds. "We should stop. We can't—"

"You're so right." He moistened his lips and she nearly shuddered at the hot, smoldering look he gave her. "But Jules, I did warn you about this being dangerous. Now it's too late."

His mouth again swooped down and plundered hers, devouring and demanding more and still more. Ripples of pleasure spiraled through her body. He aroused yearnings in her that she hadn't known she possessed. She had recently wondered if she would ever feel them for Edmund . . . until now.

He drew back, and Julia blinked up at him, struggling to

clear the sensual haze engulfing her. When clarity returned, she realized she was still intimately pressed against Edmund. His arms around her waist fully supported her, and through her riding habit she could feel his heart pounding against hers.

Flushing, she tugged free of Edmund's embrace and straightened, grateful that her legs managed to support her weight when she stepped away.

"Well, then." Her voice was breathless and sounded strange to her ears. Lifting an unsteady hand, she tucked an errant strand of hair back under her bonnet rim.

"Well, then indeed." He smiled. "I had doubts about coming home, but no more."

Her breath caught at the sultry look he swept over her. She wished she could say she was glad, too. The new Julia would have done so, but she was feeling more and more her old responsible self and a bit appalled at her brazen behavior. She tugged down her riding jacket, but refused the urge to run her fingers over her swollen lips. "So we are agreed. It is long past time we set a date and stop the run of wagers at White's."

She frowned when the smile curving his lips froze and then disappeared. After a moment, he lifted a hand to rub it along his neck in that strange, new adopted mannerism of his. "Ah, about that date. There is one minor complication in regard to that."

"Oh?" Her hand stilled. "And what is that?"

"As much as I wish it otherwise, I'm not in a position to be making any future dates with you."

"What are you talking about?" she demanded, a cold chill suffusing her, dousing the simmering embers of their shared passion. "You're not backing out of the betrothal agreement. You can't. My father would ruin you."

"Particularly after that kiss," he agreed quite amicably and leaned close to her as his eyes flashed with a spark of defiance. "But it was worth it."

She stepped back and fisted her hands at her sides, a hard ball of suspicion curdling deep in her gut. She should have listened to his earlier stammers—or warnings. She hoped it wasn't too late to do so.

"However, your father's desire to murder me would be for

different reasons than you think. I can't set a date because I am not in a position to do so, which is what I tried to explain earlier."

She simply stared at him, waiting him out. She was done talking. Done with being young and foolish and reckless. She feared she was about to pay the price for allowing herself to be so for one lovely moment.

"You see, I'm not Edmund."

LOVE
ROMANCE
NOVELS?

For news on all your favorite romance authors,
sneak peeks into the newest releases, book
giveaways, and much more—

"Like" Love Always on Facebook!
𝐟 LoveAlwaysBooks

*Enter the rich world of
historical romance
with Berkley Books . . .*

Madeline Hunter

Jennifer Ashley

Joanna Bourne

Lynn Kurland

Jodi Thomas

Anne Gracie

Love is timeless.

berkleyjoveauthors.com

Discover Romance

berkleyjoveauthors.com

See what's coming up next from your favorite romance authors and explore all the latest Berkley, Jove, and Sensation selections.

See what's new
~
Find author appearances
~
Win fantastic prizes
~
Get reading recommendations
~
Chat with authors and other fans
~
Read interviews with authors you love

berkleyjoveauthors.com